Lynn & Kirk,

Thank you!

then you enjoy:

Lies From Beechwood Drive

Michael David MacBride

D0920026

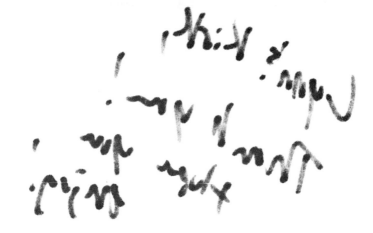

This is a work of fiction. All incidents and dialogue, and all characters with the exception of some well-known historical figures, are products of the author's imagination and are not to be construed as real. Where real-life historical figures appear, the situations, incidents, and dialogues concerning those persons are entirely fictional and are not intended to depict actual events or to change the entirely fictional nature of the work. In all other respects, any resemblance to actual persons, living or dead, events, or locales is entirely coincidental.

DEDICATION

- Roxanne Blaess (1952-2010), Paulette Ratkiewicz (1951-2017), and Jean Osborne (1946-2020).
- Mom and Dad for letting me be an 80s kid and have my own adventures.
- Paul Ratkiewicz for being my partner in crime.
- Gayle, Dylan, and Parker, for always believing in and encouraging   me.

RESIDENTS OF OPOLE, MICHIGAN

On Beechwood Drive:
- Esther and Jeffrey Fuhrman; child – Bruce

South of Beechwood Drive:
- Regina and James McKinney; children: David and Russell
- Victoria and Dean Webster; children: Barry, Mark, and Michael
- Rachele and Rodrick Williams; children: Christopher, Brandon, and Hannah
- Helena Piekarski and Brent Barnett
- William ("Bill") and Carol Daniels

North of Beechwood Drive:
- Becky and Craig Schwartz; children: Tiffany and Sean
- Brenda and Thomas Walker; children: Betsy, Angie, and Larry
- Patty and Richard Lambert; children: Jason and Rodney
- Suzy and Raymond Townsend; children: Lisa and Jane

PART I: 1987-1988

CHAPTER 1: LEUKEMIA

A moment like this was rare for Esther. It was unusual to find herself without something to say, some nugget to offer or some meaty gossip picked up on her rounds, but when confronted by someone to offer a solicited opinion, she would just as soon make something up as admit failure. The very idea that Esther, the fount of all knowledge in the city of Opole, keeper of wisdom, holder of stories, collector of facts, mobile news organization, might not know about something before anyone else did, terrified her to the point of fact-creation rather than acknowledging that someone had scooped her, or beat her to the punch.

Esther dealt entirely in "local" news. She covered the stories that the local paper, the *Opole Record*, didn't touch. To some, this was gossip, to others, someone else's business, but to Esther, it was a currency that she peddled around town to anyone who would listen (and some who wouldn't). Her reputation was built on being there first, knowing things before they were public knowledge, and by her almost omnipresence. She power-walked everywhere. But, even given the ground she covered by foot, the houses she entered (with and without permission), and the countless people she interviewed (or eavesdropped on), there was the odd time when Esther wasn't in the know.

In a moment like that, indeed in a moment like right now when she was being asked a direct question, she was at the top of her game. Because she had so many pieces of information at her disposal and knew so many nuggets about this family or that, she was often able to assemble a hunch that turned out to be true. When someone asked her, "Is everything alright with Chris and Debbie," Esther was able to see quite clearly, in a way she hadn't before because she hadn't been under pressure to do so, see that no, things weren't alright with Chris and Debbie. In fact, Esther could clearly see now that Debbie and Chris were *both* having affairs as she tugged at this memory and that to put together a convincing string of cause and effect that led to her foregone conclusion. This all transpired in a matter of seconds, before the questioner would wonder if Esther had forgotten the question, and when it came out of Esther's mouth, it was now fact. The questioner would then spread that information to another friend, because the questioner had long suspected something was going on with Chris and Debbie anyway and just needed something or someone to confirm it. Afterward, it was difficult to know if Esther had somehow inadvertently stumbled upon the truth or if the spreading rumor throughout the town caused Chris and Debbie to distrust one another, pushing them into the comforting arms of another. Either way, Esther took credit for her truth-finding.

Today's question was a simpler one. The questioner, one of Esther's few actual friends, Victoria Webster, was folding laundry when Esther barged into her house. Some neighbors saw Esther's intrusions as impositions, but since Vicky was a friend, Vicky didn't mind at all—at least that was what she said to Esther. Vicky folded her son's pants and casually said, "Barry said David wasn't at school today. Did you hear anything?"

In truth, Esther had not. Some might think such a question wasn't worthy of the great Esther's vat of knowledge. This was, after all, just a child who missed a single day of school.

But, since Vicky was a friend, Esther felt extra pressure to know this answer. Her mind started to wheel. What had she heard about the McKinneys? Well, for one, after ten years of not having another child after their son David was born, they suddenly had another child. That could just be happenstance, bad luck, or maybe they hadn't been trying. Maybe the second child was an oops. Or, maybe David had been the oops, and the last ten years had been restraint while they adjusted to being parents and determining if they wanted any more. Maybe, after testing the waters of having a child they finally came to the conclusion that they had this parenting-thing down, and they could handle another one. But, that wouldn't explain an absence at school. That second child, who Esther just could not remember the name of, it was right on the tip of her tongue, was over a year old now. There would be no reason for David to stay home with his little brother. What was his name? There was something she had heard on the news recently about children. She looked at Vicky folding her laundry and knew she was taking longer than usual to come up with an answer. There was an easy way out; she could just say three simple words. But to her, those words were terrible. They meant defeat. She simply couldn't say: I don't know. So, instead, she said:

"He," long pause, "has leukemia." A shorter pause. "It's terrible, actually. But little Russell has leukemia. They're trying that new treatment they were just talking about on the news. Something about a refined protocol. Even though it's terrible, the recovery rates in children, particularly as young as Russell, are very high. Upwards of seventy percent or better. The McKinneys just took him in today, and David went with them."

The moment she began to speak she remembered both Russell's name and the gist of the news story she caught last night before bed. Esther was rather proud of herself. How did she do it? Where did these ideas come from? Sometimes, when she had more time to prepare, she was careful to leave an easy out, or a reset, in case her hunch turned out to be inaccurate.

This time, she hadn't. there was a high rate of recovery that might explain Russell's sudden healthy return to the neighborhood but that wouldn't account for the confusion on the McKinneys' faces when asked about their child and his leukemia. Esther was busy thinking about how to undo this when her friend erupted.

"Jesus! That's terrible! Why didn't she say anything to me? I was just talking to Regina last night, and she didn't say anything at all."

"Regina probably didn't want to worry you," Esther said. Now an idea was formulating. What if she suggested to Vicky that Regina didn't want the story to spread around, and that it was best never to mention it to her, or anyone. To not let on that she knew. That maybe the information had been given to Esther in confidence and she really, really shouldn't have said anything. But before she could, she realized her friend was crying.

Vicky was sobbing openly into one of Barry's clean t-shirts. She kept saying, "It's so terrible" over and over again. Esther moved closer to her friend and hugged her. She did her best to comfort Vicky, but Vicky's crying wasn't stopping, and, frankly, human touch wasn't something Esther excelled at. She knew what a hug looked like, and she knew how to give one, but she never felt like she was doing it quite right. While she was happy to peddle stories and converse with people, their physical presence in her space was something she had never quite gotten used to. It wasn't even that she was uncaring; she just lacked that empathy portion of the brain that could properly console someone. She thought she said and did the right things, but it never quite worked the way it did in the movies or with other people that she'd observed. So, she held her friend and tried to comfort her, but Esther quickly realized she wasn't helping and left.

This was how it came to be that Vicky left a message on the McKinneys' answering machine, and sent flowers to the house, and told everyone she knew that the McKinneys needed their comfort and support in this difficult time. Those people, parishioners at the church, neighbors, and anyone else who heard, sent similar messages and flowers. Maybe if Esther had been better at comforting people, or had taken the time to temper the message a bit more to her friend, or had come out with the truth that the pressure of being asked a question that she didn't know the answer to about local gossip terrified her into making something up, this could have all been avoided. However, because she didn't, and because the McKinneys were actually on a short family vacation, the matter only worsened when there was no response issued from the McKinneys.

This story had legs, even without Esther providing them. In fact, it had legs despite her. She tried to do some early damage control by preemptively mentioning the story, and then undermining it. "Oh, I heard this thing about Russell McKinney having leukemia, but I'm not sure there's any truth to it." However hard she tried though, the story spread throughout the town of Opole. While small towns might be happy to spread stories of tragedy, like gawkers at car wrecks, they are also good at coming together to support one another. This story allowed them to do both: spread a tragic tale and support one another. Esther must have poo-pooed the story twenty times before she was home for dinner, and each time she was sure to mention the statistic of seventy percent, or better, recovery rate, but it was quickly out of her hands.

The McKinneys had informed the school that they were pulling David from fifth grade for a couple days, but they didn't specify why. They had spoken with his teacher about the extended absence, and requested all homework assignments and reading materials so he could work throughout the absence. They hadn't seen the need to explain what the absence was for. Also, because the idea occurred to them rather spontaneously, they didn't take the time to notify neighbors like they normally would. They did ask one neighbor to water their garden while they were gone, but he was retired and not an active participant in the community; he only shared a fence with the McKinneys and nothing more.

When the McKinneys arrived home from their vacation in

Florida, they parked in the garage and went into the house through the backdoor. Jim made the discovery first, when he went to collect the paper from the front porch.

"Gina?" he called. "What the hell is all this?"

His face was bright red from not wearing proper sunblock or having a base tan to begin with, and the redness only made him seem angrier than he was. What Jim meant to convey was surprise, not anger. But, after hours in the car, preceded by late nights and long days on the beach, he was tired and frustrated and, frankly, disappointed about having to return to work.

"Gina!" he called again.

The rest of the family came running to the front porch. They were tentative and a little afraid of his tone, but they came knowing that it was worse to avoid him. Imagine their surprise to see piles of mostly dead flowers outside their house, cards piled in their mailbox, and a small shrine on their front porch with signs offering support and prayers.

Jim started digging in the mess of well-wishes for the Sunday paper, the family only received the Sunday edition because he didn't have time to read much more, but he couldn't find it under the various flowers and packages. David and Gina marveled at the piles before them. They had no words.

David ran to the side entrance of the house. "There's more over here," he called. Jim and Regina, who was carrying little Russell, ran to the side of the house, where they in fact found more packages, flowers, and cards.

"Jesus," said Jim. "What the hell?" He moved back to the front porch and eventually pulled out his paper from the bottom of the pile. A vase of flowers had fallen over and spilled water all over it. Thankfully, the paper was encased in a plastic bag to protect it from the elements. He picked up the bag, held it as it dripped, and then carried the newspaper inside.

"I wonder how much mail we got," said David. Suddenly, he was very excited. Nothing like this had ever happened to them before. He didn't know what it all meant, but he liked the excitement. He ran back to the front of the house and checked the mailbox. It was overflowing. They hadn't thought to stop the mail, because they were only going to miss a few days. David couldn't carry all the post in a single trip, so he made two and piled it all on the table. He made a pile of things he could immediately recognize as bills and junk mail and then counted all the personal mail. Most of the mail was addressed to "The McKinney family" or "Mr. and Mrs. James McKinney and Family" or, more concisely, "Jim and Gina."

"Thirty-four," David announced.

"Thirty-four what?" asked Jim. He was flipping through the paper trying to find the score for the Lions' game. That was one thing he hated about traveling; he never could find a decent paper that would report the things he cared about back home. If he wanted to know what was going on in Michigan, even something big like the score of the Lions or Tigers (even after their 1984 win), he'd have to wait until he got home to find out. It was so rare that either team was televised, unless they were playing someone like the Yankees or Red Sox or the 49ers or Dolphins, or, in the case of the Lions, it was Thanksgiving.

"Thirty-four pieces of mail," David answered.

A slight frown passed over David's face, and he ran to his parents' bedroom. There, on his parent's bedside table, was the answering machine. It was a marvel of technology. No more missed calls. The Panasonic KX-T2300 EASA-phone. David's father loved this thing, even if he liked to grumble about paying "damn near a hundred bucks" for it. What David loved more than the actual messages it held, was the little box that indicated how many people had called while they were away. Sometimes this number corresponded to how many messages were waiting, but not everyone always left a message. Sometimes people would just call, hear the answering machine, and hang-up. So far, the record number of calls had been sixteen, and that was after the McKinneys had been gone for a week. Today, the record was shattered.

"Sixty-two!" David yelled from the bedroom.

"What?" both of his parents yelled back from down the hall, their responses were not perfectly synchronized, so one sounded like a slight echo of the other.

"Sixty-two calls!" David knew better than to press the rewind button, but he really wanted to hear how many had left a message. His finger hovered slightly, and then he dropped it to his side.

Jim suddenly appeared beside him. "Jesus!" he yelled, not realizing Regina was right behind him. He immediately pressed play.

Some were hang-ups, which Jim thought were just rude. If you call, leave a message. He didn't understand why people couldn't get that through their heads. If they had called, asking for him, and he wasn't home, they would have left a message with Regina. So, if they call and no one is home, why not just leave a message with the machine? Not everyone had machines, so it was probably just a matter of familiarity. They'd come around once they had one of their own. Of the sixty-two calls, fourteen were hang-ups, and the rest were some variation of: I'm so sorry, please call me when you can; we just heard, is there anything we can do to help; I'm surprised you didn't say anything the other day, but I also understand your need for privacy; I have a casserole in the freezer for you – let me know when you're home and I'll bring it right over; and poor little Russell, I'm so sorry.

The last ones, that actually mentioned Russell's name, were the only ones that provided any kind of clue. Even that wasn't much to go on. What had happened while they were gone? The flowers and packages and cards didn't provide much more help. They were full of "our deepest sympathies," "get well soon," and "thinking of you," but offered no further information.

At one point Jim turned to David and said, "Is this something you and your friends did?"

Even as he asked it, he knew this whole situation was as much a surprise to David as it was to him and Regina. They were sure the mystery would resolve itself soon enough. That night they cleaned off the porches, threw most of the flowers away, piled the cards and gifts on the dining room hutch, and then went about the business of unpacking and getting ready to return to the routine of their lives.

It was Esther herself who broke the news to the family that their youngest son had leukemia.

Esther had been keeping a close eye on the McKinneys' house. On a typical day, she powerwalked the neighborhood a few times. Since the conversation with Vicky, she had been doing double, or triple, duty on the McKinneys' street. Everyone within eye-shot of the McKinneys' house was gifted with extra, and extra-extended, visits from Esther, until, finally, Esther saw the McKinneys' car parked in their the driveway.

She headed over to greet them, but as she neared the driveway, she hesitated. She wanted to absolve her name from the list of people suspected of starting the rumor to protect her reputation—should it turn out to be unfounded. Honestly, she wasn't convinced the story wasn't true. Her gut was rarely wrong, and so she finally approached the side door of their house under the assumption that Russell did indeed have leukemia. Due to the circumstances, Esther thought it best not to let herself into the house as she normally did and instead rang the doorbell.

There was a small commotion as David yelled, "I got it!" and started towards the door, until Regina intercepted him and said, "No, I have it." David trailed behind his mother as she answered the door.

"Esther?" Regina wasn't asking because she doubted it was in fact Esther, she was asking because it was so uncharacteristic of Esther to ring the doorbell. Typically, she would have been in the house and chatting at Regina before Regina even heard the screen door close.

"I am so sorry to hear about little Russell," Esther said.

David was about to go back to unpacking when he saw who it was, but at the mention of Russell, he craned his neck around his mother's side and listened.

"I'm sorry?" asked Regina. "For what?"

"Oh," said Esther. "Then it isn't true?" She sincerely felt relieved that the child was fine but also sorrow at her instincts being wrong. How could she have let herself down like that, let alone the rest of the community who counted on her?

"What isn't true?" asked Regina.

"Well," Esther said. She thought quickly about how to distance herself from the rumor. The only person who knew for certain that she was the source of the story was Vicky. Everyone else heard it second, or third, or fourth hand. Esther played back the conversation with Vicky in her mind and tried to recall exactly what she had said to her friend. Did she say something about "hearing" the story from somewhere? Esther knew people's memories were faulty, so even if she hadn't attributed a source for the story, she could probably convince Vicky that she had heard Esther wrong.

"Well, I heard that little Russell has leukemia," Esther finally said. "It sounds ridiculous now that I'm saying it out loud, because obviously you would have told us, your community, about something like that. You know, for support. But when I heard it, it hit me in the gut. To think of your little boy going through that. I couldn't help but picture my boy going through that ordeal, and I guess, I didn't think to question it."

"Leukemia?" asked Regina. She was mystified. "We went to Florida."

"Florida?" asked Esther. "How long had you been planning that?"

"Why?"

"We go to Florida every year," said Esther. "It just seems like, if you were going to go to Florida, that that would have been something you would have talked to me about. Or, to ask for advice about where to stay. I could have made so many recommendations. How long did you stay?" Now that she had Florida on the brain, all Esther could think about was asking Jeffrey to make her a Rum Runner like they used to have on the beach.

"I'm so confused," said Regina. "So, someone told you that

Russell has leukemia? And that's what all these messages and cards and flowers are about?"

"Your community cares about your well-being," said Esther.

"Where did you hear that from?" asked Regina.

"I don't remember, exactly."

That was the moment that Regina called bullshit, because Esther remembered everything. She was a human sponge for stories, and her retellings of stories could last for hours as she recalled each minute detail and name of each event and person in the story. Like when Regina made the mistake of asking Esther about her youngest sister's wedding. They went through two pots of coffee and four loads of laundry as Esther rattled off the names of each guest, the cake decorator, the name of the DJ, the church and location of the reception, how the bows were tied at the end of each of the pews in the church, the song of the father-daughter dance, who had too much to drink that night, what the centerpieces looked like, and how the one gentleman, Gerald Davis, who spent every moment of the night on the dancefloor with every woman in attendance, was likely gay because he had an earring in his right ear. What type of earring? It was a tasteful gold cross with a small diamond where the pieces of the cross met. So, when Esther said she didn't "remember, exactly," Regina knew it was bullshit. Who was Esther protecting?

Regina thanked her politely for the information, indicated that, "No, in fact Russell is doing quite well," and said her goodbyes.

As soon as Esther left, Regina picked up the phone and called Vicky. Regina and Vicky weren't best friends, but their sons (David and Barry) were, and so they made attempts to get the two families together on occasion and were growing to like one another better and better. Regina also knew that Vicky's house was often the first house on the "prattle path" (this was the name that the neighbors gave to Esther's route), and while Esther and Vicky were on friendly terms, Vicky didn't have any kind of steadfast protective loyalty to Esther. In short, Vicky would give it to Regina straight.

"Did you hear about Russell?" Regina asked when Vicky finally got to the phone. Barry had answered the phone, and then Regina had to wait while the boy let the receiver dangle by its cord and smack repeatedly into the stand that held the microwave oven.

"Yes! Is he all right?" asked Vicky.

"He's fine. Who did you hear it from?"

"About the leukemia?" asked Vicky. "I'm so glad he's doing well."

"Yes. Thank you."

"Esther told me. I was surprised you hadn't said anything, since we had just talked the other day."

"When Esther told you, did she say who told her?"

"Hmm," Vicky tried to recall, but couldn't. "I'm not sure. I don't think so. Why?"

"He doesn't have leukemia," said Regina matter-of-factly.

"Oh? Wow, that's even better news," Vicky replied, but she sounded a little confused.

Then Regina dropped the bomb. "I think Esther made it up."

"Why would she do that?" Vicky asked, but she was already formulating answers of her own.

"Because of who she is," said Regina. "Plus, she rang my doorbell today. She didn't just help herself. When I asked her who told her, she said she didn't remember. And she left right away. I didn't have to try to get rid of her multiple times like usual."

"Wow," said Vicky, "she just left?"

It was true. You usually had to say, "I have some chores to do," or "Well I really need to get going on dinner," or "I have errands to run," multiple times before Esther would leave. Most of the people of Opole were too friendly and courteous to be direct with Esther, and she was too slow, or cunning, to take the hint. Jim was one of the few exceptions. He had zero tolerance for Esther and would directly tell her to get her "ass out of my house." But on this day, when Esther's scoop was at best wrong, at worst completely fabricated and wrong, she fled the McKinneys' house immediately without provocation. On a normal day, she would have wanted to hear all about the vacation, so she had a new story to spread to anyone further down her prattle path.

"Exactly," said Regina.

"Why would she make something like that up?" asked Vicky. "I had only asked her if she knew why David wasn't at school because Barry had said something to me about it. That's when she told me about Russell having leukemia and you guys pulling David to go to the hospital to be together as a family."

Regina made several other calls after hanging up with Vicky, and all signs pointed to Vicky being patient zero of the story. Everything originated there, because after Esther had left her house, Vicky called her friends, and their friends called others, and someone notified the church, and soon the whole town knew. This is how the McKinneys were greeted with a pile of flowers, packages, thirty-four cards, and sixty-two calls, albeit some of them were hang-ups, sympathizing for them and their child who, in reality, did not have leukemia.

News that Esther had been wrong spread more quickly than the original story about Russell's illness, but it didn't reach everyone in time. At school the next day, David met several administrators, teachers, and students who gave him their sympathies about his brother. David, of course, did his best to straighten out the rumor but the adults at school refused to believe David. David was just a child and had obviously gone through a very traumatic event. All day long they continued to pat David on the shoulder and encourage him to "keep his chin up" and to "let them know if they can do anything to help." The students took the corrected information in stride; honestly, they didn't really care or fully understand what leukemia was; they were just doing what their parents had instructed them to do. David didn't exactly mind the extra attention.

The whole event was a serious blow to Esther's ego and reputation. Her reputation was crafted over the years on being the go-to source for information around the town of Opole—and sometimes beyond its city limits—and now that position was in danger. Would someone else come along and attempt to fill her shoes? How could she repair her tarnished image?

Esther considered confessing all to Regina, and even headed over to the McKinneys' house. She powerwalked all the way there, but when she arrived, she found herself not quite ready to face Regina. So, Esther paced on the sidewalk alongside the home. As she did, her gaze wandered over the garage, which needed to be repainted, the roof that needed to be re-shingled, and the chain-link fence that was bent from children climbing over it. This was a house that was well-lived in, but outwardly showed the priorities of the people who lived within it. Instead of spending their money on repairs and maintenance, they were taking spontaneous trips to Florida. If they wanted to go to Florida, they should have asked Esther for her advice. She couldn't remember how many times she had been to the state, but it was definitely in the double-digits if you included both her trips as a single woman, the trips with Jeffrey before Bruce, and the trips since having Bruce. She knew her way around, what to avoid, when the best times were to go. And she felt slighted that her friend hadn't asked her. Even if she didn't value Esther's opinion, which Esther had a hard time imagining to be the case, surely Jim and Regina would want to save money. She could have done that for them.

The various cost-saving methods were running through her mind when her eyes settled on the McKinneys' laundry line. It was a nice day, so Regina was clearly taking advantage of the warmth and breeze to dry the laundry instead of using a dryer. Proof, Esther thought, that Regina did value frugality, which made the oversight of not asking Esther for Florida-advice even more baffling. Her eyes followed the sheets as they billowed and flapped, and then she noticed something smaller. Colorful. Esther wasn't sure what it was at first, and then it came clearly into focus: underwear. The cut was so different from the kind she always wore. Now she was picturing herself wearing them and wondering how they would feel. Would they ride up? Would they show lines? Were these comfortable underwear that she could wear around the house, or were these for special occasions?

"Esther?" a voice asked.

"Yes?" she replied absent mindedly. Suddenly Regina came into focus, pulling down pieces of laundry from the line. Esther hadn't noticed her because either Regina's presence had been disguised by the sheets, Regina hadn't been there before, or Esther hadn't noticed because she was picturing herself walking around in her friend's underwear.

"Are you okay?" asked Regina. She sounded concerned, which for Esther was a good sign. Maybe they were still on good footing. Maybe she could forget about the whole leukemia-thing and just move on as if nothing had happened.

"Fine," said Esther quickly. She walked closer to the fence. "I was just wondering," she said, "are those underwear comfortable?"

"Yeah," said Regina slowly. "I like them well enough."

"Can I try on a pair?" asked Esther. To her, it was not creepy at all to ask, so she didn't notice Regina's change in expression.

"No," Regina said firmly.

"Why not?" asked Esther genuinely surprised.

"Because they're my fucking underwear," said Regina. "That's why." Regina snapped the last piece of laundry from the line, tossed it in the basket, walked into the house, and slammed the sliding screen door behind her.

Esther stood for a moment trying to figure out what had happened. Clearly Regina was still upset about the leukemia-thing. She wasn't going to be able to sweep this under the rug as she had hoped. She would have to start small and work her way up again. That was the way she established her reputation in the first place. She had started with a small cohort of friends and made it her business to know their business better than they did. Once that foundation was created, she expanded her scope and incorporated more and more households until she finally reached the point where she had been just prior to the leukemia-debacle.

She would just have to begin again. She'd have to find a new circle to work her way up from, and hopefully, eventually, she would regain the trust of her original inner circle. If she could do that, then she would have successfully expanded far beyond her original scope. Maybe instead of a catastrophic failure, this could all work to her benefit? Esther smiled. Just maybe.

CHAPTER 2: HER ROUNDS

Esther had been moving in the same circuit to spread information for so long that she forgot how she initially gained her reputation. After the leukemia-debacle, she took a week off and spent time thinking about how best to cultivate a new audience and new sources for her information. Ultimately, she decided on a rather simple approach. Instead of making a large loop to the south of her house, she would make a large loop to the north. In truth, the houses to the north were a largely untapped resource for her. Esther knew a few families up that way, but she rarely spent time with them. Her kids made friends with kids from the south, and even on Halloween when there was the potential of free candy to be claimed in the northern neighborhood, they stayed in the southern neighborhood. It was silly, really. Nothing more separated the two areas except for the way the road jogged around the elementary school, and yet that little jog did seem to cut the area decidedly in two.

Esther decided she wouldn't ignore her friends to the south, but if anyone asked why she was venturing into northern territory she would say she was expanding her circle of friends. She knew the Lamberts fairly well but hadn't actually stopped by in quite a while. And there were the

Walkers. Their daughter was in the same grade as her son, Bruce. With those two entry points, Esther was sure she could ingratiate herself into the rest of the northern neighborhood. In truth, it worked out even better than she had hoped.

Monday, the first day of a fresh new week, Esther saw the kids off to school. Her husband was already gone to work, so she locked up the house and powerwalked around the little jog in Beechwood Drive. Before long, she was standing at the Lambert's front door. The question was, should she knock or just go in? With people on the southern route, she just let herself in, but she hadn't established herself here in the same way yet. However, if she did just let herself in, she would assert her authority and comfort with these families and maybe that would add a sense of normalcy to her suddenly being north of the jog. Before she a chance to decide, a decision was made for her.

Little Rodney Lambert opened the door and looked up at her. Rodney was just three. "Hello, lady," he said.

"Hi," she waved at him. "I'm Esther."

"Easter?"

"Esther.

"Easter."

"Can I come in?" Esther asked, as she opened the screen door.

Rodney kept an eye on her as she stepped into the entryway.

"Patty?" Esther called.

"In here," Patty responded.

Esther walked into the living room, turned the corner, and found Patty in the bathroom, cleaning the mirror.

"Kids," Patty said, barely looking at Esther. "Look at this mirror. Toothpaste and water all over the place. You can hardly see yourself in it." She squirted more Windex on the mirror and wiped again with a fresh paper towel. There were still streaks.

"How have you been?" Esther asked. "It feels like forever since I've been over."

"Not that long," Patty said. "We saw you at the church picnic, uhm, two weekends ago?"

"Right, but not at your home."

"Not much has changed here. Same furniture. Same paint. I suspect it doesn't look any different."

"You've updated the pictures in the hall," Esther said. She had a keen memory and an eye for details.

"Oh, you noticed. We tried that new photographer in town. I really think she did a great job," said Patty. She was giving up on the mirror even though it was far from perfect. There was a bit of a hazy film over most of the lower half of the mirror. "It takes a special knack to get smiles like that out of a child, much less out of several of them," Patty laughed.

Esther laughed as well. "I'll have to remember that and give her a try. I've been disappointed with Sears the last couple times we've gone, but there always seems to be coupons that make it hard to pass up."

It was true. Every time they went to Sears, she swore it would be the last, but then, when October came and she started thinking about the need for fresh family photographs, she would receive a flyer from Sears Photography with 50% off this or 25% off that. Sometimes she would shop around, but it always happened that Sears still had the best prices. Other times she wouldn't bother shopping around because it felt like too much work. By the time the actual photographs came in with the cheesy backdrops, the limited number of poses, and the few actual "good" images she had to choose from, Esther would swear up and down never to use Sears again. And then she would. Maybe this time she wouldn't. Esther decided to test the waters a bit.

"The new photographer is Carol, right?"

"Right. She has that shop downtown, next to the bank," said Patty. She moved out of the bathroom, down the hallway, and into the kitchen, where she put the Windex away under the sink. "Well, the bank we use anyway. The one that used to be the credit union?"

"Opole Savings?"

"That's the one." Patty said. "Want some coffee?" She poured herself a cup.

"No thank you," said Esther. "Her husband, Bill?"

"Right."

"Bill, I thought I remembered right. Did you hear that he's been laid off again?"

"Doesn't surprise me," said Patty. "He's a heavy drinker."

"I guess he came in a little tipsy a couple days ago," said Esther. "So, fired is more accurate."

Patty didn't respond.

"I said laid off, but I should have said fired."

"I hadn't heard that," Patty said. "Though, it doesn't surprise me. He can't seem to hold onto a job to save his life. Good thing Carol has a good eye for photography and reasonable prices." Patty paused as she drank from her coffee. "Just so you know, Suzy and Becky are coming over in a little bit. We usually get together around this time."

"Great," said Esther. "I'd love to meet them."

Suzy Townsend and Becky Schwartz arrived shortly after with their preschool-aged children in tow, and Esther found she fit right in. They were chatting and swapping stories like old friends. Becky remembered meeting Esther at a school function or two, and Esther apologized for not remembering. It was unlike her. She had such a good memory. Esther actually doubted whether or not Becky had met her before and thought that maybe Becky was just trying to become more familiar with her. This was fine for Esther. That's why she had come here after all. A knock on the screen door interrupted the conversation.

"Hell-loo." Even after all these years, Esther immediately recognized that voice. It was Brenda Walker's trademark "hell-loo." Esther met Brenda in seventh grade when they were locker partners. Esther had just opened the locker and was hanging her coat on one of the hooks when someone tapped on the open door and said, "Hell-loo."

"Hi, I'm Brenda. Brenda Walker," she said.

At the time, Esther wasn't sure what to make of this girl,

but she had a hunch, given Brenda's proximity to Esther, that this might be her new lockermate. She had requested her friend, Janet, but apparently that request didn't mean much of anything.

"I like saying hello as two distinct parts," Brenda had explained. "That way I can say HELL," she laughed a little, "and loo."

"As in skip to the loo?" asked Esther. Maybe this Brenda person wasn't so bad.

"Exactly!" said Brenda.

"So, you're saying, hell toilet?" asked Esther.

"Pretty silly, isn't it?" replied Brenda. "Hell toilet."

Esther agreed that it was, and Brenda appreciated that someone "got" her joke that she'd been telling all these years.

So, when Esther heard it again, now twenty-eight years later, she immediately knew who it was. The two were friends all through high school, and then went their separate ways after graduation. Brenda went to college, and Esther began working at the local dentist office. They lost touch until Brenda returned to town, pregnant, and a year and a few credits shy of graduation. The distance created over the intervening three years was a lot for their friendship to overcome, and they remained friendly, but not friends. It didn't help that the father of Brenda's soon-to-be baby girl was Daniel, an ex-boyfriend of Esther's.

After Daniel left for college, he and Esther had tried to maintain a long-distance relationship, but ultimately—even though his college was only an hour away—he broke up with her, in a letter written in his neat penmanship. The letter didn't provide much in the way of an explanation but instead waxed poetic about philosophy and how college was changing his outlook on the world. If Esther had cared more about Daniel, his sleeping with Brenda would have ruined their friendship, but truthfully, Esther had moved on well before Daniel's letter arrived. Not that she had cheated on him, but she no longer felt the connection she once had. Still, whenever Esther saw Brenda's daughter Betsy (who was turning eighteen this year), she couldn't help but feel a little sting from Daniel and Brenda's betrayal.

Brenda walked in the front door and her eyes immediately found Esther. "Hey stranger," she said. "Someone turned the big three-five, this year, right?"

Esther was a little surprised that her old friend remembered. "A lady never speaks of her age," she said in her best impression of a coy southern mistress.

"I'm wondering if you have any advice for me because I only have a month left," said Brenda. "Then I'm only five years from, oh my . . . the big 4-0."

"I never would have guessed you had a decade on me," said Suzy. "You both look so young."

"Great complexion," said Becky.

Before an awkward silence could take hold, Patty changed the topic, inadvertently, to an even more uncomfortable one. "How is Daniel?"

Upon hearing his name, Esther's mouth turned to a sneer, and she tried to hide her revulsion by looking at her lap. But Brenda caught the look and laughed.

"Oh, not that Daniel," Brenda said, grabbing Esther's hand. "He's long gone, believe me. Just a coincidence that my husband's name is Daniel, also."

Somehow the news of her old friend's nuptials had escaped her knowledge. It was a good thing she was extending her reach into the northern region – who knew what other useful and interesting information was flying under her radar.

"When did that happen?" she asked.

Brenda locked eyes with her friend, and it was as if the rest of the women were no longer there. "Four years ago." She rubbed the side of Esther's hand with her fingers. "We have a little boy. He's two. My mother has him today. Larry."

"I'm so happy for you," said Esther. "I heard about how awful Thomas was, and then how terrible the divorce was. That must have been difficult." Esther caught Brenda's fingers in her hand and squeezed them gently.

"It was."

"I'm sorry that I wasn't there for you," said Esther. "I was stupid. Shouldn't have let that old stuff bother me so much."

"Me, too. It was a two-way street, and I should have reached out sooner. But, you know how it is with kids. I was a single mom then, had to finish up school, and I never got a break from Betsy. It took my parents a while to come around and accept me and her. When they did, so much time had passed. I wasn't sure how to approach you," Brenda said. "I'm sorry."

And like that, the old friends were back in business, and Esther found her new crop of women. From Patty, Suzy, Becky, and Brenda, Esther would meet plenty more. In a week or two, she'd be walking in their front doors like she belonged there, like she had in the southern neighborhoods, and she'd find their houses open to her as a source of local news.

The northern route also took her past stores she had nearly forgotten about. There was a cute cheese shop, Horatio's Cheese Shoppe, that she must have driven by dozens of times without every stopping in, and now that her new route took her right past it, she'd occasionally swing in. Even her husband, Jeff, appreciated her new routine because she also stopped by the local bakery to get fresh pretzels on her way home. Granted, the pretzels weren't fresh and warm when he got home, but they were better than no pretzels at all.

On Monday, Wednesday, and Friday, she did her rounds, and on Tuesday and Thursday she volunteered at the school. Sometimes she cut and stapled projects for whichever teacher needed the help. Other times, she was in a classroom working with students. She preferred working in Bruce's classroom because then she could see her son, but he was getting to the age when his mother embarrassed him. Bruce was in Mrs. Adkins' class, which is where Patty's older son (Jason), and Brenda's middle child (Angie) also were. Prior to her new rounds, she hadn't paid much attention to these children. But after finding a rhythm with the northern neighborhoods, she found herself noticing them more and more. Angie was bright and reminded her a lot of Brenda. Jason, however, needed a lot of help with reading, and Esther regularly helped him with something Mrs. Adkins called "guided reading."

Despite enjoying the familiar children in Mrs. Adkins' class, Esther hated volunteering in there. Mrs. Adkins always spoke down to her and made even the simplest task cumbersome and overly complex. When she first introduced Esther to "guided reading," Mrs. Adkins provided her with a written set of instructions and then proceeded to read them to her.

"This is the list of names I'd like you to work with today," she said. "Go to the first child on the list, and ask him to choose a book. It can be a book he is already reading, or a new one. It's up to him. Then take him and two chairs—one for you and one for him—into the hall. Ask him if he wants to read the whole thing aloud, or if he just wants to go back and forth with you. He could either read a sentence and then you could read a sentence. Or maybe he could read a paragraph and then you could read a paragraph. Or maybe, if he's really good, he could read a page and then you could read a page." And on, and on, and on. Mrs. Adkins moved her finger to each part of the written instructions as she read to Esther, and then smiled. "Any questions?"

Esther had questions. Like, why did it need a fancy name like "guided reading?" Wasn't that how anyone taught a child to read? Let them read some, as much as they could, and then help them if they got stuck? Why did Mrs. Adkins assume the worst of her students? She never said "if," she always said "when," as in: "When he gets stuck on a word." Most importantly, Esther wanted to ask, "Why do you trust that I can help these children read if you can't trust me to read the instructions for myself?" But, she didn't ask any of those. She just took the slip of paper from Mrs. Adkins and went to find the first child on the list.

Thankfully, today she wasn't in Mrs. Adkins' class. She was in Mr. Poole's, one of the few male teachers at Opole Elementary. Esther didn't know much about Mr. Poole, but she did know she liked how he ran his classroom. Barry and David were in this class, but she rarely had an opportunity to work directly with them because there were other students who needed more of her attention.

At present, she was the only person in the classroom. Mr. Poole was at the teacher's lounge, and the students were out at recess. Her task was to make sure each student had a packet of handouts on their desk before recess was over. She was nearly done. As she dropped the papers on Barry's desk, a folded note fell onto the floor. Esther picked up the note and automatically unfolded it. She was too curious to do otherwise.

The top of the note read, "Mock Raid." She didn't know the kids in this class well enough to know whose handwriting it was, but given that it was on Barry's desk, she assumed it was either his or David's. Those two were thick as thieves.

It took Esther a moment to process what was on the note and realize it was an overview map of the school. It was a terrible drawing, and it was obvious whoever drew it had never seen an overhead view of the school. Vicky's husband Dean, after getting his pilot's license, had flown over the city and taken aerial photographs of the city. Esther remembered Dean coming by the house to show Jeff his handiwork, and among the photographs was one of the school. There was also a clear photo of Esther and Jeff's house, which Dean gave to them. In either case, the drawing looked nothing like the photograph Dean had taken. Thankfully, someone else had labeled parts of the school, and those labels made it abundantly clear what Esther was looking at.

There were also six stick figures surrounding the line-drawing of the school. Each figure was labeled with the word "team" and a corresponding number, one through six. A dotted line extended from each figure into a different entrance of the school, and then traced a path through the school. At the bottom of the map was a list labeled "supplies." The list consisted of the following: walkies, bbguns, smokebombs (at least twenty), camo, facepaint. Esther wasn't sure what it all meant, but it seemed like a trip to the principal's office was warranted.

Carlos Perry was a nice enough man. Esther saw him

occasionally, usually during fundraisers or at a church event, but she didn't know him well. Her son Bruce was never in the principal's office. As she walked to his office, she worried about what might happen to Barry and David. She was already on the outs with their parents and didn't want to cause the rift to widen. But, the map she held in her hand, coupled with the mention of guns and smoke bombs, concerned her. She was pretty sure she was doing the right thing; she just wasn't sure if Regina and Vicky would see it that way. Esther flipped the map over and over in her hands as she waited for Carlos to invite her into his office. When he finally did, she didn't feel any more certain about what she was doing.

"What brings you in, Mrs. Fuhrman?" Carlos asked, and closed the door behind them. He walked around the side of his desk and took a seat.

"Esther, please," she said. "I was helping out in Mr. Poole's class, and I found a note."

"A note?" Carlos asked. "What kind of note?"

"I'm not sure," she said. "It just feels a little," she struggled for the right word, one that wouldn't be too alarmist, one that would temper her anxiety about the note she had found, and finally settled on, "concerning."

Carlos raised his eyebrow. "Can I see it?"

Esther handed the note to him, but did so slowly and with great reluctance. When he finally extended his arms fully across his desk and his fingers gripped the edge of the paper, she let go. Esther watched his eyes dart around the note. She could see that he was taking in the words "mock raid" at the top then darting around the outline of the school. His eyes didn't linger on the map, and she figured he immediately recognized the poorly drawn rendering of the school. His eyes did settle on the list portion of the note where he read and read the words.

"This is concerning," he finally said. "Do you know what a mock raid is?"

"I know what the words separately mean, but I don't know what they mean together. And I don't understand what any student here would have to do with whatever it is."

"Whose desk did you find this on?"

Here it was. The moment of truth. Did she come out with it? She could easily have said she just found it on the floor. Maybe Mr. Poole would be able to identify the handwriting? Maybe he wouldn't. Maybe Principal Perry would have all the parents come in and see if they could identify the writing? Eventually it would come out. It may as well be from her. She found herself saying, "It fell off of Barry Webster's desk."

At first Carlos said nothing. He just flipped the paper over in his hands, much as Esther had when she first found it, and read and re-read the words on the page. Then he said, "The *Weekly Reader* ran a story about mock raids last month. Some religious organizations and other militia-type groups have been conducting mock raids to check the preparedness of the communities."

"Preparedness for what?" Esther asked.

"An invasion," Carlos said. "From the Russians."

"Oh, I do remember reading something about that. But I thought that was in Kentucky."

"There have been several. Most were in the south."

"So, you think this means the kids are planning to do a mock raid here?" Esther asked. "At the school?"

"Seems like the most logical conclusion to draw, don't you think?"

"But, Barry and David are good kids. They wouldn't do anything like that."

"I'm sure they mean no harm," Carlos sighed. He set the map down on his desk and rocked back in his chair. "There are six stick figures here. I think you're right that it's Barry and David, but who are the other four?"

Could her Bruce have been involved? Maybe even Barry's younger brother Mark? Or Patty's Jason? She couldn't believe that this would be going on under her nose without her catching some whiff of it.

"Mrs. Fuhrman?"

"Esther, please," she said. But she was stalling. How did these kids get such ideas? Carlos said it was from the *Weekly*

Reader, but that was just a newspaper for kids. It couldn't be responsible for an idea like this, could it? She'd read the *Weekly Reader* with Mrs. Adkins' class a number of times, and she never saw anything in it that was objectionable. It was just simplified news.

"Esther?"

"I don't know." And it was the truth; she really didn't know. "I have no idea who could be involved. Frankly, I have a hard time believing that Barry and David would do anything like this, let alone anyone else at this school. They're just fifth graders."

"I know, but you never know what it will lead to. It's best to catch this type of activity early," Carlos said. "Thank you very much for bringing this to my attention. I have some calls to make now though. So, if you could excuse me?"

"Of course," Esther said. She stood, pushed in the chair, and left his office.

When Bruce came home from school, Esther practically pounced on him. It turned out, he was not involved in the mock raid, which was a huge relief to her, but he had heard the boys talking about it. For once, being in Mrs. Adkins' class was a blessing, because it meant that her son was isolated from the potential trouble. Barry and David were the masterminds, but they hadn't thought to reach outside their own classroom for participants. Instead, the guilty parties consisted of all twelve of the boys in Mr. Poole's class. Each stick figure on the map actually stood for two boys, not one, which was why they were labeled "team" one through six. She collected versions of the story over the next twenty-four hours before delivering the definitive account at Brenda's.

"Those little shits were going to attack the school!" she started animatedly as soon as their cups were filled with coffee. Brenda had invited over the usual women (Patty, Becky, and Suzy) and a few others Esther was just beginning to get to know.

"Really?" one asked.

"Attack how?" another asked.

"They were going to pretend to be sick, and then meet outside the school in a group of trees. One of them was going to have hidden face paint and camouflage clothing there. They were going to get changed into their fatigues, and then," she was interrupted.

"Wait, they were all going to call in sick? Half of Mr. Poole's class?" asked Brenda. She had heard a version of the story from Esther before all the pieces had been finalized.

"Didn't they think someone would notice?" Suzy asked.

"They are nine or ten; you expect them to have a perfect plan?" asked Esther. "They were going to go in teams of two. One would light smoke bombs, another would open a door, and the last team would throw the smoke bombs into the school. They all have those ridiculous bb-guns that are shaped like M-16s. You know the ones."

There was a chorus of uh-huhs. Each of their boys had wanted one enough to actually save up all their birthday money, Christmas money, and to do extra chores around the house. At the time, the parents thought it was just harmless fun. Kids playing wars. But now, in light of the "mock raid" the whole thing took on a much more sinister feel.

"And then what?" asked Patty.

"I don't think they got that far," said Esther. "Barry said they just wanted to make sure the school was ready for an attack, like they had read in the *Weekly Reader*."

"We should get rid of that thing," said Becky. "It's putting twisted ideas into their heads."

"It's just a newspaper for kids," said Esther. "I've read it before. It's harmless."

"Hardly harmless," said Patty. "Just think what could have happened if you hadn't found the note and foiled their attack."

"I'm going to suggest at PTO that we form a committee to preview the content of the *Weekly Reader*," said Becky. "We can't have this type of thing happening again."

From there, word spread that Esther had foiled an assault on Opole Elementary. Each of the children involved received detention after school, had to write apologies that they read before the school at a special assembly, and most received additional punishment at home.

One notable exception was David McKinney. Jim and Regina fought the after-school detention and argued against David's involvement in the school assembly. Principal Perry finally convinced the McKinneys that the punishment could have been much worse, and the threat to the school was very grave. At home, David received no additional punishment. In fact, his father commended his ingenuity.

"Well son, I think it's fucking hilarious," Jim said.

"Jim, language!" said Regina.

"What?" he asked. "Like he hasn't heard it on the playground. God, when we were kids, we did all kinds of stupid shit like this. Well, not exactly like this, not nearly as creative, but stupid shit nonetheless. I'm proud of you. Nobody was hurt, nothing was broken. Hell, you didn't even get a chance to enact your plan. Everyone has their panties in a twist over nothing. Just some kids having some fun."

Jim was an involved parent, but most of the parenting decisions were left up to Regina. It was rare that he took such a stand about something related to the kids. Her lack of response was as much about her surprise as it was about not wanting to have this fight about punishment.

"And you know, while we're at it," Jim said, clearly enjoying being on a roll. "Fuck Esther and her shit. I mean, leukemia? Who makes that shit up? And now saying our boy is going to attack the school? Who hasn't dreamed of killing their teachers before?"

Regina could think of at least one person that hadn't thought of killing her teachers before, but she was hoping this whole conversation would just go away, and they could move on with their life.

Though David appreciated his father's approval, he knew he could never tell his friends, because they were all in deep, deep shit. They would hate him forever. So, David kept quiet. When he was asked about what his parents did, he deflected the question by asking, "What did yours do?" And then followed it up with, "Yeah, basically the same."

Despite all the trouble and worry, it was a great moment for Esther. She gained back whatever authority she had lost from the leukemia-debacle and advanced to number one on Jim's shit list. She had always been in the top five, but now she was indisputably numero uno.

CHAPTER 3: WIANKI

Even though only a small percentage of the population of Opole, Michigan was Polish, the town was once a thriving ghetto for Polish immigrants. The city of Opole, Poland was one of the oldest cities in Poland and was the thirty-seventh most populous city in Poland around the time Opole, Michigan was being settled. There are conflicting stories about why the people in Michigan chose their namesake from such an unexceptional city. One story claimed the founder was born in Opole, Poland, but the birth and baptismal records of Bruno Fabian, the founder, were eventually discovered in a trunk in an attic. Both clearly showed that Bruno was born in France, not Poland. Additional letters found in that same trunk confirmed that Bruno Fabian had lived in Poland, but there was no record of his ever stepping foot in Opole, Poland. Krakow, yes; Warsaw, sure; Rzeszow, yep; but Opole, no. Another founding story claimed that the decision was the outcome of a bet during a card game.

The less well known but probably most likely claim is that there were two cities in Michigan vying to use the name Krakow. In this account, the two towns battled to prove themselves more Polish than the other one by displaying the genealogy of their townsfolk, celebrating all the Polish holidays (even the most obscure ones), and by producing the best paczki. Polish family trees were displayed prominently around each town and were tastefully decorated. However, because the genealogies were all crafted according to the memory of people living in the town, it was quickly discounted as a method of proving a town's superior Polishness.

An unforeseen consequence of the increased number of opportunities for celebration was that it actually brought the towns closer together. While the town leaders initially became anxious when one town celebrated a festival and another town didn't (how could they have neglected this ancient tradition?), they quickly fell into the joy of simply being connected to human beings through drink, food, and dance. Eventually, the one definitive criterion that the towns settled on to determine which was truly more Polish was the paczki.

The eventual visitor who wandered into one of these towns and encountered a paczki for the first time was at once puzzled by the word and mystified by all the excitement surrounding a jelly donut. The townsfolk were more than happy to help the visitor pronounce the word. Most pronounced it poonch-key, but there was a distinct contingent that insisted on poons-key.

"No ch-sound," they would insist.

A battle between the rival experts would ensue and the visitor would be forgotten, until he or she asked, "What's so special about these jelly donuts?"

Then the factions would unite and animatedly instruct the visitor that, "This is *not* a jelly donut, this is a paczki."

The visitor would politely wait for further explanation, but the townsfolk saw no need to elaborate. Their case was clear. The visitor's curiosity would eventually get the better of him or her and ultimately the visitor would order, "One, just to try it."

Sometimes then, after the mouth was filled with deliciousness, one of the townsfolk would explain that in the old days, "Way back, they used to be filled with pork fat." That would give the visitor pause. The chewing would stop. "Not any more. Today we use lemon, or plums, or raspberry, or, sometimes, chocolate." Another townsfolk might mention,

"There is a small amount of alcohol in them because alcohol keeps them from absorbing too much grease in the fryer. Plus, who doesn't like to drink while they cook?"

After the visitor finished their paczki, they inevitably ordered several to go. And this is how the word spread of the amazing paczkis in Michigan.

The two neighboring towns enjoyed challenging each other's skills with paczki bake-offs during the many Polish celebrations. Thousands of pastries were consumed at each event. Every time a contest was held, an argument broke out over the "proper" method for baking the paczki. And for what criteria should be used to determine whether a paczki was the "best." Initially, the towns went with a simple method of determining who sold the most, but it was decided that was too easy for someone with an appetite and extra money on hand to manipulate the outcome. Other times, they went with "most traditional," which of course caused debate over whose tradition they were basing the evaluation on and how far back they wanted to go. Occasionally, they'd settle on "most original," which resulted in new fillings being used like: vanilla pudding, whipped cream, and bacon. It was hard to consistently determine which town was best, and how that "best" would be decided. As time went on, the towns began to intermingle more. People from one town married people from the other, and before long it was hard to remember where the boundary between the two towns was.

One day, after thousands and thousands of paczkis, the leaders of both towns decided to join forces to become a single city. It was an option they had never considered before.

"Why didn't they choose the name Krakow?" visitors often ask.

Indeed, they had the opportunity to have the name they both had sought and argued over for years. But that name was tainted now by the division it had caused, and they wanted something they could agree on. Something without the baggage of the past. They called the elders together to discuss Polish towns and cities, and various lists were made. Elders told stories about the histories of the Polish cities they remembered, and why they were significant. Some names were immediately discounted because of tragedies that had occurred within them; others were eliminated because they were too well known, or too symbolic, or too hard for Americans to pronounce.

At one point, Bruno Fabian asked, "What about Opole?"

The consensus response was, "What about it?"

No one had considered the name or knew much about it. It hadn't appeared on any of their lists or been spoken by any of their elders. Yet, the more the people considered it, the more they liked it. It wasn't hard to pronounce. It wasn't overly symbolic. It didn't summon up unpleasant memories, and it was decidedly Polish. It was decided. The leaders announced it to the townsfolk at a general meeting, and there was a general shrug of acceptance. More importantly, no disagreement was voiced.

As time went on, the obscure festivals and celebrations fell by the wayside—after all, a lot of work went into organizing and preparing for them—but one remained: Wianki. This was an old festival, and one that was most closely associated with Krakow, so it was fitting that it should remain.

Wianki translates to "wreaths" in English, and the festival involves creating wreaths and floating them down a river. The festival originally honored Kupala, the goddess of harvest and love, who was associated with both water and fire. So, in addition to creating beautiful handmade wreaths, huge bonfires were also made. Couples were encouraged to float wreaths together and jump through the fires, and single men and women, seeking love, were encouraged to participate individually. As Opole aged, the festival became an opportunity for couples to express their love for one another, and for singles to find matches while seated at the fire, while creating wreaths or casting them down the river, or while dancing to whatever live music was present. Of course, no Wianki festival attender was satisfied until they had eaten one, or maybe a few, paczki.

Today, Opole still celebrates Wianki, though few call it that now. The kids call it the "Polish potluck" because everyone brings a dish to pass and baked goods to sell in the town square. The thirtysomething generation likes to think of it as a "city-wide block party" because that's the easiest way to explain it to people outside of Opole. Wreaths are still made, but now you can purchase premade ones if you don't have the time to commit to the construction of one. The bonfire is gone, but bands now play on a stage constructed at the main four corners of town, and they play late into the night—the festival is held on the longest day of the year, after all. Occasionally, Opole even pulls in national acts to play the stage.

On June 21, 1987, Rodney Cone was the big draw at the Wianki Festival. Tabitha Cooke, the mayor of Opole, had booked Cone before his hit "Faultless Quakes" made him popular in the United States. Cone originally recorded the song in 1985 in the UK with some success, but when Cooke snagged a booking in early 1986, it looked like Cone's moment of fame had come and gone. To Cone's credit, when the song did explode in the U.S. a few weeks later, he didn't try to back out of his commitment, though he didn't exactly advertise his appearance in Opole either. Cone's eleven-date tour in the States began in April of 1987 and wrapped up June 12. There was a nine-day gap between his show in Opole, which did not appear on any of the tour merchandise or flyers, and the previous show in Madison Square Garden. Anyone who was following Cone probably assumed he went back to England after playing New York to rest up. They didn't know that Cone had settled into the one and only hotel in Opole, Michigan. He found the town to be quaint, and everyone there polite. Even though people knew his music, he wasn't recognized, and he enjoyed the anonymity that he didn't get in large cities.

Of course, when Cone opened his mouth and his English accent spilled out, the citizens of Opole knew he wasn't a native. They wondered where he was from, but they were polite enough not to ask. That is, until he encountered Esther Fuhrman at the gas station.

"Who are you?" Esther asked abruptly as Cone browsed the candy bar options.

"I'm Rodney," he said.

She held out her hand, "Esther Fuhrman."

Rodney went back to looking at the candy bars. M&Ms were always a safe bet. He rather liked Junior Mints. Cone didn't care for any of the fruity candies, like Starburst or whatever a Skittle was. But he had his eye on a 100 Grand; he wasn't sure what it was, but the description made it sound pretty good: "Chewy caramel & milk chocolate & crispy crunchies."

"Yes, but who are you?" Esther interrupted.

"Pardon?"

"Rodney," Esther said. "Obviously you're not from Opole. And I can tell by your face that you're somebody, but who?"

"Cone," he said. "Rodney Cone."

"Okay, but there are thousands of Coneses. What I'm asking is, where would I recognize you from? What do you do? Who are you?"

"Let me buy this candy bar, and then we can talk outside," Cone said. The few people in the gas station were beginning to notice the conversation. "Ever have one of these?" he asked, showing the 100 Grand to Esther.

"I don't care for chocolate," she said. "It makes me gassy."

Outside, Esther waited for Rodney to buy his candy, and then waited some more while he opened his 100 Grand and took a giant bite. The chocolate was of poor quality with a waxy texture, but he loved the combination of the flavors. He wiped his lips with the back of his hand and a satisfied look on his face and finally turned his attention to the ever-intrusive Esther.

"I'm a singer," he said bluntly.

"Oh, for Wianki," Esther said.

"Huh?"

"The festival," Esther said. "It's the Polish festival to

celebrate the summer solstice."

"Oh, I didn't know that," said Rodney. "Never heard of it before."

"Do you play any songs I'd know?"

"Probably," he said. "A couple years ago, you wouldn't have. But now my songs are pretty much everywhere over here. It's good for business, but a bit embarrassing."

"You shouldn't be embarrassed," Esther said. "It's hard to make it in music." She paused and looked at his half-eaten candy bar. "What song might I know?"

"'Faultless Quakes'?" he suggested tentatively.

"That's a title?"

Instead of answering, he sang an acapella version of the song to her. Esther was captivated.

"Oh, I do know that," she said. "But it's so much better than on the radio."

"Thank you."

"There's some real desperation and sadness in there."

Cone didn't answer.

"Sometimes things just don't work out, I guess," Esther said.

The two walked quietly up to the corner of the block and waited as the crosswalk sign changed from "do not walk" to "walk." Cone began to cross, but Esther remained on the curb.

"It was nice meeting you," she said.

Rodney Cone turned, tipped his head slightly, and said, "Likewise."

Typically, Esther's walk was faster than most people's jog, but today, unaware of what she was doing, she slowed everything down. Her arms didn't swing from hip to shoulder as she walked. Her hips didn't twist and her ass didn't jiggle. She just walked, holding the newspaper that she bought for Jeffrey. They should probably subscribe to the paper, since she ended up buying it on most days for him, but she wasn't thinking about newspaper subscriptions today. She wasn't even, for the first time in a very long time, thinking about who she would tell her news to. She was still lost in Rodney Cone's words and how he was able to so effortlessly carry the tune without accompaniment.

When she got home, she put the paper at Jeffrey's place on the table and sat in her chair in the dining room. Usually she would be thinking about what to make for dinner, or how many minutes she had before Bruce came home from school, or if Jeffrey would be late. Today she just sat there replaying her private moment with a superstar and watched the memory on loop in her mind. When Bruce walked in the door, she snapped out of it and sprang back into her usual mode, but the moment with Rodney Cone was not forgotten.

The day of the festival marked the first time that Esther's old circle of influence met her new one. In the past, the southern and northern neighborhoods had combined, but Esther hadn't given it much thought. Now, since Esther had lost favor with her old group and gained favor with a new one, she was extremely conscious of the melding of the families north and south of the jog in Beechwood Drive. By thwarting the assault on the school, she had gained back some of the respect of the southern families. Indeed, most of the families she once visited routinely now saw her as a hero. Even Regina McKinney seemed to have come to appreciate that Esther had prevented her son from doing something that would have greatly impacted his future.

Regina's husband Jim, however, was another story. Esther knew he never really liked her, and now he liked her even less. It was rare for someone to so blatantly not like her. Esther knew people talked about her behind her back, or at least she assumed they did, because she talked about them behind their backs, but she could count on her hand the number of people who openly expressed their dislike for her. Of the ones she could think of, Jim was the only person in Opole that made her feel uncomfortable. This was largely because she couldn't predict how he would behave. Sometimes he would be pleasant enough while other times he would pointedly ignore her. On occasion his anger would flare up and he'd yell and curse at her. "Get the fuck out of my house!" She wasn't used to being treated this way.

Jeffrey and Jim were having beers with Ray (Suzy Townsend's husband), Rick (Patty Lambert's husband), and Dean (Vicky Webster's husband). The men stood close, but not too close, and all the men were laughing. When one told a joke, the others rocked politely on their heels and laughed out loud. Rick was telling one now, "I heard they found the cure for AIDS." The other men look surprised.

"Oh?" asked Dean.

"I read about this, something called AZT?" asked Ray.

"That's that gay disease?" Jim asked. "I don't want to be anywhere near that." He crushed the beer can and looked for a cooler for another.

"Come on, you saw Princess Diana shake that guy's hand. She didn't have any gloves on," said Dean. "Just because someone's gay doesn't mean you're going to catch it."

"Right, right," said Rick. "Anyway, the cure is to sit down and keep your mouth shut."

"Oh, this was supposed to be a joke?" asked Ray.

There was a little polite chuckling, but no rocking back on their heels.

"I have one," said Ray. "What do you call an Amish guy with his hand up a horse's ass?"

"Sounds like a veterinarian," said Jeffrey.

"A mechanic," said Ray. He smiled at his own joke. The others laughed a little and then the men shifted their conversation to world affairs.

"Has anyone heard anything new about that West German kid, with the plane?" asked Ray.

"Guilty," said Jeffrey. "He's going to spend four years in a labor camp."

"Not if Gorbachev tears down that wall like Reagan told him to," said Jim. "Then that kid will get out early. Plus, he's not really a kid; he's like nineteen."

"Did you guys feel the quake a couple weeks ago?" asked Rick. "Patty swears she felt it. I told her we were too far away to feel anything like that."

"I didn't, but I heard other people saw things moving on their shelves," said Dean.

"Patty said she was sitting on the couch and sat bolt upright because it scared the crap out of her," Rick says. He laughed a little. "No way she's that sensitive."

"People in Canada felt it," said Jeffrey. "I guess I'd believe her. Where were you?"

"Working late," said Rick.

Esther didn't hear all of their conversation, but she picked up enough to get a sense of what was being said. Patty and Rick were clearly having problems. Jeffrey was opening another can of beer and she absently wondered how many he already had. She filed the information away and turned her attention to the children. They were gathered in a circle like the men, but instead of beer they were drinking Coca-Cola. Unlike the adults, the children didn't segregate based on gender; the boys and girls mingled together and chatted.

"You are so lucky that your dad let you see *Adventures in Babysitting*," said David.

"It was no big deal," said Jason.

"No big deal? It's rated PG-13!" said Bruce.

"It wasn't like there were any tits in it," said Jason. "Just language."

"Like what?" asked Angie.

"They say fuck a couple times," said Jason. "And shit, and asshole."

"I heard all of that in *Spaceballs*, and that was only PG," said Barry. "My mom flipped and almost dragged me out of the theater when they dropped the f-word. But my dad stopped her."

"All I got to see was *Harry and the Hendersons*," said Bruce. "You could tell it was just a guy in a costume. So, lame."

"Less than two weeks until *Pee-Wee's Big Adventure*!" said David.

"That should be good," said Barry. "I saw the ad for it on Saturday."

"Me, too," said Angie. "But, it didn't look like anyone from the show was in it. No Chairry, or Jambi, or Magic Screen. It looks like it is just about him trying to find his bike."

A silence fell over the small group as they sipped their sodas and tried to think of what to say next.

"Any new astronaut jokes?" Bruce asked Barry.

Barry was the resident joke collector, and his specialty, since the *Challenger* exploded last year, were forbidden astronaut jokes. Barry couldn't remember which ones he'd told already, but his uncle had told him a new one recently. Barry looked around to see who was listening. He noticed Esther but figured she was too far away to hear.

"How many astronauts can fit in a Volkswagen?" he said, barely louder than a whisper.

"I don't know," said Jason. He was Rick and Patty's oldest and always felt the need to fill any silence with sound.

"Two in the front, two in the back, and seven in the ashtray," Barry said with a smirk.

David and Angie laughed at the same time, but it took Jason a minute to get the joke. Then he began to laugh. Only Bruce didn't laugh.

"I don't get it," he said.

"How many astronauts died on the *Challenger*?" asked David.

"Seven," said Bruce. He began to see where the joke was going but said, "But they weren't cremated. I thought they found pieces of them on the beach." He paused and waited for a beat. "Plus, when someone is cremated, there are a lot of ashes. When my grandfather died, it filled this whole thing. His ashes never would have fit in an ashtray. No way there'd be room for seven."

"It's a fucking joke," said Barry.

"But jokes are supposed to make sense," said Bruce.

The younger kids, Jane, Lisa, and Michael, lingered on the fringes of the older kids' circle. They poked their heads into the ring occasionally and tried to listen to see if they could pick up anything interesting. But more than anything they were just observing and taking careful notes about how to behave. Esther had heard the joke and shook her head. She was glad that her Bruce didn't find the joke funny, but was a little disturbed it was based on a technicality. Ever since she found those plans of the school, she couldn't quite look at Barry and David in the same way, and now, to hear Barry telling these tasteless jokes, she was even more disappointed. She walked casually away from the children and toward the stage where the band *Velcro Soldiers* was setting up. Esther didn't know what type of music they played, but she had heard they were from East Lansing.

As she neared the stage, she saw Regina and Vicky standing a little back from the fray near the Ben Franklin store. Carol, the photographer with the unemployable alcoholic husband, was chatting intimately with them. It stung a little to feel excluded, but Esther was nervous about approaching her old friends. Regina had mostly forgiven her for the leukemia-debacle, though, honestly, Esther had never fully admitted to inventing the story. Everyone assumed she was at fault, and that was enough to convict her in the court of neighborhood opinion. In their position, she would have done the same. She didn't fault them. She had even considered confessing, but instead held onto that small thread of untruth. Who knew when it might be useful.

Esther approached the group slowly and feigned interest in the sidewalk tables selling handmade goods or distributing information about local organizations or charities.

"I just heard that Fred Astaire died," said Regina.

"A month ago," said Carol.

"Oh?" Regina asked. "Clearly I'm not as up on my famous people as you are. I guess he was almost ninety."

"Eighty-eight," interrupted Carol.

"That is almost ninety," said Vicky.

"He lived a long life, but it's still sad. I can't help but imagine him as an old man remembering being able to dance like that, and looking down at those legs and knowing that he wouldn't be able to do that again," said Regina.

"Wow, thanks for that, Debbie Downer," said Vicky. She sipped from a thermos, but it wasn't clear to Esther what her friend was drinking. In the old days, they would slip liquor into thermoses. In the last couple years, they had opted for coffee mixed with Kahlua. Esther hadn't been invited to meet up with them this year, so it was anyone's guess what they'd settled on for their thermoses.

"You want a real downer, let's talk about poor Heather O'Rourke," said Carol. "I really don't know what Crohn's disease is, but she isn't doing so well. And she's only eleven."

"Wait, who?" asked Regina.

"The girl from *Happy Days* and *Poltergeist*," said Vicky. She knew the name, but had no idea about her age. "Eleven? By god, that's almost our kids' ages."

"Or younger than your oldest," said Brenda, walking up to the group, "If you're a college dropout like me."

"Hey Brenda," said Regina. "Welcome to the party. Any depressing news you'd like to share with the group?"

As Regina and Vicky turned to welcome Brenda into their conversation, they caught Esther eying the group.

Esther had been working her way closer and closer but had not quite worked up the courage to approach the group. As she picked up a flyer from a table, she overheard someone, she thought Vicky but she wasn't sure, say, "Here she comes; Esther on the prowl. She's limping like a little puppy that's been naughty." Outwardly, Esther ignored the comment. She didn't flinch, even though it felt like she'd been struck. She looked at a flyer she had picked up and placed it back on the table.

During her gradual, circuitous approach over the last seven minutes, she had worked through several opening lines. She considered: "Happen'en?"; "Hello, gals"; "Long time, no see"; and "Hey, hey, hey." None of them felt quite right. Finally, Esther jutted her chin up a tiny bit and walked purposefully to the group, taking her place beside Brenda. She opened her mouth and said the first thing that came to mind.

"Regina, does Jim still like to record things off TV?"

"He does," Regina answered. "Anything in particular you're looking for?"

"The Live Aid concert from a couple years ago," said Esther. "Any chance he has a copy and would be willing to let me borrow it?"

"You could always go ask him," said Regina. She knew this was a particularly mean thing to say because she was well aware that Esther didn't like her husband.

"Okay," said Esther.

"Why do you want to watch that?" asked Brenda.

"Have you ever heard of Rodney Cone?"

"The guy who's playing tonight?" asked Vicky.

"Yeah," said Esther. "I thought the name sounded familiar, and I think it's because I remember him playing a song there."

"Just one song?" asked Regina.

"Most of the musicians didn't play very many," said Esther.

Esther had actually watched the live event, but hadn't thought to ask Jeffrey to record it for her. Live Aid had been hyped to be such a big deal that Esther couldn't help but tune in. She wasn't a big fan of music in general, but when someone described something as, "A once in a lifetime event," as Bob Geldof had, Esther felt compelled not to be left out. ABC only played three hours of the concert, but apparently the concert had lasted for closer to sixteen or eighteen hours.

Esther remembered sitting on the couch watching it. Such a big deal was made about *Led Zeppelin* reforming, but to her, it didn't sound very good. Afterward people speculated about if they had even rehearsed at all. Plant and Page dispelled these rumors, but blamed the poor performance on Phil Collins, who had filled in on drums for the deceased John Bonham. Somewhere in the three hours of television that Esther watched, she did remember a quiet single-song set from a man behind a piano. If someone had asked her about this prior to her meeting with Rodney Cone, it would never have stood out to her. After hearing him sing to her on the sidewalk the other day, the sonic memory flashed, and she couldn't get it out of her mind. She had to see the video again.

"I remember that," said Carol. Then she turned to Esther and said, "Hi, I'm Carol Daniels."

"The new photographer in town," said Esther. "I'm Esther."

Their little group of women grew as Becky, Suzy, and Patty all joined them on the sidewalk. Esther's tension and anxiety began to fade as the two circles of friends found a rhythm to their conversation. Vicky even offered Esther a drink from her thermos, and the two friends shared the quiet secret of the liquid inside. Esther decided she liked Carol, even if she seemed a little too focused on celebrity gossip. Carol might turn out to be a good connection, and she could always use her friendship for a discount on photography.

Velcro Soldiers finished their set of mostly covers, and roadies began setting up for Rodney Cone's performance. The men meandered over and met and mingled with their wives, and the group took up a sizeable portion of the area to the right of the stage. Occasionally a parent would glance in the direction of the children, or ask, "Shouldn't we get them to bed?" But, ultimately, the decision was made that this was a special day, and the parents should just enjoy the peace and quiet. Besides, it was nearly time for the final show to begin. The stage lights dimmed, and Cone walked right past their group. His eye caught sight of Esther, a friendly face in the crowd, and he smiled and winked, though he wasn't sure if she could see it. No one else noticed, but she did.

Rodney Cone could have performed an abbreviated set and still fulfilled his obligations, but he didn't. He played the full setlist that he had played on the rest of the tour and even added some songs that he hadn't played in a long time. He played "Dayglo Sunshine," which was his first single from 1983, "Come Over for Tea" from 1984, and an early version of "Sundrop Sorrow," which wouldn't be released until next year. The crowd might not have been Madison Square Garden or the Bronco Bowl, but the people of Opole were locked into the groove of Cone's songs and loving every minute of it. They danced. They enjoyed themselves.

When the show was over, the group lingered. The consensus of the men was that they were surprised by how much they enjoyed Cone's music. They had expected, given that he was on a piano, that it would be more of a chick thing, but they found they recognized a number of the songs and enjoyed it. The women universally loved Cone and enjoyed the opportunity to dance with their husbands. On this night, they had danced without stopping in a way they hadn't since they were in their teens or early twenties. They had also drank in a similar manner and were all, well most of them, very, very drunk.

All night, everyone had treated Esther warmly, acting almost as if nothing had happened. But for Jim, everything wasn't all right, and he hadn't forgiven Esther. The group was now gathered in a long line, waiting for the Port-a-Potty. As they waited, the party goers expressed their surprise and dismay that the town only had a single Port-a-Potty at either end of the festival area. How had someone not planned better for this? They knew Wianki was well-attended. The group shifted their weight from foot to foot as they waited for their turn and made small talk with those closest in line to them.

Suddenly, out of nowhere, Jim pushed Esther. Jim hadn't meant to push her so hard; he just meant to give her a little shove to let her know that he wasn't okay with her. Esther had betrayed his son by doing what she always did, sticking her nose in other people's business. Jim knew this drove everyone else batshit, but they weren't willing to say anything out loud. He felt like he had to speak for all of them. Even still, he probably would have swallowed his pride and kept his hands to himself if he hadn't just overheard Esther saying something that sounded suspiciously like "leukemia." That reminder of Esther's meddling in his son's business, a child who didn't realize the implications of the rumors the town gossip had started, boiled his blood. It didn't help that he was drunk. Still, he never could have anticipated that his shove would end up with Esther bleeding so profusely. He had only meant the shove to say, "Hey, I heard that and you and I are *not* okay," but Jim wasn't always very good at moderation. It also didn't help that Esther hadn't been expecting to make a sudden movement, and though she wasn't drunk, her reaction time was slowed by the alcohol she had consumed.

Jeffrey was in the Port-a-Potty when it happened, so he didn't see Jim shove Esther, but Rodney Cone just happened to stroll by when it went down. He saw the man push Esther and saw the blood gushing from her nose as she lay surprised on the ground beside the Port-a-Potty line. Cone had zero tolerance for violence against women. He rushed over to Esther's side and caught the eye of the man who had pushed her. In that moment, Cone was giving the man an opportunity to apologize or to prepare for a punch. Jim did neither. Jim was obviously drunk, but Cone was angry in a way he hadn't been in a long time.

Cone, born in England, had moved to Canada during his teen years and then moved back to England to attend the Royal Northern College of Music. He had three younger brothers, and while they occasionally wrestled and fought with one another, Cone wasn't necessarily a brawler. When he moved to Manchester for school, most of his focus was on music, but he also found himself drawn to Buddhism. There was one time at Peveril of the Peak, Cone's favorite Manchester pub, that he was pushed a bit too far. Cone was sitting at the bar, talking with friends, but he kept noticing a couple that was arguing at a nearby table. The woman was obviously tired and frustrated, and the man was drunk and belligerent. She wanted to go home, but the man with her demanded they stay for another drink. When she got up to leave, the man blocked her way. Cone was trying to listen to his friend, but the man raised his hand like he was going to slap the woman, and that was too much for Cone. Cone walked over to the man, confronted him, ducked the man's punch, and then laid him out with a blow to the jaw.

Rodney Cone hadn't hit anyone since that day, and his fist ached to do it again. He clenched his jaw, squared his feet, and delivered. Jim went down. Jeffrey emerged from the Port-a-

Potty just in time to see blood streaming down his wife's face and one of his friends getting knocked out.

CHAPTER 4: THE PORN RING

The morning after, Jim stood at the Fuhrman front door. His face was bruised, but he was dressed nicer than his job required. If Jim had rang the doorbell, Esther would have heard it right away, but he was a man who knocked, and his knocks got overshadowed by the vacuum Esther was pushing in the living room. Eventually, she saw a shadow at the entryway and went to investigate.

"Jim," she said.

"Esther, I'm really sorry," he said. He held a box in both arms.

"Oh, don't worry," Esther said.

"No, I really need to apologize. I've never been very nice to you, but last night was uncalled for," he said. "I'm sorry."

"Aren't you late for work?" she asked.

"Not very," he said. "Besides, the city can wait a bit. I didn't want to wake anyone up. I know it was a late night for everyone. Is Jeffrey still here?"

"No, he left about thirty minutes ago," she said. "Want to come in?"

"Thanks, but no," Jim said. "I just came to apologize and to give you this."

He handed her the box. It wasn't as heavy as she expected

it to be.

"What's this?" she asked, as she opened the lid.

"Gina said you wanted a copy of the Live Aid concert," he said. "I got most of it, but had to change tapes every 90 minutes or so." Jim looked up at her. "That means pieces are missing here and there, but we do have BBC." Jim kept waiting for Esther to say something, and when she didn't, he continued to fill the air with his words. "Here in the states, it was the only way to get the whole concert. ABC only carried a couple hours of the show, but BBC had it all. I got as much as I could. Like I said, there are gaps, but it's mostly there."

He paused again, waiting. Still nothing. Then he remembered, "Oh, I almost forgot. Gina said you really wanted the tape for that singer from last night," he laughed slightly, "the one with a solid right hook."

That caught Esther's attention. She had been staring at the VHS tapes in the box slightly confused by them while listening to Jim drone on. The mention of Cone caught her attention. Still holding securely to the sides of the box, Esther froze as Jim reached over and started flipping through the tapes. Suddenly he stopped and held up a tape.

"This one," Jim said, holding the tape where Esther could see it, "has Cone's performance on it. It took some doing to find it, and to isolate it, but I didn't go to bed until I had it for you."

He hadn't slept much at all last night, and definitely was going to pay for that today. Probably around lunch time, Jim would start to drag and want a nap. But, getting punched last night had really shaken him up. Even if he hadn't been digging through the VHS tapes all night to find the Live Aid tapes from 1985, he wouldn't have been able to sleep. His jaw was sore, heck his whole face was sore, and his mind was spinning. It was hard to sleep when that happened. Jim had a lot of tapes to dig through. Blank tapes weren't cheap, but Jim was firmly convinced that being able to re-watch shows had a value beyond dollars. He recorded almost anything he even vaguely might want to watch again. Regina was pretty convinced it was a disease, but occasionally she was grateful that Jim had captured a show that she wanted to see again.

"Thank you," Esther said finally. She would look forward to watching it today.

"He only did one song," said Jim. "Flew all the way to England to play that one song in the middle of a tour. Cone told me that last night. He's a stand-up guy. He might have knocked me out, but he made sure I was taken care of afterward."

"Thanks again, Jim. I really do appreciate it. Do you need these back?"

"I haven't watched them since I recorded it two years ago. You take your time, and if you want to keep them, go ahead. If you don't, then you can throw them away or send them back. Your choice," he said. "Now, I am off to work. The city will wait, but only for so long. Eventually someone's going to need an inspection and wonder where the inspector has gone."

Esther carefully set the box of tapes on the coffee table, finished vacuuming, and then wrote a note to Bruce that she would be back after some errands. She left the note near his cereal bowl at his spot on the table to find when he eventually woke up. Then she closed up the house and headed out the door.

As soon as she was gone, Bruce got out of bed, read the note, and called Barry.

"She's gone for a bit," Bruce said. "Want to see what I got?"

He hung up the phone and a few minutes later, Barry and David were at the door. They gave the special knock, even though they knew only Bruce was home. It was more out of habit than anything. Bruce yelled, "Come in. Finishing breakfast."

"So?" asked Barry as he walked into the dining room.

"We were over at Uncle Kenny's last week," said Bruce.

"And you're just telling us now?" asked David.

"It's been crazy," said Bruce. "I haven't had time. Anyway,

I took four magazines. They're in my backpack, under my bed. Go check them out while I finish. I still need to brush my teeth and clean up."

At the words "under my bed" David and Barry took off to Bruce's bedroom. They heard, but didn't really listen, to the rest of what he had said.

Uncle Kenny was Esther's older bachelor brother. He owned a home forty minutes from Opole, just inside a larger city. His house was tastefully decorated, not like the normal bachelor pad. Kenny considered himself as an artist, though few recognized his talent. He had a good eye with color and unusual pairings of finishes. In fact, he would have made a great interior decorator if he could take instructions from clients. That was Kenny's flaw. On the rare occasion someone commissioned a work from him, he went in his own direction regardless of what the client actually wanted.

"What the hell is this? I paid you to do _____."

And Kenny's response would be, "You have no idea what you really want; this was calling to me from the canvas."

As a result, Kenny wasn't gainfully employed as an artist. Instead, he worked mixing paints at Ann Arbor Paint and Wallpaper. It was a small business, and it was often overshadowed by its bigger competitors, like Sherwin Williams and Benjamin Moore and Pittsburgh Paints, but Ann Arbor Paint and Wallpaper had a large enough client base to keep it busy.

Mixing paints at A2PW, as Kenny called it, provided him employment that was adjacent to his true love of art, but not directly dependent on his creation of art. When a client brought paint chips or a paint sample to him, his job was to match the colors the best he could with the paints he had available. He was good at it, too. The customers requested him by name, and some learned that Kenny was an authentic artist. Then, inevitably, they would make the mistake of commissioning him to create a work that would fit into the scope of their renovation, and all were dissatisfied as Kenny veered far from the script. Inevitably, those customers who returned to A2PW requested to have him not mix their paints or they went to a different store.

In addition to his fine eye for color-matching and mixing, Kenny also had an extensive collection of pornography. He had *Playboy* and *Penthouse*, but he also had: *Hustler*, *Oui*, *Celebrity Skin*, Juggs, and For Men Only. It was Kenny's eye for porn that drew the attention and admiration of his nephew Bruce. For the most part, Bruce was bored when the family went to visit Kenny's place. The house was immaculately decorated, and Uncle Kenny did not have toys for Bruce to play with. He did have the Nintendo and every game for it that Bruce knew of, and several he had never heard of before, but even those got boring after a while. Invariably, his mother would interrupt *Donkey Kong, Super Mario Bros., Duck Hunt, Castlevania, Punch-Out!!,* or, Bruce's favorite, *Spy Hunter,* to remind him it was important to actually "visit" with his uncle and not just play his games. When Bruce failed to respond, particularly if he was trying to line up his G-6155 Interceptor to drive into the back of the weapons van to acquire new equipment, his mother would say, "And this is exactly why we don't have one of these systems at our house." Occasionally, Kenny and Esther would go out to a local restaurant to talk, or shop, or do something together, and they would leave Bruce behind at the apartment. Kenny and Esther assumed he was fully immersed in his video game world, and Bruce worked hard to project that illusion, but as soon as they left, he would abandon whatever game he was playing and make a beeline to Kenny's office.

In the office, next to the file cabinet, Kenny kept boxes filled with his magazines. Many of these dated back to the founding of the magazine. Kenny had the full run of *Oui* (1972-present), *Juggs* (1981-present), *Celebrity Skin* (1986-present), and *Hustler* (1974-present). Bruce wasn't sure how far back Kenny's collection of *Playboy* or *Penthouse* went, but there were a lot of issues to choose from. When he knew how much time he had, Bruce would browse a bit. The older issues of *For Men Only* were almost entirely stories and articles. He never took any of these for his friends due to the lack of pictures, but

Bruce read through many of the issues. The stories were mostly adventures, and the subscription was kept current. If Bruce was short on time, he would just reach into the middle of a box of *Oui*, *Penthouse*, or *Hustler*, and grab one or two magazines at random.

By the time his mother and uncle returned, Bruce was back in front of the television. He was a sneaky little bastard, too. He always remembered to carry a backpack filled with toys and books over to his uncle's house to smuggle the contraband safely out of the house without anyone being the wiser. To this point, he had never been caught. At least, if his uncle noticed anything, he never said so.

Bruce was putting his cereal bowl away when he heard David and Barry gasp in unison.

"This is last month's!" David yelled down the hall.

"Yeah," Bruce yelled back, as casually as he could. He closed the dishwasher.

"Usually you get shit from way back in the seventies!" yelled Barry.

"It looked like a particularly good issue," Bruce said. He was almost to his room now. As he turned the corner in the hall, he could see his friends hadn't even opened the April 1987 issue of *Oui*. "Guys, you haven't even opened it yet."

"This is Samantha Fox on the cover," said David. "She does that song, 'Touch Me.' It's hot."

"She's hot. I don't know about the song," said Barry.

On the cover, Samantha Fox was holding boxing gloves over her breasts. "You know she moves those boxing gloves inside, right?" Bruce said.

"I'm more interested in this '1987 Amateur Nudies' than what Samantha's boobs look like," said David.

"Not a boob guy, huh?" asked Bruce.

"Boobs are fine," said David.

Barry flipped through the pages as Bruce and David looked on. They stopped occasionally to examine a photo more closely, and then continued. David was clearly keeping count of something. When they were done, Barry closed the

MacBride

magazine and flipped it back over.

"Thirty-five," said David. "There were thirty-five pictures that we can easily sell for a buck or two. More pictures if we count some of the smaller ones, and the ones that aren't full nude. We're going to make a killing on this one."

"People really like her music," said Barry. "I think we can jack the usual prices up because of that and because this is so, so, current."

"You haven't even looked at the other three," said Bruce.

"Are they as new as this one?" asked Barry.

"Two of them are older, and the *Celebrity Skin* is just from last year," said Bruce. "Those usually go quick, because sometimes people have seen the girls in movies."

"Yeah, and those aren't usually even nude," said David.

Suddenly it occurred to Bruce that he wasn't sure how much longer he had before his mother returned. He wasn't exactly sure how long ago she had left, and how many errands she had to run. She could be extremely expedient, or she might run into someone and end up talking for hours and completely forget about him. It was a gamble. He'd have to get things moving.

"My mom left me a note with some things to do, so I need to get busy," he said. "Do you guys mind taking the magazines to the fort?"

The fort wasn't the traditional kid-fort. It wasn't in a tree or a large hole dug in the ground. The fort was in the rafters of the McKinney garage. Jim McKinney, running out places to keep junk in the house, had nailed down some plywood across the rafters of the garage to disperse the weight of the items he kept there. For the most part, that consisted of boxes. But there were also some spare parts to the lawn mower, or an old lawn mower he was supposed to have gotten rid of, and other odds and ends he wasn't yet willing to let go. Regina McKinney wanted nothing to do with that part of the garage, and so Jim was able to hide whatever he wanted up there. It wasn't that she didn't know the rafters contained things she'd rather not possess anymore, it was more that as long as she didn't have to

56

see it, she was okay with it. It wasn't in the house anymore, it wasn't underfoot, and so she was fine. If you wanted to get into the rafters, you had to drag a ladder from one side of the garage to the opening in the plywood. Then you had to be able to lift yourself up the remaining foot and a half or so and drag yourself onto the plywood. Getting up wasn't so bad, but getting up also meant you had to be able to get back down.

The kids, however, didn't mind. It was a great place to hang out with little effort. Both Regina and Jim knew the boys went up there. Occasionally they would half-heartedly say, "Boys, be careful up there" or "Please don't mess with the boxes," but they never did anything to keep the kids from claiming the rafter-area as their fort. In fact, Jim and Regina even began to think of that area as "the fort."

At first, Jim worried the boys would mess with his "things." He didn't express this concern to Regina, because it would mean admitting that he had "things" in the rafters (a fact she already knew, and he was pretty sure he knew that she knew). Jim used to climb up into the rafters to make sure everything was still in order, and then decided that the kids were being respectful of his things. In fact, the more he thought about it, the more he liked that they used that area as a fort. It meant they had a place to play that was outside of the house, but not subject to the weather. Regina didn't mind either. She was mostly concerned that someone would fall and break their neck, but as Jim had found, the kids were careful and no one had broken a neck yet.

"The boys" primarily meant Barry, David, and Bruce, but sometimes included Jason Lambert, and when he was good, Barry's younger brother Mark. Occasionally, Angie Walker would join them, as she was considered an honorary member of "the boys," but she rarely visited the fort. The boys enjoyed finding treasures to keep in their fort, and Jim often gave the kids shit about going through people's garbage for their treasures. The first fort had been constructed entirely from garbage collected during Spring Clean-up. One time, David brought home a box of forty-some hubcaps. Jim asked him what he was going to do with them, and David said he wasn't sure. The two looked at the hubcaps for a long time, and finally Jim said, "I'm not an expert, but I'm pretty sure you could sell these to the junkyard." They went to the junkyard and cashed in the hubcaps for twenty dollars.

"It's more than you started with," Jim had said. That became the mantra for the friends. Anything they saw, they wondered how much it was worth and if they could sell it. Most of the time, it didn't amount to anything, but occasionally, as with the hubcaps, it was enough for them to buy some candy and a new toy of some sort—often GI Joes, but sometimes a plastic model car.

Among the assorted items in the fort was an old toilet. The toilet wasn't one of their finds, but rather one that Jim found on his own. He was driving to work one morning and saw it at the end of someone's driveway. He pulled his car over the curb, killed the engine, and thought for a moment, then dashed out of the car, grabbed the toilet, and not knowing what else to do with it, hauled it up into the rafters before Regina could see what he'd dragged home. Jim didn't know whose house he was parked in front of. On the one hand, that was a good thing. It would be embarrassing to be garbage picking from a friend or neighbor. He was far enough away from the usual neighborhood, so he wouldn't have to worry about Esther reporting that Jim McKinney was collecting junk like his kid. On the other hand, not knowing was almost worse. Since he worked for the city, he wasn't sure who might recognize him and who might not; even if they didn't recognize him today, they might call for an inspection and then suddenly think, "Hey, isn't that the guy who took the toilet from our garbage?" Jim was pretty sure if he ever saw someone picking through his garbage, he would remember it for the rest of his life. What if he was confronted as he had the toilet half in his trunk? What would he say?

Jim decided he was being ridiculous. These people obviously didn't want the toilet anymore, and they wouldn't care how it was removed from their premises, as long as it was.

He was willing to offer that service for them. He got out of the car, and circled the toilet. No gouges. No cracks. No obvious signs of damage. It was in great condition. Why on earth would these people be throwing away a perfectly good toilet? He couldn't imagine a scenario where someone would remove one from their house. Did they suddenly decide they had too many bathrooms in their home? Did they upgrade their toilet to some kind of new model? Had there been some kind of innovation in toilets that Jim was unaware of? He gave the toilet another glance, unlocked his trunk, and hefted the toilet into his car.

The McKinneys didn't need another toilet, and Jim knew that. He knew if he told Regina about his find, she'd demand that they dispose of this perfectly good toilet. In fact, maybe this scenario is precisely what resulted in this toilet being left at the end of the driveway of the house he was taking it from. The saga of the toilet might have begun long ago by a man who found this undamaged toilet, brought it home, and then found his treasure rejected by his wife, and that cycle was about to be repeated by Jim. Stranger things have happened. Jim eventually decided he would take the toilet home, back the car into the garage, and heft the thing into the rafters. Regina would never know, and should one of their toilets crack or become damaged, he could be a hero for saving them money. "Funny story," he imagined himself saying, "the other day"—which could mean anything from, literally the other day to six months or a year ago—"I found a toilet on the side of the road and kept it up in the garage." Future-imaginary Regina would be so pleased. He hauled the toilet up to the rafters where it was all but forgotten. In the years it had been up there, none of their toilets had cracked or became damaged in anyway, and Regina was none-the-wiser.

Eventually, the forgotten toilet became an essential part of the fort. It happened like this. When Bruce first showed one of Uncle Kenny's magazines to David and Barry, they were stunned by the images within. They had, of course, heard of sex, and David's parents had even given him an uncomfortable "sex talk," but they wouldn't have a full-on "sex education" class until next year. They studied that first magazine from cover to cover, even reading some of the letters and articles. But, after the novelty wore off—around the tenth magazine— the boys' thoughts turned to the question of what to do with them now. It was Bruce who suggested selling them. Immediately, they were hit with the sense of opportunity they had here. Barry was the one who pointed out that, "this is a hundred bucks; no one could afford it." Then David suggested selling the magazine an image at a time. Genius. Refinements of the idea fell out of their mouths: big images could go for two dollars, smaller ones for a buck or fifty cents, and they'd make a killing.

For the boys, the forgotten toilet became an ideal place to hide their porn until they could sell the pictures. The porn rarely stayed in the toilet for long. During the school year, they took it to school in their backpacks, safely sandwiched flat in special folders, and they would sell the images, cut from the magazines, on the playground during recess or before school. Their biggest buyer was Jason Lambert. As the richest kid on the block, he had the most disposable income. He always had the coolest, newest toys, and a seeming endless supply of cash for the candy store. The boys didn't mingle much with Jason outside of school. His wealth kept him out of the "Bruce, Barry, David" social circle. Ironically, Jason bought the porn largely because he wanted an excuse to spend time with the boys. He didn't really need more naked pictures (he'd already purchased a decent collection from them and the novelty had worn off long ago), but he remained a dependable buyer. Unfortunately for the boys, Jason had been gone most of the summer. With their top buyer out of the picture, the toilet was getting rather full.

David and Barry arrived at the McKinney household with their latest stash and started to head up to the fort when David was called into the house by his parents.

"Just a minute!" he yelled. He turned to Barry and whispered, "Get the stuff up into the fort."

"No problem," said Barry.

David ran into the house, and Barry went to the garage. He moved the ladder, climbed to the top, dragged himself up onto the plywood, and opened the toilet. It was packed to the rim, so instead Barry laid the new issues on the floor and sat down to flip through a couple magazines from the toilet. He was lost for a moment in the allure of nudity when he heard a car start and the garage door go down. No worries; he would just go out the side door of the garage, climb the fence, and head home. Barry stuffed all the magazines into the full toilet, but then worried he was bending and damaging the valuable images. So, he pulled a couple magazines from the toilet, pressed them flat, and set them behind the toilet. He knew this wasn't protocol, but he was pretty sure Bruce and David would understand why he did it. Besides, they'd be unloading the magazines soon enough. Jason was finally back in town, so most likely the boys would meet up tomorrow for a cutting session to get ready for their best buyer.

If they had just cut the images from the magazines right away, they could have fit more in the toilet than they could with full magazines; however, as ten and eleven-year-olds, it didn't occur to them. They always met and cut together. Each brought a pair of scissors and a backpack from home. They'd sit and cut the images, make small talk about anything that had happened since the last time they'd met, and comment on particularly striking images, new poses, or anything novel they found in the magazine they were working on. When they were done, they'd put the images into the nondescript folders they each had in their backpacks. Finally, they'd clean up the scraps and put them in plastic bags to toss in the dumpster behind the local businesses.

This all came to a screeching halt the day that Barry broke with protocol and left three magazines behind, not in, the toilet. He waited a couple seconds after the garage door shut, then climbed down into the empty garage, replaced the ladder, exited through the side door, and climbed the chain-link fence as he headed home. About an hour later, the McKinneys returned to their house. Jim McKinney liked to back into the garage, and if he had been driving, who knows how things would have gone differently. Today, however, he wasn't driving; Regina was behind the wheel. Jim almost always drove, but on occasion, he would get a migraine headache that rendered him useless for driving, or about anything else. Today, in the middle of their visit to Sam's Clothing Store where they were trying to find new pants for David, a migraine struck Jim and shortened their errand.

Regina waited for the garage door to fully retract, and as she did so she was grateful that her husband had a migraine. Not because she was a terrible person, but because she knew if he didn't have a migraine, he'd be giving her shit for not backing into the garage.

"It makes it so much easier to pull out," he would be saying, "and it doesn't take that much longer to back in. And, it's good practice for parallel parking when you go downtown."

Regina didn't buy any of these arguments and was tired of hearing them.

"When you drive, you park the way you want to, and when I drive, I'll park the way I want to," she always said.

It happened about every fourth time Regina drove. They'd have the argument; she wouldn't drive for a while because it was easier for Jim to just do his thing than for Regina to have to put up with his nagging her about how to park; then she would drive a couple times to test the waters, and Jim would keep his mouth shut; and then suddenly the argument would happen again. When Jim announced he was heading to the car because he needed to close his eyes and couldn't handle the artificial light in Sam's Clothing Store, Regina knew she had a free pass on parking, and could park however the hell she wanted.

The entire drive home, Jim criticized Regina's driving.

"Why do you keep jerking the car around?" he asked.

"It's the wind!" replied an exasperated Regina. Just because Jim drove all the time, he seemed to think he was some expert about driving. Regina was a perfectly good driver, and she resented his constant corrections or suggestions.

It had become very windy while they were out. The trees bent over sideways and the leaves and garbage were strewn about the street. The gusts of wind shook the car as Regina waited for the garage door to full open. Jim grumbled.

Regina pulled in and parked as the wind burst through the open garage door and swirled through the rafters. It invaded every available space in the garage and jostled the toilet slightly. Unfortunately, it also caught the three magazines that Barry had left lying behind, not in, the toilet. The wind grabbed the magazines and dropped them from the rafters. They fluttered down and landed squarely on the hood of the McKinney family vehicle.

David was in the back of the car, and Jim had his eyes closed, but Regina saw the whole thing. She didn't realize at first that it was porn, but she did see something had fallen from the rafters. She knew that Jim kept his "things" up there, even though he wasn't supposed to. She was perfectly happy to ignore that fact, as long as she didn't have to look at it. Jim had done his best with the plywood to obscure the fact of his "things" from sight. But now something had fallen from the rafters. Three magazines, and the wind was whipping through the pages of the magazines, which meant Regina knew exactly what type of magazines these were. Her first thought was, "Is this the kind of shit he's keeping up there? Does he climb up there and beat off in the garage? In David's fort?"

"JIM!" she yelled.

As much as Jim wanted to be in the comfort and darkness of his bedroom with the curtains drawn, he knew that tone. Something had happened, and his wife assumed he was at fault. "What?" he asked, trying to find his way out of the car without opening his eyes.

"WHAT. IS. THIS?" she asked.

David couldn't quite see what was going on. He was working his way around to the front of the vehicle when his father stepped in front of him.

"Regina, can we talk about whatever this is later?" Jim

asked. "My eyes feel like they're being pushed into my skull right now."

"NO! NOW."

Jim worked his way around the car, trying to get as far away as possible from the light streaming through the open garage door. Despite the wind, it was a very sunny day. He felt along the side of the car, and then felt where the side panel ended and the bumper assembly began. He opened his eyes. The light burned, but he immediately registered the images in the magazine pages whipping back and forth in the wind.

"Jesus!" he yelled. He closed his eyes again.

By now, David had worked his way to the front of the car. His stomach dropped. Slowly, he began retreating as nonchalantly as possible.

"THIS IS WHAT YOU KEEP UP THERE?" Regina yelled. Her focus and fury was on her husband, but her words smacked her son as if they were intended for him.

"You think that's mine?" asked Jim defensively.

"Who else's would it be?" demanded Regina. "I can tell you I'm about to find out."

Regina dragged the ladder across the garage floor. David headed toward his room. Jim stood there confused, eyes tightly shut.

"I swear, they're not mine," said Jim.

"Are you blaming this, this filth, on our son?" yelled Regina. The ladder was in place now, and she was climbing it. "That's low, Jim. Where would he even get such a thing?"

As she said this, her mind started spinning. Was it David's? Maybe he got it from Barry? That kid was always trouble. Or, he stole it? Jesus, was her son a thief? Maybe David and Barry were working together – one distracts while the other steals? That was even worse. She heaved herself up onto the plywood and heard the cheap plastic toilet seat rattle from the wind.

"Regina, you have to believe me. I swear," Jim pleaded. He was still keeping his eyes closed, despite wanting to make eye contact with his wife to show her how sincere he was. He could hear the rivets on her Levi's scraping on the plywood.

She was in the rafters. He couldn't have made eye contact if he even wanted to.

"Jesus Christ!" Regina screamed from the fort. She had opened the toilet and was tearing the magazines out of it. She threw the magazines down from the rafters. "You are a sick, sick man."

"There's more?" Jim asked, as the magazines fell on him. He crouched down and gathered up the magazines. There were at least fifteen, maybe twenty?

"Of course, there's more!" Regina yelled. "I found your collection!"

"I don't know what to say," Jim said. He was just as surprised as she was, but he couldn't think of a way to convince her. "Look, come down here and let's talk about it. Maybe we could go into a dark room, so I can deal with this fucking migraine, and we can talk about it?"

He hadn't noticed, but Regina had already climbed down the ladder, and now she was just standing there crying. "Honey," he said. "Look, they really aren't mine. It's got to be the boys. Nobody else goes up there."

Regina started crying harder. Regina had many complaints about her husband, but Jim was an honest man. As much as she hated the idea of her husband having a secret stash of porn, she really, really hated the idea of her son having one. They would have to confront their son about his collection of pornography. Giving David the "sex talk" had been awkward enough for all involved; she could only imagine how this one would go.

Jim and Regina went inside and retreated to their room. Regina pulled the curtains and the blackout shade, which they had bought precisely because of Jim's migraines, and talked about how to approach the matter. Then they called David into the darkened room. Ironically, his father had suffered a migraine on the day of his "sex talk" and the room had been dark then, too. Both David and Regina had wondered if Jim had faked the migraine in hopes of getting out of giving the "sex talk." If he had, his plan failed because Regina just hosted the conversation in the darkened room with all present. The darkness was somewhat of a blessing for David, and he imagined today it would also help take some of the sting out of whatever they were going to say. He would have to look them in the eye later over dinner, so it was only a temporary reprieve.

"David," Regina started. "I found some magazines in the garage, and I'm pretty sure they are yours. Please tell us the truth about this. Remember, it's always better to come clean than it is to lie and get caught later."

"We're pretty good at finding out," said Jim.

David didn't say anything. Because it was dark, his parents couldn't see if he was thinking about an answer, or if he was picking at his fingernails, or if he had fallen asleep. They gave him a couple minutes to respond and sat in darkened silence.

"David? Are they yours?" asked Regina.

"Not technically," said David.

"Did you steal them?" asked Regina.

"Not, *technically*," stressed David.

"Oh Jesus," Regina said. "It's what I was afraid of. You and Barry are distracting clerks and stealing pornography from stores!"

"What?" asked Jim.

"What?" echoed David.

"No?" Regina asked.

"No," said David. He was playing with different answers in his mind. He could always go with, "I found them." But then he'd have to explain where and how he found so many. Maybe go with, "Someone gave them to me." But then he'd have to rat out who and why they had given them to him in the first place. He could blame his friends, but then his friends wouldn't be his friends for very long.

David was convinced that the argument that he "found them" was laughable, but had he tried that defense, his father would have vouched for him. Jim might have even said, "No, honey, that checks out." Because, as a boy, not much older than his son, Jim and his buddies had a stash of pornography as well. They were far too afraid of their parents to keep them anywhere near their house, and so they hid the magazines in the woods. The first magazine, which they had stumbled upon purely by chance, was ruined the first time it rained. Steven, Jim's best friend, suggested if they should ever find another magazine, that they keep it in a plastic bag. Soon enough, while exploring in the woods, they stumbled upon another magazine. By accident, they had stumbled on the secret porn stash that belonged to another pair of friends. Steven and Jim couldn't believe their good luck. Because it was in the woods, there was the odd chance that someone else might find your collection, just as they had, and walk away with it. Or, sometimes they might tell someone else where the stash was hidden, and then a magazine might go missing with no one to blame. Deniability was the best part about keeping pornography in the woods. Regardless, if David had just said, "I don't know. I just found it," Jim would have accepted that.

Suddenly Regina realized she really didn't care how David got the magazines, or why they were in the attic. There was a more important message here for him.

"Look, David," his mother started. "Sex is supposed to be something between two people who love one another. It's not supposed to be like, that, that stuff you saw in those magazines. It's, oh, I don't know. Jim?"

"Remember our talk?" Jim asked.

"Yes," said David. He definitely remembered. He would remember it for the rest of his life.

"Like that," said Jim. "Like your mother said. Two people who love each other. Sometimes to have a baby; sometimes just for fun. But, she's right; it shouldn't be like what you see in the magazine. That shouldn't be what you think about, or how you see women."

In the darkness, Jim couldn't see his wife's expression, but she was looking at him very fondly, as if she had never loved him more than right now.

"I'm sorry," said David.

"Do you understand why we're upset?" asked Regina.

"I do," said David. "I'm sorry."

"If you ever want to talk about stuff, sex, women, whatever, even drugs or alcohol," said Jim, "I want you to know you can always come to us. Either of us, or both of us. Okay?"

"I know, Dad," said David. "I love you."

With that all cleared up, the magazines were thrown away without comment, and the discussion, which had gone better than any of them had hoped, was never brought up again.

Two days later, on garbage day, Esther was powerwalking the neighborhood. Since the Wianki, she had bridged the gap between her two routes and now had to cover twice the distance in the same amount of time. She spent a little less time with each family, but managed to collect easily twice the information. Life was good. She saw Jim McKinney wheeling his garbage can out to the curb. They hadn't seen one another since Jim came to apologize and to present the peace offering of the Live Aid tapes, so Esther crossed the road in time to catch Jim's attention. He saw her approach and waited for her.

"Morning!" she said. It was a beautiful morning, and she was well-caffeinated.

"Hey, Esther," said Jim.

"Garbage day today," Esther said.

Jim nodded at the garbage can, now parked at the end of his driveway. "Yep."

"Thanks again for those tapes," she said.

"No problem," he said. Jim began to walk back up the driveway. If he stood here, Esther could go on this way all day, and Jim knew it. He backed away. "I need to get to work, Esther. Have a good day."

"Thanks!" she said. She stepped to the side of his driveway and waited as Jim got into his car and drove away. She waved. He waved back.

She began her walk again, when she noticed a piece of paper in the grass. She scooped it up without looking at it, and walked back to the trash. She hated litter. She had argued for stricter enforcement of the litter laws and harsher punishments at city hall, but the mayor lacked Esther's conviction for the issue. Esther even pointed out that Keep America Beautiful was over thirty years old now, and that Opole should be held to a higher standard than the rest of the country. This was a small, beautiful town, and it needed to set the standard. Esther opened the lid to the can, and was about to toss the piece of paper in without a second thought when she noticed the naked women starring up at her. Lots of naked women. Clearly, one of the McKinneys was a pervert. Maybe both of them. Maybe they were the type of couple who looked at pornography together? To think she thought she knew them.

CHAPTER 5: A MOB THEORY

Esther's spider-sense had been tingling ever since she found the pornography in the McKinneys' trash. It didn't sit right with her, but she wasn't sure what to do with the information either. Normally she would have gone to talk it over with someone else, or the information would have just fallen out of her mouth during a casual conversation, but she felt like she was just getting back onto good terms with the McKinneys and didn't want to risk damaging the friendship again. The leukemia-debacle had definitely been a misstep; she could see that now. There was also the incident with Regina's underwear; Esther still didn't quite understand why Regina had gotten so angry about that, but she understood it left them on uneasy footing. In her reckoning of events, Jim's shove, the resulting bloody nose, and the peace offering of VHS tapes just barely brought Esther back to ground zero with the McKinneys. As a result, Esther was more cautious than usual, but she didn't like not being able to share such an explosive piece of news.

There were still a couple weeks of summer vacation left, and Bruce was particularly alert to his mother's mood especially since the porn had been discovered. Bruce began to wonder if his mother was onto him and was just waiting to see if he would confess. What could she know? David said that he hadn't outed any of his friends, that he had shouldered the burden of the blame entirely himself. What if his friend was lying? Or, maybe Regina or Jim had told Esther about the whole thing, just assuming that Bruce was part of it. David had said that his parents were embarrassed about the whole thing, so it was unlikely they would just tell anyone, much less his mother, unless they also suspected him.

Bruce knew that his mother was the town gossip. He heard people talk about her and didn't try to defend her. There was no defending her. Bruce saw the way she behaved, barging into people's houses and nosing around the neighborhood. Frankly, he was a little embarrassed. She was terrible at keeping secrets, and he knew it, which was why it was so puzzling that she seemed to be keeping one now. What if his parents were getting a divorce? The only family he knew that had divorced parents were the Walkers. Bruce had heard his mother talk about Brenda Walker any number of times. Whether she was telling the story of how Brenda had Betsy out of wedlock with Esther's boyfriend, or about her first failed marriage, or about how Brenda was working on husband number two, but "partner number three." If his parents were getting divorced, what if he had to choose which parent to live with? How would he make that decision?

"Mom?" Bruce asked. He decided to try take the matter head on. "Are you okay?" Well, not precisely head on.

"Huh?" Esther shook her head. "What?" She had just poured milk all over the table, missing the cereal bowl, and it was dripping onto the floor. She looked at the milk and then looked back at Bruce.

"You seem distracted. Are you okay?"

"Sure, sure. I'm fine," said Esther, mopping up the milk with a towel. "Are you okay?"

Now the pressure was on. Maybe she was simply returning the question out of politeness, but maybe, just maybe, she was turning the tables and testing him for a confession before she had to beat it out of him.

"Fine," Bruce said. He knew he had to do better than that though, and he was stalling a bit for time. "I heard something the other day." He said. "I'm not sure if it's true though," he paused. "But, I know you always tell me to be honest with you." He said this, even though his intention was not to be honest with her. "Someone said, I don't remember who, that the cheese shop …"

"Horatio's Cheese Shoppe?" interrupted Esther.

"That one," said Bruce.

"What about it?" Esther was very interested now. Her funk over the McKinneys' pornography was momentarily forgotten, and she was entirely focused on her son.

"Well, they said it was a front for the mob," said Bruce.

"A what?"

"A front for the mob. You know, like gangsters run their gang out of there?"

"That's ridiculous. In Opole?" asked Esther. But, as she asked it, she realized it wasn't so ridiculous. Mobs were everywhere, and the whole point of a front for the mob was to hide in a place no one would suspect. What better place to hide than a cheese shoppe?

Bruce and Esther had a good relationship, but he rarely offered information about his school day, much less a juicy rumor like this, without prying. When Esther asked, "How was your day?" she was often greeted with, "Fine" or "Okay" or, sometimes just a shrug of the shoulders. None of these provided much for Esther to work with, and she'd had to try other approaches. The thing was, since Esther volunteered at school, she knew about his day, and Bruce knew this. He knew she was trying to make polite conversation, but he didn't see the point of it.

Esther would come back with, "What about that art project you've been working on?" and Bruce would offer a minimal response.

He found that the less he said, the more likely Esther was to stop asking. The conversation he was having now was proving his point. He threw out a nugget about something he heard at school, and suddenly he was being peppered with more questions. If it hadn't been such a desperate situation, and he hadn't been so concerned about her finding out his connection to the porn ring, he would never have mentioned Horatio's Cheese Shoppe. It was a Hail Mary, he knew his mother wouldn't be able to resist it, and he was absolutely correct. Her full attention was now on him. Her excitement about this possibility trumped her dubiousness about her son giving her unsolicited information. Bruce, however, knew the whole thing was a joke and a ridiculous idea.

"That's what I heard," said Bruce. In fact, he had heard this from someone else when he visited the library last week. Two high schoolers were talking at a table, and Bruce was trying to find a book on the shelf behind them. One of them said exactly what Bruce reported to his mother, "You know that cheese shoppe? It's a front for the mob." And the other one laughed and said, "You're fucking with me." The first one, who had made the comment, held a straight face for a couple of seconds, and then cracked, "Yeah, but wouldn't it be funny if it were? We need some excitement in Opole." The two high schoolers laughed. Bruce wasn't precisely sure what a mob front was, but he definitely filed the information away for later use. After he found his book, he went up to the librarian and asked if she could help him find information on the mob, and mob fronts.

"What?" asked the librarian.

"Mob fronts," said Bruce. "I want to know what a mob front is."

"Okay," said the librarian. "Is this for some kind of school project?"

"No," said Bruce. "Just curious."

"Where did you hear about mob fronts?"

"Around," said Bruce.

"I'm afraid I can't think of any titles that would be appropriate for your age level," said the librarian. "I can tell you a mob front is just a place, like a store, that the mob uses to hide their illegal activities. Does that answer your question?"

"What's a mob?" asked Bruce. "And what kind of illegal activities?"

"I'm trying to think of an easy way to say this," said the librarian.

"I'm a smart kid, and I read a lot," said Bruce. "Just give it to me."

"Well, the mob is a group of people. In this context, we're talking about a gang of, like, mobsters. Do you know what those are? Or gangsters?"

"The ones with the Tommy-guns?" Bruce mimed holding a Tommy-gun. He had seen a few movies about gangsters.

"Sure," said the librarian. "Right. That kind of thing. They rob banks and launder money and that kind of thing."

"What does it mean to launder money?" asked Bruce.

"Honestly, I'm not very sure myself. It has something to do with making it look like the money is yours, instead of stolen. I think," said the librarian. "But, I have no idea how they do it."

"So, a mob front is a store they use to launder money?" asked Bruce.

"I don't know they use the store to actually do the laundering, but they use the store to hide the fact that they're mobsters."

"Okay, thanks," said Bruce. "I also need to check this out, please." He slid his library card and *The Beggar Queen* onto the counter."

"Oh, Lloyd Alexander," said the librarian. "I haven't read this series yet, is it any good?"

"I like it better than the Prydain series," said Bruce.

He left the library, book in hand, and knowledge for later use, which he used now to good effect. He could see his mother's gears turning. She had taken the info and was running with it, even though she was questioning it.

"You really think so?" Esther asked.

"I don't know," said Bruce. "Like I said, it's just what I heard. I thought you might like to know. Should we call the police?"

"No," said Esther. But, she knew if there really was a mob-fronted cheese shoppe, that is exactly what they should do. Like the pornography in the McKinneys' trash, she itched to tell this story to someone. First, she needed some proof. Later that day, while she did her northern rounds, she walked by the cheese shoppe. She decided to just keep an eye on it, and see for herself. If there was enough evidence to go to the authorities with, then she would report it. But, first she had to do some reconnaissance. Esther barely said goodbye to her son as she walked out the door. She had a new purpose, and for the moment, the pornography was forgotten.

The door closed, her feet hit the pavement, and she was powerwalking up Beechwood Drive, around the jog, and northward. Nothing could stop her. She finally spotted Horatio's Cheese Shoppe when she was about a block away. She noted the new yellow awning out front. The old one had torn in a recent storm and been faded by the sun. The new one was bright yellow, and it looked like they had even put a fresh coat of yellow paint on the storefront. There wasn't much to the store, just a large window, a door, and a sign that read: "Horatio's Cheese Shoppe: charcuterie and cheeses." Esther had never been inside. She didn't know anyone who had, which is why Bruce's story seemed plausible to her. How could this little store exist for so long in this era of Kraft singles and boxes macaroni and cheese? Maybe it was a front for the mob.

As she approached the store, she noted that the sign hanging on the door sign read "Closed." There were no hours posted on the door. It was already after ten o'clock, but most stores in Opole opened by nine. Yet this little yellow store was closed and there was no sign of when it might open again. She'd have to come by tomorrow, midday, and see what was inside.

Since she was north of the jog, Esther decided to swing by Brenda's. She had almost kicked the powerwalk into high gear when she remembered that Carol's photography shop was over in this direction. Esther had seen Carol's work on the Lambert family and was pretty impressed. She was curious to see what else Carol had done, and more than anything, just wanted to see the shop and nose around a bit. Esther crossed the road and found the shop, having remembered Patty's directions from a couple months ago. The sign on the front also said "Closed," but Esther tried the front door anyway. Signs like that were for other people, not Esther. It was open, and she went in. She just wanted to see samples of Carol's work, after all, and, surely, there would be some in the shop.

The front room was simple but tastefully decorated. There were several photo albums displayed on a coffee table. Esther sat on the couch and flipped through one of the albums. She recognized almost all of the faces, but there were a few that she assumed were from out of town, or maybe even family members that Carol was using to pad her display book until she had more "real" clients. The couch was comfortable, and Esther didn't really give any thought to the fact that someone else might be in the shop. Then she heard the noise.

It sounded like a telephone dialing, but louder. The dialing was followed by a weird pinging noise, and then distortion of some kind. It sounded like a machine was screaming. She was curious. She sat on the couch for a moment to see if the sounds would repeat, but they didn't. Then she puzzled through the sounds she had heard in her life to see if one of them matched the sounds she had heard. They didn't. Esther got up from the couch and went in the direction of where she thought the noise had come. She went through a doorway that was obscured by a black curtain, turned a corner, saw one of the studios where Carol must take photographs, and then was about to step into a smaller office, when she stopped. This was probably Carol's office. Film cannisters were neatly stacked on a desk, envelopes were held by a rubber band, and the inbox on the desk was filled with release forms. There was another door that led into a smaller room, which Esther guessed— correctly—was the darkroom. The door to the darkroom was ajar.

Directly in front of her, with his back turned to Esther, was Carol's husband Bill. He was seated at a large desk facing a window with the curtains drawn. In front of him, was a computer. Esther had seen personal computers before, and knew this was an IBM, or an IBM-clone. Jim would be proud that she remembered that IBM was a specific manufacturer of computers and not a type of computer. People might say, "I have an IBM," but what they really meant was, "I don't have an Apple." On the screen of Bill's IBM, or IBM-clone, was an image of a naked boy. That it was a male nude would have been enough to shock Esther, but that it was actually a boy, maybe twelve, nearly the same age as her Bruce, nearly forced a gasp out of her. But, fortunately for Esther, the image startled her beyond words and gasp, and she quietly backed up and left the shop. On her way out, she closed the door as carefully as she could and, as disgusted as she was, she was just as grateful the boy wasn't anyone she knew.

She didn't have enough information to report Horatio's Cheese Shoppe as being a potential mob front, but she definitely was going to report Bill Daniels. Immediately. Esther powerwalked faster than she ever had, directly to the police department and told them what she had seen. No, the boy was not anyone she recognized. Yes, she was absolutely sure of what she had seen. No, she had never seen Bill act strangely around anyone that she could recall. She did know that Bill had a difficult time keeping a job, but always thought it had to do with his alcoholism. No, she didn't know Bill very well. Yes, she had spoken with Carol before and she seemed nice enough. No, she had no reason to suspect that Carol might know about what Bill was up to. Yes, she would be happy to provide a statement. Yes, she would be happy to be a witness should there be any kind of legal action against Bill Daniels. No, she did not know where the Daniels lived. No, she didn't know if Carol was in the shop, too. No, she wasn't sure what that sound was that she had heard. She did her best to replicate it for the police, but wasn't sure she got it quite right. Yes, they absolutely could call if they had any further questions.

Esther left the police department and returned home. She was tired from the whole ordeal with the police and to learn that someone in her community was looking at such images.

That makes two families of perverts, she thought, but clearly this one was far worse. Her powerwalk home was erratic. When she got home, she found Jeffrey was waiting for her.

"There you are," Jeffrey said. "I was beginning to wonder. It seemed kind of late for you to do your rounds."

"I told him you might be headed to Horatio's," said Bruce.

"But we expected you back by now," said Jeffrey. He was stirring something on the stove.

"Brucey," Esther said. "Go to your room, please."

"Why?" Bruce asked. Bruce was confused. Had she figured it out? She only used the name Brucey when she was feeling nostalgic or trying to comfort him, but why would she ask him to leave the room? Maybe she finally decided to have the talk with his dad about divorce? If so, he wanted to be here for it. Bruce looked around and saw the table wasn't set. "I was just going to set the table," he said. Surely, she wouldn't send him out of the room if he was doing one of his chores.

"I just need a moment with your father," Esther said.

Now Bruce was really nervous. He hesitated for a moment, but walked to his room and closed the door. By closing the door, he hoped to give them the illusion that he wouldn't be able to hear them. In truth, he could hear just fine through the wall. If his mother was going to announce to his father that she wanted a divorce, there would probably be some yelling and then he'd be able to hear them either way. Unfortunately, he couldn't hear anything. They were talking too quietly.

Five minutes later, his father knocked on the door and called Bruce to dinner.

The next day, the news was everywhere. Esther was able to the break the news to Regina and Vicky first, but by the time she made it to the northern group, the *Opole Record* had been delivered. The headline read, "Local man arrested for child pornography." The story revealed how William "Bill" Daniels, husband of the local photographer Carol Daniels, was trading child pornography through a series of bulletin board systems (BBS) using his modem and personal computer. As far as authorities could tell, his wife was completely unaware of his actions. Further, none of the children in the images found on the suspect's computer matched children from the neighborhood. Authorities were working to identify the exploited children and to track down the people Bill was exchanging the images with. The *Opole Record* would be following the story as it developed. Esther was not mentioned by name, but the article did indicate that police were tipped off by a "local citizen." She did not feel slighted by the exclusion, and in some ways even appreciated the anonymity. Of course, her invisibility was immediately dispelled when she recounted the story to anyone. "That local citizen? That's me. I did that."

The people of Opole reacted in different ways. The most immediate reaction was to lock their doors. However, locking their doors was an unnatural behavior, and it was forgotten by most households after a month or less had passed. All the children received a refresher course on not talking to or taking candy from strangers. Some parents explained why and others simply said, "It's always a good thing to remember."

Vicky and Dean were straightforward and blunt with their children, Barry, Mark, and Michael. Though Vicky wanted to protect her children's innocence, she and her husband also realized their actual safety was more valuable. Such straightforward honesty meant awkward conversations about sex, sexual preferences, predatory behaviors, and pornography. The latter of which, of course, Barry knew more than a little about. Dean was careful to point out to his children that just because Bill Daniels was looking at naked boys, it didn't mean all child molesters were homosexual.

"Remember," he said, "Your Uncle Chester is gay, and he doesn't like little boys. There are plenty of molesters out there that go for little girls, too."

Vicky thought he was scaring the children, and tried to temper the language. But Dean insisted, "No. It's important they don't think that gay is the same as someone who likes little kids. My older brother is not the same as Bill Daniels."

Unfortunately, children often only remember the last things

from an adult's mouth, and so the youngest Webster, Michael went to school the next day and told all his friends, "Gay people like little kids, and my uncle is the same as Bill Daniels. That's what my dad said."

Another consequence of the Websters' conversation with their kids was that all the other parents who had taken a different approach with what to tell their children had to deal with a lot of questions when their children came back from school that day. "Barry Webster said..." and "Mark Webster said..." and "What's a homosexual?" and "Do all adults look at pornography?"

For Esther, the revelation of a real-life child molester in the small town of Opole meant that her eyes were now wide open for crime. Everywhere she looked, she saw crime. She expanded her route to include uptown and stayed out later and longer. When she saw abandoned bicycles, she assumed they had been stolen and reported them to the police. If Esther saw a suspicious light on after hours at a store uptown, she went to investigate. When a man with a winter hat went into the Opole Savings Bank, she notified the authorities; just in case.

Esther even went so far as to invest in a modem of her own and learned how to connect to various BBS (she knew the lingo now). She became acquainted with the dinging and pinging and hissing and screeching that the computer made when it connected to another computer. Esther didn't find any more illegal pornography, as she had both hoped and feared, but she did meet some interesting people. Esther found the anonymity of the message boards freeing, and it was easy to talk to these people she had never met before. One user, fizzwanna, was originally from California. Esther and fizzwanna struck up a friendship. Esther wasn't sure whether fizzwanna was a male or female, though she assumed everyone was female in the message boards, since she was female. From their conversation, Esther learned that fizzwanna's home state had a "sex offender tracking program." In fact, fizzwanna informed Esther, it had been on the books since 1947. The information lit a fire in Esther, and she campaigned hard for such a program in the state of Michigan.

"If we had such a registry," said Esther, "we'd know where the perverts are."

While the authorities agreed it was a good idea, there were two main problems with it. First, people who served time were supposed to be free to start a new life, and such a registry would make it hard for them to do that. Second, for the list to be useful, it would have to be easily accessible to the public; how would they do that? With easy-access came difficulty for people to reintegrate into society, and without it, compiling and updating the list only meant more paperwork without anything to show for it. Disappointed, Esther lost interest in checking the BBS. Occasionally, she would still log in to talk with fizzwanna or the few other people she had made connections with, but for the most part the BBS-part of her life, short as it was, was forgotten.

Instead, she increased her surveillance of Horatio's.

If finding a child molester in her town did nothing else, it reassured Esther that the reality of a mob-fronted cheese shoppe was now distinctly possible. Esther asked everyone she knew, and many she didn't, if they had gone in Horatio's Cheese Shoppe. It became an embarrassment for her son, and he almost regretted telling her the story in the first place. Esther would approach people selecting cheese at the grocery store and ask them, "Have you ever been to Horatio's?" The shoppers would look at Esther and shake their heads in confusion. Then she had to explain what Horatio's was, and where it could be found. Had Esther's approach been softer, she would have been a wonderful, albeit unintentional, walking advertisement for the cheese shoppe. Most people in Opole had no idea that they even had a cheese shoppe.

Finally one day, her efforts paid off. It started with the usual question, "Have you ever been to Horatio's Cheese Shoppe?" But, instead of the confused look that said, "Why is this stranger speaking to me?" the man shrugged and said, "Yeah, a couple of times." He was an older man, and looked Mediterranean. Maybe he was Greek? Esther wasn't sure. If he was Greek, she thought, that would make sense that he'd be the one person in town to have gone into Horatio's.

"What was it like?" she asked.

"It was like a cheese shop," replied the man.

"Do they have good cheese?" she asked.

"Yes, but a bit expensive."

"Lots of cheese?"

"Yes, lots of cheese. Also, salamis and meats and stuff. There's a word for it, but I can't think of it," the man squinted and seemed to be concentrating.

"Charcuterie," filled in Esther.

"Yes," said the man. "That's it. I go sometimes when I need something special, or when I need prosciutto. Stores like this one never carry it. Also, sometimes I go there for pastrami."

Esther took this all in and recorded it carefully on the lobes of her brain. She had so many questions for this man, but ultimately just asked one more, "What are their hours?"

The man laughed. "They seem to keep irregular hours. I've gone in on Thursday afternoon. Around two. But sometimes I also go on Saturdays, and they're open." Then the man said something that really caught Esther's attention, because it seemed to confirm Bruce's theory. "It's kind of funny, but I've always imagined the owner to be very wealthy who didn't need the store at all, but just kept it for fun."

"Have you ever met the owner?"

"Horatio?" asked the man.

"Is that really his name?" Esther asked.

"It would be silly to name the place after someone else," the man said. He laughed. "I've met him before. Nice guy."

Esther thanked the gentleman, and decided it was time to go into the cheese shoppe herself. In the Bill Daniels revelation, she had almost forgotten about the idea that Horatio's might be a mob front, but then she heard two kids talking about it at school when she was volunteering in the classroom. Esther didn't know this, but the one girl who was telling the other girl that Horatio's was a mob-front, was the little sister of the high schooler who had originally told the joke in the library. Because that "joke" received a laugh from his friend, he retold it a few more times, and eventually his little sister overheard it. She, like Bruce, didn't know what a mob-front was, but knew that it wasn't supposed to be in a cheese shoppe, so she told her friends at school, and now Esther heard it. She heard the story again from another child in the classroom, who had heard it from the first girl, and then Esther heard it for a third time before her volunteering was done. A theory was practically humming within her, and Esther was barely able to contain her excitement at being able to break another story.

Esther wondered if she should tell the police first, just in case there was trouble, or if she should risk going alone. Maybe she could convince someone to go with her? Maybe that would be suspicious. Ultimately, she decided to see if Vicky was up for it. Esther went home, put the groceries away, and then powerwalked over to Vicky's house. On instinct, she attempted to throw the door open and almost smashed her face into the locked door. Good, she thought; the Websters are still securing their domicile. Because Esther usually just let herself in where ever she went, she hadn't taken a strong stance on knocking or ringing the doorbell before. The last couple weeks had forced her to confront the reality that faced most people when they wanted entrance to someone's home. The doorbell had a harsh sound to it, and Esther didn't like it. She didn't want to introduce her presence that way, and preferred the knock. Esther's current policy was that she would start with a knock and only progress to a doorbell if her knock wasn't answered in a reasonable amount of time. But this matter, today, felt like it was doorbell-worthy. She rang.

"Esther," said Vicky. She was wiping her hands on a decorative hand-towel.

"What are you doing?" asked Esther.

"Right now?" asked Vicky. "I'm talking to you, at my front door."

"No, no, no," said Esther. "I mean, are you free? Can you

go with me? I have an important job for us to do."

"I guess. What's the important job? Will it take very long?"

"Grab your purse and lock up," Esther said.

"Okay." Vicky was surprised to see her friend so frantic. Whatever this was, it seemed important, and Vicky was curious. She grabbed her purse, put on her shoes, and met Esther on the front porch. She locked the door and turned to her friend, "Ready. Where are we off to?"

"Horatio's Cheese Shoppe," said Esther.

Vicky was puzzled, but curious. She had heard of Horatio's Cheese Shoppe, but she had never been in there. Vicky also knew that her friend was suddenly obsessed with the place. Esther, who usually had an impeccable memory, had asked Vicky in the last month at least three times if the Websters had ever gone to the cheese shoppe. It was unlike her. Vicky had also been with Esther on various occasions when she badgered other friends and random people they encountered about the cheese shoppe. Vicky wasn't sure exactly what was going on with Esther, but she sensed that some kind of conclusion to the mystery would occur at the shoppe today.

Miracle of miracles, the shoppe was open. Esther held the door in her hand, took a deep breath, and then charged inside. Vicky followed. There were four or five cute little café tables surrounded by chairs, a short counter with a cash register, and a large glass deli display case. Vicky and Esther both took deep breaths and filled their senses with cheese and dried meats. It smelled delicious. Vicky was delighted, but Esther was deeply disappointed. Then it occurred to Esther that this was the perfect front! A delicious smelling store that actually sold cheese and meat. What could be better to disguise mob activity? She walked up the counter and rang the bell.

It took a while for anyone to emerge, but eventually a man stepped through a door in the back of the shoppe. He closely resembled the potentially-Greek individual Esther had chatted with in the grocery store earlier. He had the same olive-colored skin and was roughly the same height. This man had dark, almost black, hair that was slicked back tight to his scalp. The man must use some kind of wax in his hair because Esther could see the lines left behind by his comb.

"Can I help you?" the man asked in a friendly voice.

"Horatio?" asked Esther.

"That's me," he said proudly.

"Your name, is it, Greek?" Esther asked.

"Haven't you ever read Shakespeare?" Vicky interjected. "Horatio is Italian." She paused, and then looked to the man for confirmation. "Right?"

"Right you are," Horatio said warmly. "Second generation. You ladies want to try some cheese? I haven't seen you in here before, have I?"

"No, first time," said Vicky.

Esther stood mute, and stared at Horatio.

"Well, I have a delicious aged parmigiana that came in last week. Or you could try our fontina – that's our most popular cheese."

"What's fontina like?" asked Esther.

"If you've ever had French onion soup, you've had it. It's that melted cheese that they put across the top of the soup," Horatio said. "Most people in Opole don't buy it for French onion soup, though. They use it for fondue. Do you fondue?"

"No," said Vicky. Esther shook her head.

"Good," said Horatio. "Waste of perfectly good cheese if you ask me."

Horatio walked over to the display case, slid the door, and selected a cheese. He brought back a small wheel of cheese and cut two slices. He handed them to Vicky and Esther.

"Thank you," said Esther.

And so it went for about fifteen minutes. Horatio wowed Esther and Vicky with his selection of cheeses and dried meats. There were so many new flavors and names that both women forgot the ones they liked best. They went on Horatio's recommendation and ended up buying six different types of cheeses and two dried meats and walked back outside.

"Wow, that was a pleasant surprise," said Vicky. "Dean and the boys are going to be blown away when I share these with them."

"Definitely a surprise," said Esther. She knew a conman when she saw one, and she was certain that Mr. Horatio, Mr. Cheese Shoppe, was indeed a conman. Yes, she had bought his cheese and meat and she would enjoy them, but that was only so as not to raise suspicion.

CHAPTER 6: EVE OF DESTRUCTION

For the kids of Opole (aka, any kid the age of Bruce, David, Barry, and Jason), Devil's Night was an opportunity to wreck some havoc. They didn't really need an excuse because they were often doing something destructive, but the day before Halloween was a day they could be honest about their intentions.

"Mom, I'm taking a couple rolls of toilet paper," they would say as they headed out to meet up. Or they might say, "I left a buck on the table for the dozen eggs I took."

This generation of parents tried to dispel any lingering nervousness they had about the night. Their parents would let them go, be a little wild, and have a little fun. But, their parents, who were born in the 1950s, lived through the 1967 riots in Detroit and, even though they allowed it, they couldn't help but be a little nervous. "It's just good fun," they would think. That generation's parents (the ones who birthed Esther,

Becky, Patty, Regina, Brenda, Vicky, etc.), associated Devil's Night with the 1943 riots in Detroit, and saw the 1967 riots as a continuation of the earlier one. Had the Civil War generation still been living, they would have talked about the 1863 riots in Detroit, and how the city had a long tradition of self-destruction. The association of Devil's Night to any of these events was erroneous though; the 1967 and 1943 riots occurred in the summer (July and June, respectively), and the 1863 riots occurred in March. And now they were essentially giving their children their blessing to go out and wreak a little havoc of their own.

It's hard to say why and when Devil's Night took hold in Michigan, but most people pointed to it starting in the 1940s or 1950s. Certainly by the late 1970s it was in full swing. By then, instead of toilet-papering trees and egging houses and cars, like today's boys were prone to do, people in Detroit set buildings on fire. The peak was set October 29-31, 1984, when the record was set for arsons during the three-day holiday. There were 810 verified arsons. By 1987, things had calmed back down, but there would still be 300-some arsons during the long Halloween weekend. That was considered a "good" year.

If the parents of the "boys" ever had concerns about their children destroying the neighborhood in a similar fashion, this year they had no such concerns; they knew what the focus of the attacks would be, and it wasn't the town. Bill Daniels was safely locked away, but everyone knew where he used to live. There was no evidence that Carol had anything to do with her husband's transgressions, but the house and the business where the photos had been found became locations for the community to vent their rage and disgust. No one had anything against Carol, but since her husband wasn't around, they had no problem taking their frustrations out on things that once belonged to him.

So it was that, on Friday, October 30, 1987, the boys set out with a clear objective in mind. This was a first for them. Typically, the revelers would take supplies, wander aimlessly around town, and pick a target at random. Sometimes it was a new family who had moved in, or someone they didn't know at all. They would throw the toilet paper into their trees, toss eggs at their house or cars, rub soap on windows, and then ring the doorbell and dash off. The pranks kids played had been passed down from participants of years past. Bruce had no idea why rubbing soap on a window was part of the ritual, it just was something you did. The eggs made sense, because they were gross and sticky, but soap? His wasn't to question. Esther didn't know it, but Uncle Kenny was one of the sources of Bruce's information about Devil's Night hijinks. One day, Bruce would get up the courage to do the flaming bag of dog shit that Uncle Kenny told him about, but at ten he was still a little nervous to play with actual fire. Bruce would never have admitted it; he was a Cub Scout after all, and what scout doesn't like to play with fire?

Last year's Devil's Nights antics began and ended with Mr. Barnett. His was the first house on the list, not because they hated him, but just because it was conveniently located directly across the street from the McKinney's and two doors down from the Webster's. The boys figured they could dash across the street, do their damage, and then dash into the Webster's backyard to hide. There were no fences between the Barnett's and Webster's, so it should be a straight and easy shot. Each boy dressed in his black ninja costume—they were all going as ninja for Halloween—and then they gathered at the McKinney house. Regina was making chili and reminding them to "Not be out too late" and "Be safe out there." The boys could see Mr. Barnett's porch light was on, but that didn't necessarily mean anyone was watching the house. It could have just been left on to scare people away. David pointed out that the jack-o'-lanterns had been pulled in, which meant the Barnetts were being careful to not leave themselves too open to attack.

Brent and Helena Barnett were well-known in the community. Brent was the Boy Scout leader, which made him very popular because with Scouts came the ability to use knives, start fires, and camp outdoors. Arguably though,

Helena was even more popular. As the den mother of the local Cub Scout troop, she was the gateway into the more "grownup" version of scouts that her husband ran. After the age of ten, kids in her den graduated to Brent's troop. Because both organizations met in the same house, the transition was seamless. However, it was Helena's life before Brent and scouting that really made her a household name in Opole. Her maiden name was Piekarski, and she was a direct descendant from the very first paczki-making Poles to inhabit Opole. Since those early days, many of the Polish settlers had left the area, or inter-married with non-Poles, and the result was a very homogenized group of Americans with non-distinct names. Helena's family was known locally as the pie-family, which was somewhat accurate. The name "piekar" literally meant "baker" and "ski" indicated "of." Those that knew the Polish roots of the name would often joke, as they approached the Piekarski paczki stand, "Ah, the pierkars of the finest paczkis in the land." It wasn't a very original or funny joke, but the Piekarskis had come to accept it as being the compliment it was intended to be. Had the boys any inkling that they would be caught tonight, they would have thought twice about offending the people associated with their favorite paczkis and their scouting career, but, as so often was the case, the boys thought their plan was foolproof.

And so, they were off. Across the street. Bruce started rubbing a chocolate bar on the window, David smashed eggs on the side of the house and porch, and Barry was throwing a roll of toilet paper from the porch to a nearby tree. Bruce knew you were supposed to use soap, that's what Uncle Kenny told him, not chocolate bars, but he couldn't convince Esther to part with any soap, and he thought Baby-Ruth bars were garbage anyway. Bruce looked at his friends and realized they were done. He stopped rubbing the chocolate on the window and rang the doorbell. They ran.

Mr. Barnett had started the night by lingering in the family room (that the family never used) watching the front door, but after two hours of no action, he was bored. The porch light would keep kids away, and he remembered to bring in the pumpkins, so there was nothing to smash. He joined his wife and kids in the living room for after dinner television. Friday was one of his least favorite nights to watch TV, but his kids loved *Full House* and *Mr. Belvedere*. Personally, he was a fan of *Night Court* and *Miami Vice*; his wife loved *Dallas*. Right now, if he was being honest with himself, he really didn't care what they were going to watch; he just wanted to sit in his chair and fall asleep; it had been a long week. Then the doorbell rang. Instantly, he was reminded what night tonight was. This was karma coming back to bite him in the ass for his participation in Devil's Nights past. It didn't mean he was any less irritated now that his evening was being interrupted. He raced for the door, flung it open, and chased after the black forms scrambling across his yard.

Having rang the doorbell, Bruce was the last one off the porch. He hit the ground running and encountered a problem he hadn't anticipated. The grass was wet. His sneakers didn't so much sneak as slip, and he found himself sprawling on the wet grass. His friends were calling to him from the backyard, "Come on!" But then he found himself being lifted off the grass before he could stand himself. Mr. Barnett didn't look pleased.

"Come on. I saw you," Mr. Barnett yelled. He couldn't actually see the others, but he knew they were there. He heard them calling to their friend as he approached the fallen boy. "Or are you just going to let him take the fall for all of this?"

Reluctantly, David and Barry emerged from the darkness and joined Mr. Barnett and Bruce. Mr. Barnett refused to let go of the back of Bruce's costume, and pushed him in the direction of the porch.

"Look at this mess!" Mr. Barnett said. He pulled the mask off of Bruce's head, and confirmed his suspicions. It was disappointing, but not surprising. He didn't need to see who was under the other two masks, because there were only a handful of kids that Bruce ran with and were the right age. It had to be David and Barry. But, even if it was Jason, or Angie, or Mark, it didn't matter.

"You're going to clean this," Mr. Barnett said to the boys. Then he opened the door, "Helena!"

Helena responded half-heartedly, "What?" But then her footsteps could be heard walking towards the front door.

"Get a bucket of water, soap, and a few rags, please," said Mr. Barnett.

"What is going on out here, Brent?" she asked. She eyed the mess, recognized Bruce, and figured out who the other two were. She sighed.

"Just, please. Get a bucket of water, soap, and a few rags."

The kids stood mute. Helena returned with the requested supplies, shook her head at the mess, and then went back to the living room and her television. That night, the boys learned that egg is hard to get out of brick. There are many small nooks and crannies. If they had a hose, it would have been easier, but the outside water had been turned off for the season, and the hoses had been brought in already. Mr. Barnett had no plans of making this easy for them. When they were done, Mr. Barnett gave them a quick motivational speech. "I expect better from you. Don't be dumb. Don't be dumb. Don't be dumb." Then he went inside and closed and locked the door. The kids, disappointed in how the night had gone, returned home without saying anything else to one another.

So it was that one year later, on Friday, October 30, 1987, the boys set out with a clear objective in mind. Tonight, they would redeem themselves of last year's debacle. Bill Daniels was safely locked away, but everyone knew where he used to live. Despite Carol's innocence, her house and the business where the photos had been found became locations for the community to vent their rage and disgust over the preceding months. No one had anything against Carol, but since her husband wasn't around, they had no problem taking their frustrations out on things that once belonged to him.

The boys gathered their supplies, dressed in their darkest clothing, and headed out into the night. The photography shop was their first stop. Halfway there, Jason joined them. He wasn't typically part of the crew, but sometimes he joined David and Barry. Though none of them would admit it, going out on Devil's Night held a measure of danger they weren't quite old enough to feel comfortable with. So, because there is safety in numbers, Jason was invited to join. He acknowledged them with a casual head nod barely visible in the dark. When they arrived at the photography shop, they found they were not first. Another group of kids was already in the middle of making mischief on the studio's exterior. This group was older, and the younger group approached them with caution.

"Hey," called Bruce, the de-facto leader of the younger group.

"Hey," responded the older boy who was clearly in charge of the other group. He wasn't actively participating in the destruction, but he was obviously orchestrating it. "Don't forget the van," he said.

As he said that, two boys ran over to the van parked outside of Carol's Photography. Barry and David were already by the van, letting air out of the tires.

"Don't do that," one of the older kids hissed. "Like this." He drew a knife from his pocket and stabbed the tire. The blade bent. "Ugh. What the hell," he said.

"Yeah, screwdrivers are better for that," the other boy said. He removed a Philip's head screwdriver from his pocket and jammed it into the side of the tire. Air leaked around the sides of the screwdriver. All the air whooshed out, and the van groaned as it resettled. The boy went around to the front tire. Then he whispered, "You want to do it?"

Neither Barry nor David knew who he was talking to, so both ran to join him and said, "Sure." He handed the screwdriver to Barry, and Barry turned it over in his hand. He swung his fist with the screwdriver in it, but it bounced and refused to go in.

"No strong enough," said the older boy. "Give it back."

The older boy grabbed the screwdriver and quickly punctured the front tire. Barry and David rejoined their crew, but found the older kids had already done quite the job on the place. Toilet paper was hanging from everywhere the kids could think to hang it, eggs were splattered all over the sides of the building, two tires were flat, and someone had spray-painted "PERVERT" on the building and van. The younger kids all looked at Bruce who just shrugged. As they left, the older kids broke a few windows with rocks, and then ran off into the night.

Barry's crew wandered the neighborhood in hushed tones as they tried to find the pedophile's house. When they arrived, they found others had beaten them here as well. Lights were on in the house, but either that was just a ruse to make it seem like someone was home, or Carol didn't care to do anything to prevent the vandalism. Bruce and Jason threw a few eggs at the house, but their impact was hardly noticed among the rest. Barry threw a roll of toilet paper, and David just watched. The message to Carol and Bill had been delivered loud and clear. The boys went home early. It wasn't surprising that someone else was at Carol's Photography, but the thoroughness of the vandalism did surprise the boys. They had never seen anything quite like that before and would clearly need to rethink their approach to Devil's Night from here on out.

The boys had planned to sleep over at the McKinneys, and Jim and Regina were surprised to see them return so soon.

"Everything okay?" asked Jim.

"Yeah, Dad," said David.

"Not much fun tonight," said Bruce.

The eggs were thrown away and the toilet paper would be used. Not much else was said. The kids watched a movie, and then went to bed fairly early for a sleepover.

Halloween morning, Esther was surprised to find Carol Daniels on her front step. Carol had rung the doorbell, which Esther found quite rude considering it was before nine in the morning. It didn't matter that Esther was typically up at this time on a Saturday. She opened the door and invited Carol into her home nonetheless.

"I don't know what to do," Carol said.

"About what?" asked Esther.

"You know. I was at home last night, and I just watched everyone come and throw eggs and toilet paper, and pop the tires on my car, and kill my grass with gasoline. I watched it all. The light was on; everyone knows Bill is in jail and I'm there by myself. I guess they need to get it out of their system." Carol paused. She wasn't going to cry, but it was obvious she was choosing her words carefully. As near as Esther could remember, she had never spent any time with Carol one-on-one before. Coming to her like this must have taken some effort. "How do I fix this? What do I do? I didn't have anything to do with what Bill was up to. It disgusts me, too."

Esther was pretty sure she knew the answer to the question that she was about to ask, but she went ahead and asked it anyway, "Why did you come to me?"

"Because you know all of them," Carol said. "If you vouch for me, they'll listen."

That's about what Esther figured. She looked at Carol and considered her for a long moment. Maybe she could use her influence to bring Carol back into the good graces of the neighborhood. She had never intentionally spread news to discredit someone, or to diminish their reputation, but she realized some of the stories she spread had that effect. Had she ever spread a story that had helped someone? She couldn't think of a single example of telling and retelling a positive story. Why was she so drawn to other people's misery? Perhaps the better question was, why was everybody else so drawn to the misery of others? If they wanted and enjoyed happy stories, Esther was certain she would have worked those in. But no one did. She shared a story now and then about so and so having a baby, or something like that, but nothing close to the ego-reducing tales she delivered on a more regular basis. If she had said, "You'll never believe who's getting perfect grades on their report card!" or "So and so is a stand-up man and has never made an ass out of himself when he was drunk," no one would have cared. They might listen, but they wouldn't ask questions like they did when Esther shared something sad.

They never said, "Oh, tell me more about all the children who didn't get detention" or "Those parents really do a wonderful job." No, she traded in stories that broke down illusions about people, and the people on her route ate it up.

"I will take your case," said Esther.

"Case?" Carol sputtered. "Are you a detective?"

"That's a good one. You have a sense of humor. We can use that," said Esther. "Tonight's Halloween; it's a perfect opportunity for you to patch things up. Go out and buy boxes of full-sized candy bars. The good stuff. Like, Snickers and Reese's Peanut Butter Cups and MilkyWay; forget those circus peanuts, or that rock-hard bubble gum. Maybe even buy a box of those new Airhead candies, the kids are loving those, or pouches of Big League Chew bubble gum. Go all out."

"How much should I buy?" Carol asked.

"Enough for, I don't know, two hundred kids?"

"That's a lot of candy."

"Right, but it will be worth it. The kids will love it, they'll tell their parents, and that will be the start," said Esther. "You need to go now though."

"Why?"

"Get shopping. I need to get out on the route and say a few nice words for you," said Esther. "Otherwise, they'll never want their kids going to a pervert's house to get candy."

The Halloween of 1987 passed in the same tradition as all the years previous: the same people who had vandalized houses the night previous, returned to the scene of their crimes in disguise and requested candy. The candy was readily given, and the events of the previous night were forgotten. Except this year, the focus of nearly all the Devil's Night attacks had been concentrated on Carol's house and shop, and the rest of the houses were spared. This meant the owners of the other houses, Mr. Barnett included, handed out candy with a little more joy than on previous years. They were no longer eyeing each costumed individual wondering if this person was responsible for that egg, or that person was responsible for this roll of toilet paper.

Esther had, as promised, visited everyone on her route to spread the word about the full-sized, or king-sized, candy that Carol Daniels would be handing out. The news was met skeptically, but Esther assured everyone Carol wasn't involved with Bill's perversions. Esther was typically the most skeptical of anyone she knew and the least forgiving, but she found it hard to convince even her most Christian friends that Carol was innocent and should be given another chance. She even went so far as to make up stories about how Carol and Bill hadn't had sex in over ten years, and how they were practically estranged but just remained married, legally, because Carol was trying to help Bill get treatment for his alcoholism and didn't want to abandon him. Esther did the best she could that night, and then returned home to get her house ready to distribute candy to ghouls and goblins.

When Bruce came home, Esther asked him if he had gone to Carol's. Bruce shook his head.

"Why not?"

"She's a perv, Mom," Bruce said.

"I'll have you know, Carol is a very nice woman," she almost launched into a full-on defense, but she was interrupted by her son.

"Fuck that noise."

"Excuse me?" she said. But she had heard him perfectly well. She was stunned into silence, and by the time she found the words, it was too late. Bruce was in the bathroom brushing his teeth and getting ready for bed. She should have gone in there and given him a piece of her mind, but she felt like the moment had passed. Esther rarely cursed, and she hated it when other people did, particularly when they cursed at her. It was something akin to her kryptonite. Something about the vehemence of the words, or the harsh sound of the consonants. It rattled her. Fortunately, only Jeffrey really seemed to know this about her, and he didn't often take advantage of it. There were moments when she knew he was reaching the point of fatigue in their argument, when he would reach into his back pocket and toss an s-, or f-, or b-bomb, and simply end the discussion. Later, after she had recovered from the blast, she would come back to Jeffrey and let him know she was sorry, because if it had come to that last resort, she had surely been out of line.

"Did you hear that?" Esther asked her husband now.

"Huh?" he asked. He was watching the made-for-TV movie, *The Midnight Hour*. It wasn't very good, and he had this nagging feeling he had seen it before, but he'd rather be planted in front of the TV than deal with distributing candy to the neighborhood brats.

"Never mind," Esther said. She settled in next to him on the couch. "Haven't we seen this?" she asked.

"Not sure."

"Yes, we have. Remember, a couple years ago?" She was correct; it had first aired in 1985. "The town is being overrun by the living dead, and there's someone who read an old spell, and they have that find that spirit ring or whatever to end it."

"Jesus, thanks for ruining it for me," said Jeffrey. It wasn't even that he was particularly enjoying the movie, but he hated when someone talked during a show, and it was worse when they gave away the ending.

"I didn't say anything about who died or if they were successful," said Esther.

Now that Esther mentioned it, the storyline definitely sounded familiar, and he remembered the whole thing. The one thing he really did enjoy about this show was the soundtrack. There were some great songs by Wilson Pickett, CCR, and that song that went, "Hey there little red riding hood"; he wasn't sure who did that, but he enjoyed it. Jeffrey sighed, and pressed the button on the clicker. He glanced over at Esther, but she didn't seem to be paying attention.

"Looks like a new episode of *The Golden Girls*," he said. "Want to watch that together?"

She cuddled up close to him on the couch and they settled in. Jeffrey never openly admitted it, but he loved *The Golden Girls*. He might never turn it on without qualifying it with something like, "Hey, Esther, your favorite show is on" (Esther thought it was so sweet that he thought of her), but he also never changed the channel, or grumbled about it interfering with something else he would rather be watching. Esther cuddled into Jeffrey, and the warmth of their bodies caused them to both nod off. They saw the part of the episode where Rose wrote a letter to Reagan and Gorbachev because she was worried about nuclear war, but missed the part of the episode where the Soviet emissary read Rose's concerned letter because he thought it came from a child.

Bruce emerged from his bedroom just long enough to see the tell-tale sleepiness of his parents, and then went back to sort his candy and wait. He made four piles. Pile one consisted of his favorites. Pile two was ones he liked, but he was willing to trade. Pile three was ones he wanted to get rid of, but was pretty sure he could easily find someone to trade with. Pile four wasn't worth the hassle of trying to trade, so he dumped this pile straight into the trash. There was one piece of candy that was not sorted into any of the piles, and that was a Bounty bar. He hadn't heard of it before, and wanted to see what it was. Even though he had just brushed his teeth, Bruce tore open the wrapper and took a bite. The mint from his toothpaste didn't help, but even on a good day, Bruce wouldn't have enjoyed it. It had coconut in it. He spit out what remained in his mouth, and then went to check on his parents. He was pretty sure they were asleep.

He wandered into the guest room and turned on the computer. While Esther was learning how to use BBS, Bruce had been learning too. He watched his mother, curiously, and learned how to connect. He found her list of bulletin boards, and watched as she typed her passwords. Even if he hadn't paid attention, the pad of paper next to the computer contained all her login and password information. Esther had no reason to suspect that she needed to keep that information private or secure, and she needed an easy way to remember it all. Bruce had seen his mother operate the computer and modem a number of times, and he had no problem dialing up and logging in himself. He ignored the message boards, and instead went right to the software that was available.

Unfortunately, most BBS sites had a ratio that users had to maintain. This meant that Bruce was only able to download so many times, before he had to upload something of his own or find a new place and start over. It was difficult to maintain a decent ratio, when the games he wanted to download were worth so many points. If he had been interested in the text files and other things available for download, he might have had an easier time. But, since he wanted the latest and greatest games, he had to juggle several BBS against one another. Most sysops wouldn't count uploads toward your ratio if they already had that particular item. So, Bruce would visit one BBS, download something he wasn't particularly interested in, but that other BBS sites didn't have, and then upload it to those sites. Once his ratio was inflated, then he could download a game or two before he'd have to repeat the cycle again. Bruce didn't care about LOTUS 1-2-3, or Word Perfect, or any of the other latest versions of software for the PC; he only cared about games.

Bruce dialed up to Exec-PC or Inner Circle or Hot Spot or Interforce, and downloaded whatever the latest uploads were. This took time; often he left the computer running over night. He just had to remember to disconnect before his parents tried to use the phone in the morning and were greeted with the terrible noise of the modem on the line. Then another night would be dedicated to uploading whatever he grabbed to Dragon's Lair or Lightning BBS or Technically Speaking or Baytec Zone or Wildcat!, and sometimes he would dedicate several days to uploading his loot to all of them. Once the sysop registered his upload and adjusted his ratio, Bruce could take his time downloading what he really sought. The funny thing was, Bruce wasn't even really that big into gaming. He was into profit. Most of his time on the computer was dedicated to getting software to upload in order to get more games. Then he sold the games.

When the porn ring went down, Bruce's spending money

took a serious hit. As a kid, he didn't need money, but he liked to be able to buy things when he wanted without his parent's permission. Often, he wasted money on candy and other things that were ingestible, or disposable, or intangible (like arcade games), because that way he didn't have to worry about explaining to his parents where this or that suddenly came from. Buying things gave him a weird sort of joy he couldn't quite explain. Spending money made him feel grown up. With the income from selling porn gone, he needed a way to get some money. As he watched his mom one day, he asked about the non-message-board parts of the bulletin board. She was busily composing a message to one of her BBS friends and casually said, "People sometimes trade software on these." It didn't cross her mind that Bruce might become one of these "people" that traded software, and, honestly, even though she did try to explain how the computer and modem and BBS worked, she wasn't sure her son was paying any attention. But he was.

Just as the boys had become famous at school for their easy access to pornography, Bruce became known as the kid to go to for the latest games. Each interested party had to provide Bruce with enough disks for the desired game, plus one. The additional disk was part of his fee, and his way of acquiring disks for his own use without having to spend money. He preferred to deal in 3.5 floppies, but he would also accept 5 ¼ disks if that's all their computer supported. In addition to providing the disks and a bonus disk, the game cost each buyer two dollars per disk. Many games took at least three disks and most five or six, but this was still a steal because these games easily went for fifty dollars or more. What Bruce learned from this new venture was that kids hadn't not bought porn from the "ring" because they couldn't afford it. It was because they didn't want to hide it or they were embarrassed by it. Jason had been their biggest porn customer, and the boys assumed it was because he had more money than anyone else. To Bruce's surprise, Jason was not Bruce's biggest buyer of illegal computer games. Where the other kids got the money, Bruce didn't know and didn't really care. They brought their disks and dollars, and he was happy to oblige them.

Personally, Bruce was a fan of games like *Roadwar 2000*, *Phantasie I and II*, and the entire *King's Quest* series, but by far his biggest seller was *Leisure Suit Larry*. The game followed the same basic format of the *King's Quest* games, but instead of an adventurer the character's mission was to have sex. For someone like Bruce, who had seen so many naked women, this low-res, softcore-porn adventure held no interest. As near as Bruce could tell, the gag of the game was that Larry never "got the girl." It also surprised him that the very kids who wouldn't buy porn before would buy this game. It was almost as if the real thing were too frightening, and this was just edgy enough. Whatever the case, his sales of *Leisure Suit Larry* more than made up for the lack of income from the porn ring, and the money he made from selling other games was just gravy. Most of those other games were adaptations of the arcade games, and Bruce didn't understand the appeal of them either. While they worked great with a joystick at the arcade, it never translated as well to the computer. Bruce found them more frustrating than anything. But, if kids were willing to buy them, then he'd continue providing them.

That Halloween night as his parents slept on the couch and the *Golden Girls* prattled on in the background, Bruce began the hours long process of uploading software, downloading games, and copying games. His timing was pretty good, but on occasion they'd catch him at the computer. When they did, they were often too tired to realize what he was doing, and they'd just say, "Bruce, you should have been in bed hours ago" and then head to their bedroom assuming that he'd follow suit. He usually did. In the morning, he always remembered to disconnect the modem, if the line hadn't already timed out or a sysop hadn't already disconnected him, and then shut down the computer. At that point of the day, his parents were busily getting ready and didn't notice him fiddling with the machine.

This year the day after Halloween was a Sunday, and his

parents slept in. By the time they got up, Bruce had already taken care of disconnecting the modem and was playing *King's Quest* when Esther poked her head it to say, "Good morning."

After breakfast, Esther decided to check in on Carol. She knew Bruce hadn't gone over there last night, but she hoped other kids had. Carol had cleaned up some of the mess from Devil's Night, but there still was a fair amount of toilet paper in the trees and something, Esther assumed egg, stuck to the side of the house. Esther knocked and waited. She knocked again, and waited. She could see Carol's car with the flat tires and knew she hadn't gone anywhere. Finally, Esther rang the doorbell. It was ten in the morning, surely, Carol was awake.

"What?" Carol asked as she opened the door. The Carol that came to the door did not look like a woman who had been awake prior to the doorbell ringing. "Oh, sorry." She opened the door and invited Esther in.

"Are you okay?" asked Esther.

"I slept like shit. The doorbell wouldn't stop ringing." Carol shuffled around the kitchen and prepared a pot of coffee. "I think they finally quit coming around three."

"Who? The trick or treaters?"

"I don't know; anyone and everyone I'd guess."

"Didn't you hand out the candies?"

"Practically no one came for candy," said Carol. "I practically threw handfuls of them at the kids who came because I had so many left over. Most times, when someone knocked or rang the bell, I'd go check and no one would be there."

"I'm so sorry," said Esther. "I went around and told everyone, like I said I would. I don't know why they didn't come."

"That husband of mine has royally fucked me this time," said Carol. She leaned on her countertop as if it was holding her up. "You want some? Coffee?"

"No thanks, I already had a cup. Jeffrey says I shouldn't drink so much," Esther said. "I'm already wound tight enough as it is." She was trying to make jokes at her own expense in an attempt to make Carol laugh, but it didn't seem to be working. "You know how it is? The caffeine-overload shakes? Jeffrey says I burn ruts into the sidewalk when I've had too much coffee. I just powerwalk until I run out of gas." Esther laughed a little, but it was awkward and the only sound aside from the coffee percolating.

"I really appreciate all you did," said Carol. "I just need to figure out what to do now."

"If you need help cleaning up outside, let me know. Jeffrey and I could come over and help."

"Why bother?" asked Carol.

"Well, it has to be cleaned up at some point. Doesn't it? Otherwise it will litter up the neighborhood."

Carol shrugged. "I cleaned up the mess from Devil's Night. The stuff you saw outside is just from last night."

"They did that on Halloween?" gasped Esther. She hadn't heard of anyone being destructive when candy was being handed out for free, much less full-sized candy bars.

"Yep, that's all from Halloween." Carol tipped her head in the direction of the dining room table. There were stacks of candy there. "Do you think the store will take that back? I kept my receipts."

Esther knew the answer to this because one year she overbought candy for Halloween and tried to return it. The store would never accept it. She could tell Carol didn't need more bad news, so instead she said gently, "It wouldn't hurt to try." This was, of course, the truth. "Can I at least send Jeffrey over to help patch your tires? He could bring his air compressor and fill them for you, too."

"That would be great," said Carol. "Otherwise, I'm looking at getting it towed into town and paying a premium for new tires. Can't really afford that."

"I'll go get him," said Esther. She left Carol's house and headed home.

When Esther got home, she noticed her brother's car was in the driveway. Kenny kept saying he was going to upgrade to the new Mustang, but he just couldn't seem to let go of his

Monte Carlo SS. Esther had to admit there was a simple kind of beauty to the black car and the red stripe around the ground. It was rare to see Kenny on a Sunday, especially at their house. Kenny wasn't a religious man, but he had his own Sunday routine that he rarely broke. Esther wasn't sure what that routine was, because she never asked, but whenever she invited him over for Sunday supper, or any activity on Sunday, her brother always said, "Can't, I'm busy." Yet, today, here he was.

Kenny wasn't trying to keep his Sunday routine quiet; he just found it easier to say "Can't, I'm busy" than to explain his routine to his sister. Kenny was a compulsive collector, and Sunday was the day that he expanded his collections. As a kid he collected anything that he could find more than one of; sometimes that meant rocks or bottle caps, but it also could mean something actually, potentially, valuable like stamps or baseball cards. The value, if there was any, was always "potential" in Kenny's case, because he never sold his collections. He could tell you how much everything he had was worth, but in practice they held no actual valuable because Kenny never intended to sell them. Over the years, Kenny had cut down on the collections he maintained and now only held onto things that other people assigned potential value to. Gone were the stones and bottle caps and found objects. At one point, Kenny had quite the collection of action figures, but then he found they took up too much room. His house wasn't big enough to accommodate large collections and he hated justifying his collections when people came over and saw them, and so he had to give some thought to what he could best collect, given the confines of the space he had available, how to keep the collections out of view. Kenny hated answering questions and justifying his need to collect, and he also hated it when people touched his things; hiding the collections seemed to solve both problems.

Every Sunday, Kenny woke up around eight or nine, showered, got dressed, and headed to his favorite breakfast place by ten. The restaurant was about halfway between his house and his next destination, and so it helped break up the drive. His breakfast usually consisted of Huevos Rancheros, but sometimes he could be convinced to have corned beef hash or the French toast—The Nomad stuffed their French toast with strawberries and some kind of cream cheese filling. From the Nomad, Kenny went to the Gibraltar Trade Center. It opened at ten on Sunday and closed at six; Kenny spent most of the day here, browsing the booths and buying and trading when he found something that interested him. Most of the items for sale at the indoor flea market didn't interest him, but when he found a booth that did, he could spend an hour going through their stock. Kenny decided, given his limited space and desire to hide his collection from sight, that magazines were what he would focus on collecting. He could easily preserve them in boxes and stack the boxes out of sight. Who would question what he had in boxes?

The first item Kenny bought was *Charlton Blue Beetle* #1, which contained the first appearance of The Question. This was a comic book that he had as a kid, and he remembered loving it. When he saw it for sale for three dollars, he scooped it up. Charles Victor Szasz, aka Vic Sage, aka The Question, was an investigative journalist, which wasn't horribly original. What was special about The Question was that, unlike Superman and even Batman, The Question had no qualms about letting a criminal drown; he would notify the police about where to find the criminal, but he would not extend his arm to save one. Kenny hadn't been an avid comic book reader as a kid, but that changed when he read that first issue. After *Charlton Blue Beetle* #1, Kenny continued to collect comics of various kinds. At one booth, he came across issues of the *For Men Only* magazine. It seemed out of place, so he picked it up. He intended to point it out to the vendor, assuming that it had been filed in the wrong box, but as he waited for the vendor to finish a sale with another customer, Kenny began reading the stories inside. They were adventure stories, mostly, but they often included a female in distress, and there was sometimes sex. The vendor finished, and Kenny asked, "Do you have any more of these?"

"Yeah, I got a few more. Not too popular; they don't have as much skin," the vendor said.

"You have stuff with skin?" asked Kenny. It wasn't that he was ignorant of pornographic magazines; he just didn't expect to find any out here on the trade floor.

"Sure, most of us do," winked the vendor. "You just gotta ask."

Kenny began asking, and then began collecting. He had his favorites, but ultimately it was the drive to have a "complete set" that kept him going more than the pornography itself. Some of the writing—articles and fiction—in the magazines was really good. But, let's not kid ourselves, Kenny also enjoyed the nudity. In addition to his collecting at the Gibraltar Trade Center, he also maintained twenty-two subscriptions to keep his collections current. Some of these subscriptions were to "normal" magazines, like *Rolling Stone*, but the majority were split evenly between pornography and comic books. He loved each subscription for different reasons, but the problem became that he only had so many hours in a day and more than enough reading (or viewing) material to fill that time. Some of the magazines or comics were thoughtfully placed in a box for later. He always meant to get around to reading all of them, but as his collections increased in size, he couldn't keep up. If he had dedicated his "free time" to reading or viewing, then he might have been able to accomplish this feat, but he also loved television. And that was the second part of his Sunday ritual.

After leaving the trade center before it closed at six, he'd stop somewhere for dinner, and then head home. Unlike the breakfast part of his routine at The Nomad, he had no such prescribed dinner establishment in mind. Kenny would just stop at a place that sounded good. By the time dinner rolled around, he was always hungry because he never bothered to stop for lunch. While he took his time with breakfast at The Nomad and knew many of the staff there, he hurried through dinner so that he'd be home in time for his favorite shows on the new Fox network. His evening would start at seven with *21*

Jump Street, which he loved; and then sometimes he'd watch whatever Fox had at the eight o'clock hour, which he didn't love; then *Married with Children*, and finally *It's Garry Shandling's Show*. After that, he was pretty cooked from television and usually went to bed. Occasionally he'd flip to see what the NBC Sunday night movie was, but when he did, he usually fell asleep before it was over. This Sunday, Kenny had forgone his trip to The Nomad, and was eating into his vital trade center time.

Esther popped in the house, and found her brother chatting with Jeffrey.

"Jeffrey," Esther said. She knew Jeffrey hated to be interrupted mid-conversation, but Esther wanted to make sure to grab his attention before he made plans to do something with her brother. The two men didn't often do things together, but when they did, it meant they both disappeared for a whole day. Carol needed Jeffrey, and Esther was just trying to help her out.

"Yeah?" Jeffrey said. He didn't seem as annoyed as usual. Maybe they hadn't been planning anything together.

Esther quickly explained what she needed, and Jeffrey made his exit.

"Good, because I need to talk to you, sis," Kenny said. "About your kid."

Esther looked at her brother and tried to get a sense of what he might be talking about. What did he know, and how did he know it?

"I have a large collection of magazines," said Kenny.

"Oh, okay. What does this have to do with Bruce?"

"Well, he's been into them."

"How do you know?"

"Because some are missing," Kenny said. He was trying to avoid saying what type of magazines precisely, because he knew his sister would freak out.

"But that doesn't mean he took them." Esther knew her son wasn't perfect, but she found it very hard to believe that he'd steal something, much less something from his uncle.

107

Bruce loved Uncle Kenny. He wouldn't steal from him.

"He's the only one who's in my house, alone, ever," said Kenny. "It's definitely him."

"What if someone broke in while you were gone?" asked Esther.

"It seems extremely unlikely that someone broke into my house, ignored anything else of value, found their way to my office, found the boxes of magazines, and removed selected issues from the boxes, without disturbing anything else."

"Why would Bruce want your old magazines? We have plenty to read here, and he goes to the library all the time," Esther said. She looked at her brother and tried to puzzle it through. Then it occurred to her that Uncle Kenny might have a type of magazine that Esther and Jeffrey didn't subscribe to. But she had to be sure. "What type of magazines are missing?"

"Now Esther, don't freak out," said Kenny.

But she did.

"BRUCE!" she yelled a moment later.

Bruce knew that Kenny was here, but since his uncle had been chatting with his father, Bruce had no reason to remain in the room. He figured, if the family was going to do something together, that they'd let him know. Currently, he was reading *Animal Farm*. It wasn't required reading until eighth grade, but Doug Barnett—Helena and Brent's oldest child—liked to read and had recommended it one night when Bruce was over for his Cub Scout meeting. So far, it was a little strange, but Bruce liked that it was different from other things he'd read. The only other thing Bruce had read with talking animals before was *Charlotte's Web*, and this definitely wasn't *Charlotte's Web*. Bruce put *Animal Farm* facedown with its pages spread wide, and went to see what his mother wanted. He didn't have to wait long to find out.

"Did you steal magazines from your Uncle Kenny?" Esther asked immediately when her son emerged from the hallway.

It was clear from the tone of her voice that his mother knew the answer, but Bruce played with different possible attempts at denial. None seemed very plausible, and Bruce could tell his mother wasn't going to give him much time to think about it. Instead of trying to come up with an excuse, Bruce tried to calculate the best way to honestly answer the question with the least amount of repercussions. His father liked watching the show Matlock, and on occasion Bruce would watch it with him. He remembered an episode where a witness was being given advice. The character, Bruce couldn't remember who but it wasn't *Matlock*, said, "Listen, just answer the question you're asked. Don't give them anything else to work with. I learned to KISS in the Navy." The witness asked, "Kiss?" And the other character clarified, "Keep it simple stupid." Bruce might not have loved the show as much as his father did, but Bruce definitely filed this information away for later use, and here was that opportunity. He answered his mother.

"Yes."

It had the desired effect. His mother was caught off guard. There was no lie to try to make sense of, there was nothing for her to find traction with. She struggled to come up with a response. The best she had was, "You did?"

"I did," Bruce answered. "Sorry, Uncle Kenny."

"Well, you won't be surprised to know that I want them back," said Kenny.

"I can't give them back."

"Why not?" asked Kenny.

Esther was glad Kenny had stepped in, because she was still trying to make sense of her son's response, and what had just happened between them.

"I sold them," said Bruce.

That wasn't an answer that Kenny had anticipated. He imagined his nephew might have bent the magazines some, or that something would have gotten folded as they were tucked into a new hiding place, or that some pages might be stuck together, but he had not imagined that his nephew would no longer have the magazines. Kenny would have taken them back even if they were damaged, because it was less about the condition of the magazines and more about the completeness of his set. It was the gap in the dates that brought the theft to his attention in the first place. Initially, Kenny thought he had misplaced one of his issues, or that it had been put away in the wrong box. The more he dug through his boxes, the more issues he found missing. He made an itemized list and was flabbergasted by the number of missing magazines. How had he not noticed before now? It should have been a sign to Kenny that he didn't really need all the magazines, because who knows when they first went missing, and how many Bruce even took at a time? If he wasn't going to read them, or look at them, then what was the point? But, Kenny would deal with that matter at a later date. Right now, he wanted to deal with the fact of the theft and righting the wrong that had been done to him.

"Well, I'm going to need them to be replaced," Kenny said. He turned to look at his sister. There was no way Bruce was going to be able to afford to replace all that he had stolen.

This Esther had an answer for before Bruce had a chance to say anything. "No, my son is not buying pornography."

"What?" Kenny asked.

"What?" Bruce echoed.

"He's not old enough, and I won't have that stuff in my house."

"I don't think you understand," said Kenny. "He took a lot of magazines. We're talking about, easily, a couple hundred dollars' worth. And that's for copies in shitty condition. Some of these are real collector's items and are out of print. You can't just go to the store and buy new ones."

"Well, that's good. Because he isn't going to buy them. His money isn't going to be used for, for, that."

"Mom, I have some money," Bruce said. And, of course, he did because of his software sales, but he didn't want to get into explaining where that money was coming from, so he didn't specify how much he had.

"I won't have it," said Esther.

"What are you going to do about my magazines then?" asked Kenny.

"I'll deal with my son about stealing, but we're not replacing your filthy magazines. You can buy them again, or do whatever you want. But no Fuhrman money will be used to assist you in your perversion."

Bruce was shocked. This was going much better than he expected. He wasn't sure what his mother had in mind in terms of a punishment, but it would likely be short-lived and forgotten soon enough.

Kenny was shocked, too. This was not going well at all. Whatever punishment his sister gave his nephew wasn't going to replace the magazines, and, really, that's all that Kenny cared about right now.

Esther was also shocked. She was completely surrounded by perverts. First the McKinneys with the nude images in their garbage, then Bill Daniels with his computer pornography, then her brother and his disgusting collections, and now her son? The only thing that saved her son, at least in Esther's mind, was the fact that he sold the magazines. The McKinneys had thrown theirs away, but Esther was convinced they, like her brother, had more where those came from. Just what the hell was going on in her neighborhood? She would have to become even more vigilant.

CHAPTER 7: PROGRESS

In the next two weeks, Esther broke three big stories. All three stories involved the school system and changes that were brewing. Education was something that was particularly near and dear to Esther's heart. She loved school and always wished she had gone on to college, but she couldn't afford it, and then she was married and had a kid. She made up for her lack of higher education by trying to help out in the school as much as possible. Esther volunteered at the school so regularly that the staff no longer noticed her, and she often picked up chatter from them. Sometimes she found memos lying around and being who she was, she read them. Often the memos addressed inane subjects, like dress codes or proper etiquette for dealing with parents during conferences, but in the month of November, Esther happened upon three particularly interesting documents. One was about computers, another about foreign languages, and the third about a major change in the way the school operated. As a parent, Esther hadn't been part of the context of the content of these memos so she was a little mystified at first, but she quickly got up to speed, or at least assumed she did.

The first memo was a call for an all staff meeting regarding the possible addition of IBM computers—whether these were actually IBM or just IBM-clones, the document didn't specify, and Esther wondered if the writer of the document even knew. Up to this point, there were only a handful of computers in the school, and they had been donated by Apple. In 1987, the Macintosh was three years old but still functioned fine. Opole Elementary, the only elementary school in town, had a single computer lab with five Macintosh computers. Students would rotate being sent to the lab for short bursts during the week and supervised by a staff member. The computer lab was only used by the fifth graders because they were, everyone assumed, the most responsible. Because there were only five computers, the students were easy to monitor. This memo called for a "large investment of IBM computers to be in all classrooms." Esther immediately wondered where they would get the money for it, how many computers constituted as "a large investment," and would students be able to learn with that technology distracting them from the teacher?

The second document read as if a decision had already been made with regard to the "issue of second language education," but this was the first that Esther was hearing about it. She didn't think learning an additional language was a bad idea, but how would they manage to fit that into the kids' already busy schedule? According to the memo, "Spanish immersion schools have been successful in other states, like Minnesota, since 1976." Who cared about what Minnesota was doing, and what worked there? There was nothing to say that what worked there would work in Michigan, and she didn't like the sound of "immersion." Regardless, who cared about Spanish? Wouldn't French make more sense with the Canadian border only an hour away? Never mind that Quebec was French-only and Montreal was almost ten hours away from Opole; it was far closer than Mexico or Spain.

Esther took advantage of her invisibility as a volunteer and listened for clues from the staff. She heard none, so one day she casually asked the secretary, "What's Spanish immersion?"

The secretary responded, "It's when students learn entirely in Spanish. Supposed to really teach them the language."

Then the secretary turned her attention to an incoming phone call. Esther returned to the classroom and asked the teacher, "Do you speak Spanish?"

The teacher shrugged and said, "Un poco. I took four years in college, but it never really stuck."

Right, thought Esther; kids would fill up their brains with this useless stuff and then forget it two days later.

It was the third document that really riled her up. It discussed a shift to a "school without walls" approach to education. Her first thought, ridiculous though she knew it was, was that they might get rather cold in the winter. What did catch her eye was a reference to "following the successful model of the Community High School." She knew exactly what that was. That was that super hippie liberal high school in Ann Arbor where all the druggies went when they were kicked out of other schools. The kids there wandered around during the day and didn't learn anything. Esther was pretty convinced they were just given a diploma for not killing one another. She remembered when the school opened in 1972; she had just graduated from high school two years prior, and the neighborhood was all abuzz about Community High.

"How forward thinking!" people said.

"What a wonderful concept!" others chimed in.

The papers claimed that the school was going to allow high school students to come and go at will, and even to design their own coursework and classes. How on earth would that prepare anyone for the real world? Esther was baffled. She would have loved to be able to do that, and she would have designed thoughtful classes that allowed her to focus on her strengths, but other people? She knew the Daniel Byrds of the world would spend most of the time smoking pot. Esther also remembered how, two years after it opened, Community High selected a gay man as their homecoming queen. John Arden Rhyne. Just what the hell was the world coming to? How could a man be a queen? And why would they want to celebrate someone being like "That"? Now Opole wanted to make the elementary school like that? Over her dead body.

Of course, none of the conclusions that Esther drew from the documents were very accurate. Still . . .

"It's true!" she told Becky.

"Can you believe it?" she asked Vicky.

"Seriously! That's what the memo said!" she told Patty.

"Why would I make this up?" Esther asked Regina.

"I know you don't have any children, but I think you should be part of this," Esther told Carol. "It would be good for repairing your image.

Everywhere she went, Esther's news was met with skepticism, surprise, and then outrage. How dare the school system attempt to pull something like this behind their backs? An emergency potluck was called for the women to gather at Esther's house the following evening to discuss the next course of action.

PTO and school-related issues were designated as an area where women held domain. So, while the women met at Esther's, the men and children divided their presence between the McKinney and Barnett households. The children ran wild in their bedrooms or the basements, and the men drank beer, chatted, and sat around a television that none of them were really watching.

The women, however, were organized. Not only had they prepared meals for their families, they brought a dish to pass at the potluck at Esther's. This was the single largest gathering of Opole females since the Wianki, and it took a little time to get all the small talk out of the way before they could get down to business. Esther took the lead.

"Thank you all for coming over tonight. As you know, this is a serious business. The changes that are being talked about will affect every kid K through 12. At first, I thought it was just the elementary level, but I've since learned it will also impact the middle school." She hadn't actually learned any such thing but had come to the conclusion on her own.

"That means," said Becky, "ladies, that if you think you're out of this conversation because your kid is moving on to sixth grade, then you better think twice."

Heads nodded. Lips were pursed.

"Even if that weren't the case, just think of the future generations after ours," said Patty.

"We have an obligation to all children," said Carol. No one tonight had really spoken much to Carol. The women had been polite enough and didn't exactly ignore her, but they didn't go out of their way to strike up small talk with her. She took this opportunity to show she was invested in a matter that really didn't affect her as a woman without children at all. "Education isn't something to," she paused for effect, "fuck with" she finished. It had the desired effect. The women were smiling, nodding, and a couple were laughing at the boldness of her language.

"I'm not typically one to curse," said Esther. "But Carol is right."

The neighborhood wives talked, ate, and made plans. The next PTO meeting and the next city council meeting wouldn't know what hit them. The PTO meeting came first. Even without the additional nine women, the meeting was well attended, but their presence required that the meeting be relocated to a larger room with more seating. This had never happened before. Traci Matthews was the PTO president, and she called the meeting to order.

"Welcome everyone. So nice to have such a great turn out," Traci said cheerfully. "We don't have enough copies of the agenda, so it would be great if you could share with one another. As you can see," Traci paused to look at the first bullet point on the agenda, but she never had a chance to finish.

"I don't see any mention here of the planned Spanish immersion," interrupted Esther. She looked at the others in attendance, mostly women; she saw a few surprised looks. This wasn't how PTO meetings typically went, and they had no idea what Spanish immersion was. Of course, like Esther earlier, they understood the meaning of the words separately, but they didn't understand them in tandem. "That's right," said Esther. "They're pulling the wool over our eyes." Esther was standing now and all eyes were on her. "Maybe, madam president, you'd like to enlighten the citizens gathered here, or should I?"

Traci hesitated. She had heard something about Spanish immersion but only in passing. The information was clearly above the PTO president's pay grade. She was at a loss as to how Esther might have found the information. Did she know more than Traci? How could that happen? The main reason she joined PTO in the first place was so she could understand the direction the school was going in and to know things before her neighbors. She liked knowing things. She liked being first. Traci decided to call Esther's bluff, "No, please. Go ahead. It's not on the agenda, but you're welcome to take the floor."

Esther should have been more prepared, but she really hadn't anticipated Traci giving her the floor. The way Esther had seen it going was she would call Traci out, and Traci would spill the beans and answer questions. Esther had more questions than answers, but she wasn't going to let Traci show her up. "Well," she started, turning to look at the gathered parents, "they're going to immerse our children in Spanish. They're going to make them learn a worthless language, and use up valuable classroom time when they should be learning math, science, and English."

Her emphasis on the last word was meant to suggest English is the language they *should* be learning. The uproar from the parents was exactly what Esther wanted and needed. She had nothing else to offer, no other information actually, and so she stepped aside as chaos reigned.

Traci Matthews was inundated with questions that she didn't have answers to. The agenda was thrown out the window. Esther didn't even have a chance to mention the two other issues she had come prepared to fight the PTO over. The meeting eventually ended, and Traci did her best to extract herself from the gathered chaos, saying that she'd follow-up on their questions and get back to them as soon as possible.

When the neighborhood women entered the city council meeting the following week, they were joined by parents from the PTO meeting and others from around town—word had spread. Opole had six city council members, and all of them were present. Council members sat behind desks at the front of the room and wondered to each other why there were so many citizens in attendance. There wasn't anything particularly novel or interesting on the agenda today; there rarely was. Esther attempted to take charge at the start of the meeting, as she had with the PTO one, but Gordon Welch, who had been Esther's tenth grade history teacher, interrupted her.

"Excuse me, Ms. Fuhrman," Gordon said. "There will be an opportunity for you to speak, but now is not it. Please take your seat and wait your turn." His tone was kind, but firm, and it immediately transported Esther back to her high school days. She sat without further comment and felt embarrassed about her outburst.

After the agenda items were addressed, Randy Kowalski opened the floor. "Esther, I believe you had something you wanted to say?" Randy asked.

Esther stood and said, "Thank you." She had notecards this time, because she wanted to make sure she addressed all of her main points. "Thank you," she said a second time and then realized she had just repeated herself. She plunged on. "I, I mean, we have recently heard about several concerning changes regarding the school system in Opole. We'd like to put a stop to them."

"Oh?" asked Gordon. "What changes?"

"First, the computers," Esther said. "I think, we think, it's a particularly dangerous idea to have computers in the classrooms. Not only will they distract students from listening to their teachers, but there's also the concern about what else they might find on the computers."

"Such as?" asked Randy. He was a big fan of computers, and in fact he ran one of the bulletin boards that Bruce downloaded games from.

"Well, in the wake of," Esther paused and looked at the people behind her. She found Carol Daniels in the audience and tried to apologize with her eyes. "In the wake of Bill

Daniels, I'm concerned about pornography on the computers."

There was a sudden uproar and Gordon had to bang his gavel and ask for order repeatedly before it simmered down.

"There will be no pornography on the school computers," said Gordon.

"How can you be so sure?" asked Esther.

"Because they won't have modems," said Randy.

"What if someone brings the pornography to school and puts it there?" asked someone from behind Esther. Other similar questions peppered the council members, and again Gordon had to call for order.

"Nothing has been decided on this issue; it's just a discussion" said Randy. "The problem is right now we have Apples in the elementary and middle school and IBMs in the high school."

"IBM clones?" Esther asked.

"No, actual IBMs in the high school," corrected Randy. "We just want to sync these up for a more seamless transition from K-8 to 9-12. Not to mention college." Esther's mob seemed to be simmering down. "And, again," he said, "it hasn't been decided yet. It's just a discussion." He had no idea how Esther got her information, but he was definitely annoyed. Of all the people in town to acquire this information, Esther was the one he would least want to have it.

"That's not all!" said Esther, raising her voice to gain whatever ground she had just lost by Randy's reasonable response. "What about the new plan for a school without walls?"

"What?" the council members asked almost in unison.

"They're planning to turn our beloved school system (which works just fine—thank you very much!) into an imitation of that neo-liberal-hippie-Community High School in Ann Arbor," Esther said emphatically.

Again, the council members were at a loss.

"Don't deny it!" people in the audience yelled.

"Finally, tell us about the Spanish immersion!" yelled Esther. She was really getting into it now.

This was a topic that Liz Nowakowski knew quite a bit about. "I can't speak to the other issues, but I can certainly tell you a little about language immersion," she said.

Everyone turned to look at Liz and a hush fell in the room.

"The idea is simple; if you want to teach kids a language, you need to immerse them in it. They don't learn by doing something for an hour at a time for a couple years," Liz paused. "How many of you took language classes?"

A couple hands went up.

"And how many of you remember how to say much more than 'my name is' or 'what is your name' or 'where is the bathroom' or something similar?"

The hands went down.

"Right," said Liz. "So, if we want our kids to learn a language, we need to immerse them in it. The idea is, you're already teaching them English at home, so we can teach them another language at school."

The crowd muttered and considered her words.

"And, as a city founded by Poles, we should be particularly proud to do something like this," Liz added.

It was obvious no one in the room had any idea what Liz was talking about, but Esther wouldn't admit to being one. She countered, "But they're not teaching Polish; they're going to do Spanish!" The crowd around her became united in their anger and their discontent was made evident.

"Who speaks Polish any more, anyway?" asked Gordon.

Randy and Liz raised their hands. No one else did.

"Well, except for you guys, of course," Gordon said and rolled his eyes good-naturedly.

"The point isn't to teach Polish," said Liz. "The point is to carry on a proud tradition of giving students a life skill. It was the Polish immigrants to the US in 1619 that fought to get the same rights as Englishmen, and to be taught lessons in Polish." Liz looked out at the people of Opole as she spoke, fully realizing that few of them recalled their Polish roots. She did, however, and she was forever trying to re-educate people about the town's Polish origin story.

"But Spanish?" asked Esther. And her question was echoed by the people behind her.

"Why not? It's one of the fastest growing populations in the United States," countered Liz.

It was a reasonable question and a fair point, but this wasn't a reasonable audience. Esther and her gang countered with a cacophony of uninformed, and sometimes unintelligible, response. Still, Esther couldn't let Liz think she had the upper hand, so she hit the city council members below the belt: "Computers in our classrooms! Spanish immersion! And what about the schools without walls, and gay homecoming queens?"

The first two statement got roars from her supporters, but when she lobbed the third accusation the response was mixed and confused. A collective "huh?" seemed to fill the suddenly quiet room. Esther had gotten ahead of herself, which is what happened sometimes when she got too excited, and she was definitely excited now. Even her friends, with whom she had discussed her discoveries over potluck and attended the PTO meeting with, were confused. She needed to recover quickly, or all would be lost.

"Don't play stupid with me, council members," she said. A good insult always worked wonders with an angry mob. She could feel the support from her friends and likeminded citizens coming back to her now. "The plan to convert our wonderful schools into some kind of communistic haven, like that place for druggies in Ann Arbor."

There was a chorus of yeahs, but they weren't as strong and confident as they could be.

Esther plowed on, "Do I have to spell it out for you?" She didn't give the council members a chance to respond. "The city wants to adopt the model of the Community High School, and let your kids come and go when they want, and decide what they want to learn. How the hell is anyone supposed to grow up with the skills they need, if they get to decide what those skills are?"

It wasn't as precise a message as it could have been, and it certainly wasn't something that was chantable at a protest, but it worked. The people in attendance shouted down the council members as they attempted to, first, figure out what the hell Esther was talking about, and then refute and respond to the allegations. Their attempts were not successful.

The city council meeting ended much as the PTO meeting had. The members of both groups were confused about where this information had come from, were unprepared for the assault, and left feeling beaten and abused. Clearly, they needed to be getting paid a whole lot more to do this job. Furthermore, neither was really the correct venue for the discussion that Esther wanted to have. Even though she volunteered regularly at the school, she wasn't a regular member of the PTO and never really gave much thought to how the school was governed. She assumed things were going well, and the people running the school were the best qualified people to make decisions about how to govern it.

Had she bothered to ask anyone about how to address her concerns, they would have pointed her to the school board meeting, not the PTO or city council. Even if someone had told Esther to raise her concerns at the next school board meeting, she wouldn't have been willing to wait until they're next meeting. The school board only met on the second and fourth Mondays of most months, and November was one of the few months they had only one meeting, and that wouldn't be until after the Thanksgiving holiday. Furthermore, Esther never would have tolerated being limited to the three minutes the school board allowed to non-scheduled speakers. Announcing her presence wasn't her style.

As it turned out, Esther's course of action, though not the "proper" method, was the most effective. Members of the PTO and the city council both left their respective meetings frustrated at the members of the school board for leaving them out of the loop. How dare they? As such, these members did follow the proper protocol, registered their interest in speaking to the school board in advance, and attended the November 30, 1987 meeting of the school board.

The meeting was called to order and roll was called. Those present and the one absent member were noted for the minutes. Good news items were shared. The board recognized visitors attending the meeting. Consideration was made of the current agenda; no additions were made. Consent items were brought up, and motions were made and seconded. The board accepted the retirement of one member, the resignation of another, and approved contracts, both certified and not. The minutes were approved from the previous meeting, old business items were discussed, old business action items updated, and new business discussion items were brought forth. During the new business items, members of the PTO and city council addressed the concerns that Esther had brought before them. Each speaker was granted fifteen minutes, because they made their request to the Superintendent known at least seven days in advance, but few of them actually took all fifteen minutes. At least three of the speakers were done in less than the three minutes they would have been given had they not made prior arrangements for more time. The school board heard their comments, logged their remarks, and promised to investigate their concerns and report back. They suggested forming a specific committee to address each individual concern. New business was concluded, reports from existing committees were given, and a list of important dates were shared with the audience. The meeting adjourned.

Esther was not present, but her presence was certainly felt. It would not have gone as smoothly if she was there because the school board members would have spent much of the time reminding her of the basic etiquette rules for speaking before the board. She might have, for example, been reminded that, "The meeting cannot be used to make personal attacks against a Board member," even though Esther would likely have plenty of dirt on each of the board members. They might also have had to redirect Esther and ensure she didn't veer off course on a tangent, or make some wild claim that was not pertinent to the "matter at hand." The board might have also had to remind Esther to keep her unruly mob in check, by pointing to the guideline specifying that "If large groups are in attendance, their representative is the spokesperson for that group and is responsible for the behavior of the group."

Who knows what would have happened if Esther had been present, but in her absence, her message was delivered and her desires were achieved. The school system did want computers in the classrooms, but they knew they could never afford as many as they desired. The decision was ultimately made to switch from Apple computers to IBM-clones in the elementary and middle schools because they would be less expensive and would provide familiarity to the systems students needed in high school and, if they continued in their education, at college. The compromise was that the computer lab of five computers would be doubled to ten, and each classroom would receive a single computer in the classroom for special projects. This price tag was much easier to accept, and for the school administrator who wrote the memo that Esther had stumbled over, was a huge victory. That particular person had never dreamed of receiving that many computers, she knew it was a pipe dream, but had only posed the idea as a hypothetical; as in, "Can you imagine when each student has his own computer in the classroom?"

Because Esther read this as a foregone conclusion and raised the issue before the PTO and city council as if it were on the docket pending final approval, Esther inadvertently made the nameless she, because Esther failed to note who wrote the memo, a happy, happy administrator who could brag to her fellow administrators at sister schools around the district about having computers in every classroom. On the issue of computers in the classroom, Esther also felt as if she had won, and so did everyone else involved. The members of the PTO and city council saw this decision as their doing the good work that they had hoped to achieve when they all had originally joined their respective groups.

No one had ever seriously intended to convert the schools of Opole to language immersion schools, Spanish or otherwise.

There was no fight to be had here. The memo had only meant to point out that Minnesota, and other states that Esther failed to mention, had been offering Spanish immersion schools for quite some time and found it to be a successful program for actually teaching students a foreign language. The memo also pointed out the failings of traditional language classes that were offered in schools, and that the Opole schools were well behind the curve by only offering language in the high school; by this point in their development, it was much more difficult to teach students a language than it was if they had begun in the elementary schools. The memo went on to recommend that the very least that the Opole schools could do was to offer optional language classes for families that were interested. This matter was already being addressed prior to the writing of the memo. The school district was in the process of hiring two language educators to begin the next academic year. One would teach Spanish and the other French. When the news came out, Esther claimed responsibility for the French-language teacher and for staving off the Spanish-conquest of Opole schools.

Finally, in the matter of the "school without walls," the memo-writer was merely suggesting that students have some freedom with regard to their assignments. The memo-writer pointed out that when students are given a topic for an assignment, they typically turn in lackluster results. What if, teachers gave them the freedom to choose their own topic? This wasn't a particularly revolutionary idea, but it was not one that all teachers at Opole Elementary adhered to, so it did require a little convincing. Esther was on the side of the memo-writer for the first half of the memo, because as a student she had longed to write about topics that teachers never assigned and would never allow her to pursue. Esther quickly became enraged when she read, "To go so far as the Community High School in Ann Arbor and its school without walls strategy." That was too far, Esther thought. Indeed, the memo-writer thought that as well, because the memo-writer had included the word NOT directly in front of "to go so far as," but Esther overlooked that little word. Since no one on the school board, PTO, or city council, wanted to adopt the school without walls strategy, the idea was dropped without further discussion.

Esther was, as far as she could tell, three for three with her battle against the school. She took credit for all of it, and the people who had seen her speak in front of the PTO and city council praised her for the victories. Some even went so far as to bring baked goods to her house with handwritten thank you notes.

CHAPTER 8: SURVEILLANCE

Esther might have continued in her position of education gatekeeper, but she opted to leave on a high note and turn her efforts back toward fighting crime in the city. As much as she valued education, and she was proud of her recent work to ensure it continued in the direction she deemed best, what good was a sound educational system without a moral and upright city to raise students of that educational system in? No, she felt secure that the school would think twice about making drastic changes without consulting her, and that their recent defeats would make them gun-shy from trying anything else this year. Her attention needed to be directed where no others knew a problem existed: Horatio's Cheese Shoppe.

Esther began staking out the shoppe. She could have just gone in when it was obviously open and asked Horatio what his hours were, but that wasn't her style. She powerwalked up to the shoppe on Monday morning, found a bench across the street, and despite the cold, sat outside reading a new book from the library called *Patriot Games* while keeping an eye on the store. It didn't open, she got cold after waiting two hours, and went home. Tuesday, she went up town a little later in the morning and found the shoppe was already open. She approached the store carefully. Rather than entering directly, she circled the parking lot around it. Nothing suspicious. There were no cars. Did that mean Horatio walked to work? Did he live nearby? Maybe someone dropped him off. Esther wasn't sure. She finished her exterior observations and went inside.

Before Esther stepped into the shoppe for the second time, she paused and wondered if she should have worn some kind of disguise, or if she should, at least, give a fake name. The disguise was immediately discarded as being a step too far; what would she have worn anyway? It's not like she could just press on a fake mustache, and even if she could, Horatio would see right through that (even if she were a man). Possible fake names rattled around in her brain. Had she given her name the first time she came in the store? Esther couldn't remember. What if she had given one name then, and another name now? Horatio's was not a bustling mega-mart, and he might remember meeting her. As her back foot crossed the threshold and the door closed behind her, she decided to be straightforward and honest. What did she have to hide anyway? She wasn't the one with secrets.

"Be right out," said a man's voice from the back of the shoppe.

The shoppe had been decorated for the holiday season with a light touch. There was a wreath on the door, some lights around the display case, and a small tree in the back corner of the café area. Esther took a seat at one of the tables. As she sat there, she wondered, did people eat here? Did they buy cheese and meat and then decide they couldn't wait to get home to consume it? Did Horatio offer sandwiches? She saw no menu or any condiments or means of sandwich assembly. Who knows what he had behind the counter. Someone must take the time to sit in these chairs, because there were five or six tables surrounded by two to four chairs each. If someone wasn't sitting here, why would Horatio bother putting them out? Maybe it was a simple matter of trying to fill the empty space? Had the cheese shoppe been a different store previously? As far back as she could remember, it had always been Horatio's Cheese Shoppe.

"What can I help you with?"

The voice startled Esther, and she turned to look. There was Horatio, standing near her with a white apron around his neck and covering a dark collared shirt.

"You came in a couple months ago, right?" he asked.

So, he did remember. "Yes, I'm Esther." She stood and put out her hand. Horatio wiped his hands on his apron, shook her hand, and then sat down at the table in the chair across from her.

"What brings you in today?" he asked. "As I recall, you don't fondue. Right?"

"Correct," she said. And then decided to try a little humor with him, "I fon-don't."

Horatio smiled broadly, but did not laugh. "I'm going to file that away to use, if you don't mind."

"Not at all; please do," Esther said. Did this man seem like a mobster? He seemed nice enough. Maybe he wasn't actually involved in the mob. Maybe he just had to pay protection money, or maybe the mob was holding his family hostage and threatening them if he didn't allow them to launder money here.

"Let's see how good my old memory is," Horatio poked a finger at the side of his head. "You, and there was another lady, right?"

"Right."

"You and her left with the aged parmigiana, some fontina, and a couple different meats," he paused. "How did I do?"

Esther didn't remember the names of the cheeses she had bought on that day because she had been so overwhelmed by actually being in the cheese shoppe. Also, she had been disappointed then that there weren't obvious signs of mob-front activity. So, she trusted Horatio's memory better than her own. She just nodded.

"You don't look like you're in a hurry today, or am I wrong?"

"No, not today. I'm just up and around and thought I'd come back and spend a little more time here. You don't mind, do you?"

"Not at all," Horatio said. "But, you'll have to forgive me if another customer comes in and I go to tend to them. I want to be a good host, but business is business."

"Absolutely."

"Do you want an espresso?"

"I thought this was a cheese shoppe," Esther said.

"It is, but I'm not a savage." Horatio smiled again. "The machine is really for me, but sometimes people come in and spend a little time; I'm happy to share." He got up from his seat and went behind the counter.

Esther remained seated and listened to the sounds of his finding this or that. She asked, "So, I was trying to remember, has this shoppe always been here? Or was it something else before?"

"Sorry, say again?" he asked.

She got up from her chair and moved over to the display case where he was working. Esther eyed the contraption he was filling with water, and asked, "What's that?"

"This is my espresso maker. I brought it home from Italy," he said. "I'm sure they have better ones now, but this was my grandmother's, and I always liked it. It still works, so," he shrugged.

The appliance was stainless steel, had a cord, and didn't look like it was particularly ancient. "How old was she when she passed?"

"She's still kicking at ninety-five, but we put her in a home three years ago," Horatio laughed. Then he said, "This isn't like some ancient piece of technology, or any kind of old family heirloom or anything. She bought it probably in the fifties? I just always liked it. The company is Vesuviana."

Esther repeated her earlier question about the cheese shoppe.

"Mom and Dad had more a deli back in the sixties. You know, sandwiches and a soda fountain."

"When did it become a cheese shoppe?"

"Seventy-two."

"Really? I would have thought I would have noticed that," Esther said. She was doing the math in her head, and realizing that she would have been twenty when Horatio's Cheese Shoppe opened.

"We didn't do a big grand opening or anything, so I don't know many people even knew there was a change of ownership." Horatio opened a cupboard and found two mugs. He placed them next to the espresso maker and waited for it to finish producing coffee in the carafe. When it was done, he foamed milk using the attachment on the side of the device. Then, he poured the coffee, added the milk, and walked back over to the table holding the two mugs.

Esther joined him. "But, didn't you change the sign, and wasn't there some kind of announcement in the paper?"

Horatio shrugged. He seemed to do that a lot. "I don't think anyone cared. It wasn't like Mom and Dad's place was integral to the history of the town of Opole, and everyone was sad when it went away. It did okay business, but there were places that did better. If people came in asking for sandwiches, I still had the workings to make them one. Eventually I got rid of the soda fountain because it just took up space and no one was asking for it anymore."

The espresso was delicious. Esther was a coffee drinker, but she had never taken the time to discern "good" coffee from the bad, and was perfectly happy with her instant coffee in the morning. Having had this though, she was having second thoughts. She wondered if she could find the little device for sale somewhere.

"This is good coffee," she said. How bad could a man who made coffee this good, be? She was seeing no evidence of the cheese shoppe being a mob front. Time to turn the screws. "Why did you decide to sell cheese?"

"Why not?"

"I mean, your parents had a delicatessen, why not just keep doing that?"

"Because I didn't fall in love with sandwiches. I fell in love with cheese." Horatio sipped his coffee.

"How did you fall in love with cheese?" asked Esther.

"By the time I turned forty, in 72, I was ready to settle somewhere. Maybe it was one of those midlife crisis things, I don't know. I had spent half of my life running away from my parents and wandering Europe, and by the age of forty, I was ready to be home. I was born here, in Opole. My parents were first generation immigrants from Italy in the thirties. We didn't get along, but I loved my grandmother. So, as soon as I could, I hopped a boat and went back to the motherland."

"And there you fell in love with cheese?" Esther asked. She was helping keep him on track.

"Eventually, but only after seeing the world and trying out everything else." Horatio sipped his coffee again, and Esther realized she had completely forgotten about hers. She picked hers up and drank some as well. "I wrote my parents, telling them I was coming back, and they were very excited. We had made up through letters over the years. I had grown up and realized they weren't the enemy, and they had time to forgive me for being an idiot. But travel takes time, and I wasn't sure about flying, so it took longer than it really needed to. When I got home, Dad was in the hospital. He had a heart attack. Mom didn't know what to do. She'd never driven a car before; Dad always drove. There were so many little things like that, that my dad always did and so Mom just never bothered to learn how to do them."

"I'm so sorry," Esther said.

"He didn't die," Horatio said. "You keep thinking everyone in my family is dead, first my grandmother, then my dad. Geez." He laughed. "Dad got better, but they decided they were done running the store. They wanted to travel. So, just as I come back, they're ready to leave. Life is too short they said, which had always been my line."

"Where they'd go?" Esther asked.

"Everywhere, but mostly they spend their time around Italy," said Horatio. "Back home. A lot has changed for them since they were high school sweethearts in the thirties."

"That's great," Esther said. "I'm glad everything worked

out for them. But you still haven't answered, why cheese?"

"Do you do the grocery shopping for your family?"

"Why?"

"Just stick with me for a second. Do you?"

"Yes," Esther said.

"Okay, so you probably are like most people, and I'm guessing you buy your family Kraft singles," Horatio said. "Am I right?"

"Sure. They taste pretty good, and are easy for sandwiches."

"Did you know they're not actually even cheese?" said Horatio.

"What are they then?"

"That's what I'd like to know," Horatio chuckled a little. "Okay, so they go for, what, $1.47 for twelve, or sixteen slices?"

"Sixteen, and yeah, $1.47 sounds right," said Esther. She wasn't sure where he was going with this.

"That's only twelve ounces, so it's not even a pound of whatever it is, certainly not cheese," said Horatio. "If you adjust it, and make it a pound, then you're talking about $1.95 per pound of Kraft singles."

"Okay."

"Any guess what I sell a pound of, hell, cheddar for?"

Esther shrugged. She hadn't bothered to look at his prices and didn't remember how much she and Vicky had paid the last time they were in. She was pretty sure they hadn't bought cheddar so it didn't really matter.

"$3.06," said Horatio. "A pound of my most basic cheese goes for a little more than a buck more than that Kraft garbage."

"You should lower your prices," said Esther. "Remain competitive." She was beginning to see why the cheese shoppe wasn't very popular among the people of Opole.

"No, I shouldn't lower my prices," said Horatio. "That's just the thing. Kraft is elbowing everyone else out of the market. They're trying to push cheese shoppes like mine out of business so they can peddle this garbage on the American public." Horatio paused and sighed. "You know their ridiculous claim that there are five ounces of milk in every slice?"

"We must see that commercial six times a night," said Esther. "Why is it ridiculous?"

"Well, you're supposed to think that it means that each slice has as much calcium as five ounces of milk."

"It doesn't?"

"No. Not even close," Horatio said. "Besides, they're pumped full of preservatives. They're not made to be cheese; they're made to have a long shelf life." He stood up and walked to his display case. "This," he gestured at the cheeses on display, "this is cheese. Making it takes time, and effort. And it doesn't last forever. It's not made to last forever; it's made for flavor. You might not like all the flavors, but there's a cheese for everyone. Why cheese? Because someone has to stand up to the Kraft Singles of this world and offer an alternative." He paused and finished the last drops of his coffee. "Plus, in seventy-two, cheese shops were more popular than they are now."

It was definitely not a romantic explanation, but it was all true. "Sadly, I missed the cheese-craze of the sixties, and by the time I opened this shoppe, the cheese business was already fading. I just didn't realize it." Horatio realized he was diminishing the quixotic inspiration for the cheese shoppe, and quickly added, "But, even knowing that, I wouldn't have done anything different."

His story was compelling, and Esther almost lost sight of her original mission.

"How can you afford to run this place, with the prices you charge, and, I'm sorry," she asked suddenly, looking around the empty shop, "the lack of customers?"

No one had interrupted their conversation this whole time. Aside from Esther and Horatio, or maybe an enzyme or bacteria on some of the cheese, there was no sign of life.

Horatio pushed his chair back and stood up. "Want another espresso?" he asked.

"No thank you. I've had enough coffee today." Maybe if she tried a softer tone. "I just mean to say, it must be hard. I really don't know many people who buy cheese from you."

He worked his way behind the counter and began making himself another espresso. "It's not so bad. I have regular customers, and every now and then a new one like you. Plus, the place is paid off, and I get money from Italy sometimes."

There it was. The first evidence of what Esther suspected. She wished she had brought Bruce's Sony Walkman so she could have recorded the comment. Maybe she could get Horatio to say it again when she had it with her. She would definitely be coming back.

"I'm going to need to get going," said Esther. "But, before I do, what are your hours?"

"It depends what's going on," said Horatio. He was rinsing out her mug. "I don't usually work Monday, but sometimes during the holidays I do. Probably starting two weeks before Christmas, I'll do that. Otherwise, I'm usually here between ten and four. Sometimes I stay open later. If I know someone's coming, then I'll be here."

"Why not Mondays?" Esther asked.

"Two reasons," said Horatio. "First, Mondays are always slow. No one comes in. Second, most restaurants are closed, and they don't need cheese."

Esther knew that most restaurants were closed on Monday, but she never had understood why. This was her shot. "Why are restaurants closed on Mondays?"

"Because it's the slowest day of the week for them. Most people eat at restaurants on the weekend, and the chefs need a day off."

"Do you sell a lot of cheese to restaurants?" Esther asked.

"Yeah, probably half the cheese I sell is to them."

Esther was surprised to learn this, but, now that she thought about it, it made sense. She filed the information away in her brain. "I'm off," she said. "Thank you for the espresso."

"Thanks for coming in and for the chat," said Horatio. He was pouring his second mug, but he waved over his shoulder with his left hand.

The month of December went like this. Esther frequented the shop, Horatio made espresso, and they chatted. He told her about his misspent youth in Europe, she told him the stories she gathered from around town, and she looked for cracks in cheese shoppe façade. She began buying cheese from him, instead of the Kraft Singles from the grocery store, and her husband Jeffrey enjoyed the surprising variety of cheeses that he had never encountered before. Bruce was less impressed by the replacement of his Kraft Singles; at school lunch he removed the replacement cheese from his sandwiches and threw them away. When New Year's neared, Esther nervously approached the cheese shoppe. She wasn't sure how Horatio was going to take the news. Her family wanted to fondue this year.

"I thought you fon-didn't?" he asked and winked at her. "No worries, no worries. Fontina is a beautiful cheese. You'll see; it melts like butter. Better than butter."

"The cheese police aren't going to arrest me?" Esther asked.

"Nah, they'll just issue you a warning this time. Don't let it happen again."

Jeffrey's family used to have a fondue pot in the sixties, and it was because of him that the Fuhrman family was breaking their traditional New Year's Eve meal of prime rib, cheesy potatoes, honey-drenched carrots, and oranges. Prime rib was always one of Jeffrey's favorite meals, but the family couldn't afford to have it as often as he might like. So, when they did, like on New Year's Eve, Esther took special pride in taking her time preparing it for him. She always made a call, weeks in advance, to the butcher in a neighboring town, to dry age a prime rib for the family, and then she'd drive to pick up the prime rib when it was ready. This was a fairly big deal for Esther because she didn't drive often, and when she did, she didn't drive far. But, for Jeffrey, on this special occasion, she would happily do it. She seasoned the meat, and then she'd slow cook it, with the oven barely hitting 200, for hours. Then, just before they were ready to serve it, she'd crank the oven to 500 and let it cook another ten minutes. Finally, though Jeffrey wanted to tear into it immediately, Esther would demand on letting it sit for a couple minutes before cutting and serving it. While they waited, Esther would use a little red wine to deglaze the pan and make an au jus for the dinner. She wasn't a big meat-eater herself, but she loved the dish almost as much as Jeffrey did. Bruce didn't care so much one way or another; he just ate what he was served. This was the tradition that began December 31, 1975, the first year they could afford the luxury after being married for just over a year.

But, the twelve-year streak was coming to an end this year.

Apparently, when Esther wasn't tuned into the conversation at the Wianki that summer, Jeffrey, Dean, and Jim discussed the possibility of doing a joint-family New Year's Eve bash at the McKinney house. Jim said his family always did fondue to ring in the New Year, and Dean and Jeffrey both had expressed their interest saying, "We always did that, too!" and remarked that "It's been a while." So, it was decided. Jeffrey swore he told Esther immediately, but she denied hearing any such thing.

"My hearing works just fine," she said.

Jeffrey countered with, "Yes, but sometimes your memory is full of other people's stories," and that had quieted her.

Fortunately, the reminder of fondue with the McKinneys and Websters came before Esther had made any arrangements with the butcher about the prime rib, so no money was lost. Esther asked Jeffrey what they should bring, and he said, "We're supposed to bring cheese. The Websters are bringing chocolate, and the McKinneys are going to provide things to dip."

So, Esther headed up to her favorite cheese shoppe and acquired various cheese. She got fontina, of course, but she felt cheap just bringing a single type of cheese to a celebration, and so, upon Horatio's recommendations, she also purchased cheddar, gruyere, and Emmentaler.

"If you're going to fondue," Horatio said, "these will blow

their minds. Emmentaler is the Swissest of Swiss cheeses. It's one of the oldest cheeses."

The evening went well enough, but Esther wasn't sure anyone's minds were blown by the cheeses she brought. There were lots of comments and questions, mostly just "What is this one again?" but no one said, "This cheese has changed my life." The kids didn't like the cheeses at all, and much preferred dunking fruit in chocolate that the Websters had brought. But, everyone seemed to have a good enough time

Regina and Vicky both wondered why Esther had been spending so much time at the cheese shoppe, but Esther brushed their questions off. She wasn't ready to reveal what she knew. In part, she wasn't sure precisely what she knew. Now that she was becoming more and more friendly with Horatio, she was also becoming more reluctant about turning him in.

Everyone stayed up late, watched the ball drop, the husbands kissed their wives, they raised a drink to the new year, and then everyone lingered another half hour before walking back to their respective homes.

The new year officially began on a Friday, and Esther wasn't sure if Horatio's would be open or not. She assumed not, but since nothing exciting was happening at her home, she decided to walk up there. Jeffrey was watching football, even though he didn't follow college sports he somehow enjoyed all of the Bowl games that played on New Year's Day. Bruce was already over at Barry's probably playing *Mega Man* or *Wizards & Warriors*—Barry always seemed to get the latest and greatest game for the NES as soon as they came out—or maybe they were playing that *Punch-Out!!* game they seemed to enjoy so much. Esther didn't see the attraction of video games, and refused to buy a game console for the Fuhrman residence. Her refusal just meant that the kids played at other people's houses. In a way, Esther had a hard time blaming them for wanting to be indoors. It was cold, and there was about two inches of snow on the ground. Still, she didn't see any value in whatever the Nintendo had to offer.

As she approached Horatio's Cheese Shoppe, she was surprised to see the parking lot full of vehicles. All the vehicles were black. Most of them were Lincolns and Cadillacs, but a few were Mercedes-Benz's. Esther had never seen so many black cars gathered in one place before. Just what the hell was going on? The closed sign was on the front door, but it was obvious something was happening inside. The inside of the shoppe was packed with people. Esther attempted a casual walk-by, but ended up pausing periodically to stare at the people inside. No one paid her any attention. With few exceptions, the people in the shoppe were men, and they all had their hair slicked backed against their scalps. Most were about Horatio's age, a few a little younger and a couple a little older. Some were holding mugs of, what Esther assumed to be, espresso made from Horatio's little machine; others were drinking beer from bottles. All of the men were dressed in nice, but dark, suits. The few women that were present were formally dressed as well and had long black hair. They milled about carrying glasses of wine. Esther couldn't help but stare. She didn't see Horatio anywhere, but that wasn't surprising given the crowd of faces. Then one face did stand out to Esther, but it wasn't Horatio's. The more she stared at the man, the more she realized everyone was vying for his attention. The name came to her just as the man's eyes locked onto hers: John Gotti.

Holy shit, Esther thought, and started powerwalking faster than she'd ever powerwalked before. She took off with such a start, that she didn't even pay attention to the direction she was headed. Instead of going to the police department as she had intended, she was blasting towards the edge of town and away from everything. She settled her breathing and turned just as she saw a black Lincoln coming towards her. It turned the same direction she had, and her heart began to pound. If she had had another speed, overdrive perhaps, she would have used it, but she was topping out. The car was moving slowly and keeping pace with her. She wanted to look to see who was driving, but was afraid to turn her head. When the car had first turned, she had noticed it had tinted windows, so she wouldn't have seen the driver anyway. Then, out of the corner of eye, she noticed one of those windows was rolling down now.

"Miss? Miss?" a voice said to her.

She ignored it and walked on.

"I think I missed my turn," the voice said again. "Miss?"

She slowed and turned her head. There was no sense in running, the car could easily catch her, regardless of how fast she ran. If she needed to though, she could out-maneuver it. On foot, she could hop fences. Nobody knew the town better than Esther Fuhrman.

"Yes?" she asked.

"Horatio's," the voice said. It belonged to a man dressed like the others she had seen inside the cheese shoppe. The voice had a thick Italian accent. Either it was a first-generation immigrant or someone who was just visiting. "Did I pass?"

"No, not yet," she said. "It's one more road up."

"Thank you," the voice said. The window rolled up, and as the car pulled away, Esther swore she could hear sinister laughter coming from inside. She watched the car creep up the block, and then turn out of her sight.

She waited to make sure the car wasn't going to double-back, peeked around the corner to see if the car was waiting for her, and then powerwalked on to the police department. Sergeant Jake Busko was on duty. Esther knew his real name was Jacek, but everyone called him Jake. It made him sound more American than the Polish pronunciation, and Jacek was also the common name of the hyacinth flower, which he thought made him sound girlish. Esther went to school with Anita Busko, his sister, so she knew all the dirt on Anita's big brother Jacek. When Anita first told Esther about the floral connection to Jacek's name, the two girls had made fun of him and spread the word around the school.

"He's a flower child!" everyone shouted. "Pansy Busko," the other boys called him; even though pansies and hyacinths shared nothing in common, aside from both being flowers.

When Jacek complained about his name to his parents, his

father sat him down and told him how Hyacinthus was a beautiful Greek man that attracted the attention of both Apollo and Zephyrus, the god of the West wind.

"Wait," Jacek interrupted, "Weren't those both male gods? You named me after a gay Greek?"

His father quickly pointed out that wasn't the point; the point was Jacek was beautiful and strong. His father left out the part about Apollo killing Hyacinthus with an errant discus-throw, but the damage to Jacek's ego was already done. Why did they give their only son this name anyway? It didn't have anything to do with the Greek myth; it just happened to be an old family name that the mother and father liked. They learned about the story of the Greek gods battling over this young man after the fact, and thought it was kind of a neat story. They never gave the homosexual overtones much thought, nor the tragic end of their new son's namesake.

Once Jacek made it known that he'd rather be known as Jake, it did hurt his parent's feelings a little, but they understood and tried to respect their son's wishes. Jacek announced to his teachers, friends, and coaches that his real name was Jake, and did everything he could think of to exert his masculinity. Football? Check. Wood shop? Check. Vocational Industrial Clubs of America? Check. Auto shop? Check. Smoking? Check. And then, after school, he joined the police academy.

Jake hadn't been working the day Esther came to the police department to report Bill Daniels, and since Esther rarely drove anywhere and was a law-abiding citizen, she hadn't crossed Jake's path in a number of years. In fact, since his hyper-masculine make-over, she didn't wind up in similar circles with him or any of his friends. Perhaps he had forgotten about the teasing or who she was entirely. At least she hoped so. Of course, it was also possible that Jake had grown and matured past the phase where he no longer cared about high school name-calling and now was a professional peace keeper. It was possible that he'd listen to her with an open mind because she came to him with a problem, and he held the key to solving it.

Except, he did remember her. As soon as Esther walked through the door, he recalled her taunts of "flower boy" and how quickly it had spread at school. He pretended not to notice her, as though his brief eye contact had only been a passing glance as he worked on some serious police work. He shuffled papers and ignored her.

Esther approached the desk, waited, and then said, "Detective?"

"Sergeant, ma'am," he said, looking up finally.

"Isn't that a military rank?" Esther asked. She hadn't been sure what to call him. Officer seemed too demeaning, and she wanted to try to flatter him. Detective seemed just right, but he had corrected her.

"It's both," Jake said. "What can I do for you?"

"I need to report a crime."

"What sort of crime?"

"It hasn't happened yet."

Jake couldn't help rolling his eyes; it just happened. First, a blast from the past, then all the bad memories associated with his past, and now this? What kind of weirdo was she. Had she become a wasteoid in the intervening years? Had Esther become a druggie? His memory of her was always as the perfect little angel, teacher's pet, homecoming queen, and all that sort of thing. Had she fallen on hard times? That would bring him a measure of joy, though he knew it shouldn't.

"I mean," Esther tried again, "it's more suspicious activity."

New Year's Day was a miserable day to work, but it wasn't nearly as bad as having to work the Eve. Today, for the most part, people were tired and hungover and kept to themselves. Jake had hoped for a quiet day in the office, but now Esther was here, and Jake suspected she was about to send him on some wild goose chase. Unfortunately, she had said the key words "suspicious activity," and that had to be investigated. However ridiculous it sounded, if something was suspicious, he'd have to dig in. It could be the Commies or who knows what. If word got back to the Chief that a report of suspicious activity had come in and he hadn't investigated it, or even done a cursory report, he would be in trouble. So, Jake dropped the dubiousness, looked beyond the high school grudge, and tried to make this as painless as possible.

"Esther, right?" He knew how to work people, and if he reached out as a human being and made a little gesture, he might get to the bottom of this quicker and without additional hassle.

"Yes," she said. "I wasn't sure if you'd remember."

He debated about going with something like, "Oh, I remember!" or "You think I would forget?" but instead plowed ahead with the relevant questions. "Where is the activity that you'd like to report?" As he asked, he reached for a pen and his legal pad.

"Horatio's Cheese Shoppe," Esther replied.

"That's open today?" Jake asked. Maybe there was a break-in. Maybe Esther had seen a broken window or a door that had been kicked in.

"That's part of why it's suspicious," Esther said. "I didn't think he'd be open today."

"Well, a cheese shop being open on New Year's Day isn't particularly suspicious. Horatio keeps his own hours and can open whenever he chooses. That's not something the police monitor or control," Jake said. "Is there something else that made you suspicious?"

"There were a lot of people there," said Esther. As she said it, she realized that sounded stupid. If it was open, then it would make sense that there would be people inside. "But the door said closed."

"I thought you said the cheese shop was open?"

"Well, I don't know if it is or isn't. The sign said closed, but there were a lot of people there." She could tell she was losing his interest. The pen fell out of his hand, and he was resting his hand on the legal pad now. He wasn't vocalizing his thoughts, but Esther could read his face. "I know it sounds ridiculous, but the cheese shoppe is full of mobsters. Gangsters. They all have those black cars, Lincolns and Cadillacs, and they're dressed in their dark suits, with their slicked back hair." Jake was picking his pen back up again. "I've never seen so many people at Horatio's. That place is almost always empty. I've been spending my days up there talking with him for the last month, and I see maybe a couple of customers a week, maybe ten in a whole month, and now this?" She paused. "I saw John Gotti," she stammered, almost certain she had seen him.

"Get out of here." Jake was looking doubtful, but it was clear he wanted to believe her.

"I'm not sure of course, I've only ever seen him in the newspapers and on news, but it sure looked like him." Jake was scribbling notes now. Esther wished she had more information for him, but she had given him all she had, and she found herself waiting uselessly for further instructions.

Jake had no instructions for her. He was thinking as he scribbled. The mob was known to be operating out of Detroit; Jack and Tony Jack and Tony Z were running the Detroit Partnership, so a mob presence in the town of Opole wasn't impossible. In fact, it might even make sense. This was a natural halfway point between Detroit and Ann Arbor, so maybe the mob used Horatio's as a cover. There was a plausible logic to it. He would need to scope it out before he went any further. If it was Gotti, then Jake would probably need to involve the State Police, and he didn't really want to do that. He could make a case for this being Opole jurisdiction, but they also didn't have the manpower to handle as many people as Esther was talking about. Then he realized Esther hadn't specified how many people there were.

"How many do you think were in there?" he asked.

"Fifty?" Esther said. "The place was packed. I've never seen so many people crammed into a small place like that."

"Alright, come with me," Jake said and gestured for Esther to come behind the counter. "Diane?" he called.

"Getting coffee," a voice from the back said.

"Cover the desk," Jake said. "I'm going out on a call."

Esther followed Jake through a maze of hallways, out the backdoor, and then into the patrol car. She'd never been in a police car before.

As they approached Horatio's, Esther could see even more cars were parked than before. They had overflowed the parking lot and were parked on the streets of the neighborhood nearby. Jake said nothing as he took it all in. The cruiser drove by the cheese shoppe at a regular speed. Jake didn't want to draw attention to his presence. A mile or two up the road, Jake pulled over to the side of the road and turned on his hazards.

"Wow," he said.

"I know!" Esther said. "What do we do now?"

"Well, I need to get you back to the station before I do anything else," Jake said.

"Why?"

"Because, if something goes down, I can't have civilians in harm's way," said Jake. He was trying to buy some time. If all those cars did belong to mobsters, then some serious shit could fly. He wasn't sure if he was ready for that. He needed to think through the proper order of things. There was a need to move quickly, because the mob might relocate or disband. But, he also wanted to be sure not to go in half-cocked. That balance of speed and caution was a difficult one to juggle. Jake pulled away from the curb, turned off his hazards, and returned Esther to the station. She would have preferred to be dropped off at home, but she didn't want to get in Jake's way and didn't want to ask for any more favors.

By the time Jake returned to the station, he had come to the conclusion that, as much as he hated to admit it, he should really let the troopers deal with this. So, he made some calls. They assured him he was doing the right thing, and even allowed him, and the four other officers of the Opole Police force, to tag along. It took the troopers a while to coordinate and organize their efforts, and some of the black sedans had since relocated, but there were still plenty of people in the cheese shoppe to raise suspicion. Jake had expressed his concern to the troopers about the gathering, but had not precisely indicated what the suspicious activity was, or what he thought might be going on. Instead Jake led with, "John Gotti and a bunch of mobsters are in my town," so the troopers didn't ask further details; they were excited by the possibility. Gotti had been wanted for quite a while for a crime related to the 1986 assault of John O'Connor, a union official, but nothing had been able to stick. Maybe this was their chance?

If the sudden appearance of two dozen uniformed officers surrounding the cheese shoppe made anyone inside nervous, they didn't show it.

"What can we do for you?" one dark-suited men asked. "Horatio's got the best cheeses in all of Michigan."

"Gotti," said the lead trooper.

The dark-suited man shrugged and motioned with his head to the left.

The troopers followed the direction and a sea of dark suits parted for them. Eventually, they were face to face with John Gotti who was sitting at one of the little tables enjoying some cheese. As soon as they saw actual cheese in front of the mob boss, the officers knew this was headed south. All their excitement about pinning charges that might stick to Teflon Don and putting him behind bars faded, and the lead trooper did his best to save face.

"Just seeing if you're enjoying the cheeses this fine town has to offer," the trooper said.

"I am," said Gotti.

"Nothing funny going on?" asked the trooper.

"Everyone knows Horatio's is the place for cheese," said Gotti. "He opened up special for us."

"Enjoy Opole," said the trooper. "We'll be watching."

"Horatio!" said Gotti. "This is some of the finest. Can you send our friends home with a meat and cheese tray for the office? Put it on my tab." Gotti smiled his shit-eating grin that made him so famous.

The troopers would have loved to bust him for just about any infraction, but there was no law against mobsters buying cheese. Trooper Emanuel Curtis would remember Horatio and his little shop though, and he would be back. Sometimes to buy cheese, because the trooper had to admit it was some of the best cheese around, and other times to make sure everything was in order and that this wasn't some kind of front for the mob.

When Esther didn't hear from Jake about raiding the cheese shoppe, she powerwalked up to the station to inquire. He was less than thrilled to see her again, and gave her an abbreviated account.

"It's like I figured; nothing was going on. Just some people enjoying cheese," he said.

Esther walked out of the police station at a pace much slower than she had arrived. Based on Jake's excitement yesterday, she assumed something big was going to go down. He was downright surly this morning, and even less friendly than when she had first arrived at the station the previous day. What had happened? She wished she had stayed to watch whatever might happen between the police and the mob, but she also feared she might get caught in the line of fire. So, she went home like Jake had instructed her to. She called a few of her sources, but they had no information to provide other than, "There are a lot of police cars and black sedans." No gunfire, no high-speed chase, and as near as anyone could tell, no arrests. A little dazed by the turn of events, Esther decided to swing by Horatio's to see for herself. If nothing else, they could chat, and maybe have an espresso or two; she really was beginning to enjoy the coffee he made in that little Italian device.

When Esther approached the cheese shoppe, she saw Horatio switch the little sign from "Open" to "Closed." Had he seen her coming and done that on purpose or was it just a coincidence? She couldn't be sure because her mind had been wandering, and she hadn't really been paying attention to what was going on in front of her. Her feet were on cruise control. She trusted them to get her anywhere the sidewalks and streets of Opole would take her. She was confident that if she knocked on the door Horatio would open for her. Surely, he'd want to have a chat like usual. She knocked on the door and was only met with silence.

The next day the cheese shoppe was closed, and the next, and the next. Esther tried again the following week, but could never manage to find a window of time that Horatio's was open, and she assumed it was no longer a coincidence. She stopped trying.

Meanwhile, Horatio was now having some serious struggles with the state police. He was suddenly being audited, and there were periodic raids of his home and shop. One day he was even taken into custody. He was held for three nights, and when he was finally released and returned to the shoppe, he found the power to his deli cooler had gone out. It was possible it was a random short in the wiring or that a sudden surge had occurred, but he had a sneaking suspicion that someone executing the search of the premises had "accidentally" been responsible for power outage. Everything else in the shoppe had power. The result was he lost a lot of cheese, and received the message loud and clear.

CHAPTER 9: SISTER CITIES

Esther was disappointed about the lack of mob activity at Horatio's, but she was even more disappointed in the loss of her espresso-making, cheese-mongering, friend. This surprised her. Most of her friends were women, but Horatio, maybe because of his age, somehow filled a strange void she didn't realize she had. Horatio was a kind man who was willing to take the time to listen and share stories with her. Esther loved hearing about Europe and his life because it was so different from her own. Unlike her other friends, whose lives she mined for gossip, she told no one about the things Horatio shared with her. Now that was gone. She did see him one day buying fruit at the grocery store. He caught her eye, smiled slightly, shrugged (like he did), and then left the produce section. She wasn't sure how it got back to Horatio, but she understood at that moment that someone had told him Esther was the source of the police raid. Her friendship with Horatio had to be the shortest friendship she'd ever had; it started in November and ended in January. So, there it was. She was minus one friend.

Whether it was because of the loss of the new friend or a reaction to the grayness and longevity of winter, Esther became a recluse for February. Temperature-wise, it was a surprisingly warm month for Michigan, but Esther felt cold and lonely. She began making regular visits to the Opole Public Library and stocked up on things to read during her days of being a recluse.

One day, in the first week of February 1988, she stumbled into the periodical section of the library. Esther had given up monitoring Horatio's Cheese Shoppe and had yet to restart volunteering at the school. She felt unsettled and out of sorts. She didn't feel charitable, and didn't think surrounding herself with kids would help with that. Esther wasn't a big newspaper reader, that was more Jeffrey's realm, but since she had found herself in the periodical section, she settled in. She read the *Detroit News, Detroit Free Press*, and *USA Today*, but found the most interesting news in the *Wall Street Journal, New York Times*, and two papers from England. The Opole Public Library subscribed to *The Guardian* and *Newbury Weekly News* because Opole's sister city was Hungerford, Berkshire.

Town twinning, as it was originally called in 1931, began with Toledo, Ohio, when it chose to be a sister city with Toledo, Spain. The two cities shared nothing in common, other than just the name, which was a point that was raised when Opole was selecting its own sister city.

"I don't understand; who has twins and names them the same thing?" a thoughtful citizen interjected when the history of "town twinning" was explained to the audience.

It was a good point. Since then, other US cities found sister cities, or "town twins," for various reasons. Some stuck with the tradition of "Oh, we share the same name!" despite the obvious flaw with that logic. Other towns and cities tried to find similar-sized or populated towns or cities to twin with, or they found a place that shared a similar industry or value. When Opole was looking for its twin in 1962, the committee narrowed the search based on population. They quickly found there were many, many towns with 6,500 and 7,500 citizens. Given the Polish roots of the town, they tried to find one from Poland that was a good match for their town but couldn't reach a consensus. This group of people had connections to this region, and that group of people had family ties to that region, and this group of people hated that part of the country, and so on, until eventually all Polish cities were eliminated from the running. After weeks of wrangling, Chester Webster offered up a suggestion that no one could object to: Hungerford.

The general response was, "Huh? Where?"

In all fairness, that was also the response the people in Hungerford gave when their mayor mentioned the town of Opole, Michigan.

"Hungerford," said Chester. "In England." He had recently gone to England and had enjoyed his trip quite a bit. Chester was a newly-minted twenty-year-old and wanted to explore the world before he figured out what he wanted to do with the rest of his life. He considered various places in Europe to travel to but ultimately settled on England because it would, he thought, provide the least amount of difficulty with language. When he got to England, he found the variety of accents off-putting, and struggled to keep up with conversation. By the time he was finally getting the knack of it, his time abroad was winding down. Near the end of his trip, Chester found himself in a pub, trying to decide out how to spend his final days in England. As the pub filled up, a young man asked if he could share a table with him.

"I'm Nick," he said.

They had a few beers and chatted. Chester learned that Nick was a young artist from a small town called Hungerford. Chester had never heard of it before.

"Why would you?" asked Nick, laughing. "There's not much there."

Nick was a recent graduate of the Chelsea College of Arts. This was something Chester had heard of before.

"What's your medium?" Chester asked.

"A little of this, a little of that," said Nick. "I think I like sculpture the best."

"Right, but what kind of sculpting?" Chester asked. "You're not carving marble are you?"

"Nah, fiberglass," said Nick. "Much lighter and easier to

work with."

They left the bar and found their way to Berkshire, and then more specifically, to Hungerford. Nick showed Chester where he grew up and showed him a couple works in progress. Unlike other people Chester had met who claimed to be artists, Chester could tell Nick really was an artist. He had a unique vision and perspective on the world and the work in a way other people simply didn't. Chester only had a few days left, and since Nick was, as he put it, "only sketching out ideas," the two ended up spending quite a bit of time together. Chester enjoyed finding a like-minded artistic spirit and the sleepy the little town. It reminded him, vaguely, of home.

When the city council began running out of possible twin cities for Opole, Chester offered up Hungerford as a possibility. There were no objections, and so it was decided to reach out to Hungerford. Chester's new friend Nicholas Monro's was an obvious liaison, so he was consulted by the mayor of Hungerford and the mayor of Opole. The townsfolk of Hungerford had heard of other places having sister cities, but none really understood what the benefit was. They understood, for example, that this American city was reaching out to them and saying, "Hey, we share something in common with you." They also understood that there was no monetary benefit to becoming a sister city, and that it was purely a symbolic gesture indicating a desire to exchange cultural experiences and histories. There was also no loss of money or obvious downside to becoming a twin or sister city. The people of Hungerford were convinced, the people of Opole were excited, and the two cities were united through an artificial, completely arbitrary bond.

As time went on, people from Opole visited Hungerford, and people from Hungerford visited Opole. A student exchange program was developed to encourage students to experience England and for English students to experience Michigan. Opole residents enjoyed Hungerford's relatively close proximity to London and Oxford; it is sixty-eight miles west of London, and thirty-five miles southwest of Oxford.

And Hungerford residents enjoyed Opole's close proximity to Detroit, Ann Arbor, and even Canada. In addition to exchanging students and residents, each town also subscribed to the other's newspaper. Neither newspaper had the infrastructure required for international subscribers, so it fell to the local librarians to send a copy through the post to the other country. This wasn't a high priority, so the other town's newspaper was typically a month or so behind by the time it arrived in its twin's library. Though this partnership started as little more than a whim, by 1987, the two cities were as close as two cities with an ocean between them could be.

This is why, on this day in February 1988, Esther was reading the *Newbury Weekly News* dated August 23, 1987. The frontpage was dominated by a single story about a young man named Michael Robert Ryan who on August 19, 1987, killed sixteen people, injured fifteen more, and then killed himself. Esther was flabbergasted. First, how could something like this happen? How had Hungerford's sister city not heard about it? She read every inch of the newspaper, and then went back through it again. The murderer had been twenty-seven years old and apparently very angry. He burned down the family house. He shot his car because it wouldn't start. He shot a dog when it got in his way. He used a pistol and two semi-automatic rifles. One of the people he killed was his mother. The other fifteen people killed by Michael were in the wrong place at the wrong time. There was no other known connection between Michael and his victims. One man was mowing his lawn, a mother was on a picnic with her children, a woman worked as a cashier where he happened to stop for gasoline for his car, a father of two was walking a dog, another man was a taxi driver. Young and old, the killer didn't discriminate. That really got Esther. The story made her sick to her stomach, but it also made her curious.

Esther went up to the librarian's desk and asked if she had the latest issue of the *Newbury Weekly*.

"No, it hasn't come in yet," she said. "I fear it's a little slow, particularly with the holidays. When it does come, we'll probably get a couple packed together."

"Did you read about what happened over there?" Esther asked.

The librarian hadn't, so Esther told her.

"That's terrible!" the librarian said. "But, it doesn't surprise me. We had that shooting in Florida not that long ago."

"What?" asked Esther.

"Oh yeah, in Palm Bay or something? I remember reading all about it because my father lives down that way," the librarian said. "It was an old man who was angry and sad. You know, he used to be a librarian. So, watch out. You never know who's going to snap one day."

"I don't remember hearing anything about that," Esther mused.

"I think he only killed six though," the librarian said. "You said the guy in Hungerford got seventeen?"

"He killed sixteen, hurt fifteen others, and killed himself," said Esther. She didn't like the tone the librarian was using. It seemed callous to say "only got six" when they was talking about human lives. "What did they do in Florida to stop it?"

"Stop it? Well, they used some kind of stun-grenade and tear gas," said the librarian.

"But that's just stopping the one guy, what about if someone else tries it?" asked Esther.

"Well, you know, we have the second amendment," said the librarian. "Not much you can do with that. There was also that guy in Arkansas; I think he got sixteen or twenty? That was just in December."

"What?" asked Esther. Now she was really angry, partly because of the language the librarian was using and partly because she had somehow overlooked all this.

And just like that, Esther had her new purpose in life: Ending gun violence.

The librarian called Esther the next week, saying the latest six editions of the *Newbury Weekly* had arrived. Esther sped back to the library to get caught up. Since last week, she had read all about William Bryan Cruse and his rampage in Florida and Ronald Gene Simmons and his shootings in Arkansas. She even dug into the archives to find stories about previous similar shootings. She was surprised so many had occurred, and she hadn't even noticed. There was a welding shop shooting in Miami, a nightclub shooting in Dallas, a McDonald's shooting in California, and a post office shooting in Oklahoma.

She did remember the post office shooting in Oklahoma. That was just in 1986, but at the time she hadn't given it much attention because instead of focusing on the loss of life, everyone seemed obsessed with the new phrase "going postal." There was an almost universal empathy for the killer because of the drudgery of his work, and that was something the generally blue-collar workers of Opole could relate to.

She even heard Jim McKinney say, "The city drives me nuts, I tell you. One day, I'm going to go postal."

Her husband, Jeffrey, had come back with, "You work for the city, not the post office," and the two men laughed.

Now Esther was seeing the Oklahoma shooting in light of the tragedy in Hungerford and other cities, and she didn't think it was funny at all. What good did it do to shoot your coworkers anyway? They probably hate their jobs just as much as the killer did.

She dug into the *Newbury Weekly* and got caught up. The people of England were outraged by the attack. It wasn't isolated to Hungerford. The government was talking about banning guns. Esther wondered how they could even do that. How many guns did the English have? Esther realized she knew very little about England. She pictured them hunting with dogs in the countryside and maybe chasing foxes, but she really didn't know if the average Englishman hunted like the average American did. Maybe it would be easier to remove guns from England; she wasn't sure.

She didn't have an answer to the problem, so she continued reading to see what they might come up with. Esther hoped they'd have an answer that she could borrow and propose to the Opole city council. As the story unfolded, the proposed legislation in England shifted from an outright ban of all weapons, to banning only automatic and semi-automatic rifles. Those, the people in the *Newbury Weekly* argued, had no place in a civilized society. Esther found herself copying one line from the newspaper onto a pad of paper she brought with her: "There is no legitimate sporting or leisure interest that would be seriously damaged or even significantly impeded if the more lethal firearms were prohibited from normal sale and could not be kept by the private person in his own home. I refer to self-loading full-bore rifles, carbines and shotguns." She liked that and thought she could use it.

While Esther was working to combat mass shootings, her son found himself outgrowing his bb-gun. It was shaped like a M-16 and all his friends had one, but it still was just a single-pump bb-gun. It could shoot pellets, but the loading mechanism was awkward. He had tried loading the pellet backwards, thinking it would work like a hollow-tip bullet, but it didn't seem to make much of a difference. David and Barry both swore that backwards pellets ripped huge holes in targets, and Barry also claimed it was a backwards pellet that had taken the head clean off of a sparrow one day. Bruce couldn't attest to either of those claims, but he did notice that loading the pellet backwards made its flight less predictable. In either case, Bruce found his bb-gun to be boring and wanted something new.

He had amassed a fair amount of money from selling computer games. In fact, part of the problem was that he actually had too much money. Before, with the money from the porn, the boys would receive sporadic payments for their product and then have to split it three ways. He never had much money at a time and quickly spent it on candy or smoke bombs; he very rarely saved it. Now he had more buyers for computer games than they ever did with the pornography, and he didn't have to split his earnings with anyone. The money, quite literally, piled up faster than he could spend it.

Wilson Hubbard, the barber that cut hair for all the boys, also had the best collection of magazines this side of the library. It was actually at Wilson's Barber Shop that Bruce encountered his first pornographic magazine. Wilson kept *Playboys* and *Hustlers* behind the counter for his adult customers because he knew some of them "enjoyed the articles." When an adult was done with the magazine, he, or she but usually he, was supposed to return it to the basket behind the register. One day, Bruce found a *Playboy* sitting in the pile of regular magazines and had almost made it to the centerfold before he was caught and the magazine was confiscated. Since the porn ring, Bruce didn't really have much interest in pornography, but he still enjoyed Wilson's library of magazines. Bruce would often arrive a little early for his appointment to leave a little time to read Wilson's magazines. Lately, it was *Guns & Ammo* that had his attention.

Wilson's magazine collection included current subscriptions and older, sometimes years' older, issues of the magazines. When Bruce arrived for his most recent haircut, his eyes lit up. The March 1984 issue of *Guns & Ammo* was sitting right on top of the stack of magazines. The cover featured a picture of an UZI with the headline, "Exclusive: UZI, Assault Pistol." Bruce was familiar with UZIs because some of his GI Joe action figures came with them. He had also seen them on TV during some of his favorite shows, like *The A-Team* and *Airwolf* (by 1988, both of those shows had gone off the air, but Bruce still loved them). In addition to the magazine featuring an UZI, there was also an August 1987 issue with a .357 magnum on the cover. Bruce knew it was a .357 magnum because he had seen *Dirty Harry*. The headline said, "The .357 Magnum... Is It Dead? Not by a Long Shot!" That same article also included an article about special ammunition for the .44 magnum that was "more powerful than ever!"

Bruce flipped through the pages. Unlike the pornographic magazines, which Bruce occasionally did read for the articles, Bruce only cared about the pictures and advertisements of guns in *Guns & Ammo*. The prices blew his mind. When he wanted to buy his M16-shaped bb-gun, he had to work to save up ninety dollars for what seemed like forever. Dave and Barry already had theirs, and he was dying to have one.

He begged his parents to help him, "Please, it will prepare me for when the Commies come," he said. "Please, I'll be able to practice for when I join the Marines," he said. "Please, it will be good for when I'm in Boy Scouts and can get my rifle merit badge," he said.

Jeffrey and Esther were not interested in arming their son. Bruce begged them for chores that he could do, so he could earn money, but the Fuhrmans were also the cheapest parents on the block. He might get a quarter for folding all the laundry or a dollar for mowing the lawn. At that rate, Bruce argued, it would take forever to earn enough money.

"It might as well be a million dollars!" he said, getting frustrated one day. It never dawned on him that they really didn't want him to have a bb-gun, and that they were intentionally making it difficult. Fortunately for him, and unfortunately for his parents, Bruce's birthday and Christmas came during the time he was saving for the air rifle. They had to hand it to him, he was dedicated to the cause. Eventually, he managed to scrape and save enough money to buy the bb gun.

Now, as he sat there staring at the back of a *Guns & Ammo*, he realized he could buy almost any gun he wanted. Here was a Browning 9mm pistol for $395, an UZI pistol for $579, a 22-caliber pistol for $265, a badass Dirty Harry-style 357 Magnum for $390. He might not be able to afford the $1,495 MAS 223 semi-auto rifle, even though it looked totally awesome and would be worth every penny, but he was close to being able to afford the UZI carbine, with a 25-round clip, for $679, and could definitely afford the Winchester 12-gauge shotgun for $350, or the Mitchell AK-22 semi-auto rifle, with a 29-shot magazine, for $265. He had almost $500 saved up, which meant nearly all these weapons were within his reach.

The problem was Bruce had cash but no means of turning it into a check, or whatever a money order or COD was, which was what all the advertisements required. He did write the various firearm companies to receive the catalogues they offered, but he kept running into the same problem: They wouldn't accept cash in the mail. And, unbeknownst to Bruce, his mother often intercepted the catalogs and threw them away. When the first one arrived, she assumed it was a fluke. When they kept arriving, she figured it was some prank her brother was playing on them. Esther wasn't always the one who got the mail though, and so enough of the catalogs found their way to the intended recipient. Bruce never realized more than half of the ones he ordered had been disposed of.

Even something simple, like requesting a catalog, was a bit of an ordeal for Bruce. Bruce knew if he asked for stamps and envelopes, his mother would ask why, and he knew if he tried to mail things from the mailbox attached to their house, that she would wonder why envelopes were clipped to the box waiting for the postman to pick them up. His mother was inquisitive and relentless, and nosy. Mostly, Bruce knew his parents wouldn't approve of his trying to buy guns, so he went to the postal office and bought his own book of stamps. He also went to the drug store, which had a small selection of "office" supplies, and bought a box of envelopes. Then, when he wanted to request a new catalog, he wrote the necessary note, addressed the envelope, sealed the note within, stamped it, and walked the requests to the post office himself. Even though Esther did destroy a number of the catalogs before Bruce received them in his grubby hands, the Fuhrman address was added to that company's mailing list, and sold to others, and, of course, Bruce was requesting more and more. So, the gun catalogs bombarding the Fuhrman mailbox compounded, rather than decreased.

From *Guns & Ammo* Bruce learned that there were gun shows that happened regularly. One was at the Gibraltar Trade Center, but Bruce also had no wheels to get to any of these. Even if he had known his Uncle Kenny went to the Gibraltar Trade Center regularly, he probably wouldn't have had the balls to ask Kenny to take him along, especially after the whole stolen magazine fiasco. It was unlikely that his porn-loving uncle would have allowed Bruce to buy a firearm without the approval of Esther and Jeffrey anyway.

It was safe to say that Jeffery and Esther did not want their son to have a semi-automatic weapon. His father might have said yes to a rifle or a shotgun, but the rub would have been that Jeffrey would never say yes to the purchase of ammunition for the gun. Jeffrey could be cruel like that at times. Bruce knew he was overlooking something whenever his father readily agreed to anything. If Jeffrey said yes too easily, it made Bruce immediately second-guess his request. Was it a trap? Sometimes it was, and sometimes it wasn't. Bruce once asked for a pet, and his father surprised him by immediately saying, "Sure." The next day, Bruce asked if they could go to the pet store to pick one out, but his father said, "Oh, your pet is already here." The boy was overjoyed, "Where?" he asked. How on earth did his father know what he wanted? Jeffrey walked Bruce into the garage and pointed up at a large black spider sitting in a spiderweb. "I figure you'll name it Charlotte, like the one in that book you like." All this is to say, it was unlikely his parents or uncle would be assisting Bruce in acquiring a firearm.

So it was that Bruce found himself complaining to his friends on the school bus on a cold day of March.

"You could buy a machine gun?" asked Dave.

"No, not a machine gun," said Bruce. "But a semi-automatic."

"Wow," said Barry.

"You should see the catalogs, and the prices aren't much more than what we paid for our bb-guns," said Bruce.

"How much do you have?" asked Dave.

"Almost five hundred dollars," said Bruce.

"Jesus," said Dave. "What are you going to do with it all?"

"Aren't there gun stores?" asked Barry.

"Not within the distance of my bike," said Bruce. "And you know my family isn't going to help me get a gun."

Gerry White had been splitting his attention between listening to the younger boys talking and listening to Bon Jovi's

Slippery When Wet. The kids were loud and distracting, but he also loved guns, and so he was trying to track their conversation to see if it would provide him an opportunity to interject. Side-A ended with the final notes of "Wanted Dead or Alive," and Gerry was opening his Walkman to flip the tape, when he heard the words, "Five hundred dollars." This definitely caught his interest. He opened the player, flipped the tape, but didn't hit play immediately. Soon Gerry realized he didn't just have an opportunity to interject, he flat out had an opportunity.

"I've got some guns," he said. He stood up and leaned his elbows against the back of Bruce's seat. Even though Gerry was a junior, he was a young junior and didn't have a license yet. This was a sore point for him. He hated riding the bus with the little kids, but he also didn't have many friends. The few friends he did have that had their licenses either didn't have cars to drive or didn't want to give him a lift.

"Oh?" asked Barry. "What do you got?"

"What are you looking for?" asked Gerry.

"I'm the one looking for guns," said Bruce.

"Okay," said Gerry. He turned to look at Bruce directly. "What are you looking for?"

"MAS 223, or Bullpup, or maybe just an UZI," Bruce said as casually as possible.

"Yeah, I'm not really an arsenal or anything," said Gerry. "I do have some handguns and hunting rifles."

"44 mag?" asked Bruce.

Dave and Barry watched the conversation bounce back and forth like a tennis match. Neither knew much about guns. They knew what an UZI was, and they assumed a "44 mag" was short for 44 Magnum, but they didn't know what the Bullpup or MAS 223 was.

"I don't think you could handle it," said Gerry. "Do you have any idea how much kick comes with a Magnum like that?"

"Of course, I do," said Bruce. But he didn't. "I go shooting all the time." He didn't.

"Well, I don't have one anyway," said Gerry. "I do have a 357, a 12-gauge, and a Beretta 9mm." These weren't actually his weapons, but Gerry was getting excited about the prospect of duping this kid for all of his money. Gerry hunted with his dad, but he mostly shot a 30-06. He had shot the 357 before, but he wasn't a very good shot with it.

"Is the 12-gauge sawed off?" asked Dave. He had seen *RoboCop* last year and remembered a scene at the beginning where criminals used sawed off shotguns. It looked pretty cool. Regina and Jim didn't know that their son had seen the movie. They had forbidden him from seeing it because the movie was so violent it almost received an X-rating, in part for the very scene that Dave remembered it by.

"What are you, a gangbanger?" asked Gerry. "Only fools saw off their shotguns."

"Yeah," said Bruce. Though, he thought a sawed off one would be cool, too. It was Uncle Kenny that had taken him and Dave to see the movie that inspired this thought. He had to act like he knew what he was talking about. "Dave, that shit's just in the movies."

"Look, if you buy it, you can do whatever you want with it," said Gerry. He turned his attention back to Bruce. "So, are you interested?"

"How much?" asked Bruce.

"The shotgun has a tactical grip, custom stock, and breaching barrel," said Gerry. He was counting on Bruce not knowing what any of those things were, and hoping they would justify his inflated price tag. "Plus, it's a Remington."

"Whoa," said Barry. "That's like the Cadillac of shotguns, right?" Barry had also read a fair number of the magazines at the barber shop, but unlike Bruce he didn't obsess over them. Despite that, the brand Remington stuck out in his mind.

"More like Lamborghini," said Gerry. But he was nodding his head at Barry, and thinking, "That's right kid, help me out here."

"So, that's probably worth like, what, three hundred?" asked Bruce.

Gerry blew air out of his mouth and snorted. It was more than the gun was worth, but he wanted to get as much of the aforementioned five hundred dollars as he could. "Five or six, at least." Gerry paused. "How much ya got?"

"Five!" said Barry. He was trying to help, but he wasn't.

Gerry feigned his best look of disappointment.

"No way it's worth that much," said Bruce. "I know the prices in the mags, that kind of shotgun goes for three, maybe four, with those improvements. But those are for new. You're talking a used shotgun. Come on. You're trying to rip me off." He was pretty confident with the pricing, but he also had wanted both a shotgun and a pistol, and at this rate he was only going to end up with one of the two.

"Supply and demand, kid," said Gerry. "You got any better offers?"

Bruce didn't. "I'm going to want to see them," he said.

"Sure," said Gerry. "What should I bring tomorrow?"

"All three," said Bruce. "I want the shotgun for sure, but I also want a pistol."

"I'll bring them," said Gerry. "But I'm not getting screwed by some fourth grader who thinks he knows guns better than I do."

"Fifth grader," said Dave. "We're fifth graders." He, like his friend Barry, wasn't helping.

Gerry didn't answer as he clicked play on his Side B of his cassette and enjoyed the rest of the ride with his mind fully occupied by Bon Jovi.

The next day, Gerry brought the guns as promised. Instead of his usual backpack, he had a duffle bag with him. As the bus bumped along, the kids passed the handguns and shotgun around. Dave and Barry and Bruce remained low and hidden behind the seats. It wasn't that they thought they would get in trouble for having guns on the bus; it was more that they didn't want to share their experience with anyone. This was their private moment to enjoy. Bruce tested the weight of each weapon in his hand, sighted the shotgun, and braced himself against the imaginary kick of the 357 Magnum. They were impressive. Dave and Barry were even more excited than Bruce was. They had never held a real gun before, and the possibility of their friend owning one or more of these weapons was exciting; much like a swimming pool, the only thing better than having one yourself is when your friend has one. All the excitement with none of the clean-up or maintenance. Bruce wanted all three, but it was pretty clear to him that Gerry wouldn't let them all go for the four hundred, eighty-three dollars that Bruce had in his wallet. He remembered back to when his father was buying the new family vehicle, the Plymouth Voyager, two years ago.

Bruce had been bored out of his mind, but his parents said he wasn't old enough to stay home alone, and no one else in the neighborhood was around to watch him. He had brought a book, and he tried to settle in. The Plymouth showroom was loud, and it was hard for Bruce to focus on the words in front of him with all the announcements going on and people hustling around. Instead of reading, he ended up listening to various conversations. Bruce knew, from the car ride in, that his parents wanted to buy the Plymouth Voyager. It had been rated one of the *Car and Driver's* 10 Best cars of 1985. His father liked the room it had and that it could haul lumber if he needed it to. His mother liked that it drove more like a car than the other vans they had test-driven but still had additional height so she could see over most traffic. Knowing how much his parents were already sold on the vehicle, it surprised him that they didn't just go in, pick out their color, pay the man, and drive off the lot. Instead, his father and mother were hemming and hawing and pretending that the salesman needed to convince them.

"I don't know, Esther," Jeffrey was saying. "It's awfully expensive for something that isn't quite a car and isn't quite a van. Just what is this thing?"

And Esther was saying, "The one you have on the lot isn't really the color we'd prefer, and it has some additional features that we don't want to pay for."

To Bruce's surprise, the family was leaving the dealership empty-handed.

"Where's the new car?" asked Bruce.

"They're not ready to deal yet," said Jeffrey. "I give them maybe two days."

"No, he's stubborn," said Esther. "Probably a week."

"You see, kid," said Jeffrey, "you can't let them know you want it bad, or they'll rake you over the coals and take you for everything you're worth."

"It's part of negotiating," said Esther. "In a week," Esther started, but was interrupted.

"Two days," corrected Jeffrey.

"A week, or sooner," Esther said, "that salesman will call us, and he'll be ready to make a deal. We already want what he has; we just want it for less than he's asking."

"We could save a couple grand," said Jeffrey. "Patience. Never buy something when you need it. It puts you in a bad position."

The salesman contacted them three days later with a deal, the Fuhrmans countered that offer, and they had a new family vehicle later that night after they finalized the paperwork.

Impulsively, Bruce wanted to give Gerry whatever he wanted for the guns. It was magical holding something he had only ever seen in movies and on TV before. The longer he held the weapons and reflected back on his parent's advice, the more he realized they were right. Gerry needed to wait. Bruce didn't need these guns now. In fact, he really didn't need them at all. This was pure want. He could use that to his advantage. So, he handed the guns back to Gerry and said, "Thanks for bringing them, but I need to think about it a bit more."

Gerry was dumbfounded. He didn't want to have deal with the guns at school. He had been so convinced that the kid would buy them from him, he hadn't even considered if the duffle bag would fit in his locker. If he had sold the guns to the kid, it wouldn't be his problem, but now he was left in a bind. "Come on," said Gerry. "I thought your mind was made up."

"They're pretty scratched up," said Bruce. "And, I thought

you said the shotgun had a pistol grip?"

Gerry didn't remember exactly what he had said about the grip on the shotgun; he had intended to talk over the kid's head so he could justify the inflated price he was asking. "Did I?" he asked. Gerry looked at the duffle bag and thought it would probably fit in his locker. "Well, think it over. Let me know if you want to see them again."

After school, Bruce tried to play it cool again. The bus picked up at the elementary first, then the middle school, and finally the high school. When Gerry climbed onto the bus, he was surprised that Bruce hadn't saved him a seat. He walked by Bruce and found a seat behind him.

"Hey," said Gerry. "You think about it?"

"Yeah, I don't know," said Bruce.

Gerry slumped into his seat. "Want to see them again?" he asked.

"Sure," said Bruce.

Gerry slid the duffle bag into the walkway and around to Bruce's waiting hands. Bruce opened it, and felt each of the pistols in his hands again. They were so heavy, but the weight felt good. He felt powerful. He passed the 357 to Dave, who was sitting next to him, and then removed the shotgun from the bag. Bruce stood up, pressed the stock into his shoulder and leveled the gun. He mimed shooting things out the window, and then swung it around again in order to sit down.

Unfortunately for Bruce, the bus driver suddenly caught a glimpse in his rearview mirror of a person holding a shotgun and slammed on the brakes. Bruce smashed into the seat in front of him, and the shotgun fell from his hands and onto the heads of the people in the seat in front of him. Everyone was surprised by the sudden stop and more surprised by the falling weapon.

"What the hell is going on?" asked the bus driver. The bus had barely come to a complete stop and he was already halfway to Bruce's seat.

"What?" asked Bruce, somewhat lamely.

"You can't bring guns on the bus," said the bus driver.

"They're not mine," said Bruce. "They're Gerry's."

Gerry tried to defend himself, "They're not loaded. We weren't going to hurt anyone. He was just thinking about buying them from me. That's all."

"You've got to be kidding me," said the bus driver. "An arms deal on my bus? I don't even allow chewing gum or eating food." The bus driver took the duffle bag, put the guns away, and then returned to his seat at the front of the bus. "You two," he said pointing at Gerry and Bruce, "Do not get off the bus. We're going back to the office after we drop everyone else off."

It was a long and quiet bus ride. Typically, Bruce's house was one of the first stops on the way home, but today he got to see the full route. Finally, it was just the bus driver, Gerry, and Bruce. They pulled into the front of the school and walked straight to the office. The bus driver explained what had happened and then left. Sheryl Duncan, the office secretary, called Gerry's and Bruce's parents, and they waited for the parents to arrive. Gerry's father came first. He was shaking his head as he entered the office and greeted his son with a smack to the head.

"What were you thinking?" he asked. Gerry had no answer.

Jeffrey arrived a short time later. Rather than smacking his son, he walked in quietly and sat next to his son without saying a word.

"Thank you both for coming," Sheryl said, when she noticed Jeffrey had arrived. "Principal Graham will see you now."

Bruce had never been to the principal's office before, let alone the high school principal's office. He had no idea what would happen. He understood with greater clarity that the bus was not the ideal location to buy guns, but he also thought everyone was overreacting. The guns were not loaded, and Gerry hadn't even brought any ammunition. At least he thought Gerry hadn't. Even if he had, what did the school think they'd do? Shoot up the bus? Who would want to do that?

Gerry and Bruce sat quietly as the adults spoke, but neither was engaged in the conversation. The principal was saying, "This is a very serious matter," and the fathers were nodding and agreeing. Both boys knew the real conversation would occur at home, away from mandated reporters.

Now the principal was saying, "No, there was no need to confiscate the weapons, or report this to the police."

Gerry's father was asking about possible suspension.

"We'll have to review the case, but I don't know that expulsion can be avoided."

Gerry's father was particularly animated about that response and began to raise his voice. "Nothing has been decided." Pause. "We'll definitely be in touch."

They were escorted out of the office and each father and son went their separate ways to their respective vehicles.

If Gerry had been trying to sell his father's guns, he would have been in even more serious shit. As it was, he still had to explain where the pistols came from and why the hell he had taken guns to school.

"Even without ammunition, you had to know that was a stupid thing to do, right?" his father asked him.

At the time, Gerry hadn't thought it was as stupid thing at all. Kids sold and traded things at school all the time. It was usually candy, or gum, or school supplies. But, the way his father phrased the question, it was obvious that it would be best if Gerry accepted fault and did not put up any resistance. He nodded at the appropriate moments, responded in an apologetic tone, and gave no backtalk to any of the criticisms lodged at him about his intelligence or his ability to think critically and know the difference between right and wrong. He would be grounded, his father would take away the shotgun for the foreseeable future, and they would wait to see what the school decided to do with him. If he was to be expelled, then he'd work his ass off to prove himself worthy to return to school, and to fill the time, he'd do additional work around the house and find himself a job to see what the "real world" was like for high school dropouts.

Jeffrey said nothing on the way home, and Bruce wasn't sure what to do with his silence. His father wasn't a big talker, but he also wasn't prone to extended silences like this. Bruce's mind raced for something smart to say, which was something he was typically good at, but nothing seemed appropriate. He could apologize again but what good would a third or fourth apology do? He could attempt to explain, but he couldn't come up with a way to justify his actions now. Before, it made total sense to him. He had money; Gerry had a gun; they just wanted to exchange those things. The incident on the bus only happened because Bruce had been following his father's example of making the salesman sweat, but Bruce knew it was a bad idea to place the blame on his father. He could imagine how that conversation would go, and he wouldn't come out ahead.

The Plymouth Voyager turned into their driveway, Jeffrey got out, closed the door gently, and went inside the house without waiting for his son. Bruce gathered his things and followed. He could hear raised voices as he opened the front door. Inside, his parents were standing on either side of the kitchen counter. Their conversation ended and their heads turned in unison to look at their son. Then they looked at one another and began anew. Bruce put his backpack down and walked to the kitchen. He stood there, waiting for his punishment. Jeffrey was catching Esther up to speed. Esther was alternating between expressing her shock and rage and peppering her husband with questions. Bruce's head swam, and he faded in and out of their conversation. Finally, his father said something that caught his ear.

"I want to know where the hell he got that kind of money."

There was a brief pause, and then both adult heads turned to look at the child.

"Well?" asked Esther.

Bruce didn't answer fast enough for them, and Jeffrey filled in a possible answer with a question of his own, "Is it drugs?"

"No!" said Esther. "It isn't drugs, is it?"

Compared to drugs, selling pirated computer software and

pornography didn't seem so bad. Maybe if he let his parents go on long enough, they'd invent more worst-case scenarios and ultimately be less upset by what he had actually done.

"Why else would he need protection?" asked Jeffrey.

"You're dealing drugs?" asked Esther. "That's even worse than using them."

"Actually," said Jeffrey, "I'd rather he dealt drugs than used them."

"Seriously?" asked Esther. Who was this man?

"Well, I'd rather him be a businessman than a junky."

Esther had to admit that was a decent point, but she didn't like the idea of her son being the source of so many other people's downfall. Yes, it was better than being junky, but not by much. At least as a junky, Bruce could get help and be reformed. He was the one being taken advantage of, not the one taking advantage of others.

"I'm not doing drugs or selling them."

Well, thought Esther and Jeffrey, that was a relief.

"Then, why the guns?" asked Jeffrey.

"Because guns are cool," said Bruce.

Jeffrey remembered being a kid and enjoying shooting things with the .22 his grandfather had at the farm, but he never had the urge to own a rifle of his own. He was fine with the gun staying at the farm. He could shoot it whenever he visited, but what on earth did someone living in the city need with a rifle?

Esther didn't understand the appeal of guns at all. They were good for hunting, but who needed to hunt with grocery stores in every town? As far as Esther was concerned, the only place for weapons was for people who lived in the country or the military. The fact that her son was attempting to buy guns hurt her in a way that surprised her. It meant that somehow his values were very different from her own and the way she thought she had raised him. The more she thought about it, the angrier she got.

"What the hell would you do with a gun?"

"Shoot it," said Bruce.

"Okay smartass, at what? And where?" asked Esther.

"Birds? In the woods?" suggested Bruce. Suddenly he was realizing he hadn't given much thought to where he would actually shoot his guns. His backyard was tiny, and the place he referred to as the "woods" was really a city park where he and his friends snuck off to shoot birds with their bb-guns.

Jeffrey shook his head. Had he raised a moron? What the hell was going on in this kid's mind?

"Do you know what a 357 or shotgun would do to a bird?" he asked, but didn't wait for an answer. "There wouldn't be anything left of it. It would, quite literally, explode. And don't you think people would wonder who the hell was shooting in the city park? It's not like sneaking off with your stupid little M16-shaped bb-gun and playing war, or whatever you kids do there."

So, they knew what Bruce did. He was a little surprised. He thought he had been sneakier than that. He wanted to say, "The guns felt so good in my hands!" but knew that wouldn't win him any points. Even he was now realizing that buying something for its weight and the way it felt was a pretty stupid reason for spending hundreds of dollars on it.

"I'll ask again, where did the money come from?" his father asked slowly.

Bruce hesitated but figured at this point there wasn't anything left to lose. Since his parents had already jumped to the conclusion that he might have been dealing drugs, he hoped his software sales would come as a relief.

"I've been selling computer games."

"What?" asked Jeffrey. "You make your own computer games?"

This was not a conclusion that he assumed a reasonable person would come to. Bruce would love to make his own computer games, and actually he had several good ideas for them, but he had no knowledge of how programming worked. He had done some BASIC programming in school, but that was a far cry from what Sierra Games or Activision was producing. He remained silent for a bit to see what would

171

happen.

"Well?" asked Esther. She hoped it was true because at least this was a marketable skill he could use in the future, but somehow she doubted it. She knew that Bruce spent time on the computer after they went to bed, and she had on occasion picked up the phone to hear the tell-tale sounds of a modem connection. But programming games? That seemed a little more complicated than the tinkering she assumed Bruce was doing.

"I get games from bulletin boards, copy them, and sell them to kids at school," Bruce said finally.

"That's kind of genius," said Jeffrey.

"Don't encourage him," said Esther.

"How much money have you made?" asked Jeffrey.

"Almost five hundred dollars," said Bruce.

Both parents sat in silence.

"And you wanted to spend that money on guns?" asked Esther. "Why?"

"I don't know," said Bruce.

"You must have a reason," said Jeffrey. "I mean, how much are you charging people for these games? Even if it was ten dollars a game, it isn't that much, is it? Don't answer that. It would take you a while to save up that kind of money. Why would you waste that time and money on a gun?"

"It was going to be three guns," said Bruce. He couldn't help himself.

"Okay, three guns," said Jeffrey.

"First of all, it was a good deal. I was working Gerry," said Bruce. His father gave him a blank look. "The kid I was buying the guns from? He wanted all my money for just one gun. I was going to convince him to give me all three for that price. I did my research. I shopped around in the catalogs and the magazines."

"You're the reason we keep getting those?" asked Esther.

"I knew what they were worth," said Bruce. "I wanted guns. You guys weren't going to take me to the store to buy them. Uncle Kenny isn't going to take me to a gun show at the

Gibraltar Trade Center."

"Is that what you brother does there every Sunday?" asked Jeffrey.

"No, he buys porn there," said Esther. She realized that wasn't a marked improvement.

"And, again, you wanted guns purely because you thought they were cool?" asked Jeffrey. "I mean, seriously, that's what you wanted to spend your money on? Of all the things in the world? Guns?"

"Why guns?" asked Esther.

"I don't know," said Bruce. He did know, but clearly his parents didn't really like the answer he had given. Now it was easier to plead stupid and hope the whole thing blew over.

"I can tell you what I do know," said Jeffrey. "You no longer have a bb-gun or a gun of any kind."

"We are also taking away your camouflage, your face paint, and all that garbage that puts these ideas in your head," said Esther.

"We will also be taking that money you earned and put it away for college for you. It can earn interest for you while you mature enough to be able to use it," Jeffrey said. "And, I'm guessing you're going to be suspended from school."

"Could he be expelled?" asked Esther.

"Maybe," said Jeffrey. "But, I don't think so. Technically, it was the high school kid that actually brought the guns to school. Bruce was just handling them."

Jeffrey was correct about Bruce not being expelled. The school did come down a little harder on Gerry, because he was older, but neither kid was expelled. Bruce received a three-day suspension, and Gerry received five days. Gerry did work his ass off around his house, doing chores and helping out wherever he could. An unintended consequence was his father and him actually grew closer because of the incident. They bonded over putting in a new half-bath in the basement, and Gerry earned a new appreciation for what it took to maintain a household. Bruce spent most of his three days writing letters to all of the catalogs he had requested, asking them to cease and desist. The modem and Bruce's bb-gun were destroyed by Jeffrey who found more satisfaction in smashing and destroying them than he could have imagined possible.

This also meant that Esther's crusade for gun control was over. Once the "attempted arms deal on school property" headline hit the news (as the *Opole Record* reported the story), Esther didn't have much credibility left on the matter. How could she justify regulating how others used guns if she couldn't control them in her own household? She continued to follow the story in Hungerford and England in general and watched as that country grew nearer and nearer to outlawing the weapons used in their mass shooting, but she was helpless to enact any change at home.

CHAPTER 10: APRIL FOOL'S

Regina was enjoying coffee with Vicky at the McKinney residence when Esther let herself into the house. If her recent setback with regard to gun control was bothering her, Esther didn't let it show; she seemed like the same old town gossip Regina and Vicky knew but did not necessarily love. It was always a little annoying when an uninvited party showed up. Esther always just let herself in and made herself at home, as if they were all the best of friends. Which they weren't. Neither Regina nor Vicky trusted Esther. Both women had used Esther's proclivity for spreading gossip to circulate stories they wanted shared, but they liked to be able to control the flow of information, and Esther was anything but controllable or predictable. She was great when, if for example, you forgot to send out invitations to a gathering and needed the information out there faster than the post office could deliver it. In that kind of situation, Esther was the best tool for the mission.

Vicky had just finished the sentence, "That one-handed pitcher at the U of M," when Esther burst in.

"What pitcher?" she asked, dragging a chair from the dining room to be next to the couch where Regina and Vicky sat.

"Abbott, I think his name is," said Regina.

"We were just talking about how handicapped people were

all in the news this week," said Vicky. She didn't feel like fighting Esther's intrusion, and figured it was easier to just get her up to speed.

"Oh, right," said Esther. "I did hear something about him, and then there's that deaf thing."

"You mean the first deaf college president?" asked Regina.

"Well, first deaf president of a deaf college," said Esther.

"I think he's the first deaf president of any college, deaf or otherwise," said Regina. Her sister had suffered hearing loss as a child, and so Regina was particularly tuned into the deaf community.

"Okay," said Esther. "Whatever. What about the pitcher? What were you saying about him?"

"He's amazing," said Vicky. "How he pitches and then puts his glove on like that."

"He was selected for the Summer Olympic team," added Regina.

"Really?" asked Esther. She didn't follow sports. It was definitely a gap in her arsenal of information.

The three women sat in silence as each considered what to say next. Regina waited for Esther say something; she was the intruder, she was the last to arrive to the conversation, it was her turn. Vicky wanted to talk about the Democratic caucus, but she was never quite sure where her friends stood on the political divide. Her interest in the selection of a Democratic Party candidate didn't necessarily indicate her party of choice because anyone vaguely interested in politics might be paying attention to such a thing, but she was afraid that if either of the other women were Republicans they might start an argument with her about her positions and she didn't feel like having to defend herself or her values. Esther had noticed a moving van on her rounds today, and she wanted to tell her friends the news, but she felt like she was always the one leading the conversation, and so she paused and waited for one of them to go first. Vicky broke before the other two did.

"Gephardt is out," Vicky said. "And Dukakis is taking the lead over Jesse Jackson." It really wasn't a conversation starter so much as an information dump. She immediately regretted the way it had come out.

"Did you like Gephardt?" asked Esther.

"Not really; he didn't seem like he'd be good for the Union," Vicky said. She meant the United Auto Workers union, which governed the Big Three automakers in Detroit, which nearly all of Vicky's family worked for.

"Huh," said Regina. She didn't follow politics very closely. She always voted, but her decisions about who to vote for in November were made in November shortly before arriving at the poll.

"What do you think about a black president?" asked Esther. Jackson had run before in 1984, and Esther vaguely remembered when Shirley Chisholm was a candidate in 1972. Her interest was not really in the answer the women gave to the question, but rather the opportunity to steer the conversation towards the new people she saw moving in. They were black.

"I don't care about his color," said Regina. "I don't know that I agree with all his policies."

Vicky wondered if that meant that Regina was a Republican, or if there was something specific she didn't like about Jackson. Instead of asking it outright, she coyly asked, "You like Dukakis better?"

Regina shrugged.

"Those eyebrows," Esther said and shivered. "Huge."

Unlike Vicky, Esther automatically assumed everyone shared the same values as she did, so it never crossed her mind that her friends might actually be Democrats. Esther thought Reagan was doing just fine, and Bush would continue that trend. Normally, Esther preferred more seamless transitions in conversation, but she couldn't see an easy way to redirect this one. "Speaking of black people," she said.

"What policies of his don't you like?" asked Vicky. She wasn't quite ready to give up on this conversation. She personally liked Jesse Jackson quite a bit. She liked that he was a reverend, that he wanted to invest in American infrastructure, change the direction of the War on Drugs, and truthfully, she also liked that he was black. He was different from the same old white guy, and Vicky thought something different would be good for the country.

"Oh, I don't know," said Regina. She didn't know. Regina had just meant her comment to be a polite indication that she was in fact paying attention and participating in the conversation when in fact, she hadn't been and wasn't. She vaguely remembered something Jim had said about Jackson's platform, but she couldn't quite put it together. Then, suddenly there it was, "That whole reparations thing really seems dangerous."

"Speaking of slaves," Esther tried to interject.

"Why?" asked Vicky. "We treated those people terribly; we need to do something for them, or we can never heal as a nation."

Hearing her friend put it that way, Regina had a hard time arguing with it. She remembered Jim had said something else about why it was a problem, but for the life of her she couldn't remember what it was. She really had no problem with black people, and she knew they had been treated terribly ever since they were brought to the United States. There was only one way out. "What were you saying, Esther?"

Esther jumped at the chance. "We have a new family moving in to the neighborhood!"

Regina and Vicky both knew the Dawson house had sold, but they hadn't noticed anyone moving in yet. Neither had been very close with the Dawsons, and their house was a little off the normal traffic pattern, so it wasn't like they walked or drove by the house regularly. Clearly, Esther had been expanding her route if she had noticed activity over on Maple Drive.

"Oh?" asked Regina.

"They're from Detroit," said Esther. Actually, she didn't know this for sure. The people she had seen were wearing Tigers hats, but those could have been movers for all she really knew. And, just because someone wore a Tigers' hat, didn't mean they were from the city. Hell, half the kids in Opole wore hats with the old English D on it, and they probably had never even been to the Motor City.

"Any kids?" asked Vicky. She really wanted to steer the conversation back to the election but was sincerely curious about the possibility of new neighbors.

"I'm not sure," said Esther. This was surprisingly honest of her. She could have assumed that the people moving in had children since the Dawson house had three bedrooms and a finished basement, but she had learned a thing or two from being burned when making assumptions about things, like say, whether or not a certain child had leukemia.

"What are they like?" asked Regina.

"They are black," said Esther. Again, this was based on an assumption. The African American men she saw unloading the moving truck could have been professional movers. In either case, it wasn't really what Regina was asking.

"But, I mean, did you stop and talk to them? Are they nice?" Regina asked.

"They were busy," said Esther. "I'll talk to them after we're done here."

Vicky thought, but didn't say, "That never stopped you before," and "You can go whenever you want." Instead, she actually said, "We should bring them cookies or casserole to welcome them to the neighborhood."

Decisions were made, and after several lulls in the conversation, Esther was bored and got up to leave. She walked slowly up and around the neighborhood. Her hope was that the moving van would be empty, and she would be able to meet the new family. As she approached the Dawson's old house, the moving van was nowhere to be seen. The screen door was propped open, as it had been to allow the movers to come and go with greater ease. Whoever was moving in had a stroke of luck with this March being much warmer than nearly any March before, which meant their front door could be left open without experiencing winter inside their new home. Esther walked right up to the open door, and poked her head inside.

"Hello?" she called.

"In back," hollered a voice.

Esther navigated the boxes on the floor and found her way to the back of the house. She had never been in the Dawson's house before, but the layout was nearly identical to all the houses in this neighborhood. Frequently the plan was flipped one way, or a room or two were swapped around to make each house slightly more unique, but for the most part, this was the same house that everyone else had. At the end of the hall, the bathroom was to the left, one bedroom was to the right, and two bedrooms were directly in front of her. From what she figured, the voice was coming from the room to the right of the bathroom where a bunkbed was being assembled. She stepped into the room.

"Hello, I'm Esther," she said. An African American man was holding part of the bedframe together, and a woman, probably his wife, was sitting on the floor. The woman got up.

"Oh," she said. "I thought maybe we had forgotten something in the moving van. I'm Rachele." She gestured to the man, "And this is my husband, Rodrick." Rodrick was wearing a Tigers' hat.

"Welcome to the neighborhood," said Esther. She smiled at them both. "So, you moved from Detroit?"

"Actually," Rodrick said, putting down the bedframe and coming to shake Esther's hand, "Bloomfield Hills."

"Oh?" Esther said.

"Rod's been working with the U of M for a while now," Rachele said, "and this was much closer." She smiled at Esther. "We don't have much to offer you at the moment, but I could get you a glass of water if you'd like. We've only unpacked a few things so far."

"That's fine. No need," said Esther. "I didn't mean to intrude." But, of course, that's precisely what she had done and what she had intended. "I'm guessing by the bunkbed, you have some children?"

"Three," said Rodrick. "Two boys and a girl."

"Chris is eleven, Brandon nine, and Hannah, our little girl, is just four. But growing quick," Rachele said.

"My husband and I just have the one, Bruce. He just turned eleven as well," Esther said. "And there are plenty of other kids in the neighborhood. I'm sure you'll meet them soon enough." Esther found herself staring at Rodrick and Rachele; their dark skin mesmerized her, and she had to remind herself that staring wasn't polite. She also wanted to make eye contact with them to show the couple that she was listening to them. She had seen black people before, but never up close like this. And she had never been in their houses. This house looked just like hers, and they were doing things just like she and Jeffrey did. Their furniture didn't look so different from the furniture in the Fuhrman house. Right now, the house was decorated with brown boxes, but she could imagine, when it was unpacked, it would look nearly indistinguishable from any other house in the neighborhood. They had kids, just like everyone else in the neighborhood, too.

"Where are the kids?" Esther asked looking around.

"Out on their bikes," Rachele laughed. "Those were practically the first thing off the truck."

"Even the little one?" asked Esther. She couldn't remember what they had said her name was.

"Oh yeah," said Rodrick. "Hannah has to keep up with her big brothers. She's burning rubber somewhere on that Big Wheel of hers." He picked up a socket wrench and began tightening a bolt. "Where do you live?" he asked.

"Up a block on Beechwood," Esther said. "It's the green house. Jeffrey was crazy about that color when we moved in. I've never been so sure. But, it definitely stands out."

"You're the first neighbor we've met," said Rachele. "Then again, we've only been here for two hours." She laughed again. Esther was struck by how beautiful her smile was.

"Well, on behalf of the Fuhrmans—that's Jeffrey, Bruce, and me—welcome to the neighborhood," she said.

"We're the Williams," said Rachele, flashing another smile.

"I'll let you get back to it," said Esther.

"It was nice to meet you," Rodrick said as Esther headed back down the hallway.

"Do you want this front door open or closed?" Esther asked when she reached the front door.

"It doesn't matter," said Rachele from down the hall. "It's nice enough; it feels good to have some fresh air in this stale house."

Esther walked through the open door and left it that way. She had to agree; the house did smell a little stale. How long had it been on the market? The Dawsons had moved out after Christmas, she remembered that, but she wasn't sure when the For Sale sign had actually gone up. Maybe a month or two before that? In either case, it probably remained unoccupied for a good three or four months. She was glad she stopped by and had a chance to meet the Williams. They seemed nice. She imagined they were about the same age as she was, based on the ages of their children, but realized Rachele and Rodrick seemed oddly ageless in appearance. Their hair was dark, no signs of gray; she didn't see wrinkles or crow's feet, or anything like that. She knew it was probably a silly thought, but she found herself wondering if blacks didn't maybe age differently than whites. If Rachele had told her that she was twenty-five, Esther wouldn't have had any reason to doubt it. And her husband, his skin was tight, and he had a good head of hair. They could be twenty, or thirty, or older, and Esther would be none the wiser.

Esther was lost in thought and not paying attention to what was in front of her when Hannah Williams nearly ran her over with her Big Wheel. The two locked eyes and froze momentarily. The Big Wheel's momentum kept it going forward as Hannah's feet hovered in the air above the pedals. Esther tried to decide which direction to jump, and at the same time, tried to read the mind of the little girl barreling toward her; would she turn to avoid the collision, and if so, which direction would she choose? Fortunately, Hannah did veer slightly to the left, and Esther leapt to her left. Disaster avoided. Hannah continued on, and Esther paused for a moment to let her heart stop racing. Two black boys zoomed by in the street on their BMX bicycles, and she realized she had now "met" the whole Williams family.

Like Christopher and Brandon Williams, Bruce Fuhrman was also on his bike. He had in fact already crossed paths with the two boys. They nodded as if they had known each other their whole lives, and then Bruce continued on to "the woods." This was the favorite destination of "the boys" for just about every endeavor. They went there to shoot their bb-guns, play war, discuss school, talk about girls, and make plans. Today they were discussing their second favorite day of the year: April Fool's day. Their favorite day, of course, was Devil's Night, but April Fool's day was a close second. While some kids would be satisfied with jokes like, "Look up (pause), a dead bird!" the last couple years, David, Barry, and Bruce had elevated their game to pranks. This year, they were kicking it up a notch further. Instead of Vaseline on doorknobs or plastic wrap covering the toilet bowl (but not the seat) or mustard squeezed into toothpaste tubes (which was difficult to accomplish, but had a satisfyingly hilarious effect), they were going to superglue the cabinets and drawers shut in the McKinney kitchen.

The McKinney house was selected because Jim and Regina were the youngest parents (well, unless you counted Suzy Townsend, which the boys didn't because she didn't have any children their age), and they also were the most forgiving. Even though Jim and Regina had been upset by the pornography being stored in their garage, David had barely been punished for the ordeal. Barry hadn't been punished at all, but that was only because his parents never found out about the porn ring. Had they known, he would have (the boys assumed) been in deep shit, because Barry's parents were strict. They were consistent in their strictness, which meant that Barry always knew what to expect. When something like the idea of supergluing cabinets came up, he was quick to say, "We can't do it at my house." Which is something that his parents, had they known that their son had spoken up for them, would have appreciated. They could have chosen the Fuhrman house, but

Bruce was quick to point out he'd been in enough shit lately. So, the McKinney house it was.

The school board anchored the Opole school Spring Break to Easter. Technically, the school wasn't taking off a religious holiday; they were only celebrating the end of a session and taking a spring break. Because the date of Easter was still calculated using the Julian Calendar method, the dates for the Opole Spring Break could vary greatly. Generally, it was the end of March or beginning of April, but the date for Easter, technically, could be any time between March 22 and April 25. This meant that usually, the kids were able to celebrate April Fool's day while they were on a break from school. This year, April 1 was also Good Friday, and they were on break until Monday. Had their spring break come later in the year, or earlier, they might not have been able to figure out a way to sneak into the McKinney house to glue the kitchen drawers and cabinets shut on a school night. To do so, they would have had to either sneak into the house early in the morning, or in late at night. Both would have presented problems.

This year's prank should have been easy, because they had the time off and could spend the night at the McKinney's house. They would have easy access to the kitchen whenever they wanted it. But that wasn't the way they operated. They liked a challenge. And, even though David was okay with the prank being played on his family, he wanted plausible deniability in his involvement. If he was sleeping in the house when the prank occurred, it became much more difficult to plead ignorance. As the boys hung out at the "woods," they discussed various possibilities. The McKinney house was the best mark for many reasons, but it did have some drawbacks, and those were often connected to the very reasons it was the best mark. For example, Jim and Regina were cool and easy going, but they stayed up late.

While David's parents liked to think of themselves as being young and hip, at thirty-three and thirty-four, their age was beginning to catch up on them. They no longer were the twenty-something version of themselves that pulled all-nighters and partied until the wee hours. They might not "go to bed" until three o'clock in the morning, but they often fell asleep on the couch well before then. David had, on occasion, woken up in the middle of the night to find his parents asleep on the couch. Maybe he was headed to the bathroom, or maybe he had a bad dream, but he was always surprised to see the television light pouring down the hallway. Sometimes the television had become off-air static, and other times David saw old Westerns or kung-fu shows on the screen. He would walk down the hall to get a closer look, and then find his parents slumped on the couch; sometimes they were on opposite ends of the couch, but most often they were cuddled against one another.

The first time he found them like that, he quietly said, "Mom?"

And then his father was wide awake, "What are you doing up this late?"

Before David could explain, his father said, "We weren't sleeping." He readjusted on the couch and looked at his wife, "Well, she is," he said. Then, before David could say much more, his father would be snoring against Regina once more.

"The TV can be our cover," said Bruce.

"Right, they'll never hear us come and go," said David.

"Are you sure you want to do this?" asked Barry. Even though it wasn't his ass on the line here, he was pretty sure his friend was going to get in deep shit for this one.

"Yeah, it will be fine," said David. "They'll think it's hilarious."

"I'm thinking maybe just one or two of us should go in the house," said Bruce.

"Why?" asked Barry.

"Too much noise," said Bruce. "Actually, how about this. Two for the kitchen, one to open things and the other to do the gluing, and the third can stand watch by the couch. If David's parents wake up, then the third person can say we just stopped by the house to get something."

As the boys worked out their plan over the next couple

days, the rest of the neighborhood descended on the Williams' household to make them feel welcome. Esther brought them scalloped potatoes and ham. Regina brought chocolate chip cookies. Vicky brought her Opole-famous brownies. The three mothers hung around chatting with Rodrick and Rachele for a while, but only Vicky really stayed long enough to get to know them better. Esther made the excuse of having to make dinner for her own family, and Regina bowed out at almost the same time with a similar explanation. They met the children on their way, said hello, and went their separate ways.

"Well, I'm sure you'll meet the rest soon enough," said Vicky.

"There are more?" asked Rachele. "I don't know where I'll put any more food," she laughed gently.

"I think you'll find the people of Opole are very inviting," said Vicky. "Just make sure you all come to the Wianki this summer, and prepare yourself to eat way too many paczkis." She paused. "Do you know what those are?"

"Bloomfield Hills is only thirty minutes or so from Hamtramck," said Rodrick. "We've had our share of paczkis. Can't wait to see what the ones in Opole taste like."

"Are you from Bloomfield Hills?" asked Vicky.

"No, he's actually from Benton Harbor," said Rachele. "I'm a Chicago-girl."

"Chicago, pssh," said Rodrick. "She's from Calumet City. Trust me. I've been there before. It's no Chicago."

"It's Cook County," said Rachele. She glared good-naturedly at her husband.

"Please," Rodrick laughed and swatted at his wife's shoulder. "It's practically Indiana."

"Don't say that!" said Rachele. She was laughing now, too.

"Wait, is something wrong with Indiana?" asked Vicky. She'd driven through Indiana, usually on the way to or from Chicago, but had never spent much time there.

"It's basically the South," said Rodrick. "No idea why people living in that state have a thicker accent than my grandma from Georgia."

"Enough of that," said Rachele. Vicky seemed nice enough, but Rachele really didn't want the discussion to go down the road of accents and racism.

"Where did you guys meet?" asked Vicky.

"We met in the art museum in Chicago while looking dreamily at that goofy painting *American Gothic.*"

Vicky's expression didn't change.

"You know," said Rachele, she scooted behind Rodrick and he mimed holding a pitchfork. "That one?" "Rachele finished.

Vicky laughed. "Something tells me, you've done that a time or two before."

"Only every time she tells the story," said Rodrick. He rolled his eyes, but it was clear he loved it nearly as much as his wife did. "You know, something she doesn't often share, is that *American Gothic* originally sold for $300. Any idea how much that's worth now?"

"A lot more than $300?" asked Vicky.

"Right," said Rodrick. He nodded.

"Anyway," said Rachele. "That was some high school field trip of his. I just happened to be there for the day because I love art. We both got into Wayne State in '64, and four years later we were moving into a place together."

"I might as well say it before she does, but," Rodrick leaned closer to Vicky and whispered, "she's real smart. she skipped a grade."

Rachele shook her heard. "I don't make a point of saying that," she said. Then grinned widely. "But it is true."

"How cute, you two," said Vicky. "What do you do, Rodrick?"

"I do finance," said Rodrick. "And, Mrs. Williams is a lawyer." He was proud of his wife's accomplishments.

"Oh?" asked Vicky. This was a total surprise to her. "I didn't realize, you work, too?"

"I do," said Rachele. "I took time off when each of the kids were born, and I'm just working on getting back into the swing of things now that Hannah is getting older, but I love the law."

"So, are you an actual attorney?" Vicky asked.

"Yep. I do family law," said Rachele.

"Lots of divorces to handle out there in Bloomfield Hills," Rodrick laughed. "We both graduated with our undergrads in '68, which meant there almost wasn't a school to graduate from." Rodrick shook his head. "The riots were nuts."

"But, that was my inspiration to do law," said Rachele.

"Right," said Rodrick. "Which meant she disappeared into that school again for another five years before she came out the other side. I barely saw her during those years. Then again, I was busting my ass to pay rent."

"I think we turned out alright," said Rachele. She winked at her husband. "Everything happens for a reason."

"It sure does," said Vicky. "So, why Opole? Of all the neighborhoods you could have chosen?"

"It's cute," said Rachele. "Rod's been working at the U since '77, and I found a firm that I can work with in Ann Arbor, so why not? A shorter commute would be nice."

"Good schools, nice neighborhood," said Rodrick. "And great neighbors."

"So far," said Vicky. She laughed to try to cover up the truth of her statement. "You haven't met us all, yet." Though, she was thinking, if they've met Esther they have a good sense of the worst of them.

Vicky headed back home. She liked this couple. They would fit right in. Though she wouldn't ever outwardly express this idea, she was excited by the idea of having black friends. As a lifelong Democrat, and one supporting Jesse Jackson, she felt a bit like a poseur never having personally known anyone black, or brown for that matter. Now she could speak from experience. She could use her connection to the Williamses to extrapolate the experiences of other black Americans. She was sure that Rodrick and Rachele were Democrats, how could they be anything else, and so they at least had that in common. There was also the fact that both were college educated. Vicky didn't have a college education herself, but she read a lot and lived on a college campus while Jim was finishing school. What Vicky didn't know was that both the Williamses had voted for

Reagan in 1980, and they were undecided going into the 1988 election cycle.

None of the families had any plans for Spring Break this year. Most didn't have the extra money to indulge, and so everyone was home. The boys floated from one house to another, and each set of parents took their turn feeding and housing them. Barry offered to host the first night so they could watch the movie *The Princess Bride*. He had saved his money and bought the VHS the day before when it was first released and wanted to share the movie with his friends.

The Webster's downstairs was the coolest place to be because Dean had finished it himself and created a large entertainment room. There was a wet bar, comfortable sectional seating, and the centerpiece of the room—a 37-inch television. The TV was huge. Dean and Vicky brought the kids popcorn, made sure everyone had sleeping bags, said goodnight, and then left them to their show. Dean and Vicky would have been hard-pressed to even estimate how many times the boys had slept over here, or at the Fuhrman's or McKinney's. The first sleepovers had been awkward affairs with a steep learning curve for all involved. The host-parents who thought they knew the others parents well enough, were often surprised by the things the visiting children claimed to get away with.

"Oh, we always have a snack right before bed," one child would say.

Another might complain that he always had a light on at night, "Don't worry; I fall asleep with it on."

And, of course, someone would claim his bedtime was much later than it really was. Eventually the parents learned to call bullshit rather than checking in with one another, or to simply enforce "house rules" and be done with the conversation. The kids also had an adjustment period where they learned that not every house had Apple Jacks as a breakfast option or allowed toys to be left out or didn't like kids to stand on couches or beds. Bruce was delighted to find extra freedom at his friends' houses and a little embarrassed by the rigid rules that were enforced at his own. After years of practice, the sleepover was a well-oiled machine. Everyone knew what to expect, and as a result, supervision was greatly reduced.

Though Dean and Vicky were saying "goodnight" to the boys at 9PM, they would stay up another hour or so before actually turning in. The boys all knew this, so when *The Princess Bride* ended, Barry rewound the tape and started it again, even though they had no intention of watching it. They huddled up went over their plan once more. When the tape ended for the second time, Barry was sure his parents were asleep, but David wasn't sure his were. They waited another hour, and then another, until it was finally one o'clock. Then they set out. They were careful to be quiet, and Barry made sure to leave the exterior door to the house ajar so they wouldn't get locked out or make extra noise. He did this often. Initially, David had suggested they wear their ninja costumes, if they still fit, but Bruce was quick to point out that they didn't want to raise suspicions. If David's parents woke up and found them in their house dressed in black, they'd know something was going on. If they were dressed regularly, Jim and Regina might buy the story that they just happened over in the middle of the night to get something that David had forgotten from his room.

They crept across the street and down to the McKinney house. The side door was unlocked because time had passed since Esther's crusade against crime and it no longer felt necessary. David crept into his own house, checked to verify his parents were asleep, and then signaled for Bruce and Barry to join him. Barry was going to stand by the couch and watch the sleeping parents, David was going to open the cabinets and drawers, and Bruce was going to do the actual gluing. This meant that David could, in all sincerity, state that he did not glue the kitchen cabinets and drawers shut, because he actually and truthfully didn't. Bruce did. The plan went off without a hitch. David led the way out of the house, Bruce followed, and Barry brought up the rear, leaving the house just as he would have left his own. Back at the Webster house, the boys collapsed into their sleeping bags. The thrill of the prank was over, and the adrenaline was wearing off; they quickly fell asleep.

The closest the Websters came to sugared cereal was Honey-Nut Cheerio's, but the boys ate it without complaint. They told a few silly April Fool's jokes, so as not to arouse suspicions and because they actually enjoyed silly jokes. When David went to go home, he found that Dean had tied his shoelaces together. David looked over his shoulder and found Dean looking at him and the two started laughing.

"April Fools!" Dean said.

David untied his shoes from one another, and then headed out the door. "Thanks for having me over," he said, as he left.

"You're welcome. Say hi to your mother," Regina said. Regina was cleaning up the kitchen after breakfast.

David didn't feel any sense of dread about returning to his house, but now that he was getting closer and closer to his front door, he began to regret what he had participated in last night. What if his parents didn't think it was funny? He was pretty sure they'd think it was, but what if they didn't? He could imagine their faces as they tried to open one of the cabinets, or pull on a drawer and it didn't budge. He wished he had been there to see it when it first happened. That would have been so funny, but then he would have had to control himself so they didn't know he was involved. It would have been hard to do. David laughed easily, and wasn't great at keeping secrets. He reached the front step, opened the door, and found both parents sitting at the dining room table. They were both holding their heads and looked frustrated. Maybe they were having an argument. He'd have to navigate this carefully.

"Hey mom. Hey dad," he said.

"You don't know anything about this?" his father asked. "Do you?"

"About what?" David asked.

"Our kitchen!" his mother burst out. There were literal

tears running down her face. This was not a reaction that David had predicted.

His father was not crying. His voice was even-tempered. He was not yelling. He seemed defeated. "I didn't think so," he said.

"What happened?" asked David.

"Someone," his father said, "broke into our house last night and glued all our cabinets and drawers shut."

"What?" asked David.

"It appears so," said Jim.

"They broke in?" asked David. "How do you know they broke in? Did they take something?"

"The door was left open," said Regina. "We always close that door at night." She paused and looked at David. "You didn't," she said, "come over last night, did you? Maybe you left the door open?"

"No Mom," said David. "I was at Barry's all night. We watched *The Princess Bride* two or three times." Had he hesitated in his delivery at all, it might have changed the way things went down, but he didn't hesitate. He and his friends had practiced this and rehearsed what he would say. Bruce roleplayed as David's father and Barry roleplayed as David's mother. When the question came from his actual mother, David delivered the line they had settled on. And then he waited. The boys hadn't been able to anticipate David's parent's reaction from that point forward. If they didn't believe him, then David was to directly repeat what he had said with greater sincerity in his voice. Of the group, David and Bruce were the best liars. Barry wasn't very good at lying because he didn't practice it. He didn't lie on a regular basis. His two friends lied regularly about anything and everything. Bruce was probably the better liar because he had learned to base his lies on reality and only to diverge slightly. David was well-practiced as well, but sometimes he lied when a lie wasn't necessary. At times his parents caught him in a lie and asked him, "Why did you lie about making your bed?" (for example). He would, quite honestly, not have a good reason. He knew his parents would find out that his bed was not in fact made, and yet he couldn't seem to help the lie sneaking off his tongue.

In this moment though, his parents didn't badger David at all. They were too upset about the damage done to their kitchen and the money it was going to cost them to repair it. David had expected more of a drawn-out discussion with his parents, but as soon as he answered their question, they moved on with their own discussion and forgot about him.

"Should we report it to the police?" asked Regina.

"I don't know," said Jim. "Let's ask around and see if anyone else had anything happen like this."

They did ask around, and found that no one else had any damage done to their property. Dean McKinney immediately asked, "Do you think it's an April Fool's joke?" But the idea was quickly dispelled because nothing similar had happened in Opole before. The kids might play goofy pranks, like most of the adults had when they were kids, but nothing destructive like this. There was also the matter of the open door. While people might not always lock their doors, they always made sure to close the doors. At least it gave the illusion of being secured.

By the time Regina and Jim arrived at the Fuhrman house, they were feeling pretty low. Jim told Esther and Jeffrey about what had happened, and Jeffrey repeated Dean's idea that maybe it was an April Fool's prank.

"No, I don't think anyone here would do something like this," said Regina.

"No one you know," said Esther. "But what about someone who just moved in?"

And then all four adult minds raced in the same direction towards the Williams.

"You don't think," started Regina, but didn't finish.

"How would they know the doors would be open?" asked Jim.

"They come from Detroit," said Esther. She shrugged. "They sure know how to do Devil's Night there; maybe this is how they do April Fool's Day there, too."

While his parents were checking in with other families, David met up with his friends at the woods. He gave them the rundown of what had happened this morning.

"Huh," said Bruce. "I didn't see that coming."

"Me neither," said Barry.

"We need to make sure it never comes back to us," said David.

"I have an idea," said Bruce.

"What's your idea?" said David.

"What if we blame some other kids?" asked Bruce. "Like, Mark, or Jason? Or the girls?"

"My brother isn't taking the heat for this," said Barry.

"It seems shitty to let Jason take the blame," said David. "He's always been nice enough. I'm not sure girls do things like this. Do they?"

"Well, then there's only one other thing we can do," said Bruce.

"Come clean?" asked Barry. He really wasn't comfortable with the dishonesty.

David shrugged, like maybe that was a good idea. Bruce frowned and said, "No, we break into some of the other houses."

"Jesus, that's a terrible idea!" said Barry. "We'll get in even more trouble!"

"No, we'll be careful," said Bruce. "No one stays up as late as the McKinneys anyway, so we've already done the most difficult house."

"I don't know," said David. "If we just left their doors open like someone," he glared at Barry, "did at my house, then maybe that's a good idea."

"Do you think people would notice their doors were open?" asked Barry. He wasn't trying to be difficult, and he certainly didn't want to get in more trouble, but he really wasn't sure if it was going to be worth the effort to go around at night pushing doors open if no one noticed.

"Good point," said Bruce. "My mom would just assume my dad forgot to close it or went out to get his paper in the morning. With families that have more kids and people coming and going, it will be harder for them to know that the door was left open after a break in."

The boys sat quietly and thought.

"We'll take something small, but noticeable," said Bruce.

"Now we're going to steal," said Barry, "from our own parents?" He shook his head. "No, I'm out."

"Come on, Barry. Don't be such a wuss," said Bruce. "We'll give it back. We just need to take the heat off of us for a bit. It will go like this. We pick a house each night for a couple days and break in. Take something small but something that will be noticed and leave the door open. We'll keep the stuff for a while in a safe place. I don't know we'll come up with some place, and then a week or two later we'll put the stuff in a weird place. Someone will find it and think, oops, I guess that's where we put that. No big deal."

So, that's what they did. The neighborhood was hyperaware of the possibility of a break-in and took the precaution of trying to remember to lock their doors at night. But, this was an inside job, which meant the kids could come and go as they wanted. Once they had taken things from the Fuhrmans and McKinneys and Websters, they called an end to their crime spree and waited. The parents should have realized that theirs were the only houses that had been targeted, but somehow the invasiveness of the break-ins distracted them from the obvious. Eventually, they reported the break-ins to the police. Proper reports were filed, and the police increased their presence on the streets of Opole at night. Esther's claim that the break-ins, thefts, and vandalism were a result of the new neighbors gained traction. These kinds of things never happened before there were "those kinds of people" living here, became a frequent refrain. The people she spoke with agreed that they didn't quite feel as safe as they once did. The increased police presence should have made them feel safer, but instead it did the opposite.

Esther was quick to point out that it was just last year, with the arrest of Bill Daniels, that she had personally taken decreasing crime in Opole on as a pet project. She had encouraged people to lock their doors to keep themselves safe from predators. "But," she shook her head when she said this, "just look how easily we fall back into old habits."

The Opole Police were puzzled as to how people were able to "break-in" to the houses without damaging the doors until they investigated the locks that were standard on most of the houses. Tom, the locksmith, suddenly made a quick fortune installing deadbolts and updating locks. The first month after the break-ins, Esther noticed that most of the doors of Opole were locked to her when she was on her rounds. As before, she was both relieved and annoyed by this. She had to go back to knocking and ringing doorbells, and sometimes she saw people were in fact home even though they didn't answer their doors. Rather than assume it had something to do with her, she chalked it up to people not feeling safe in the neighborhood anymore. Who knows who might be knocking on a door and what might happen if you answered it?

When she was allowed in, she found that several Opole residents had purchased firearms. At first, she was shocked and disgusted. Who needed guns in their home? In her investigation after the Hungerford shootings, and the various mass shootings in her own country, she remembered reading that a gun owner was more likely to be killed by his or her own gun than to actually kill a criminal with it. She was quick to share this tidbit of knowledge—even though she couldn't remember where she had read it, or who had said it, or if there was any statistical information to back it up. It sounded good to her, she didn't like guns, thus it must be true. Plus, because of her son's fixation on weapons and his suspension from school as a result of it, she was more than a little sensitive to the idea of owning a firearm. As she visited people's homes, she found that more and more families were choosing to buy a pistol, or two. Just. In. Case. That's what they all said. Maybe it was time for Jeffrey and her to rethink their position on guns. Esther worried about sending a confusing message to Bruce because she had so adamantly shot down his desire to own a gun. His position of "guns are cool" was indefensible, and Esther still didn't agree with the position, but she was beginning to consider the wisdom of guns for protection.

Unlike the last time the town went through their "lock the doors" phase, this time it stuck. Esther kept trying the doors and kept finding them locked. As with before, she was both glad about this and frustrated. It meant that she no longer had the easy access to her readership or her sources of information, but it also meant the town was safer. The only house that remained open to her, and seemingly oblivious to the whole ordeal, was the Williams' house. In her mind, Esther thought it was because they were from Detroit, but the reality was they hadn't been included in the loop of information distribution about the break-ins. It was one thing to consider them the source of the vandalism and break-ins, and it was quite another to do say something to their faces.

While the neighborhood made a good showing when Rodrick, Rachele, and the kids first arrived, the rumors about their possible involvement with the break-ins halted further efforts at friendship. Rodrick and Rachele had moved a couple of times, and weren't too surprised that people were uninterested in getting to know them better. People meant well, they said the polite niceties, but in the end, most were too self-absorbed to include a new family in their social circle. The Williams had hoped it would be different in Opole, but odds were only a fraction of the people they met would become "friends" anyway. Vicky seemed committed to their friendship and visited often, Esther stopped by occasionally, and there were always work-friends. The kids kept Rodrick and Rachele busy, too, so they didn't fully appreciate the cold shoulder they were receiving.

If Vicky had a question she needed an answer to, she came right out and asked the question. Esther preferred to nose out the truth. Rather than asking how they met, Esther noticed a wedding photo of Rodrick and Rachele and asked, "Oh, when was this taken?" and "Where was the wedding?" and "How long were you engaged?" Similarly, she picked Rodrick's baseball cap up off the table and asked, "How long did you live in Detroit?" instead of asking, "Where are you originally from?"

The questions irritated Rodrick who saw through Esther to her preconceived notions about the family, but he answered them and used his answers as a way of upending Esther's engrained racism. Each new layer about the Williams family surprised Esther. They had never lived in Detroit. They both had college degrees and advanced degrees. They clearly could afford a bigger home in a bigger city, but chose to come to Opole. Rodrick liked baseball, but his favorite sport was actually tennis.

"Tennis?!" Esther had blurted in surprise. She wasn't aware of anyone who liked to watch tennis; play it, sure, but watch it? Rodrick was a huge fan of Jimmy Connors. He didn't really care for Agassi or Pete Sampras, and he thought the violent displays by McEnroe had no place in the game.

Rachele was full of surprises, too. For one, she worked. For two, she was a lawyer. For three, she primarily handled divorces. For four, Rachele did not watch any soaps. None of the other ladies of Opole, that Esther knew of, worked, let alone held a higher degree, and only Brenda Walker was divorced. There were only so many surprises Esther could take in a day, so Esther didn't stay as long as she might have at Vicky's or Regina's.

Because no additional crimes had occurred since they'd started locking doors and increased patrols, everyone assumed what they were doing was working. As promised, the boys did return the stolen items to the houses and left them in obscure places. Finding them took a while. When one of those items was found, not a single one of the parents thought, "Huh, so it was here the whole time" or "Boy, we really jumped to conclusions we shouldn't have" or anything similar. Instead, they kept locking their doors and kept assuming the worst of their new neighbors. Eventually, their behavior became the norm, and they stopped thinking about why they were doing what they were doing, and just did it.

The whole year of 1988 passed by with the homes' doors remaining locked. It was the same in 1989. And in 1990. And pretty soon the practice of locking doors was firmly entrenched. Children were scolded, "You didn't lock the door when you came inside" and "You want someone to take all your toys?" and "There are criminals out there; it isn't like the old days." Esther still made her rounds, but neighbor avoidance became the norm. Opole still held its annual Wianki, and the townsfolk gathered and mingled. Attendance to that event increased as the population of Opole grew, but the people who did gather only mingled in small groups and rarely cross-mingled.

The Williams family never quite shook the rumors of being the source of the April Fool's hijinks, and Carol never overcame her status of being the wife of a pedophile. The Williams were new to the neighborhood, so they didn't notice a shift in public opinion toward them. As far as they were concerned, the neighbors were polite but kept to themselves. Carol, however, had lived in Opole for most of her life. She had known the highs of being accepted, and certainly experienced the lows of not being accepted. She divorced her husband, sold her Opole home, and moved out of the state for a fresh start. When Bill was released from prison ten years later, he had no reason to return to Opole. His mother died while he was inside, and his wife left him and the state behind. He was required to register on the relatively new Sex Offender Registry, which meant he was never truly invisible to those that wanted to find him regardless of where he chose to relocate to.

In the hey-day of Esther's rounds, the neighbors were quick to complain about Esther and her gossip, but they sort of missed it when it was gone. They still got together occasionally. The women attempted to form book clubs, but none lasted very long. The McKinneys and Websters remained close friends, but gone were the neighborhood cookouts, the block parties, the random coffee get togethers. Graduation parties now served as de facto neighborhood reunions. The oldest children, Betsy Walker and Douglas Piekarski, graduated in

1991. Bruce, Jason, David, Barry, and Christopher Williams all graduated in 1994. Esther and Jeffrey found themselves with an empty nest after Bruce left for college with nothing to fill it. With the community scattering and doors closing on the houses of the families that remained, Esther and Jeffrey spent more time apart in their own home. Jeffrey worked in the basement, or the garage, where he had projects and things that he never talked about. Esther found things to keep her busy in the rest of the house, still went on her walks, and messed around in the garden. They were still invited to the occasional social outing, but Jeffrey and Esther found they had less and less in common with their old friends.

It's unlikely that if anyone had actually been pressed to admit it, that they would have cared to admit that it was Esther who had kept everyone together. In her own weird way, by invading their space and spreading their stories, Esther was a sort of neighborhood glue. And though few would readily admit it, they all enjoyed her gossip to some degree.

PART II: 2015-2016

CHAPTER 11: GETTING CAUGHT UP

Esther began her climb to 5,000 friends in earnest in 2015. She joined Facebook in 2010 because she wanted to be able to see the pictures that her son posted, particularly after the birth of her first grandchild. Before long she was reconnecting with old friends, classmates, and neighbors. Some of the neighbors had moved out of the neighborhood and referred to it as the "old" neighborhood. This rubbed Esther the wrong way. She still lived there, and so did plenty of other families. Dubbing it the "old" neighborhood seemed to suggest that it had fallen into disrepair or that it was somehow undesirable. Esther also connected with people who currently lived in the neighborhood, and so she could literally see into their world without ever having to visit their houses.

In the early days of her social media presence, Esther accepted friend requests that were sent to her, but rarely instigated connections of her own. The technology overwhelmed her at times. It felt like, just when she had mastered some part of the webpage, it moved. Or they changed the icon, or suddenly there was an icon where text had been. So, it was easier to be a passive recipient of others reaching out, than to do the reaching herself. And who didn't want to be friends with Esther Fuhrman? She had enough friend requests to keep her busy, and at times she was exhausted by the end of the day with all the information she had consumed. Brenda Walker had moved, which Esther knew because she remembered the sad day when her friend packed up and relocated, but now Esther had a virtual window into Brenda's world in a way she never had before. Brenda had fully embraced the technology. She "checked in" to various places, loved taking photographs of the meals she was about to consume, and posted regularly about what she was doing and where she was going. Brenda might post twenty to thirty times in a day, and Esther consumed everything her friend shared. Not all her friends were as prolific on social media as Brenda was, but by the end of any given day, Esther had encountered hundreds of photographs, status updates, and articles that friends recommended reading.

Esther's understanding of social media was that she had to engage with all of this information in order to be a good friend. Why would they share it if they didn't want her to read it? Despite that, Esther rarely shared anything of her own. How could she; she was too busy reading what others provided? Even in the old days of powerwalking the neighborhood, she had been a consumer of other people's information rather than a sharer of her own.

At some point, the friend requests slowed, and Esther came to a digital crossroad. She could either: 1. Sustain her current digital presence, or 2. She could learn to master the technology. By now she was less intimidated by the technology and had found a pattern and routine to her current friends' posts and photographs. Brenda rotated through the same coffee shops and restaurants and posted the same type of photograph. "Fun with the grandkids!" popped up every morning, around ten. Then, it was off to the Ann Arbor Beanery for a "delicious drink!" Then it was "lunch with the hubby!" And so on. Esther could scan the images and messages quickly to detect differences and move on. Often, she didn't even have to click "read more" to get the gist of what Brenda had to say or click on an image to enlarge it. Esther decided she needed more friends. For the first time in a long time, she thought back to her brief experience with bulletin boards in 1987. She had figured out that; how hard could this be?

As it turned out, not very. Beyond the initial motivation of wanting to fill her day with some purpose, she also found a target to focus on—her ex-boyfriend Daniel, the one who had slept with her old friend Brenda. It had been years and years since he mattered to Esther, but now she wanted to know what had happened to him. He hadn't married Brenda, but Esther realized she had no idea what had happened to him. She typed his name into the search window: Daniel Byrd. Unfortunately, it wasn't the most original name, and Facebook returned many possibilities. Some with "Daniel," others as "Dan," a couple with "Danny," and even a "Danielle" or two. But, despite the years that had passed, Esther recognized him immediately in the little image Facebook provided. He was the fifth on the list, and she clicked on him. She scrolled through every photo and post he had ever made. She went back and back and back and back. There was Daniel's first marriage, divorce, birth of his first child, second marriage, and, finally, the death of his second wife. He was single.

With her own husband dead in 2006, almost six years now, Esther had all the time in the world. When she wasn't visiting Bruce, she happily lived in this virtual world she had constructed for herself. She couldn't make the rounds of the neighborhood anymore, not physically, but online she could cover far more ground than ever before. When Jeffrey died, she had debated selling the house and moving in with Bruce. She had even started purging and cleaning out the house, and that's when she found the various stashes of bottles that Jeffrey kept hidden around the house. It shocked her and frankly, it appalled her that she knew so little about what was going on in her own house. The more she found, the less she wanted to live in Opole, so finally she brought up the idea with Bruce of her moving to Eden Prairie.

"That would be great, mom, but we need our space," Bruce stammered awkwardly.

Initially that stung, but Esther convinced herself that she liked where she lived, and her house was paid off, so why sell, why move? If Bruce had said, "Sure, mom! Melinda and the kids and I would love to have you," then she would have abandoned most of her possessions, quickly sold the house, and zipped out to Eden Prairie, Minnesota without another thought. But Bruce hadn't said that, so she stayed in Opole. Had she moved, she would have found most of the items in the house were insignificant and would have donated or outright disposed of the majority of her possessions.

Since she didn't move and was surrounded by these items all day, every day, they took on a nostalgic value that she wallowed in. For instance, her laptop was surrounded by tokens from Bruce's childhood. There was the broken ceramic thing that he made in eighth grade, which she glued together multiple times. It was tall and prone to catching on a sweater or being knocked off a shelf by an errant toy being thrown inside the house. It was fragmented and had been stitched back together with glue-lines. Honestly, she isn't sure what the "thing" was supposed to be (a blobby tree? Maybe a chunky person? Or just an abstract obelisk?), but it moved her to tears when her son gave it to her for Christmas, and now it took her right back to that moment. Beyond simple nostalgia and memory, the object also connected her current loneliness—though she'd never admit to being lonely—to that tearful happiness she felt when she was surrounded by her family and was gifted something that her son created with his own two hands. The happy tears of 1990 had somehow turned to sorrow in the present. This house was now empty of people, but full of things and memories connected to those things.

Esther's first grandchild was born in 2010, which incidentally was the year Eden Prairie was ranked to be the "best place to live," in the United States by *Money Magazine*. Her son, always a forward thinker and ahead of the curve, had arrived two years previous to this illustrious designation. Because Bruce was ahead of the trend, he was able to afford a much bigger house than anyone moving there after 2010 would be able to. Beyond the guest room, which was always open to his mother, there was even an extra kitchen downstairs. In short, there was room in the son's home for Esther, if he had wanted her to be there. Unfortunately for Esther, Bruce and Melinda believed that even if there was physical space for another person in the house, there wasn't really ever going to be enough room to contain Esther Fuhrman. Somehow, when she visited, she had the ability to fill all three thousand, eight hundred, sixty-two square feet of the Eden Prairie residence. Bruce was happy to have her visit but couldn't entertain the thought of her living with them.

Instead, Esther contented herself with two or three visits a year, no longer than three weeks in duration, with the occasional return visit of her son's family to Opole. She followed the digital images of her grandchildren (there were three by 2015), whenever Bruce or Melinda remembered to include her with updates. Kendra was the oldest, then Albert, and most recently, Opal. It rubbed Esther the wrong way that Albert was named after Melinda's father and not Bruce's. Because she was who she was, she wasn't able to contain herself. One night over dinner while visiting them in Minnesota, she couldn't stop herself.

"I'm sorry, I know it's not my place, but why not Jeffrey?"

Melinda stopped chewing the bite she was working on, glanced at Bruce, and then resumed chewing.

"Mom," said Bruce. "It's just that, well, you know, how Dad died . . . it isn't exactly the legacy we want for our son."

Silence. Esther wasn't sure what that meant. Lots of people died in drunk driving accidents. She pursed her lips and moved on to complimenting the eggplant parmesan that Melinda had made.

It seemed like Melinda was always trying to outdo herself in the kitchen because they always had these elaborate and fancy meals and never seemed to eat the same thing twice. Bruce assured Esther, "This is just how we eat; we both love to cook," but Esther had a hard time believing that. She was convinced Melinda, not Bruce, was the reason Esther wasn't living in Eden Prairie. To Esther, Melinda was exerting her authority through the meals she made.

"Look," Melinda seemed to say, "I have everything under control. We do not need you."

Melinda certainly seemed to have the household in order. Esther kicked the tires and checked under the hood, but she found nothing awry with the way things were being maintained. It was a big house, but Bruce and Melinda didn't have a maid. Yet, Esther found no dust behind picture frames or ringing the display objects on shelves. Her daughter-in-law even did chores while Esther watched, and refused to accept her help.

"No, don't worry about the windows," Melinda said. "The vacuum takes some getting used to," Melinda said, "I got it. You're on vacation, just relax and enjoy."

These were all the right things to say, and yet they felt hollow and passive aggressive to Esther. Esther really didn't want to do the chores at her son's house; she was only asking to be polite, but when her help was rejected, she suddenly did have the itch to dust and vacuum, or to clean a toilet or two, or even cook. She cleaned at her own house, though not as often as she used to. These days, nobody came to call, and so what was the point of keeping the house polished as if they did. Then again, even in the "old" days, Esther was usually in other people's houses, not a host of parties at her own.

Prior to 2015, Esther had been a consumer, not a generator, of information. While she greedily ate up all the content her friends produced, she contributed very little of her own. As the calendar flipped from 2014 to 2015, it abruptly changed. She began with following the example of her friends and started posting photographs of her grandchildren. People, she found, loved kid pictures, and they liked the hell out of her posts. Every time she had a new notification that someone had liked or commented on one of her images, she felt a little tingle of excitement. Her first post to get more than one hundred likes was a status update announcing the birth of baby Opal.

Some of the people who had liked or commented on the image weren't even friends of hers. They were friends of friends, or friends of friends of friends. She was amazed by the attention this simple thing drew and the joy that its attention gave her. It was not so different from the warm feeling she had when she proudly remembered reporting Bill Daniels to the police, or even the prouder moment when she could tell her friends, "That local citizen, that was me." Only here, there was no downside to her joy. Bringing down Bill Daniels was obviously a good thing, and something that benefited the neighborhood, but it also meant that Carol Daniels was caught in the fray. Sharing a photograph of a baby? This was all to the good. No one was being harmed. She sent friend requests to everyone who liked or commented on the photograph, and her friend-base expanded.

Facebook kept suggesting friends to Esther, saying "you might know." Some of those people she did know, and others looked nice enough or they shared enough mutual friends. If Facebook recommended them, or they were friends of friends, how bad could they be? She started to send more friend requests and they were accepted. By the time of President Obama's 2015 State of the Union Address, Esther had reached one thousand friends. Her computer desk was in the same room as the television, and her desk chair was the most comfortable chair in the room. It was a Herman Miller Aeron, she paid a pretty penny for it, and she hardly ever left it.

Ever since the Aeron debuted in 1994, Jeffrey insisted that it was the most comfortable chair in the world. He bought one for the house, and when one broke (usually because a kid was abusing it), they replaced the Aeron numerous times over the years. Even after Jeffrey died, Esther kept up the tradition and bought a new one in 2014 after one of the grandkids broke the old one. She kept the couch and the La-Z-Boy, but she very rarely used them. The Aeron was her chair of choice.

As Esther accumulated more friends on Facebook, she was exposed to different ways of inhabiting the digital landscape. Many of the newer people she had friended didn't follow the normal habits that her "older" friends did. These people wrote whatever was on their mind. Sometimes they ranted about things she didn't understand, but she was intrigued by their enthusiasm, and other times they reported about news she hadn't heard yet. She followed their links and read what they had to say and filed the information away for later use. Since hitting 100+ likes, Esther had itched to feel that level of excitement again. She tried posting photos she thought for sure would do the trick: a cute picture of Kenda's first day of preschool; Albert smashing his face into his second birthday cake. Those were well-received, but none topped Opal's introduction to the world.

Esther's fingers hovered over her keyboard as she watched the State of the Union Address. Esther was wrapped up in the words coming from the President's mouth and not thinking about what her fingers were doing. They typed the following: "I hate his stupid face. He is so smug. Even with those ears." When Obama had finished speaking, Esther looked at what she had typed. She thought it was kind of funny. It wasn't so different from what her other friends wrote on social media, so why not? She clicked "post." Esther didn't hate the president, but she did think his ears made him look goofy. The phrase "stupid face" was something she had picked up from her son from his high school days and had latched onto. Esther wasn't really one for name-calling or cursing, but, somehow "stupid face" struck her as both funny and appropriate in so many situations. She had used the phrase so many times since she first heard it in the mid-nineties that it lost its offensive edge and just became something to say.

The likes poured in. Before Esther went to bed, her update cleared two hundred likes. She was flabbergasted. In fact, she stayed up later just to see how many more likes she would get. Finally she called it a night at eleven o'clock, which was a full hour and a half later than she usually went to sleep. She checked Facebook as soon as she woke up. The tally was now over a thousand, and it had been shared fifteen times. Esther had never had anything of hers shared before. Why would anyone want to share something she had written or posted? Wasn't "sharing" something you did with news or articles? And yet, there it was. Her status update had been shared fifteen, now sixteen, times. There were so many comments that Esther had to keep scrolling to see them all. Daniel Byrd was among the commenters and sharers. The boy who got away. Well, not so much as "got away" as "slept with and impregnated Esther's best friend and then disappeared from their lives." Here he was, on her Facebook page, reacting to something she had written. She didn't know this, but he was in fact the first person to share her status update. His comments consisted of, "Right!" and "Smug lib!" and similar things as he responded to other comments that people made. Hardly profound statements, but the fact that he was now connecting to Esther made her feel pretty good about herself.

She was so distracted by Daniel's attention, the likes, and the shares, she didn't notice all the pending friend requests. Esther scanned through the faces and names; some looked and sounded vaguely familiar and others didn't, but she accepted them all regardless. Her ascent was mounting. With each new friend came more likes and comments, and of course, more information to ingest from their pages, their contributions, and their images. She gobbled it up. She hadn't felt that kind of excitement in a long time and didn't realize she had missed it. With sixty new friends just that morning, she had plenty to do and get caught up with. It was exhilarating.

Esther tried to recreate the same magic of her "stupid face" update on Valentine's Day, by sharing a story about the New York Police Department. The NYPD announced there had been a streak of twelve days without a murder in the city. As far as New York knew, that was a new record and certainly notable. For Esther, someone who had gone to New York in the 70s, 80s, and 90s, this story was truly remarkable. The New York City she knew was one of gangs, the mob, drugs, and prostitution. She remembered the city being dirty and filled with litter, but there were great parts of it that she loved visiting, too. She had heard that the city had really turned a corner, but this story about twelve days being murder free really surprised her. She shared the story, and even wrote a little about what she remembered of NYC in the 70s and how far they had come. Then she waited for response. It came, but not in a rush like the last one had.

Daniel pointed out, "That's because of all the storms. People can't kill one another when it's cold out!"

Esther thought Daniel missed the point, and she wondered if all of his comments ended in an exclamation mark. She made a mental note to keep track. The update about NYC only generated two hundred fifty likes and two shares. Listen to her now, "only," when just a few days ago, she would have been happy to have topped one hundred.

When the Oscar for best picture was awarded to *Birdman*, Esther posted her outrage. What was that movie even about? She saw the ads for it everywhere, and all her friends (virtual or otherwise) told her she just had to see it. She liked Michael Keaton alright, but she just didn't see what everyone else saw in the movie. It was weird and sad. Her post on February 22 was simply, "*Birdman*? That's the best picture this year? Are you kidding me?" She didn't expect much in response, because she wasn't sure who else out there tried to keep up with the awards shows. Watching movies was something Esther had always enjoyed, and now that she was single with her son and grandchildren living almost seven hundred miles away, she had plenty of time to keep up with that hobby.

Daniel was the first person to respond, "Over *American Sniper*! You got to be kidding me!"

Then some of their mutual friends chimed in, saying, "Clint Eastwood is a god!" and "Bradly Cooper was robbed!"

Esther noticed they all seemed to end their responses in exclamation marks, not just Daniel. She hadn't seen *American Sniper*, so she couldn't comment on whether it was more deserving or not, but based on what she was reading, it sounded far superior to the incomprehensible mess that was *Birdman*. As with her "stupid face" update, the attention drawn by her Oscar comment surprised her. Daniel and his friends were having a discussion of their own. Initially, she had the policy of "liking" everything that someone wrote in response to something she had written; she thought it was a nice way of showing that she took the time to read that person's words since they had taken the time to write them. When her Oscar post was hijacked and the discussion went in a direction she couldn't participate with, she stopped liking things and stopped trying to keep up. She hardly noticed when this post was also shared multiple times, and the likes soared into the hundreds.

When she wasn't generating her own content on social media, she was eagerly reading what others had written. She spent a fair amount of time on Daniel's page to return the favor of his commenting on hers. She tried to understand his stands on net neutrality and tried to care about "deflategate," but she just couldn't. Daniel frequently posted links to articles with no introduction of his own. It was almost as if he was saying, "Here, read this" but couldn't bother to indicate why or what he thought about it. Were these things he agreed with? He didn't say.

Occasionally Daniel did weigh-in, but it happened rarely. For example, when Bowe Bergdahl was formally charged with desertion, Daniel's preamble to the shared link indicated, "About time! Traitor!" When Mike Pence signed SB 101 into law, Daniel wrote, "Take that queers!"

Esther, ultimately, had no strong position on the LGBT community, their ability to marry, or anything concerning the way they governed their lives. She had never, to her knowledge, known anyone that was gay, or lesbian, or whatever those other letters stood for. Of course, there was Bill Daniels, but Esther had hardly known him. Now that she thought about it a little more, there was Dean's older brother Chester, but again, Esther didn't really know him. Daniel must have known more gay people because he seemed to have such a strong opinion about them. He posted regularly about the different courts that were overturning or upholding laws related to same-sex marriage.

The 2015 earthquake in Nepal affected Esther in a way she

didn't quite understand. Here was an event that was so far away, and yet she felt the pain of these people as if they were her own children. She wept openly when she saw the photographs and videos of destruction and the newly homeless. She even sent money to charitable organizations to help them. This was something she had never done. There were plenty of opportunities to be charitable over the years. Hell, in the 80s, it was hard to avoid hearing about the need to raise money for Africa. She had watched Live Aid when it originally aired, and then numerous times on the VHS tapes that Jim McKinney had given her, but she'd never bothered to send a penny to any cause associated with it. There was the "We Are the World" song, which she knew all the words to and "Tears are Not Enough" and "Do They Know It's Christmas?" and all of those advertisements, and yet she and Jeffery had never sent a penny to help any of them. Some people she knew drew the line with Africa because, "There are so many people who need our money right here at home," but that wasn't Esther. She had never been a charitable person. When hurricanes, tornados, and drought hit the United States, or even when the attacks of 9/11, Esther always kept her money to herself. But, these poor children in Nepal? She opened her checkbook and donated multiple times. Esther posted about the earthquake regularly, and when another one struck less than a month later, she reminded her readers about how sad it was. "They haven't even had a chance to rebuild!" Daniel's exclamation marks seemed gratuitous, whereas Esther felt this one was well deserved.

When a friend posted a picture of two little Nepalese children, Esther's heart broke all over again. A little boy cuddled a younger girl. There was no information provided by the friend to indicate this, but Esther was sure this was an older brother taking care of his little sister. She invented a whole backstory for these children. They lost one parent in the first quake on April 25, and the second parent died trying to rebuild their home on May 12. It was terrible. Terrible. So sad. Esther found her favorite charity and donated again. This was now her fifth or sixth time doing so, each time a little more than the previous donation. She shared the image of the children on her own page, included the backstory she now believed to be 100% accurate, and provided a link to donate to help victims of the earthquake.

The children in the photograph weren't Nepalese; they were Hmong. The photograph wasn't from 2015; it was from 2007. They weren't suffering from incredible loss or pain; they were playing in front of their house while their parents worked in a field. Both parents were alive and well. Esther had assumed correctly that they were brother and sister, but otherwise, the story provided by Esther, and now shared numerous times, was just plain inaccurate. Regardless, Esther's post was shared and shared again.

Now she had two thousand friends, and when she shared a post, her posts were shared hundreds of times. Esther liked the attention, and because she was sharing about the plight of the Nepalese, she felt like she was doing good.

She felt similarly altruistic about her reporting regarding the Clinton emails. She had moved from thinking of her updates as simple reflections or throwaway thoughts to considering it her civic duty to pass on important information. Her Facebook friends seemed to agree. They liked and shared her posts, and new friend requests poured in, who in turn liked and shared her posts. Much like the status update regarding Obama's "stupid face," Esther initially had no strong opinions about Hillary Clinton. She had never really been very politically-minded. She occasionally went to Opole's city council meetings, wrote the mayor, and tried to make an impact on the town around her. But beyond the city limits of Opole, she had never really cared all that much. That's not to say she didn't vote, because she did, but she didn't invest her time and energy into politics the way other people she knew did.

The spark for her, regarding Clinton's emails, came in the form of a comment from Daniel. It was innocuous enough, but his words got under her skin. One day, shortly after Hillary announced her candidacy, Daniel posted the news to Facebook this way, "Well, there goes the female vote!" He included a link to an article that included Hillary's video, and her tweet announcing that she was running for president. Those words, "There goes the female vote!" stuck in Esther's craw. The fact that Hillary was running wasn't really news. Every news organization had assumed as much since the 2012 election was decided and had even run articles the previous week saying, "Sources familiar with Clinton's campaign report she will make an announcement on Sunday, April 12." But until Daniel made his public assumption about who would and wouldn't vote for Hillary, Esther hadn't given it any thought. There was over a year to go before the actual election, and the parties hadn't even decided on their candidates yet. Who knows who would even be standing in November of, not this year but, next year. And now Daniel, who Esther remembered as a staunch marijuana-smoking liberal who went off to college to become even more liberal, suddenly was assuming that Esther, who had always voted Republican, was going to flip Democrat just because a woman was on the ticket?

Who was this man, and what had happened to him? How did he become this super conservative misogynist? She'd show him.

Her response was short and quippy, "What makes you so sure?"

Then she dug into the issues. The more she read about Clinton, the less she liked. Esther remembered Bill Clinton, and what those years were like. She remembered poor Mrs. Clinton having to deal with her husband's indiscretions and having their private life on public trial. She felt bad about that, but when you marry a politician, you have to expect that kind of thing. Esther knew that Clinton was a lawyer, and she hated lawyers. They were practically what was wrong with this world. You couldn't serve someone hot coffee without a warning label or go on a circus ride without there being some warning about who should or shouldn't ride this ride, and hell, even her sleeping pills had a warning label that they "may cause drowsiness."

"I would certainly like to hope they would," Esther muttered to herself.

She wasn't sleeping well these days, and the pills were one of the few things that seemed to help. Lawyers, ugh. Like her comment about Obama's ears and stupid face, she found she just didn't like the look of Hillary. She, too, looked smug. She didn't look feminine. She wore pantsuits. When she wore those sunglasses, she looked like a vampire hiding from the sun. It seemed like, whenever Hillary was photographed, she was bored, resting her chin on her hand, or sighing, or something unflattering. She definitely was not photogenic. Not that looks were everything, but a president did have to have a sort of look about him. It was funny, even as she was imagining a female president, she used the male pronoun.

Esther grew up hearing, "Anyone could be president," but knew that really meant any man could be. It took time to get a black man in the office, but she imagined that was easier for everyone to stomach than a female president. Would there be a Hispanic president, and a gay male president before a female president? Esther didn't know, but she wasn't going to give Hillary a free pass just because of her gender. In addition to all the "gut reaction" she had about Hillary, there were also all the scandals. Esther vaguely remembered something about Whitewater, and something called Travelgate, not to mention this whole Benghazi-thing that Esther didn't fully understand. Frankly, Hillary had just been a public figure for too long had too much dirt out there about her for Esther to see as a viable candidate.

Her argument against another Clinton in the White House wasn't very strong until Esther dove into Hillary's emails. Through Daniel's post, and the posts of mutual friends, Esther learned more about the Benghazi ordeal and why Hillary's emails were important. For Esther, the issue with the emails was less about what they contained and more about how sneaky Hillary was being with them. First, it's announced that "Hillary has 55,000 emails." Less than a thousand of them are supposedly about Benghazi, and almost 32,000 of them are regarded as "private." Then Hillary says she wants to make all of her emails public. But, she's been using a private email server! Esther wasn't sure exactly what that meant, but she knew it was against the rules and that it meant it could be hacked. Esther knew enough about how sneaky people worked to realize if someone was under investigation, they should not be trusted to make decisions about what is pertinent to a lawsuit against them. Why delete the emails if she wasn't guilty of doing something bad? Then, in the midst of all this, Hillary declared herself a candidate for president? Who would do that while under investigation? Only the most arrogant of people.

Though history would give credit to Donald Trump for the nickname "crooked Hillary," Esther used it first on September 24, 2015, after the announcement of the FBI's recovery of her deleted emails. The message, true to Esther's form, was short, but effective, "Now we'll find out what was in crooked Hillary's emails, or will we?"

Her readership liked the hell out of that short post and shared it widely. They loved the catchy name, and many people commented on specifically liking that part of the post. There was also the matter of "or will we?" that sparked all kinds of animated discussion. Was the FBI in on it with the Clintons? Would the public ever actually be able to read her emails to decide for themselves? Just how did someone undelete an email anyway? Was it even possible? And if so, what did that mean for the average person's privacy? For Esther, the lot against Hillary was cast. She was obviously sneaky, deceptive, and too much the polished politician for Esther to ever vote for her.

There, Esther thought, that will show Daniel Byrd for assuming otherwise.

As Esther neared 5,000 friends, she lost track of who came and went. Some of her old friends disappeared, and new ones replaced them. The old friends that seemingly disappeared didn't actually unfriend her though; they just stopped following her. Esther grasped the basic way Facebook worked, but she didn't quite understand that friends could opt out of seeing her "news" in their feed. Why would they want to do that? She wanted more and more; she couldn't imagine cutting a thread like that. When she eventually did reach 5,000 friends, just prior to Halloween 2015, Esther's news was only reaching about a thousand of them. But those thousand were so active and fervent, it felt like she had many, many more. Long gone were the days of her posting pictures of her grandchildren or lurking in the shadows commenting on the lives of her friends. She no longer cared about the coffee shop her friends were frequenting, or what delicious looking meals another was having, or what anniversary someone was celebrating, or who had recently died. Between the stupid-face comment, her rage at Obama's new policy with their communist neighbor, and the focus on Hillary's emails, she had become a political machine.

CHAPTER 12: A DIGITAL VACATION

The dance to visit her son began soon after she hit 5,000 friends. Esther would first ask about dates, then Bruce would take a few days to get back to her with, "Let me run them by Melinda." A few days later, Bruce would come back with a different set of dates for Esther to consider. They repeated this dance ritual every time Esther reached out to visit. Whatever worked for Melinda and Bruce worked for her, but she found if she asked to visit without dates in mind, the request floated without a response. When she anchored her request with some fixed time on the calendar, Bruce would reply. Eventually. Securing a date always took two or three times back and forth. Then after she bought a plane ticket, the whole dance repeated itself as they tried to coordinate when Bruce or Melinda could pick her up from the airport.

It wasn't that Esther couldn't drive; she just never had driven much. The thought of driving for ten hours to get from Opole, Michigan to Eden Prairie, Minnesota by herself made her crazy. She preferred to fly. The flight was only an hour and fifty minutes or so, and she could fly non-stop from Detroit right into the Eden Prairie airport. Those tickets were a little more expensive than going through MSP, but she practically landed in Bruce's backyard. The only real drawback to flying was that she missed the freedom of having her own car once she was there, even if she still hated driving.

The first time she visited, Esther couldn't seem to wrap her mind around not having any sidewalks. She peppered Bruce and Melinda with questions like: "How are kids supposed to ride their bikes or walk to the library?" and "How do they walk to their friends?"

"Mom," Bruce said, "kids don't do that kind of thing."

"Don't go to the library?" she asked, practically sputtering.

"Of course they use the library," said Melinda. "Our kids love to read, and they have their own library cards."

"We just drive them," said Bruce. "It's safer."

"But we drove by the library; it's barely a mile from here," said Esther. "They could easily ride their bikes there." She paused. "If there were sidewalks for them to use."

"It's just not the reality of how things work now," Bruce assured her. "Playdates are arranged by parents, and we drop kids off where they need to go."

"That way we know where they are," said Melinda. "And it teaches kids about planning and scheduling, which is so important as they grow up."

"How?" Esther asked. "You're doing all the planning and scheduling, not the kids."

"But they have to ask and think ahead if they want to have a playdate," said Bruce. He remembered being what now would be labeled a "free-range kid," so he could see where his mother was coming from. "Mom, Minnesota is a great place to live. Great schools and everything, but the shadow of Jacob Wetterling hangs over everything, and people just want to be careful."

"We had a child molester living in our neighborhood when you were growing up," Esther said. Except, she knew that wasn't quite the right word for what Bill Daniels had been.

"He was a pornographer," corrected Bruce.

"I don't think that makes a stronger argument," said Melinda. "Why haven't I heard this story before?"

"Sorry," Esther said. "Pornographer, you're right. But still, you kids could go where you wanted and had sidewalks to ride your bikes and walk where you needed to."

"Did you know about this pornographer?" asked Melinda.

"I was the one who discovered him," Esther said. "And I reported it immediately, and he was arrested."

Melinda looked at Bruce, and her husband shrugged back.

"Kids these days meet at school and in daycare, and their parents live all around the city," Bruce said. "Kendra's best friend lives in Edina."

"Is that far?" Esther asked.

"Further than any of my kids are going to ride their bike," said Melinda. She laughed.

"I appreciate your concern and care, and I know this is coming from a good place," Bruce said, "but this is how we've chosen to raise our children. It's how parents, in general, raise their kids."

And it seemed to work for them. Esther was always surprised how busy they were though because Melinda was always shuttling one of the three kids somewhere. Bruce helped out when he could, but he often worked from home in an office upstairs and was somewhat oblivious to the rest of the family. Esther would have intervened or said something more if she thought it would have done any good. Whenever the six of them ventured out during one of Esther's visits, she was quick to point out that some neighborhoods had sidewalks.

"Oh, this looks like a nice neighborhood," she would say. And it would essentially be indistinguishable from Bruce and Melinda's neighborhood of choice, except it would have sidewalks.

"Why do they only have sidewalks on only one side of the street?" she'd ask.

"I don't know Mom," Bruce said. "It's just the way they build them now." Esther could hear the "eye roll" in his voice. In reality, the biggest problem for Esther in a place with no sidewalks meant she couldn't go out for a powerwalk like the old days in Opole when she needed "air." There were plenty of moments during her visits when that was exactly what she needed.

Every time she flew to see her son, she was surprised at how different the airport looked. Something was always changing. Whether it was the security line that arbitrarily moved from one side of the terminal to the other, or whether or not she needed to remove her shoes, or which scanner she was sent through and whether she was patted down or not, the airport was constantly in flux. She remembered when Jeffrey had taken a business trip in the early 90s, and Esther had gone all the way to the gate with him and waited for his flight to take off. She had waved through the glass, convinced he could see her. Now, they hardly wanted cars stopping to drop people off—police or security vehicles hovered and reminded people to keep moving—let alone come inside the actual airport with travelers. She tried to remember if they even bothered checking identifications when you flew before 2001.

Compared to Detroit Metro, the Eden Prairie airport was a breath of fresh air. It was so small and quaint. Everyone there was so pleasant and friendly. She wondered why the Michigan airport couldn't be more like it. The Eden Prairie attendants seemed genuinely happy to be there, and it was so nice to come off the plane and not have to walk a mile or two to find her luggage. She would land and immediately call Bruce.

"Hi, Mom," he said. "You landed?"

"Yes. I'm here and ready whenever you are."

"I'll let Melinda know," he said. "I'm just wrapping up a project so I can be free for the weekend."

A couple minutes later, Melinda arrived in what passed for minivans these days. They were certainly sleeker and more elegant than the ones from the 80s. Esther reached for the door just as if on cue the door began to slide back on its own, revealing Melinda and the children inside.

"Grandma!" the three of them yelled.

"I'll grab your bag," Melinda said, as she came around the side of the vehicle.

"Oh, thank you, honey," Esther said.

"I want to sit next to Grandma!" said Albert.

"You did last time," whined Kendra.

Esther looked at the backseat where Albert sat in a forward-facing car seat, and Opal was in the rear-facing car seat on the other end of the bench seat. Kendra, meanwhile, sat in one of the two bucket seats in the middle of the vehicle. The empty bucket seat definitely looked more enticing, and was nearer to her, than the seat in the back, where she be sandwiched between car seats. She couldn't remember who she sat by last time and didn't know what to do.

Kendra and Albert were sniping at each other and their voices created a wall of sound that prevented Esther's thoughts from being able to form coherently. "Uh," she started. "Uh," she repeated. She really was trying to make a decision, or at least respond, but she just couldn't find the words among the noise.

"Guys!" Melinda snapped from the back of the vehicle. "Stop. Just stop it!" She sighed, pressed the button to close the trunk, and took a deep breath. "I'm sorry, but we're talking about a 3-minute drive here. Let Grandma sit in the seat that's right in front of her. I know it's next to Kendra, but I'm sorry. It's easiest. Grandma doesn't need to be squished into the back."

"It's not squished!" said Albert.

"It is, honey," said Melinda.

"I can see you just fine from up here," said Esther. She took her seat, clicked her seatbelt, and turned to look at her favorite grandchild.

She knew she wasn't supposed to have favorites, and regularly said things like, "Oh, I love them all for different reasons," but that wasn't entirely true.

Kendra should have been her favorite because she was the first. The truth was, Kendra was a spoiled brat. She had a sense of entitlement that drove Esther nuts. Albert, maybe because he was the middle child, seemed better adjusted, easier going, and didn't whine as much as his older sister. She was five now, but you wouldn't guess it by how quickly she melted down and screamed about every little thing. Opal was too little to really figure into being a favorite, but if Esther was being truthful, she would have said that Opal was an ugly baby. She knew that was a horrible thing to say, but it was the truth. Maybe she'll grow out of it, but for now, Esther was more than content to spend time with Albert, lining up his Hot Wheels cars, reading him Sandra Boynton books, or even sitting next to him on the couch and watching that *Dinosaur Train* show.

Esther thought the premise was stupid, but she had to admit she loved Dr. Scott and learning more about dinosaurs. The show provided an education for her, as much as it did for Albert. Her dinosaur education basically stopped when Bruce turned thirteen, so she had a lot of ground to cover. The TV show was a bit of a mystery to her because the dinosaurs looked so real, and Dr. Scott obviously grounded the show in reality and yet the dinosaurs spoke, had cities, and drove trains. Ridiculous.

Her phone buzzed in her purse, and she was tempted to look at it, but the drive from the airport was short enough. Instead, she looked around the van and out the windows.

"Esther, do you mind if we make a stop or two?" Melinda asked. "I need to pick up some groceries for dinner."

"That's fine," Esther said.

The drive was a blur of suburbia and being tugged on by Kendra and called to from the back by Albert. "Grandma this" and "Grandma that" and "Grannnndma" and all other variations of her name stretched out into different syllable counts. A few moments later they were parked outside of Lunds and Byerlys. Melinda turned around from the driver's seat and smiled at Esther.

"Do you want to come in? Or would you rather stay in the car with the kids?" Melinda asked.

Esther knew what Melinda wanted her to say, because it is the same thing she'd want herself: freedom from the kids. She and Jeffrey had only had Bruce, but even he was overwhelming at times. The solo trip to the grocery store was a bit like a mini vacation, and she could see in Melinda's eyes that she really needed this. It wasn't always in Esther's DNA to give people what they wanted. She sat there, probably longer than necessary, and weighed her options. On one hand, she would be trapped in a van with a cacophony of noise, hearing her name called a million times. On the other, she could shuffle through the grocery store with the chaos of children making the trip to "pick up a few groceries" take exponentially longer than a solo trip would have. If she did the first, then she might win some points with Melinda, which she needed. Melinda didn't seem to like her very much. Worse, Melinda's dislike for Esther seemed to have rubbed off on Bruce.

"You just go," Esther said. "We'll be just fine here, won't we?" She looked at Albert and Opal in the back and then at Kendra.

The two older kids nodded and smiled and the back of Opal's carseat said nothing.

"Thank you," Melinda said, and then added, "I won't be long." Melinda closed the driver's side door and for a moment, the van was still and silent.

"Well," Esther said. "What should we do while your mother is shopping?"

As the kids clamored on about this and that, Esther pulled out her phone and checked her notifications. So many likes and comments and messages to catch up on. As she scrolled and clicked and thumbed messages, she made sure to add a few audible "ohs" and "wows" and "tell me mores," and did, occasionally, make eye contact with her grandchildren. Between the nonstop chatter of the kids and getting caught up on what she had missed in the digital world during her flight, the time went by in a blink. Then the rear to the van was opening automatically, Melinda was putting her cloth bags in the back, opening the front door, and starting the van.

"How was it?" Melinda asked.

Esther thought she caught a glint of a smirk in the rearview mirror. "It was fine," Esther said. "We got caught up on the TV shows and favorite toys."

"Grandma was on her phone," said Kendra. She was

pouting.

"Oh, was she now?" asked Melinda.

"I was not," Esther said, which she realized was a stupid, childish thing to say, but she said it anyway.

"Did someone call?" asked Melinda.

"No," Esther said. "I was just getting caught up on what I had missed over the last couple hours. But I did not," she looked at Kendra, "spend the whole time on my phone."

"Anything good?" Melinda asked.

Esther knew she had to be careful. Melinda and Bruce were not exactly on the same line of the political spectrum as she was, and so she didn't know how much she could say without causing a fight. She didn't want her trip to start this way.

"Not really." She shrugged, not sure if Melinda could see the gesture in the mirror. She twisted to see Albert, who smiled, she smiled back, and then turned to smile at Kendra, who scowled at her. The little girl mouthed the words, "Did too."

As soon as the van pulled into the garage, Kendra and Albert were climbing over Esther to get out her side of the van. Esther unbuckled, twisted, and tried to figure out how to release the car seat.

"I'll get that," Melinda said. She was shaking her head. "Those kids," she said. "We get home, and they blast off to do their own thing. I've tried to teach them to help with the groceries, even to offer to help, but... I don't know."

Esther got out of the van to make room for Melinda.

"It's not their fault," said Esther. "They're kids. I mean, Bruce never did anything unless I threatened him or it was a punishment."

"I suppose," Melinda said.

Esther was amazed how effortlessly Melinda was able to remove the carrier from the car seat holder. Was there some kind of magic button she just couldn't see?

"I'll grab the bags," Esther said. "You have your hands full there."

"I could still get one or two," Melinda said, "but thank

you."

Bruce was already in the kitchen. "Wow, that was fast," he said.

"Your mom stayed in the car with the kids," Melinda said as she set the carseat on a bench and began to undo the straps and remove her jacket. "It's amazing how much faster a trip to the store is without three extra bodies competing for attention."

"Amazing," Bruce said. He worked to empty the bags Esther handed him. "Hey mom," he said. "Thanks for coming. Good to see you." He paused what he was doing and gave her a hug.

The hug felt good, and Esther realized it had been a long time since she had been hugged. Probably the last time she had visited. She could feel Bruce releasing her, but she held on a little longer.

"It's great to see you, too," she said. Esther gave a final squeeze and let go. She wiped her eyes, put on a big smile, and looked at her grandchildren. "Alright! What are we going to do first?"

The kids dragged her up and down the stairs to show her all their toys. Most of these she had seen before, but the kids felt it was important to update her on what their current favorites were and what those toys had been doing since her last visit in June. She feigned excitement and tried to keep all the names straight, but before long, the kids weren't so much "showing her" as they were outright playing with her sitting in the same room.

Esther found her way back downstairs where Melinda and Bruce were getting out ingredients for dinner and offered to help.

Melinda smiled and said, "We've got it."

That was probably for the best, because Esther had no idea where anything was in this kitchen, nor why they organized it the way they did. It felt haphazard. As if the couple had just emptied boxes from moving in random drawers and cabinets because they were too exhausted to do much more. Once established, they hadn't bothered to revisit the best way to organize the kitchen for efficiency. The soup ladles and kitchen knives were thrown in one drawer, and the bowls and cups were together, but the plates and plastic storage containers were stacked weirdly in one cabinet, and most offensive to Esther, the coffee mugs were in a cabinet clear on the other side of the kitchen from the coffee pot. Who does that? Esther imagined that after a while you just got used to it and instinctively knew where to find something.

"You okay, Mom?" Bruce asked.

"Oh, I'm fine," she said. "Better than fine, because I'm here with you."

"Why don't you take a load off on the couch and relax a bit," he said. "We've got this, and dinner will be ready in about forty minutes."

"Okay," she said. "Maybe I'll just read my book for a bit then."

"What are you reading?" Melinda asked, and Esther noted it sounded like sincere curiosity.

"It's called *Beautiful Ruins*," she said. "By Jess Walter, I think? I love that part of takes place on these Italian islands and it's kind of about old Hollywood. Definitely not my usual kind of thing, but a friend recommended it."

"No, I've never heard of that," Melinda said, between chopping carrots. "I'm reading *The Girl on the Train* for my bookclub. There's going to be a movie made of it next year, so we're trying to read the book before that comes out."

"I remember hearing about that one," said Esther. "Do you like it?"

"Oh, yeah, it's very good," said Melinda. "Troubled women in bad relationships, and maybe murder. I haven't gotten very far yet."

"I never really remember you as being much of a reader," said Bruce. "Did you read a lot back then?"

"I loved to read as a kid," Esther said. "But, married life and having a family, you know. It was hard to find the time, sometimes. And when you have a minute to yourself, you just want to take that time to sit and catch your breath."

"Before having the kids, I wouldn't have understood what you meant," Bruce said. "To me, as a kid, it just always felt like I was outside doing my thing and you were walking around talking with your friends. A busybody or whatever people called you."

Esther frowned. She hated that word. Who wasn't a busy? What did non-busybody people do? Just sit around and create dust?

"Back then, we got out and walked. We got together at one another's houses and would just drop by and see people. We weren't all connected like you are now." She knew she should have stopped there and just gone to read her book, but she couldn't help herself. "Of course, it was easier to get around because we had sidewalks."

"Oh geez, Mom," Bruce said. He started to say something, Esther assumed to argue with her, but then caught himself and instead said, "You seem to be enjoying the more connected world these days."

"It is kind of nice to be able to catch up with old friends," Esther said. Bruce was on Facebook, but he wasn't very active. She wasn't sure how much he knew about her presence.

"You should join Instagram," Melinda said. "That's really where we post more of our kid pictures."

"Yeah, and it doesn't have all that political stuff on there," said Bruce.

"What's wrong with political stuff?" asked Esther.

"Oh, nothing," Bruce shrugged. "But you're never going to change someone's mind on social media. You're just going to find people who agree and whip one another up."

Esther sat there staring at the countertop. She didn't like the pattern. It was too dark. How were you ever supposed to know if it was clean? Since it was laminate, it would be inexpensive to replace, and she had brought that up to Bruce several times, but he didn't seem interested in her opinion. Laminate was so cheap, it made the kitchen feel, she scrunched up her face as she thought, prefabricated, and well, cheap.

Esther wished Bruce and Melinda had listened when she told them to go with granite or marble. Those would have made a statement and elevated the kitchen from meh, to wow when someone stepped in the room.

Dinner was a blur of dishes she didn't recognize. Everything was fine, but it certainly wasn't the meal she would have cooked or preferred. The carrots were roasted, which Esther just didn't understand. Why would you roast a carrot? Roasting was for meat. Your vegetables were supposed to be steamed. She remembered her mom used to boil vegetables, and they'd fall apart on her plate, and she had to scrap the pieces up with the side of her fork. Esther always hated that, so when she read about the health benefits of steamed vegetables, that's the way she always made them. Roasted was fine, she guessed, but the carrots were a little tough. And oh boy, the salt Bruce and Melinda put on everything. She was also surprised by how little meat there was but didn't feel like arguing again.

The last time she was here, she got in a huge argument about milk with Bruce. He insisted that kids didn't need milk, and that they got plenty of calcium from other sources. What other sources? Cheese, yogurt, kale, and spinach.

"When you were a kid, we went through a gallon of milk every four days. I was so glad we only had you because we couldn't have afforded to feed another boy." She had meant that to be light-hearted, but it hadn't landed that way.

Bruce ended the conversation the way so many of their disagreements did, "It's different now; the science has changed, and we better understand nutrition."

She hated that line of his, "The science has changed." That was his answer to everything about why what she had done was wrong and why what he was doing now was right.

This time, she kept quiet and ate her food. Bruce and Melinda were constantly tending to one of the kids, and the conversation was hard for Esther to track anyway. It started with Melinda asking about Bruce's day but was derailed when Kendra asked for Ranch dressing for her carrots.

Esther was about to say, "Oh, smothering vegetables in Ranch is healthy now?" but she held her tongue.

Then Albert needed to use the bathroom, and Bruce was shuttling him out of the room. Kendra was saying something about a show she watched earlier, and then Melinda's phone rang in the other room. No one else seemed to hear it, and she almost got up to answer it, but again, she sat and kept quiet. As the dinner and conversation went on without her, she set down her fork and picked up her phone.

"No devices at dinner," Kendra said.

Esther didn't know how she had even noticed among the clanks and chewing and chatter. "It's okay," said Esther. "I just need to check this really quick."

Melinda glanced at Bruce, and he coughed.

"Mom," he said. "I'm sorry, but it's one of our table rules. Kendra's right." He patted his daughter's head. "No devices at dinner, please."

The whirlwind that was dinner transitioned into the whirlwind of putting dishes in the dishwasher and cleaning up, and then seamlessly transitioned into the "get the kids ready for bed" dance. Baths, pajamas, brushing teeth, and reading stories. Before Esther really knew what hit her, it was 9PM, and she was lying in the guest bed. This was way earlier than she normally would have gone to bed, but Bruce reminded her how important it was to keep the kids on a schedule. Besides, tomorrow was Thursday, and Bruce had to work. So complied and went to bed where she scrolled and liked and commented for a while. Eventually she fell asleep.

In the morning, she put on her robe and found the house startlingly quiet. There was no clock in the guest bedroom and she was halfway downstairs before she realized she left her phone in the room. Esther found her way to the coffee pot, walked all the way across the kitchen to get a mug, and then walked all the back to the coffee pot and poured the coffee in her mug. The kitchen setup was so stupid, and she debated just rearranging the mugs to a more sensible location, but then she heard the garage door going up and instead sat on a stool and waited to see who was coming home.

The carseat with Opal led the way and then Melinda stepped into the house and closed the door behind her.

"Good morning," Esther said. "Where is everyone?"

"Well," Melinda said, "Bruce is at work, Kendra's at kindergarten, and Albert's at preschool. It's not technically preschool; we just call it that because it's easier." She paused, tilted her head, and then seemed very interested in finding something in her purse.

"I think five is way too young for kindergarten," Esther said. "And poor Albert is, three? And he's already going to school?"

"It's important for developing social skills," Melinda said. "And, it's important to give me a break. I already have my hands more than full with this one." Melinda gestured at Opal, who was sleeping. "Well, I'm going to get a couple things checked off my list before she wakes up. Why don't you," Melinda, again, didn't make eye contact, "get cleaned up and we'll figure out how we want to spend the day." She hustled out of the room.

Esther wondered if there was something on her face, or if her hair really looked that bad. She hadn't looked in the mirror before coming downstairs, but it couldn't be that bad. Esther walked over to the fridge to see if they had half and half. That was the other thing; the coffee Bruce and Melinda made was way too strong. She was sure they got the coffee from some responsibly sourced coffee place where they hand-picked and hand-ground their beans or something, but Esther couldn't stomach it. At home, she had no problem drinking black coffee, but here? She couldn't tolerate it without some cream. As Esther approached the fridge, the stainless steel reflected her image back at her and she realized her robe was wide open. She looked from side to side, suddenly concerned that someone might see, and tied her robe as quickly as she could.

The rest of the day was spent in Esther avoiding Melinda. Sometimes she'd be reading her book or feigning sleep or even going outside despite the falling temperatures. While it was almost sixty degrees when she arrived, Thursday barely scraped forty and the rest of her stay was supposed to get even colder. Esther was used to the cold; it wasn't like Opole's climate was much different from that of Eden Prairie—they shared a latitude—but somehow Minnesota felt colder. At dinner, Melinda avoided eye contact and made comments to Bruce like, "I guess the travel really took it out of your mom" and "she's really into that book" and "somehow we never managed to connect." When dinner was over, Kendra wanted to play Chutes and Ladders.

"Oh boy, I remember this game," Esther said. "Your dad either wanted to play this or Candyland. Remember those?"

"Chutes and Ladders was definitely my favorite," Bruce said. "Especially when someone else hit that huge slide at the top of the game." Though he was smiling, Esther thought she noticed something "off" with him. She wondered if Melinda had told her about this morning, or what might be rattling around in his head.

Albert tried to join the game, but his involvement really meant that Esther was confined to holding him in her lap while she tried to bend around his body to move their figure on the board. As they played, she noticed that Kendra was cheating. Every single time she spun something that would have caused her figure to land on a chute, Kendra moved an extra space to avoid it. Esther wasn't sure whether to admire her sneakiness or to call her out on it. Ultimately, Esther remembered that she hated Chutes and Ladders and just let the little girl cheat her way to victory. Thankfully, her cheating meant the game went by very quickly and soon it was time for the bedtime routine. Melinda took the kids upstairs and left Esther to clean up the game. Bruce, who had been buried in his phone the whole duration of the game, set his phone down and looked meaningfully at his mom.

"I remember liking that game as a kid," he said. "But, as an adult? Ugh, it's so mindless and completely luck-based. It drives me nuts."

Esther just smiled and put the game back on the shelf.

"Mom, I'm not sure how to say this." Bruce frowned and then started again, "but, you know, I'm really not on Facebook."

"Yes, I know," Esther said. "I don't understand this Instagram. I know it's great for photos and people love all these filters, but you can't share things, there are no links, and I get lost in the comments. I just don't see what you like about it."

Bruce put up his hands. "If you want to learn how to use Instagram, I'm happy to walk you through it, but that's not what I was going to say."

"It wasn't?" She was so sure her son was going to cajole her to join his social media platform of choice, but now he had her attention. "What then?"

"Two things, really. First, you need to chill with your favoritism of Albert. I think it hurts Kendra's feelings."

"What?"

"Come on; it's so obvious," Bruce said and shook his head. "I don't know if it's because he's a boy and he makes you think of me, or what. But whenever you do something with Kendra, you're completely disengaged and disinterested."

"Honey, I assure you I don't have any favorites. They're all wonderful, all three of them. I think maybe it's just her age, that's all," she said.

Bruce didn't looked convinced. "There's another thing."

"About the kids? Bruce, I love all your kids. Even Opal," Esther said, and then realized that required a little more explanation. "I mean, even though Opal can't do much right now, she's just a baby so why would she be able to, but I mean, I love her, too. Just watching her figure out the world around her. I love that."

This was true, but Esther was always surprised when people said they loved babies. They didn't really do that much, and they required so much work. Everyone always said that babies were so cute and adorable, but Esther thought they looked a bit like moles. And Opal, well, she'd pointed out before, Opal wasn't a pretty baby.

Bruce shook his head, "No, not about the kids. It's about Facebook." He paused. "One of my friends asked me to check out something on there, so I logged in for the first time in a long time. I had no idea you were so active and out there."

"I hit 5,000 friends before I came to visit," Esther said proudly. She thought he'd be pleased with her accomplishment but instead could see that was not what he had wanted to hear.

"Wow. You need to cool it," Bruce said. "The stuff you say on there, it's horrible. You don't really think those things, do you?"

"Like what?"

"About Obama's face?"

"Oh come on; he's a goofy looking guy with those ears, and I am tired of hearing about him," Esther said.

"I don't know what to say, Mom, but that's terrible. He's our president, and the shit you're saying on there is downright racist."

"Racist?" Esther scrunched up her face. "I don't think so. If I were one of those cartoon guys, caricaturist, yes that's the word. No one would bat an eye."

"But you're not," Bruce said.

Melinda was calling from upstairs, "It's story time."

"Be right up," Bruce yelled up the steps. Then to Esther, "I'm sorry, but you're better than that. I love you, but on the internet you're what people would call a troll."

"I know what a troll is," Esther said defensively. "And I'm not a troll. I just say what's on my mind. I don't go after people trying to get a rise out of them. But if someone says something I disagree with, then I let them know."

Bruce was silent for a moment.

"Bruce, are you coming with stories?" Melinda called.

"I am, just a sec," Bruce yelled again. "Well, I'm telling you that I disagree with what I see there. It was hard to tell you, but I thought you should know. And coming from your son, I thought maybe it would mean a bit more." Bruce broke eye contact and looked towards the stairs. "But now, I need to get up to stories. Are you coming?"

"No," Esther said, smiling. "You go ahead. I'm going stay here. My knees are starting to feel all the stairs, the kids, both kids have had me running up and down them a bunch."

"Okay," Bruce said, and ran up the steps.

Esther could hear her son saying, "What are we reading tonight?" Kendra and Albert both said something, but Esther didn't recognize the titles. She wandered around the main floor of the house and found herself looking out the back window that overlooked a park. It was snowing. She went to the guest room, closed the door, packed her bags, booked a mid-day flight for the next day, and went to sleep. The Eden Prairie airport didn't have any open seats, so she'd have to fly out of MSP, but she didn't care. She just needed to be home.

Bruce and Melinda tried to convince her to stay, but her mind was made up and the ticket was paid for.

"It's just time," Esther said. "I didn't pack for snow. I should have known it would snow in November; aren't you guys always going on about that Halloween blizzard of 1991 or whatever?"

Melinda took Esther to the airport after dropping off the kids, and the ride was completely silent. Before she knew it, she had two hours to kill in the terminal.

She opened her phone and found she had plenty of notifications, comments, and posts to keep her busy. A lot had happened in the two days since she had left her home, but she had plenty of time to get caught up with her friends. The failed trip, her open robe, the arguments with Bruce, and her snippy little granddaughter's incessant, "grandma's on her phone," were all quickly forgotten.

CHAPTER 13: TWO BUDS

By 2015, The Two Buds Greenhouse was an institution in southeastern Michigan. Chefs, restauranters, and ordinary people sought out the organic fruits and vegetables that Regina and Vicky grew. Some people came to ask them how they did what they did, where to find the grants they had, or more practically, if they could buy some of their seeds. Most of the Two Buds customers came from Ann Arbor, not Opole. Maybe this was because Regina and Vicky didn't advertise or brag about their project with their friends, or maybe it was because the people of Opole weren't interested in organic vegetables grown year-round. Esther, disconnected from gossip since the April Fool's incident of 1988, certainly didn't know about it, but Brenda did. In fact, Brenda was a sort of silent third partner in Two Buds, but even she wasn't there at the start.

The greenhouse was born from the confluence of three disparate things: breast cancer, the Flavr Savr tomato, and becoming empty-nesters. Though not actually related, each was a capstone moment that was inexplicitly linked in the minds of the Two Buds Greenhouse's founders, Regina McKinney and Vicky Webster. Regina and Vicky always had gardens, but since their plots were small, their gardens never produced enough to do much more than create a salad or a couple jars of tomato sauce to can for the winter. When the families got together, which happened often, the two women would dream about opening a greenhouse one day.

"We could move just outside of town," said Regina. "Not far enough to live in the country, you know, but just far enough to have an acre or two."

"Right," agreed Vicky. "Maybe somewhere on Scio Church? Or in Ann Arbor township?"

"Maybe," Regina said. "That might even be a bit far."

The men, Jim and Dean, offered their support in building the structure for the greenhouse. They too dreamed of having more land.

"We'd need a riding mower then," said Jim excitedly.

"Maybe one of those zero-turning radius ones?" offered Dean.

"With that much land? I don't think we'd need one that could turn that tight," said Jim.

"How much land are we talking about?" asked Regina.

"Yes," echoed Dean, "just how much land are we talking about?"

"I'm not talking about much," said Regina. "I was just thinking an acre or two. Maybe we could get houses by each other and the greenhouse could be half-and-half on each of our properties?"

"How does commercial zoning work for something like that?" asked Dean.

"I think we're getting way ahead of ourselves," Jim said.

And then the conversation would go in a different direction, until the next time they gathered, or the Fall when they canned together and all wished they had more tomatoes, or any time the desire to eat fresh, locally grown produce emerged in the dead of winter. Like most good ideas, this one took a while to germinate. With kids to raise and bills to pay, the dream took a backseat, but it reared its head often enough to keep the idea in the minds of the two families, and it didn't require much encouragement to revitalize the excitement of the shared dream.

The first piece of the puzzle was Vicky finding a lump in her breast in 1994 that turned out to be cancer. Vicky's mother hadn't done much to prepare Vicky for sex or relationships, but she had impressed upon her the importance of self-breast exams. When Vicky had asked, "What am I looking for?" her mother had just said, "You'll know it when you feel it." Though Vicky thought it was a little odd at the time, she'd stuck with it and it just became part of her morning routine. She had never felt anything concerning before, but on the day in October she found the lump, she knew.

She went about her day as if nothing had happened, but try as she might, she couldn't stop thinking about it. By the next morning, when she felt the lump again, she made up her mind. She'd schedule an appointment with Dr. Collins and see what he had to say. Then she would talk to Dean. Dr. Collins couldn't see her immediately, so she had to try acting normal until Thursday when he could.

Thursday finally came. She had hoped Dr. Collins would dismiss the lump, but he didn't. He ordered an x-ray. Then a mammogram. Then a biopsy. Each step of the way, with each new doctor or physician, she had to tell her story again to these strangers that didn't know her at all. When the barrage of tests was done, and she was told the definitive results from the biopsy would be available in 10-15 days, she decided she'd better tell Dean. She could wait no longer.

Understandably, he was shocked.

"What?" he asked. "But you're only 43?"

"Age has nothing to do with it," she said. "I'm sorry I didn't tell you sooner, but I wanted to make sure I wasn't just being silly."

"So, it's for sure now?" he asked.

She explained about the biopsy, and then they waited. When the results came in, Dean went with her to Dr. Collins' office.

"What now?" asked Dean.

"There are some decisions to make," said Dr. Collins. "It

depends how aggressive you want to be, and what course of action you want to take."

Somehow, Vicky had assumed Dr. Collins would be providing the answers. She came to him for his expertise. What did she know about breast cancer?

As Dr. Collins spoke, the words rolled over Vicky as she stared straight ahead, nodding occasionally. Fortunately, Dean was there to scribble down notes. On the way home, Dean couldn't stop talking. The words and questions just kept coming.

"Could you please," she said louder than she meant, and softened her voice. "Could you please, stop talking?"

Dean wasn't sure if answering her would count as speaking or not, so he remained silent and pulled the car into a parking space at the library. He got out and came around to Vicky's door and opened it for her. While she appreciated the gesture, she felt like screaming, "I'm not an invalid!" Instead, she smiled and took his arm.

The Opole Public Library had a surprisingly large section on cancer, and a smaller section specific to Breast Cancer. The librarian (who had been working there forever) helped them find two books by the National Cancer Institute (*Breast Cancer: Understanding Treatment Options* and *Breast Reconstruction: A Matter of Choice*) and one titled *Breast Cancer* by Lesley Fallowfield and Andrew Clark. Susan scanned Vicky's card and each of the books.

"Would you like a bag for these?" Susan asked.

"I'll go start the car," Dean said.

"A bag would be nice," Vicky said.

As she slid the books into the bag, Susan tapped the cover of Lesley Fallowfield and Andrew Clark's book, "This one is particularly good. There are interviews with actual patients."

"Thank you," said Vicky.

"And," Susan added, "if you need to talk to someone, I had that, too." She smiled. "It's hard, but you'll be okay."

In the car, the tears came and thankfully Dean didn't try to talk over the space Vicky needed. He handed her a box of tissues from the backseat and drove with his hand on her knee.

It was during that holding pattern, while they were waiting for the official results to an answer Vicky was almost certain she knew the answer to, that they encountered: the Flavr Savr tomato. Vicky was going grocery shopping and Mark asked to tag along with her. This was a little strange, but she didn't mind the company. With Barry off at college, and Michael wanting to exert his independence by staying home alone, she and Mark become closer. It might have just been a ploy to convince her to buy him a car now that he was sixteen, but she liked having him around.

Vicky's mind began to wander as she stared at all the produce when her son broke her trance.

"Hey mom," Mark said. "I know you and Dad are going through this health-thing, or whatever."

"Wait," she said. "Health thing?"

"You know, the egg whites and eating all the vegetables and all that."

It was true, but she didn't realize Mark had noticed. She hadn't said anything to her boys yet. Maybe Dean had?

"Anyway," Mark was holding a container of tomatoes. "I've started reading labels, too. Looking for calories and sugar and all that."

Had he? Now that Vicky thought back, she did remember seeing him reading the side of a cereal box, and he had recently asked for granola instead of Honey Nut Cheerios.

"Look at this though," Mark said. "I've never seen a label like this."

"Who would put a label on tomatoes?" Vicky asked. She took the container from Mark and read the label, "Grown from Genetically Modified Seeds." She turned the container over and read the back, "To increase shelf-life, slow rotting, and ensure crisp skin and fruit."

"What does Genetically Modified Seeds mean?" Mark asked.

"I don't know," Vicky paused. "I mean, I understand all the

words, but I've never heard of anything like this before." She put the tomatoes in her cart. "We'll buy these and see what we can learn."

She dropped Mark and the groceries off at the house and immediately went to the library. Susan was there again. She smiled at Vicky.

"How are you doing?" Susan asked.

"Oh, thanks so much for asking," Vicky said. "Overwhelmed. But now I have a new puzzle to solve."

"Distractions are always good," said Susan. "What can I help you with?"

"Have you ever heard of these?" Vicky handed Susan the empty Flavr Savr container.

"Tomatoes?" Susan asked.

Vicky laughed. "No, the specific brand. And, really, more this label."

Susan looked at it and said the words, "Genetically modified."

"Right, that."

"I don't know precisely what that means," Susan said, "but there's a long history of cross-pollinating plants, and selecting certain varieties, and I know you can splice some trees and plants together. Maybe it's that?" She stepped from behind the counter and walked over to the card catalog.

Vicky followed her.

Susan flipped through the cards as Vicky watched over her shoulder.

"Hmm, maybe plant hybridization?" Susan asked. "That's an old book though and doesn't look like fun reading."

They found *Plant hybridization before Mendel* by Herbert Fuller Roberts and sat on the floor flipping through the pages.

"There's definitely stuff in here that seems relevant, but from 1929," said Susan. "What are you looking for exactly?"

Good question, Vicky thought. She and Dean had been more careful about what they ate since the diagnosis, Mark was right about that, and she certainly spent more time reading ingredients and paying attention to what she put in her body, but she'd never bought Flavr Savr tomatoes before. So, just what did she want?

"I'm just curious, I guess," Vicky said.

"Okay." Susan put the book back on the shelf. "Let me call a librarian I know at the U and see if she can help me find something for you that's more recent. Like within a decade at least." Susan laughed and climbed to her feet.

"Thank you," Vicky said.

When Vicky got home from Dr. Collins' office, she saw a message on the machine. She played it and listened to Susan.

"Hi Vicky, your books came in today. I'm afraid some of them are very, oh what's the right word. Scientific? I guess. Which is fine, I'm sure, because you're smart and maybe it will give you what you want. But, I don't know, just listen to the titles: *The Use of Single Seed Selection in Combination with Single Seed Descent for Modifying Oil Content in Soybeans* by L P Bonetti (1978), *The Status of Development of Maize with Improved Protein Quality* by L F Bauman and E.T. Mertz (1983), *Biological Effects of Radiation* by J E Coggle (1983), and *Federal Register: Part II, Department of Agriculture, Animal and Plant Health Inspection Service: 7 CFR Parts 330 and 340: Plant Pests; Introduction of Genetically Engineered Organisms or Products; Final Rule* by the USDA (1987)."

There was a pause, and Vicky wasn't sure if Susan had been cut off, or if that was just the end of her message, and then Susan started speaking again.

"But, there is one, *Genetically Modified Food* by Christopher Barclay (1994). It actually comes from our sister city's library, you know, in Hungerford? I guess this book was published over there, so they had a copy. It looks much more," Susan paused again. "Approachable? Anyway, come in when—" the tape cut off the rest of her words.

Vicky drove straight to the library. It was a bright day, and her sunglasses barely seemed to be making a difference. She parked and walked in and up to the counter, completely forgetting her glasses were still on.

"Vicky! I have your books right here," Susan scooted the

five books over to the scanner and held out her hand expectantly for the library card. "I'm sorry. I know I'm probably way too excited about this, but it's been a fun little project for me." Susan was about to say something else but stopped. "Are you okay?" Her hand dropped and she came around from behind the counter.

Susan held Vicky as the tears ran down from behind her sunglasses. Then she walked Vicky behind the counter and into the office and handed her some tissues.

"I'm so sorry." Susan said.

"I came right here from Dr. Collins'," Vicky said. "I haven't told anyone. And it's silly for me to get so upset."

"No it isn't."

"Yes, I knew, I knew the answer. I've known this whole time."

"Still," said Susan. "You're never ready to hear someone say those words."

In the silence between them, Vicky heard another voice. "What's that?"

"Oh, just C-SPAN," said Susan. She gestured and Vicky followed, seeing the television in the corner of the office.

They watched as Sandra Day O'Connor took center screen. They heard her say, "I don't have a magic wand to wave."

"Can you turn that up?" Vicky asked.

Susan did, and together they listened to Supreme Court Justice Sandra Day O'Connor talk about her experience with breast cancer. Though she was first diagnosed in 1987, she had never spoken about it before now. She talked about the shock and frustration she felt at the process, how scary it was, how many questions there were to answer, how the doctors didn't have the answers she wanted them to have, how suddenly she was expected to know what to do with her body and all the choices she had to make, and how she had tell and retell her story over and over again with each new specialist or doctor's visit—it was like none of them communicated with one another, or shared their notes. But, most importantly to Vicky, Sandra said the word mastectomy. Right there, on television, in front of however many people were watching. And that was all Vicky needed.

When Vicky and Dean went to see Dr. Collins together, she announced she would have a double mastectomy. Both men seemed a little surprised by how certain she was, but she said, "I want to do everything possible to make sure this never comes back."

And that's what she did. In the meantime, she read the books from the library and learned about genetically modified foods. Initially, she thought maybe that they were causing cancer, but eventually she understood that genetic modification wasn't so different from the long history of farmers selecting seeds and splicing plants and finding ways to produce more out of less and create hardier crops. Of course, there were differences, but the more she read, the more she understood she wanted to grow her own food, and she didn't want to use pesticides or chemicals.

She found a name for this: Organic farming. She was surprised to learn that it had its roots in England with people like Edgar J. Saxon and Frank Newman Turner and Albert Howard. Vicky read more books and shared what she was learning with Regina. The more they read, the more invested in the topic they became, and the more serious Regina and Vicky were about creating their own greenhouse.

When Vicky's five-year check-up revealed that she was still cancer-free, they made some progress. The families had a serious conversation about the dream becoming a reality and started setting money aside each month. The Websters had two of their three kids in college. Barry was graduating this year and Mark was a sophomore, but Michael was a senior in high school. The McKinneys were able to invest a little more because they only had David as a junior in college, and Russell still had four years before he graduated from high school. Still, the amount they were talking about saving was pretty meager. They set themselves a goal of learning as much as they could, and then reassessing their goals in five years.

Five years later, in 2004, Vicky was still cancer-free. While they had amassed a decent nest-egg, it came with its struggles. Each family had reduced or stopped contributions at different times, and even borrowed from the pot. But now all the kids, except for Russell McKinney, were done with college. Vicky and Regina were sitting at the Drowsy Parrot, enjoying a midday coffee, and "running the numbers." That's what Regina called it, but really it was just looking at a spreadsheet and checking the property listings in the *Opole Record*.

"Well, the numbers look," Regina paused as she scrolled up and down in the spreadsheet, "better than last year. That's good."

"Better than not," Vicky added. "Anything good in the listings?"

Regina handed her the paper without looking up from the laptop.

Vicky wasn't sure what Regina was looking for; it was the same spreadsheet they'd had going for years now. It wasn't like she was going to find a hidden lump of money buried in the data somewhere. And yet, Vicky could see her out of the corner of her eye, scrolling down and down and then back up and up. Vicky turned her attention to the paper. Nothing really exciting.

"You know," Vicky said. She had an idea and wasn't sure why this hadn't occurred to her before. "What about something in Ann Arbor Township? Maybe sticking to Opole is too narrow?"

"That's a great idea," Regina said. "Not that I think it will be any cheaper, but I bet it would give us more options at least. Do you think they have a copy of the *News* here?" She began to look around the coffee shop. There was someone reading the *Ann Arbor News*. She left the computer and walked over to the table. Now that she was standing, she could see it was Brenda Walker.

Regina and Brenda had never been friends, but they also had never been unfriendly. It was just that Brenda was more Esther's friend, and Brenda lived north of the loop. When they saw one another at the store, or at a town event, they smiled and chatted, but that was the extent of their relationship.

"Hi Brenda," Regina said.

Brenda tipped her paper down and smiled. "Hi!"

Regina was pleased that Brenda sounded genuinely happy to see her. "I was wondering if I could borrow your paper when you're done."

"I've been done with this paper for years, but somehow I find myself still looking through it hoping to find a reason to keep the subscription going," Brenda said. She laughed. "You can have it. Anything in particular you're looking for?"

"Land," said Regina. "And piles of money."

Brenda laughed.

"It's a silly dream we've been chasing for the last, I don't know how many years." Regina gestured over at Vicky.

"Dreams are important," Brenda said. "That's the kind of shit that keeps us going, right?"

"For sure."

"What's the dream?" Brenda asked. "If you don't mind my asking."

"A greenhouse."

"Oh, interesting," said Brenda. "I might actually be able to help."

"Well, join us then. Heck, I'll even buy you a coffee!"

Regina and Brenda joined Vicky at the table. Vicky's nose was still buried in the *Opole Record*, but the sound of Regina's chair scooting alerted her to her friend's presence. "This one is kind of interesting," she looked up as she tapped on a listing. "Oh, hi." She smiled at Brenda.

"Brenda says we can have her paper, but she also said might be able to help with our secret project."

"Less a secret if you include me," laughed Brenda.

"Well, I doubt our $25,577.38 is going to make it happen any time soon on our own, so why not include a third?" said Vicky.

They filled her in on the big picture idea. It didn't take long.

"That sounds pretty amazing," said Brenda. "But it is

definitely going to cost you more than the 25k you have socked away." She paused. "How long have you been saving?"

"Ten years?" Vicky said.

"Give or take," said Regina. "But it will go faster after Russ is out of school."

"Have you considered applying for a grant?"

Vicky and Regina answered her question with a blank stare.

Brenda cleared her throat and continued. "I dated a guy from Michigan State. Kyle. He was nice, but it just didn't work for us. Still friends and see him now and then," Brenda paused. "I don't remember his exact title, but he did something with agriculture and was always working on grants. If you want, I could connect you with him and see if he can help."

"I really don't know much about grants," Vicky said. "Do you have to pay those back?"

"No," Brenda said. "He was always saying, it's free money! They're just giving it away!"

"It can't be free," said Regina. "There has to be a catch."

"Sometimes you have to report back, or be part of a study, or work within a certain set of parameters. But, otherwise, it really is free."

"Free is good," said Vicky.

"I like free," said Regina.

Kyle turned out to be very helpful. He connected Two Buds with the people who would form the Michigan Greenhouse Growers Council (MGGC) in 2005, and, more importantly, connected them with the various grant opportunities available through the state of Michigan, Michigan State University, and the University of Michigan. Kyle also gave them sample grants to look at and offered his thoughts and reviewed their applications when they were done. Regina and Vicky seemed to be naturals at the process, and Kyle was surprised by how little he had to offer and how much they knew about precisely what they wanted. When they got together, they bought him dinner, but otherwise all he asked for was access to the greenhouse so he could use it in his research. And that's how Brenda became an unofficial, silent, third partner of Two Buds. They considered changing it to Three Buds, but decided it didn't quite have the same ring to it.

Two Buds wasn't the first greenhouse of its kind in the state, but it was on the cutting edge of what was possible. As a result, there was a lot of interest in their applications, and they qualified for $50,000 in funding for greenhouse construction, $50,000 from the "green fund," and another grant for $50,000 for organic farming. That exceeded their expectations, but when all was said and done, there wasn't a lot left over to buy plants, soil, or other supplies. It did mean they had no loans, didn't have to mortgage their houses, and they could invest all their time and energies into making the greenhouse work. With the 26% back from Federal taxes on the solar panels, and the 25k the families had saved over the years, they were off to a good start.

Just as Horatio's Cheese Shoppe had been a slight oddity in Opole, so it was for Two Buds Greenhouse. Kyle had assured Regina and Vicky that a "deep winter greenhouse" (that was his phrase, but not one Regina and Vicky ever adopted) was an outstanding idea, unique to the region, and would definitely bring people flocking for fresh produce year-round. Sadly, that wasn't so much the case. It was not a money-maker, but Two Buds only really needed to sustain itself as a hobby for the friends. Some years it lost a little money, and others it came out a bit ahead. When Michigan first passed the state's medical marijuana law in 2008, Vicky, Regina, and Brenda thought maybe growing weed would put them squarely in the profitability column. But then the law was tied up in the courts and legislation and so they didn't seriously pursue it.

While Vicky and Regina were the public face of Two Buds, it really was a family endeavor. The kids enjoyed working in the greenhouse, and Jim and Dean were eager for the greenhouse to turn enough of a profit so they could leave their "regular" jobs behind. It took about six years for the greenhouse to start turning a reliable profit, but by then Jim and Dean were close to retirement and the families still needed health insurance. So they kept on doing what they were doing, applying for grants, reporting their findings, and expanding as much as they could afford to.

In 2013, by the time the courts and state government sorted everything out regarding medicinal marijuana, Two Buds was ready to expand and add that as a crop. It didn't take long before that out-paced the demand for anything else they grew. It was all carefully regulated and cleverly labeled "Two Buds' bud," and they had to regularly defend themselves saying, "No, really, we never named ourselves Two Buds because we ever thought we'd grow marijuana." It was hard to convince people that was true, and yet it was.

Monetary benefits aside, both families found they were eating much healthier. Dean had already become a vegetarian a few years ago, so having fresh fruits and vegetables around was a huge win for him. Not everyone joined Dean in becoming vegetarian, but they all certainly shifted in that direction. Regina in particular lost a lot of weight. She liked the additional attention and casual whistles from Jim but was a little puzzled by everyone fixating on how thin she looked.

"Look! I don't know what to tell you," she would say. "I'm eating healthier, and I get more exercise from running around the greenhouse all day."

But even in quiet moments when Regina and Vicky were opening or closing the greenhouse, Regina couldn't escape someone commenting on her weight.

"I'm concerned," said Vicky as she deadheaded a coneflower.

"Not this again," said Regina. "I'm fine. All bodies handle foods differently. I guess mine's just really happy on this diet."

"It's not just the weight," Vicky said. "You're tired a lot."

"Who isn't?" Regina sighed and pushed her hair back, leaving a smudge of dirt on her face. "I mean, there's always something to do here. I'm always running here or there, and yeah, I get tired."

"It just seems like, you're more tired than usual."

"Maybe," said Regina. "I don't know." She shrugged. "Jim

was on me too, trying to get me to go see Dr. Collins. But, really, what am I going to say? Hey doc, I'm in the best shape I've ever been in before, I'm happier than ever, and I have a business that keeps me busy and exhausts me at the end of the day. I mean, what am I complaining about?"

Vicky caved. "I know it sounds silly. I mean, I'm turning 64 this year. So that means you're what, 61? What old person doesn't get a little tired and have some aches and pains?" She stood up and helped Regina load some pots in the wagon.

"Right?"

"We good?"

Regina nodded and that was that, until she went in for her annual physical. Dr. Collins recommended some tests and scans, and before she knew it, Regina was going through the same rigmarole her friend had fifteen years earlier. Despite the years that had passed, little had changed in the patient-experience world. Regina found herself telling her story over and over again to each specialist and having to fill out forms that she thought they would have had forwarded from the previous office. "This is 2015!" she'd complain to Vicky, and all her friend could do was console her. It wasn't until she had a clear diagnosis and plan forward that Regina told the families.

They all gathered for dinner, but hardly anyone ate. Finally, Regina put down her fork and said, "Look. I know what you're going to say. That I'm crazy to not take the radiation or do the surgery or whatever."

The looks from her husband, children, and the Websters confirmed that suspicion.

"But, it's not going to do any good. It started in my pancreas and now it's," she paused, thinking that she was going to cry, but then realized there were no tears, "it's everywhere."

The tension went out of everyone's shoulders at once.

"So, I have, maybe a year? Maybe two? I don't know. But I'm not going to spend that time sick and in hospitals. I want to go places. I want to be with you. I want to enjoy as much as I can before I go."

So that's what they did. They traveled. They did everything

they could to keep her comfortable and happy. And Regina had another reason to be grateful for Two Buds, because Two Buds' bud was one of the few things that kept the pain at bay. Prior to her diagnosis, the families had not ever really consumed their product. They tested it and occasionally the kids smoked some out back, but none of them had ever regularly indulged. Now it formed a sort of support group because they never let Regina smoke alone. When they did smoke, they talked and laughed and flipped through memories of the trips they had taken.

CHAPTER 14: GETTING THE GANG BACK TOGETHER

Overall, Esther was content with her acquisition of digital friends, but she found odd things happened from time to time. For instance, she realized one day that she was no longer friends on Facebook with one of her oldest friends in life, Brenda Walker. At first, Esther chalked it up to a computer glitch, and sent a new friend request to Brenda. Weeks later, however, Brenda still had not accepted her friend request. Esther tried to send a new friend request and was told, "You've sent this person a friend request." Esther assumed this meant that the request had gone through. She checked Brenda's page to see if there was any recent activity; there wasn't. Esther thought perhaps she just couldn't see the recent activity because they weren't friends. Could her old friend be ignoring her on purpose? Or, maybe she just didn't know how to accept friend requests, or didn't see the notification? Or, maybe her friend had fallen and needed help. Esther realized she hadn't seen Brenda, in real life, for at least a month, maybe a little more. She decided to rectify that immediately. Well, almost immediately. First, she had to figure out where Brenda lived. She no longer had her address.

Esther had so thoroughly disappeared into her virtual world that she had forgotten about the real world around her and how to interact with it. As she took to the sidewalk to retrace a route she had walked a million times before, she found herself exhausted barely halfway into the route. Had she really covered all this ground and more in those old days? Or was this just a trick of how memory distorts things? Her route seemed bigger and longer than it did before. In her hey-day, at the height of her crime-stopper phase, after she turned in Bill and turned her eye firmly to crime, she had expanded her route from moving directly between the southern and northern jog to covering a much wider swathe of the town. Now, here she was just starting and already tired. In the old days, she took a lot of breaks by visiting people along the way. Today, no one seemed to be around. All the doors were locked. Esther knocked a few times, rang the doorbell, but saw no signs of life. Off she went to the next home. Where was everybody? She left her home where she was so well "liked" and so often "shared," and found herself sweating as she hoofed it between empty houses. Esther used to own this neighborhood; what had happened in the intervening years?

Esther arrived at the door of the Websters' home. Esther remembered when they first moved in; the house was a nice mauve color, but Dean insisted on painting it before he would move anything in there.

"I'm not living in a pink house," he said.

And so they painted it a soothing blue color. But, it took a couple coats and it delayed the Websters from actually moving in. Six years ago, Vicky overruled her husband's declaration about the color, and the house was painted mauve again—albeit, a slightly different tone.

Dean said, "I'm fine with this. This, this is a nice color. That other color, ugh, it was terrible."

Esther remembered what the house first looked like, and could clearly see the current color was almost exactly the same.

Something had changed over the course of time, and Esther wasn't sure if it was the power dynamic in the Webster household, Dean's ability to discern color, Dean's willingness to accept things that his younger self would have seen as an assault on his masculinity, or maybe crossing the threshold into his sixties made him realize what fights were worth having, and which were not. Esther rang the doorbell again and waited. No answer.

No answer at the McKinney's house. None at the Matthew's. No answer at the Bennett's. The same at the Christensen's. Esther turned northward and passed the jog. No answer at the Schwartz's house. No answer at the Townsend's. No answer at the Marshall's. None at the Norton's. And none at the Bates' house. Esther was about to give up, when someone finally answered the second time she rang the doorbell at the Lambert house.

"Esther," said Patty. Patty hadn't seen Esther in quite a while. In fact, when she paused to think about it, she couldn't recall the last time she had seen Esther in person. She saw all Esther's updates on Facebook and felt like she knew what was going on with Esther, but Patty hadn't really seen her in a long time. Patty couldn't help but be disappointed with how Esther looked. The picture she had as her profile had to be twenty years old. Patty immediately felt ashamed when she realized she was judging Esther and her weight gain. Patty certainly looked nothing like she had twenty years ago, and really, who past fifty looks like their former self?

"Can I come in?" Esther asked.

"Of course, of course," Patty said. If the outward appearance of the old town gossip was a shock, then the fact that she asked permission to enter her house instead of barging in was even a greater one.

Esther found a seat on the couch and leaned on her elbows. "Where is everyone?" she asked.

"Busy, I guess. You know, grandchildren, and errands, and some of us still have jobs and haven't retired yet."

"You're the only home; I must have tried twenty doors," Esther said. "What happened to the old days?"

Patty laughed. "Well, they're called the old days for a reason. They're in the past. We all change and move on."

Esther knew this was true, but it made the news no less disappointing. When she left her house this morning, she had assumed she'd be able to slide back into her old routine and get caught up. It was definitely proving to be more difficult than she had imagined. Esther thought briefly of her computer and the ease of messaging, liking, and clicking, but then remembered why she was out and about. She wanted, no she NEEDED to know where Brenda was, and why she hadn't accepted her friend request.

"Do you ever hear from Brenda?" Esther asked.

"Oh, her house has been bought and sold three times since she moved out," said Patty. She sat on a chair perpendicular to Esther, and rested her cell phone on her knee. She pressed the side button and checked the time.

"Oh?" Esther didn't know this, but it wasn't really what she came to find out. "What about Brenda herself though, and Thomas, and the kids?"

"I don't hear from them often," said Patty. She checked her phone again. "You know, once they moved out of the neighborhood, we just saw them less and less."

"What about the others?" asked Esther.

"Well, I was never very close with Regina and Jim, but Becky Schwartz and Suzy Townsend and I still get together now and then. Craig, Becky's husband, is almost retired. They spend a lot of time with their kids, Tiffany and Sean. One of them lives out east, Connecticut I think? The other is in Arizona. Suzy and Ray are doing fine, and so are Lisa and Jane. Both girls are married now."

"Ever hear from Vicky?" Esther asked.

"A little," said Patty. She checked her phone again. "Here and there."

"And?" Esther prodded.

"Oh, I don't know," said Patty. She glanced at her phone.

The silence and curt responses made Esther uncomfortable. She decided to get to the point.

"The reason I'm here is that I wanted to find Brenda. Do you have her address? I don't have the most current one."

"Sure, here." Patty fiddled with her phone. "I'll message the info to you." She clicked and typed, and then set her phone down.

"I didn't bring my phone with me," said Esther. "I'll check when I get home." Leaving her phone at home had been an intentional choice, but it felt so strange to be momentarily disconnected from her fully-engaged digital world. She thought the walk and the chat with Patty would make her feel more like her old self, but now she wasn't so sure.

Patty kept eying her phone, and it was obvious she was bored. In the old days, Esther would be able to generate conversation by plucking it from thin air, but now she was struggling. What did she have in common with this woman? Esther ran through possible conversation points and realized she had nothing worth saying. She could talk about the weather, or say something about her own grandchildren, but neither seemed interesting. Who cared about the weather? Patty hadn't asked about Bruce. In the past, that wouldn't have stopped Esther, but something had definitely changed over time.

"Well, I should probably get going," Esther said. She really had nowhere to go, but figured she'd continue to explore up and around the town, just for the sake of completeness.

Patty stood up and opened the door for Esther. "Well, it was nice to see you." She debated offering the typical nicety of, "You look great," or "We should get together," but Patty found she was too old for that kind of thing. As she aged, she found she cared less about being "polite" and more about being direct.

"Thank you," said Esther. "See you later."

Esther took off again on the old familiar sidewalk, but she

didn't continue to bother with ringing doorbells or knocking on doors. She did pause briefly at Brenda's old house and recalled helping her plant tulip bulbs one spring. There was that weeping willow that Thomas, Brenda's second husband, bought and planted for her to celebrate their anniversary. The tree had grown substantially. Esther remembered how the boys used to break the branches off the tree and whip one another with them. Why did kids like to do that? Getting whipped by those branches had to hurt, and it was always the littlest siblings that wound up crying. Esther blamed that damn Indiana Jones for the kids' fascination with whips. She shook her head. Brenda and Esther used to scold them for damaging the tree, but the tree had come through the ordeal just fine. The kids had turned out fine, too, and no one ever lost an eye.

Esther kept walking. There was an Aldi where Carol's Photography once stood. Mieszko's Cheese Chalet now occupied the building where Horatio's Cheese Shoppe once was. Esther was amused to see the resurgence of Polish names, like Mieszko in the community. Horatio's was an anomaly at best in the 80s, but Mieszko's appeared to be thriving. The parking lot was packed. Esther worked her way into the chalet and found a serpentine line of people snaked around the inside. Each held a number and waited in various levels of patience. Though the line was long, each customer was treated with the same amount of attention that the previous one had received. Samples were offered, suggestions were made, and the attendants saw to the customer's every need. Other than the people inside, the store looked much the same as Horatio's had. Esther worked her way up to the display case.

"What happened to Horatio?" she asked.

The attendants ignored her, because their attention was focused on the customer whose number had been drawn. A man, waiting with two children, gestured towards the ticket dispensing machine. "Take a number," he said. "Like the rest of us."

"I just wanted to know what happened to the former

owner," sighed Esther.

Back home, Esther checked her phone. There was the message from Patty with Brenda's address. Esther considered the address. Should she just drop by, or should she call? Dropping by was easy when they lived in the same neighborhood, but now she was looking at a twenty-minute drive. She still didn't like to drive, but she really wanted to see Brenda. Finally Esther decided to drop in. It felt the most like what she would have done in the old days, and though she didn't want to admit the possibility, it also prevented Brenda from avoiding her by being conveniently "busy." So, she got in the car and drove.

Esther never was much of a driver, but lately she hardly ever ventured out. Since it was just her at home, she didn't have to grocery shop frequently, and most of her dry goods she was content to acquire through Amazon. The same went for her clothing. Even though she only wore the same five or six outfits regularly, she had a huge collection of clothing. With Jeffrey gone, Bruce out of the house, and the guest bedroom so rarely used, she had four bedroom closets to fill. Her closets contained clothing from the 80s and 90s, which no longer fit her. She could have donated them, but she was convinced that she'd be wearing them again someday. She rarely opened the closet anyway. Instead, the clothing she wore regularly sat in neat stacks on her dresser. Why bother putting them away if she was just going to wear them again? And, besides, who was seeing her bedroom these days? If Esther gained a few more pounds, then she had the truly "fat" clothes in the guest bedroom closet to draw from. If she lost some, then she could visit Bruce's old closet. And, if by some miracle, she dropped back to her powerwalking heyday weight, then she could stroll through her own closet. On the rare occasion she needed something new, there was always the internet. This drive to Brenda's house was going to be the longest she'd taken in quite some time.

Esther drove to the address from Patty, pulled into the driveway, turned off the car, and sat. She checked and doublechecked the address. She looked for anything familiar that would register her old friend's presence, but the cars were different, the house was unfamiliar, and in short, she recognized nothing. The garage door was open and two cars were parked inside. That meant either someone left the garage door open when they left, or someone was home. Esther was betting on the latter. Eventually she mustered her courage, left the car, and knocked on the front door. It would have been more direct and easier to approach the house through the open garage door, and knock on the house door there, which is how she assumed the Walkers (assuming this was their house) came and went regularly, but since she wasn't sure she had the right place, and she hadn't seen her old friend in so long, Esther approached in the most formal way possible.

As soon as she knocked on the door, she began to have doubts. If this were her house, and she came and went through the garage, as she assumed the Walkers, or whomever lived here, did, then if someone knocked on the front door, Esther would assume they were a stranger. Or, worse, someone selling something. Maybe they wouldn't answer the door out of principle? She didn't see any sign indicating no soliciting, but that didn't mean someone inside wouldn't see a person he or she didn't recognize and ignore the knock entirely. Esther waited longer than usual, and then rang the doorbell. She could hear the electronic sound bing-bong throughout the house. Then footsteps. Then a deadbolt was thrown. Then the knob was turned.

There was her old friend. Brenda.

"Hello!" Brenda's smile seemed genuine. If she was surprised to see Esther on her front porch, she did a very good job hiding it. "Come in."

Esther walked into the house, Brenda closed the door, and then asked her, "How are you? Is everything okay?"

"Fine," said Esther. "You? I haven't heard from you in a

while."

"Oh, we're good. Just busy, you know."

Esther kept hearing about people being busy, but frankly, she wasn't really sure what kept them so busy. If her son lived nearer, or if he allowed her to visit more—she had stopped asking and now just waited for his invitation, or if her husband was still living, maybe she would have a better sense of what they meant. She filled her days, but there was a difference between being busy and making yourself busy. Esther made herself busy, and she wondered if maybe everyone else wasn't doing the same and was only calling it something different.

Esther realized Brenda was looking at her intently, apparently waiting for some response of some sort while Esther had been puzzling out how to ask Brenda about the Facebook friendship request. It probably wasn't a big thing. There was probably a simple explanation and she'd feel silly for asking, but she couldn't leave Brenda's house without knowing. She could see her friend was just fine. Nothing bad had happened to her. Now she just needed to know the other part. Typically, she would have directly asked her question. When she was curious about Regina's underwear, she just asked. When she wanted information, she reached out and grabbed it. But now, with such an easy question, such a stupid question, she found herself floundering.

"It's silly, but I," she stammered. "I'm wondering if," she paused, unsure, "if you received my," was she really going to ask this? She was, "friend request."

"What?" asked Brenda confused.

"My friend request. Did you get my friend request?" asked Esther.

"On Facebook? Oh, I don't know. I don't spend much time on that thing," said Brenda evasively. She knew that was a copout, even if it was partly true. Brenda sighed. She owed it to her friend to be a little more honest, "Besides, it seems like you and I just have different opinions on things."

So, she did know, and she had received it. Esther was

finding some of her old confidence. "What do you mean, different opinions? And on what things?"

"Well, I like Facebook to see pictures of cats and kids, and you seem to like to talk politics," said Brenda.

"You can do both."

"I could, but I just don't care about politics, and it ruins my day when I read some of the things you and other people write." Brenda said. She was finding it easier to be direct and honest. "I mean, do you really believe all that stuff you write?"

"Of course," said Esther. Why would she write something she didn't believe? What a stupid question.

"Even the thing about Obama's face?"

"Yeah," said Esther. "I was so tired of seeing him everywhere. People talk about him like he's the best president, and his face was everywhere. Have you looked at it? Have you really looked at it? It's a pretty stupid face."

"Okay," said Brenda carefully. "This is what I mean. I don't need this stuff in my life. There are more important things."

"Like what?" Esther knew it was an inane thing to say the second the words left her mouth. There were so many more important things in life than social media, news, and politics. She felt backed into a corner. Brenda was putting down the new "neighborhood" Esther had created for herself.

"Well, of course, lots of things. Like what about Regina's dying?"

"What?" Esther heard and understood the words Brenda had spoken, but threw the "what" out there to buy time to actually process what she'd heard. "Regina's dying." No, she hadn't heard. She didn't know. A thing like this, this was precisely why she needed Brenda to accept her friend request because surely Regina's dying would have been something that would have been shared on Facebook. Right?

"When is the last time you checked in with her or Jim?"

"I dropped by their house today, but nobody was home," Esther said. Even as she said it she knew it was a lame excuse. Prior to today, she hadn't made any attempt to see them in a number of years. Maybe even a very many number of years.

"Yeah, they're not home. She's in the hospital."

"Why?"

"She's dying of cancer. They tried chemo, and it's not going well. She doesn't have long," said Brenda. She couldn't remember a time when she had information to lord over Esther, and she was enjoying the power trip more than she had expected. But she felt bad because she could see her old friend was struggling with the news.

"I had no idea," Esther said. "I hadn't heard. I didn't see anything about it."

"It's really not the type of thing you make public. Or, at least, it's not something she wants public."

"She's only sixty-one. Or is it sixty-two? I can't remember," Esther said.

"It doesn't matter. Pancreatic cancer doesn't care about how old you are."

"She has pancreatic cancer?"

Brenda didn't answer. Esther was going through the same process Brenda had when she initially found out two months ago. It was hard to process. She knew that. Of the old crew, Vicky was the oldest of them, but only by a year. Regina was two years younger than both Brenda and Esther, so making sense of the news about Regina was as much about confronting your own mortality as it was about preparing to lose one of your friends.

"Wow," said Esther. "What are her chances of survival?"

"She's not going to survive," Brenda said bluntly. She had asked the same thing, and initially the answer had been, "There is less than a 10% chance of a 5-year survival rate," but it quickly turned to 0% when Regina said she didn't want take the meds and deal with the treatments anymore. The doctors didn't say zero percent as there was always a very small chance of something happening without intervention, but it was very, very, very, very unlikely. Brenda visited Regina in the hospital a couple times a week, and they'd chat for as long as Regina was able. Sometimes Regina would be too tired to carry her end of the conversation, and Brenda would just yammer on about what her kids and grandkids were up to or about how she was trying to grow these colorful varieties of potatoes in the garden this year. Brenda and Regina hadn't been the oldest of friends, but since the 1987 Wianki, their friendship had grown, and in the last ten years Brenda came to call Regina her best friend. None of this was known to Esther.

Brenda and Esther sat there for a little while, but neither woman had much else to say. They made small talk for another thirty minutes, and then Esther drove home. Esther turned the news of Regina's cancer over and over in her mind. When she got home, she hit the ground running. She started on her old route again and tried to "share" the news the old-fashioned way. It seemed that everyone already knew. Someone had scooped her. Worse, she had been left out of the loop.

Regina died a week after Esther learned she was sick, before Esther had a chance to visit her. Unlike the news of Regina's cancer, the news of her memorial was circulated widely on social media. Even if it hadn't, Esther would have heard about it from Brenda. Esther was trying very hard to reconnect with her old friend, and while Brenda was willing, she just didn't have much faith in Esther.

The thing that brought them back together again for good, ironically enough, was Daniel Byrd—the very thing that had broken their friendship in the first place. Brenda came over to Esther's house and found her on the computer. It was a surprise drop-by, so Esther didn't have time to prepare for a visitor. Since Esther had already dropped by Brenda's house, Brenda felt no need to knock or ring the doorbell; she just let herself in.

"Oh!" said Esther, getting up from her chair.

"No, no need to get up," said Brenda. She pulled up a chair next to Esther, and looked at the screen in front of her. The browser took up the full screen, and it only had one tab open:

Facebook.

"Almost done for the day," said Esther, slightly embarrassed. If her friend had not interrupted, Esther would not have been done for the day. She would have kept on reading and clicking for several more hours.

"Anything good?"

"Not really," said Esther. Brenda made it very clear she had no interest in politics, and that was about all Esther was up to these days. "Oh, there is one thing you might find funny." She typed the name "Daniel Byrd" into the search box. His profile popped up.

"No!" said Brenda. She leaned forward, closer to the screen.

"Yes. The one and the same," said Esther. She provided a virtual tour for her friend of Daniel's page and photographs.

"Look at him," said Brenda. "He used to think he was so cool, all hot and like God's gift to women. Time has not been kind to him."

"No, but look at us. We're old, too," laughed Esther. In truth, her friend was on the opposite end of the spectrum from her; Brenda was a youthful sixty-three, and Esther looked her age, maybe even a little older. By comparing herself to Brenda, she was doing herself a kindness she didn't deserve, but Brenda didn't seem to mind.

"Remember," started Brenda. And the two friends fell down the rabbit hole of shared memories that brought them together again, as if the distance of the last decade or two hadn't happened.

They might have remained knit together like that if Esther had been a little more restrained at Regina's memorial. Unfortunately, during the walk down memory lane, Esther became trapped in the past. Memory and reflection are welcome at memorials, but Esther went a bit too far. It started well enough. She dressed appropriately, even dug into clothes from a closet she hadn't looked at in a year or more. Esther mingled nicely with everyone and looked at the photographs that were displayed around. She felt a bit like a ghost, moving in and out of groups of people without being noticed. These were people she had known most of her life, and yet no one said anything to her. Of course, they weren't here for her, she reminded herself, they were here for Regina. And yet, where had they been when Jeffrey died?

Jeffrey's funeral had been well-attended, but it was nothing like this crowd. Esther thought the room might burst at the seams. This group was truly was an "outpouring of support from the community" that Esther knew for a fact was nothing like her experience when her husband died. She felt a little miffed as she looked around at all the faces grieving Regina and comforting the family.

All "the boys" and their friends had come home for Regina's memorial and were comfortably hanging out talking. Wianki aside, this was the first time they had all been together since they graduated from high school. Esther saw Regina and James McKinney's David and Russell; Victoria and Dean Webster's Barry, Mark, and Michael; Becky and Craig Schwartz's Tiffany and Sean; Brenda and Thomas Walker's Betsy, Angie, and Larry; Patty and Richard Lambert's Jason and Rodney; and Suzy and Raymond Townsend's Lisa and Jane. Even Bruce had come. Miranda stayed home with the kids because it was too expensive for them all to come for an event that only he would fully appreciate. When Jeffrey passed, some of the kids were still in school and didn't make it back for his funeral, but now most of them were established. At the time, it seemed that everyone had reasonable excuses for not attending Jeffrey's funeral. Esther hadn't thought to question it—plus she was buried in her own grief. Now, surrounded by an "outpouring of support," she suddenly saw the excuses in a different light. They should have been there for her, too.

The "kids" stood around in a large circle telling stories as they let the past swirl around and distract them from the reason they had gathered.

"Mom never did find out that I was part of it," said Barry.

"We were so lucky," said Bruce. "I can't believe you didn't rat us out."

"Ha!" laughed David. "I think my dad was more impressed than upset, but he certainly couldn't have said that in front of my mom."

"I've always wondered," asked Michael, "was it you guys that smashed our snowmen?"

"Yeah," said David. "It was. Sorry about that. I don't know why, we just did crap like that. I remember your big brother saying we shouldn't do it, that you would get upset."

"Well, he was like five," said Barry. "Of course, he was going to get upset." Since they were coming clean about things from the past, he was wondering if anyone was going to mention the April Fool's "joke" or not. They'd never been caught. As a pretty honest kid, and an honest man, that deception still weighed heavily on him.

"A kid at school said you guys did it, but you always swore to Mom and Dad that it wasn't you," said Michael. "Geez, I believed you. Makes me wonder what else you lied about."

"Jesus, you sound like Mom and Dad," said Barry. "That was what, twenty years ago?"

"Spoiler alert: there is no Santa Claus or Easter Bunny," said Bruce a little meanly. Unlike Barry, Bruce never thought about the April Fool's joke. They had barely replaced the borrowed items before it was off his conscious and out of his mind.

"Not everyone can be an angel like little Mikey," said Jason.

"You guys were such assholes," said Tiffany.

"Were?" asked David. "Did something change? I wear that name like a badge of honor." David did sometimes think about the April Fool's event, and he was overly critical of himself. Though he brushed off Tiffany's comment as if it were a joke, he really did feel like an asshole most of the time. David had a guilty conscience, but it didn't stop him from lying; it just meant he felt shittier and shittier about himself each time he told a lie.

"I never did anything like that. Lisa, did you do shit like that?" said Tiffany. She ignored David's comment.

"No," said Lisa. "What about you Angie?"

"I don't think girls think to smash things that other people have built," said Angie. "But, my big sis certainly put me through the wringer more than once."

"Please; you had it so easy," said Betsy. "You and little Larry. I broke mom in for you guys."

"I'm so glad I wasn't a girl," said Bruce. "You never got to have any fun like we did." He was doing some quick math in his head. "Then again, Tiff, you were like three or something, right?"

"In '87? Yeah," answered Tiffany. "Angie would have been old enough to run with you boys though."

"Except, I had girl germs," said Angie. She shook her head. "Silly boys, with your porn and guns and whatever else you were playing with."

"Not that we would have wanted to play with you anyway," said Lisa. "Cooties."

Esther enjoyed listening in and was piecing together the parts of stories she'd only heard snippets of when Jim interrupted everyone.

"If I can have your attention; we're gathering in the hall for a few words."

The McKinneys weren't particularly religious, but there was a pastor who led the ceremony. He started off with a reading, and a short piece he had prepared for the event. Esther, for the most part, ignored what the pastor had to say; she was focused on what she would say. She had a few notes, and as the pastor spoke, Esther kept reading over her scratchy writing. Finally the pastor said, "And now I'd like to give up the podium for anyone who would like to say something in memory of Regina McKinney."

Esther practically flew out of her seat.

Jim had also begun to rise, but when he saw Esther was

halfway to the microphone, he sat back down. Everyone in attendance assumed Jim would speak first, or maybe one of their children, but when they saw Esther walking up, they thought why not. Regina and Esther had known each other for quite a while. Jim and the children would go after Esther.

Esther powerwalked to the microphone and set her notes down. "I'm not sure anyone doesn't know who I am, but just in case, I'm Esther Fuhrman. It's hard to believe that Regina is gone. But, there it is. She is gone. We used to be close, but then we kind of went our own way and never had a chance to reconnect. I found out too late about her illness, and never... well. Jim and I never had a very close relationship, until this one year, and then after that we got along a lot better. It has never been like what Regina and I had, but now I guess it's all we have. I lost my husband to drunk driving. Such a sad and tragic way to go. Ever since his passing, I feel like I've lost my connection to this community and neighborhood. It took me a while, but I'm working to get that back now. I get out more, and I see people. It's good for me. And I've even lost a couple pounds since I started doing that." Esther stopped and looked down at her waist, it was noticeably smaller than it had been. "I remember that great Wianki celebration when Rodney Cone sang to us. That was such a magical night. He's such a talented singer; I really don't think he gets enough credit. I turn on the radio now and it's just full of this garbage." She laughed. This was going well. "But, Jeffrey is gone. Oh, my Jeffrey. And now Regina. It makes me sad. There goes the neighborhood, I guess. Brenda doesn't even live in the neighborhood anymore. You have to drive twenty minutes to get to her house. But, Patty is still there, and Suzy, and Vicky, and, of course, I am still there. I'm still there. Thank you."

There was silence as Esther walked back to her seat. Vicky stood up. She had no microphone, but in the silence of the room, she didn't need one. She looked directly at Esther.

"This. Isn't. About. You." Vicky emphasized every word with controlled anger. "How dare you compare your husband's death to Regina. He died because he drank and drove. Regina didn't deserve to die this way. She did nothing wrong." Vicky paused and looked around the room and turned her focus back to Esther. "You know, we were polite for all those years when you barged into our houses and blathered on about this or that or prattled about all the information you collected or made up on your routes. We felt SORRY for you to have no joy in your life other than to spread half-true stories about the lives of others. And now, you barge back into our lives, into Regina's FUNERAL and pretend like you knew her or even care at all about what she has been through. Your life was sad and pathetic before, but it's even more so now. Go back to your bridge, troll. Regina doesn't deserve this here today." Vicky sat back down.

Nobody knew what to do. Esther was frozen in place as was every other guest in the hall. Vicky was sobbing. Jim looked like he was about to get up to say something but didn't quite know how to do it. The uncomfortable silence lingered over the guests until suddenly Jim got up and purposefully walked to the microphone just as Esther got up and walked toward the exit.

"Well, that was something," Jim laughed apologetically as he gazed warmly at the friends and family gathered to celebrate his wife's life.

Esther had survived many public embarrassments before and was convinced that this would eventually blow over, too. She was wrong. She never did fully recover from the public shaming Vicky Webster dealt her at Regina's funeral. Esther coped by retreating deeper and deeper into her virtual world. The people online were so much more reasonable and accessible, and the feedback so rewarding and gratifying. Esther wasn't one to swear or curse much, but whenever she found herself recounting "the incident" at Regina's funeral, a short phrase echoed inside her head, "Fuck the town of Opole. Fuck the town of Opole." The third time she said it out loud.

"Fuck the town of Opole."

She was perfectly content right where she was.

"I have friends," Esther muttered to herself. "Thousands of friends."

The End.

AUTHOR'S NOTE

First of all, thanks to all those who helped make this book possible. Among those, these people especially:

- Heidi Wall Burns, editor, collaborator, idea-brainstormer, cover-design-assister, etc,
- Chris Field, early reader, idea-generator, patient and kind critiquer (even if I don't always listen),
- Gayle MacBride, first-reader, patiently tolerates being read-to, collaborator, idea-brainstormer, and
- Denise and Keith MacBride, early readers, patiently tolerates my questions, and happily reads and re-reads things.

Some people from my hometown of Saline might also recognize glimmers of truth or faded memories within these pages. Thanks for providing a community where I could grow up, wander the streets, do ridiculous things with friends, and learn to appreciate the smaller things in life. Flashing back on the memories made me appreciate how special that time of my life was, even if I didn't initially appreciate it then.

Opole is not Saline, just as the characters that populate this novel are not me or the people I grew up with, but this novel wouldn't have happened without the town or the people. So, thank you.

ABOUT THE AUTHOR

Originally from Michigan, Michael MacBride now calls Minnesota home.

He has delivered newspapers, worked for UPS, delivered pizzas, done collections at a bank, was a roadie for a country band, was a grant-writer and funder-researcher for non-profits, taught English, Literature, and Humanities courses at universities and colleges in Minnesota, New Hampshire, Ohio, and Illinois, and held a few other jobs in between. He, his wife, and children, love reading, writing, and traveling whenever possible.

In addition to *Lies From Beechwood Drive*, he's also the author of:

- *Bidding Wars* (speculative fiction)
- *Voyager* (speculative fiction)
- *Emergency Preparedness* (short story collection)
- *The Thompson Twins* series (mid-grade, interactive detective books)

Made in the USA
Middletown, DE
27 August 2022

71393321R00165